Praise for **The Obstacles**

"Urroz's characters resound with doubts, fears, loves, and certainties, with sweat, blood, and semen. . . . They reach from one edge of time to the other. They are words in one moment, and flesh in the next. And who knows whether they are real or fictional?"
—Guillermo Arriaga, screenwriter of *Amores Perros* and *21 Grams*

"There is no border where emptiness and mirrors do not coexist, and Eloy Urroz knows this. . . . With *The Obstacles*, Urroz has written the only sort of border novel permissible in a world such as ours: one of every frontier, of every space, and of all books."—Ignacio Padilla

"Reading *The Obstacles* is a spiritual and carnal adventure into the baroque landscape of the possible."—Alberto Ruy Sánchez

"It is a perfect narrative artifact that is as disturbing as it is moving."—Jorge Volpi

"*The Obstacles* is a hymn of grace to the works of the great novelists of Hispanic literature."—Susan Schaffer

"Eloy Urroz creates a sphere in which the frontiers between fiction and reality disappear. Intellectual giddiness, artifice, and scandal electrify the reader."—John Skirius

"A literary experiment that fascinates thanks to its precise and direct prose; an intense action, and a precious textual mirage on each page."—Mempo Giardinelli

The Obstacles

Eloy Urroz

Translation by
Ezra Fitz

Dalkey Archive Press
Normal · London

For Lety

For my brother Ricardo
And the memory of my grandfather Héctor,
Who was born in La Paz
Not far from Las Rémoras

Originally published in Spanish as *Las Rémoras* by Nueva Imagen, 1996.

Library of Congress Cataloging-in-Publication Data available.
ISBN: 1-56478-427-4

Partially funded by a grant from the Illinois Arts Council, a state agency.

Dalkey Archive Press is a nonprofit organization whose mission is
to promote international cultural understanding and provide a forum
for dialogue for the literary arts.

www.dalkeyarchive.com

Printed on permanent/durable acid-free paper, bound the United States of America,
and distributed throughout North America and Europe.

The poet should prefer impossibilities that appear probable to such things that, though possible, appear improbable.

—Aristotle, *Poetics*

Because the principal work lies not in saying the truth of the thing, rather in feigning its verisimilitude, that it approaches truth.

—Alonso López Pinciano, *Ancient Poetic Philosophy*

0

Las Rémoras

(a novel)

by
Ricardo Urrutia

I

Like every night, that first Monday in August found me crouching in the closet, looking through the peephole and waiting for my mother to appear there, almost right in front of me. My bedroom was next to hers, making it seem like an extension of it, only larger and better lit. Since my father's death three months ago, the ritual was always the same: I knew exactly when it would happen, no more than half an hour after she said goodnight to me in the dining room or in the doorway of my bedroom. I would turn to the desk next to my bed, switch on the small lamp that cast a stain of light on the pillow, untie my shoes, undress slowly, and step quietly into the bathroom. Standing there in my underwear, I'd hold on for a few more seconds before releasing a long and relaxing stream of urine into the toilet while I contemplated my hairy chest in the mirror. Immediately afterwards I would wash my hands and brush my teeth. I knew there was still plenty of time left, but what I didn't know was why—why she would pick up his suits and cover her face with them, smelling the sleeves, the underarms, the lining. At first she did it reluctantly, without much enthusiasm. Later, though, she was caught up in a sickening, rhythmic swaying, the smell producing ecstasy for her: she would breathe it in deeply, holding it as if the scent were fleeing, slipping away forever. Then she would clutch the clothes even more tightly while I listened to her inhaling loudly through her nostrils. I thought that maybe this was normal, since after a few minutes smell becomes familiar and slowly loses its effect; the scent continues to linger, however; it's not extinguished, it's just that the nose and its olfactory abilities soon begin to fade or adapt. I would watch her crying, throwing herself to the floor grasping the pair of dark, pinstriped trousers that my father had worn right up until the end; she seemed to contemplate them with her nose, her face flushed, as though she knew she was being watched—but no, it wasn't that at all, it was desperation. The smell had to disappear, and with it went my mother's attempts to recover the man who was her husband and lover until a few months ago. She would lay there on the carpet with her back to me; she'd grown thin, exhausted and defeated, and was on the verge of crying. And still I waited, furtive and motionless. The closet had become a warm burrow shut off from the world: in there I was protected by coats, pants, and jackets that barely fit me. I'd learned how to keep absolutely quiet. I had to suppress any sense of modesty or shame that would force me to pull back from my vantage point, my eye to the hole in the wall, because that would make a noise. I had to protect myself from these feelings just as my mother had to protect herself from my father's ghost. I couldn't hold onto his smell; I couldn't even recognize it. She, on the other hand, recognized it—not clearly, but its vestiges, and it was as if I were being offered just a hint of that otherworldly odor. The rest didn't matter to me. The whole scene didn't bother me at all, didn't disturb a single particle of my being. Nor did my mother's slow, muffled crying. I knew that this was all a dream, and even if it weren't, it would just be an illusion, something out of touch with reality. Though it's true: it wasn't so unreal that I could move and make a sound, that what she smelled was meaningless. But again, in a certain way, the scene was unreal . . . after watching her gather the jackets and pants off the floor, after seeing her leave as if she were passing through a series of mirrors with that vaguely cynical manner in which you might gather up your hair or fold a skirt, I understood that this was all a dream or a worn-out drama that was being played out here, yes, in real life, though without any purpose or any effect. The whole thing was theatrical: there was no other explanation. Merely theatrical. But in the end, I decided that this wasn't a perfect explaination . . . there was no pleasure in it, and she must have known the same thing. My mother was possessed of a cynicism that—in a sudden, ironic way—sought to nullify reality or at least hide it. But this supposed reality turned out to be an unbelievable and utterly absurd one, not for anyone else, but for my mother alone, and so the benefits that ought to have resulted from this exhibition, put on for her and her alone, were just as unbelievable and absurd. Once I was sure that she had gone, I would leave my little hideaway with little memory of what I'd seen. There in bed, my warm body propped up on a pillow, I would try to read, starting the same paragraph two or three times, covering a page or two without really advancing. Exhausted, I would close my Federico Ross novella with the knowledge that I hadn't understood a thing and that I'd have to open it up in the morning and try again. My emotions rolling together like fog, I would fall asleep, though without forgetting about Laila, my neighbor, who was in my dreams.

2

Las Rémoras is a town not too close, or—depending on how you look at it—not too far away. It's been forgotten by most people, is barely remembered by others, and it sits in the central part of Baja California Sur.

Here is the map:

Some two and a half hours from La Paz, the capital of the state, and lying on the same Gulf of California, you'll find Nopoló, a smallish vacation town surrounded by a bay and that was founded to try and steal away those tourists who usually preferred Cabo

San Lucas, Bahía Concepción, or—traveling even further away—Mazatlán. Nevertheless, the experiment failed shortly thereafter because of a few Frenchmen, and little remains except for the two giant hotels that now stand unoccupied.

Close by lies Loreto, a city that many men and women return home to after spending the day working in Nopoló. High season for visitors is in the winter: they drive down from California in their shiny new RVs and set up in a trailer park, or—if the weather cooperates—on a beach safe enough for camping. Some of them come to exploit the families that arrive by sea in their ostentatious ships. These vessels—yachts, sailboats, and other, smaller craft—can be seen scudding along the gulf coast throughout the year, unless a storm keeps them in port. Still, the launch ramps in this region are few and far between, and for this reason it's not uncommon to run into a couple of scruffy gringos who've landed here three, four, or even five years before, waiting happily and eternally for someone to come along and fix their sailboat's broken keel, though they know full well that nobody will ever do it. They set up shop near some tavern and end up working there, becoming Mexicanized with time and gradually forgetting about their families to the North.

Although the ramparts that ring the lovely Nopoló tidelands are scant, the people there are quite proud of them: the lingering ruins of an old sixteenth-century fort, of which hardly a stone remains; the scarcely visible skeleton of what once was, when pirates and privateers lurked in the gulf and among the Revillagigedo Islands, preparing their assaults, Sir Francis Drake at the head of them all.

One of the Nopoló hotels, Isla Negra, was shut down years ago "for repairs." It seems like it's been completely forgotten, looking no different today than it did the day they closed it. The other hotel is owned by the state governor, and it takes in sordid lovers and fugitives on the run. At one time, the inhabitants of other, smaller towns like Santispac or Requesón—where there's no work, or anything else to do for that matter, except for tossing heavy fishing nets into the sea under the withering sun—would come to Loreto thinking that things would be different there. But the fact of the matter was that nothing ever came of their expectations, and today there's no more work in the governor's hotel and the surrounding area than the coast-dwellers were used to in their own towns.

Some two hundred kilometers to the north lies Mulegé, something of an oasis in the middle of the Baja California desert. Before you've past Bahía Concepción—that place of peaceful, cold-water beaches (cold enough to wrinkle even the thickest skin) and rough sand—you'll still find more trailer parks to one side of the winding highway. Unlike Nopoló—which was poorly planned and artificially situated to attract the American tourists who never came, preferring to go on spending their vacations in Cabo San Lucas, Todos Santos, or La Paz—Mulegé is home to a steady if listless commerce, barely able to support a town of about four thousand residents. It's split by a river whose delta both bathes the town and keeps it green throughout the year, while a mission and a jail—each some two hundred years old—remain standing, ancient relics still in use. Today, very few people pass through this oasis of fresh springs; though, again, for some reason the gringos will stop here and stay for years, never wanting to return to their country.

About an hour's drive before reaching Mulegé, towards the south and passing Santispac—growing ever smaller and finding itself caught in the midst of both commercial and estuarine exchanges—you'll find Las Rémoras, which is little more than a peaceful fishermen's village, an immutable, sun-dappled hamlet that lacks even a single sign to inform travelers of its name. Spread out before you is a poorly designed pier facing the sea, a few shops and run-down stands selling sundry items, a basketball court, two shut-down restaurants, a few sandwich shops with peeling paint, a colonnade which the locals have dubbed Altozano, a beautiful little sickle-shaped beach with a rocky, chipped-looking edge, and finally—perpendicular to the sea—a sort of raised avenue named Libertad, which could easily be compared to similar ones in Sitges or Vilanova i la Geltrú. They say that a Catalan engineer—lost for unknown reasons in Las Rémoras—built it years ago with the help of the other townsfolk: the only wide, paved road there is.

Right now, at the end of the beach, perched on a harsh, rocky outcropping, sits the writer, the son of the town, the only one who has the keys to the Las Rémoras library. It consists of about three hundred volumes that nobody, except for him, Rosales, and Roldán, know about. He's been sitting there on the rock for days: pensive, crestfallen, and mired in a state of apathy.

3

It was either that night or the next when I first felt the pain. It was stemming from the pit of my stomach, persistent if faint. But soon it welled up and became two, three, and four separate pains, like concentric rings surrounding the original. I had no idea what it was. I had to get out of bed and pick my way across the darkened room, tripping over stray shoes and sharp belt buckles on my way to the bathroom. Sitting there on the toilet, I realized I'd been fooled. I felt some pressure on my sphincter, but no movement in my bowels. There was no reason for me to be sitting there. I got up after a few minutes and went back to bed feeling like a spoiled child, but I knew it was all going to happen again before long. That's just how it was: an absurdity repeated several times a night. An empty feeling—which

I tried to bury beneath my arms, wrapped tightly around my stomach—remained until dawn, when finally I was able to forget about it and fall asleep.

The next morning, I couldn't find my mother. Only the maid performing some inconsequential task. Nothing mattered more than my body and this stubborn, lingering pain which migrated from side to side across my belly. A hollowness was there—that much I knew—but no matter how much I tried to will it away, I simply couldn't. I struggled to pull on a pair of pants, went into the kitchen, and quickly fixed something to eat. I ate some bread with *jocoque* and cereal, but the pain continued to grind away in the pit of my stomach, this time without abating for a moment. Worse yet, the consuming desire to chew, to eat, to gorge myself until I felt full and free, refused to wane as well.

Finally (though I don't know when) I began to feel the onset of sleep. I shivered. I went into my parents' bedroom and, still half-dressed, nestled under the smooth, warm sheets, impervious to the world outside. I turned on the TV, and the last thing I remember seeing was the scene from Alfred Hitchcock's *Frenzy* in which a woman is violently strangled. That was it—not even a dream or a hint of reality—until I felt a mist in my eyes and somebody's hand upon my forehead. No, it couldn't be my mother . . . I could sense her, close, but not there in front of me. Off to the side, hesitant, watching—sad, observing the lean body of her son curled up like a dog in its bed. Instead, I know that it was the hand of my father's friend, Humberto Lascurain, the venerable old doctor, making a house call. He represented an imprecise collection of facts about diseases, afflictions, and pains involving the abdomen.

"Get up," he said. "Let's go, you can do it."

I didn't want to listen. It bothered me to hear his voice: smooth, patient, and even tender. I didn't trust it, didn't trust his hands propped up on the headboard, his crossed legs, his glasses perched on his knee.

"Help me," I heard him ask my mother.

Without opening my eyes, I could feel three, four, and five hands, like a polyp surrounding me, trying to tug off my shirt. Then, sprawled out and exhausted, I felt the doctor's pale, jelly-like hands with their meticulously clipped nails probe at my skin. I couldn't do a thing. I was crushed, utterly spent, left without any solid point from which to defend myself against this aggres-sor, against his tepid, prodding hands, against his odd—even pointless—questions, which I had to answer in the affirmative, nodding my bony chin.

"Are you hungry? Hungrier than usual?" he asked in his clear, liturgical voice.

I responded, partly with a blink and partly with another nod of the chin, that slight bony prolongation of my face.

"Do you feel a kind of hollowness? A sharp pain you're not used to?"

Again, a quick-tempered nod and a blink. Neither of them understood. My mother sat blank-faced in the corner.

"When was your last bowel movement? Did you happen to notice if it was black?"

I answered yes and no. I realized I didn't care whether I spoke at all. Or even whether I could hear. That way, I wouldn't have to listen to such ridiculous things, like "to defecate"—or "to evacu-ate," which is even worse, I think—rather than "to shit." None of that. I hated Dr. Lascurain—Humberto, my father's friend—more with each passing minute.

"Ricardo doesn't drink, does he, Helena?"

"No, no," she stammered. I could hear the hesitation in her voice. Why? She knows I never drink. "Maybe a glass of wine now and then. Or a beer, but almost never."

"Other irritants? Coffee, or chili perhaps?"

"Yes, quite a bit."

"Good, good." I could feel his breath on my face: onions, meat, beans, a dessert pudding . . . all I knew for sure was that he couldn't have brushed his teeth before leaving his home or office. My mother must have been close to hysterics when she asked him to come. "What could have happened in the seven or eight hours I was out?" I imagined my mother asking the maid. Again, I felt my eyes flutter and well up with sadness and the bitter scent of masticated onions that permeated Lascurian's mouth. No freshness, not even a mint: it was a rotten stench, pure and simple. Processed food, grease, and a plaque-like film stuck to the roof of his mouth. Humberto Lascurain might as well have eaten his own damn shit.

"Helena, Ricardo definitely has a touch of gastritis, or perhaps the beginnings of an ulcer," Lascurain said, emphasizing the "definitely" to show that he'd decided it couldn't be anything else. "A slight fever is normal. You shouldn't worry; it comes with the territory."

"How?" I managed to say, but nobody heard me. Maybe I didn't actually say anything.

"It's not gas or stomach cramps. It's nerves. You see, what's happening is that the duodenum . . ."

I decided that this diagnosis was just a sickly-sweet attempt to seduce my mother, to take advantage of her sympathy for other people's pain and suffering . . . in this case, my own.

"If you don't notice any improvement, you can bring him by the office on Friday. Let's just let him rest for a few days. If you need to, just tell my receptionist that you have an appointment, bring him in, and we'll do an endoscopy. This young man is a bundle of nerves, Helena, and that can complicate an ulcer. As you know, the suppositories are for the fever. It will break soon."

"Did you hear that, Ricardo? You're a bundle of nerves. And

all that junk food you're eating is doing you no good, right Humberto?"

"That's right." Again with the sickly-sweet, infuriating voice.

"Did you hear that?" repeated my mother.

I heard, I heard, but I couldn't care less. How could I, if at that very moment the pain gripped me again, coursing through my body? I closed my eyes, but no clenching of my facial muscles was enough to stop this new wave of burning emptiness from battering me. I couldn't relax a muscle or even take a deep breath to circumvent this wave of pain shooting out from the core of my body. I couldn't find a comfortable position that would give me any respite—even a fraction of a second's worth—from this booming, unrelenting torment radiating all the way from my stomach to the surface of my skin. I was on the verge of sleep . . . I wanted to, but the suffering wouldn't let me. I felt a cold sweat. It might have been raining outside.

I heard Lascurain rattle off a list of medicines to my mother, who carefully jotted them down as she listened. I imagined her there, with a fixed gaze, almost desperate, trying not to miss any of the doctor's words, trying not to lose a single syllable. She stumbles over the names, exhausted:

"Zan . . . tac? Zantac tablets?"

"Yes, twice a day. Morning and night, but no more than that."

"What about milk?"

"No milk, and no sodas or juice, Helena. They're all slightly acidic, and that can aggravate the intestine even more."

I wanted to complain. So what's it going to be then? Chamomile? *Mate*? Tea all day? No juice, no sodas, and definitely no milk.

"Some doctors do suggest drinking milk, for the calcium, but I've found that to be a mistake. Lactose is always detrimental."

"And the other pills? What did you say they're called?" There was a touch of vehemence in her voice. She didn't want to hear any more of Lascurain's explanations. I could tell she wanted him to leave now, so that she could go to the pharmacy.

"Ditopax. They're chewable. And good, you know. They taste like orange, and a little chalky, but good." Here he paused and turned to me, drawing himself away from my mother. "You have to make sure you take them, Ricardo."

I didn't move a muscle. Not even to nod. I tried to will him to leave, but he refused to understand. He would stay there in our home until my mother suggested some reason for him to go. He knew this, of course, and simply took advantage of it. Surely my mother has noticed his breath by now, the nasty film covering his teeth like new moss. He should look into breath mints or some gum . . . anything to make his smell more tolerable. I've never hated anybody just because of their breath before, but there's a first time for everything. And as I was gauging the weight of my disgust, I let it flow out like the tide. Suddenly, a stentorian pain hit the pit of my stomach. It was sadness, shame: as long as those gastric juices were secreted (according to Lascurain), I wouldn't be able to hate anybody. And that's what's really sickening: our bodies are so deficient and fragile that we can barely tolerate the ill will, revulsion, and fury that it secretes. I have to calm down, be more submissive, and stop hating my fellow man. I should embrace tranquility and love him—Lascurain, and my mother, and Inés, who appeared at the door to find out what was happening. To love my fellow man through the goodness of this ulcer. To love each and every one through all the ulcers and gastritises of the world.

4

Elías contemplated the sea from his rocky crag, the last one on the beach. He scanned the steel-blue swells and silver-plated

waves. He thought: *Sometimes I worry about that woman too much.*
I can't go on like this, complaining to myself about someone for no
reason at all, letting my life grind to a halt to the point where it hinges
only on that one woman, getting me stuck in place. Roberta is right:
she's not going to change. I suffer—I do—but I don't want to, not for
anybody's sake. I don't seek out women to feel sad about, or to languish
in their shadows, their disdain, their lack of love, or the pleasure that
they may find in giving me what they've halfheartedly called love.
No, I understand her. She can't give more than that, either to me or
to herself. First, because it's true: I do not give myself wholly to her,
and she knows it. Secondly, because that's her mood, her will, her
character . . . something of a way of life, she told me so, more or less,
though not in so many words. Yes, I understand her. She makes me
suffer, but I cannot suffer in vain, receiving nothing in return, just
masochistic, forever.

Elías, who held the keys to the town library, sought nothing except Roberta's love. To feel her tender embrace, kissing
deeply until their mouths were dry and spent, like they had on
afternoons past, back when they first met. He wanted her to
seek him out, to feel love-struck (maybe even adoring) when
she saw him, but none of that—as he would find out later—was
to be. Her attitude was one of exclusion. Love, yes, but unfa-
miliar, cold, disinterested love. On that and other afternoons
spent by the sea, Elías believed firmly that love had to be a
selfish thing, a matter of life or death, urgent and necessary. It
was true: that afternoon, on the rocks by the sea, Elías suffered
from what Roberta, out of cynicism or fear, called her "way of
being."

He sat there on the outcropping, alone, watching the tide
reach its high-water mark at noon before the waves retreated
with the day and the sun gave way to the night sky. Elías suffered because of that indifferent, artificial gesture with which
she protected herself from him, from everybody, from all men

and especially the one who'd given her a son. Yes, that was it. At first, Elías was afraid of the boy (nobody wants to love someone with a child, though some people—like him—had already engaged in such vices long ago), afraid of the work she did to provide for him, and afraid of the men who frequented the Casa de Inés expressly to spend the night with her. Now, things were different. In Las Rémoras, the people who dealt with Inés, or her boss La Gringa, were almost always the same. They were all part of a family, and Inés was the young mother. In other words, she understood them all, at least a little. Most of them—the men, at least—knew something of the love that united Roberta and Elías: love, or whatever else they thought it was that united them. Nobody had any illusions about Roberta: they sought her out for pleasure, and that was all. Perhaps it left them with a good aftertaste. All things considered, she did her work carefully and unhurriedly. She did it well. She was humble and sincere, which the costal folks as well as the local Rémoranos appreciated. She was always affectionate, yet always detached, a combination that some people considered aloof. Love is in vain, her cold, agate-like eyes seemed to say. Loving her as Elías did meant suffering for that love, and very few people on earth really set out to suffer because of somebody else, because of the expectations of their lovers. And men often suffer more than women realize. Sooner or later, all the men learn this, and become humble in matters of love. At least in Las Rémoras. Even so, it's an adolescent lesson, the kind that's never fully learned. Maybe they suffered once for their wives or women, only to later become humbled all over again. They risk nothing though, and thus don't suffer, on account of some beautiful whore from Ciudad Insurgentes or Tijuana who, sooner or later, will be off to another port or another town. Elías, on the other hand, had always been stubborn when it came to love. He'd always challenged it.

The Casa de Inés—which was actually run by someone called La Gringa, a mysterious individual who lived in San Diego—was well known to everyone in Las Rémoras. Halfway down the block between Atuneros and Pescaderos, on the outskirts of town— where the streets are filled with dust and garbage and the lots are either vacant or in states of never-ending construction (or deconstruction, as the know-it-all Inés would say)— that impoverished building sits. (But, as everyone knew, the poverty was only skin-deep—inside, the place was more luxurious than any other house in Las Rémoras.) To one side there are three broken lights that nobody has ever bothered to fix, and the house, once pink, has faded in the harsh light of the sun. Although finding time is never a problem in Las Rémoras. It's a place where golden minutes offer themselves like sunbeams to basking lizards—but nobody takes advantage of this. Years ago, this same lot held a number of houses carelessly constructed with asbestos laminate, pieces of cardboard and cork board, and hastily laid stone walls that, with a heavy-footed visitor or a stiff breeze, would come crumbling down. Nevertheless, *this* house still stood, faded to a clear ocher color resembling dirty pond water—nobody knew exactly what color it was, and nobody in Las Rémoras could agree on why, given the house's function, they'd ended up calling it Casa de Inés—and Inés had recently gotten the authority to throw out the local squatters who were an inconvenience to her regular clients. She held some influence over the town councilman, a stiff little widower originally from Los Cabos who had arrived some years back, and who was well-liked by the people of Las Rémoras, especially because of his leniency regarding delinquent payments and other such latitudes. Maybe Inés took over her neighbors' outstanding debts, and—without incident—encouraged them to take off for Mulegé or places further north. Nobody was sure exactly how she'd gotten rid of them. But ever since, everyone in Las Rémoras had recognized her authority, and particularly the authority that Inés held over the town councilman, the lawyer Raimundo Rosales.

This lawyer—who, like everyone in Las Rémoras (including his friend, the supposed "architect" Iginio Jasso), was not quite what he appeared to be—had been born in Cabo San Lucas forty-three years ago, and nobody had any doubt that he'd come to Las Rémoras directly after finishing his law degree in Guadalajara. Just as nobody in town complained to Rosales, nobody ever spread the rumor that Inés had offered her personal services to the little man. As for walk-in clients, teenagers, boatmen, and fishermen of the town, she selected one of the girls she'd hired, or one that La Gringa had flown in from Tijuana: in her house, nobody got to choose for themselves. Inés set up all the pairings herself, according to her own tastes and whom she thought would best get along with whom. It was something she seemed to have a great knack for. But when the matter of Elías and Roberta was out of the box, it became more than a minor inconvenience. Depressed teenagers, lovesick no-good poets, and so-called librarians were enough to drive her mad. Worse still was a fool in love writing romantic letters and incomprehensible poetry to one of her most popular young ladies. So this business of the turtle that he, Elías, gave Roberta was without a doubt the drop that ranneth the cup over. Nobody in their right mind would ever spend his life savings on a girl like that, knowing she was half in love with somebody else. And for better or for worse, everyone in Las Rémoras knew that.

It was 7:30 or 8:00 at night when the lawyer Rosales tiptoed past the wharf. Through his small, round, metal-rimmed glasses the color of a green glass bottle, he was able to make out Elías's hunkered, immutable figure there on the crags. Even though night was falling and the figure was facing away from him, there was no doubt as to the identity of the man sitting there: always the same, recondite, gentle. He provoked neither pity nor annoyance. Nobody in Las Rémoras really worried about the writer. They may even have grown used to that effigy encrusted there like a barnacle on the crags, just one more rock whose only purpose was to make the sickle-shaped beach look chipped or unfinished on one edge.

For a while, Rosales continued on past the wharf, but then—before reaching Libertad—he stopped. He backed up a few steps, then stopped again to watch for a few moments. The young man had yet to feel the eyes staring at him from behind their dark glasses . . . yes, Rosales was almost overwhelmed by that hunched figure silhouetted against the sky, stamped there, breathing and thinking about Roberta, his impossible love. Rosales bent down and removed his shoes: he wasn't about to dirty a nice pair that had come all the way from Los Angeles and which he almost never wore during the daytime, saving them for his nocturnal visits to Inés. Not even Santa—the maid who worked for both him and the priest Roldán—touched them.

As he neared the rocks, Rosales stopped again. Elías still hadn't paid him any heed, but the lawyer felt like saying something. He wasn't sure what; something along the lines of, "Don't get so worked up, son. She loves you. I don't know why, but I believe she does. And even if I'm wrong, it doesn't matter, because there are many fish out there in those waters. You'll see." But he remained silent, whether out of fear or respect or because any words would be opaque and muted next to the sea's constant din. He retraced his steps. When he had reached the wharf again, he stopped to brush the sand off his black socks and slipped on his hand-polished shoes before continuing on. One last time, he stopped and looked back at the hieratic figure of the writer lingering there. Yes, now he knew why he hadn't spoken before: the young man's love had inspired a mysterious sense of respect in him.

5

On the same day I was born, my mother—Señora Urrutia—went to the beauty salon. Only later did she tell everyone how she thought her boy should be greeted: as if to a reception or banquet. A lovely little detail.

I can picture her reserving a taxi before leaving her mother's apartment that morning, sensing that later that evening or night she would be heading for the hospital. The pains she'd felt that night (the night before her appointment with Conchita at the salon) were what prompted her to call and schedule her appointment for no later than 10:30 in the morning—yes, 10:30, Conchita, not a minute after—because any later than that could be too late.

She didn't say a thing to anybody; my grandmother would have thought it was ridiculous, even criminal. She might not even have allowed my mother to leave the house that morning. I can picture her inventing some sort of ruse, anything to sneak out past my vigilant grandmother. A walk through the park, a visit to the neighborhood café, a trip to the post office to mail a letter to my father. Something, a pretext, an innocent little invention. In any case, she would have said that she felt perfectly fine.

Surprised, Conchita will step out of the salon and hold the taxi door and help my mother get out. A pedicurist will be ready to usher her inside and offer Helena, Señora Urrutia, a chair with a good back—she must be just about due, the poor thing! Smiling, my mother will accept the friendly assistance and welcome the helping hands that support her enormous, gravid weight. Once again, the pedicurist will prop up her feet and gently slip off her shoes. Her swollen feet and varicose veins are proof enough of her pregnancy: there's no need to touch her belly.

Odd and even a little impertinent, Conchita will ask her how she feels, and how her mother—my grandmother—is doing, since she hasn't been by the salon in almost two months. She'll brush out my mother's hair and wrap it around the curling irons. Then I imagine my mother enduring it all: the contractions in her belly, the redness and swelling, the aching feet, and the questions from Conchita and the pedicurist at her side. The pains become stronger and more resolute every time. Then comes the relaxation, the forgetting, or some distant memory to bring some temporary relief from the pain and fatigue. But again, less than a minute after the previous pounding, the pain returned with clockwork precision.

But there was enough time for Conchita to finish her hair, removing the curlers and combing it out so that my mother could have gone straight to a wedding or baptism, and the pedicurist—a bit distracted and nervous—finished her feet and even gave her hands a quick going-over as well. Then it comes, and she recognizes it: an intense, fecund pain. My mother can no longer move; she can only tap her feet while one of the women motions to the receptionist to dial Helena's number. My grandmother must have answered the phone and asked Conchita to take my mother to the hospital. They'd meet them there.

Commotion: everyone drops what they're doing, two young girls sitting in a corner scream while Conchita and another woman take my mother by the shoulders, the pedicurist following behind. I can hear my mother's groans as clear as day, and I can hear the other women's frantic attempts to shut her up or quiet her down. It's to no avail.

In Conchita's car, the one with red lettering painted on its doors, my mother sits with her legs open, fussing with her new hairdo and with the false eyelashes that the wind threatens to tear from her face. She tries in vain to roll up the window that the pedicurist has opened for her before giving up and shielding her hair with one hand while the other cups her stomach. It's a tie, a solution for life: a pregnant mother's pain is tied for her attention with her own beauty. Instead of wrapping both arms around her swollen belly to help ward off the painful contractions, she spares one to protect her eyes and freshly-curled hair. To do otherwise would be as impossible as it is unthinkable.

Now, I can imagine them roaring past another car broken down along the side of the road while Conchita asks:

"So this all happened suddenly? With no warning?"

"Actually," my mother reveals from her awkward yet anxious position, "I knew that today was the day. I felt it last night, and this morning I just knew. I can't really explain it; I just knew, Conchita."

"Then why get your hair and nails done?" Conchita asked, nervous. My mother answers her question with a question:

"What do you mean, 'Why?' Don't you see, Conchita?" She puts her hand to her face and blinks several times: a bit of dust, perhaps.

"No," the hairdresser stammered, still quite confused. "I don't."

"A child must be welcomed into the world properly. Think about what would happen otherwise," my mother says resolutely, one hand propped up on the glove compartment. "Careful! Take it easy. Don't hit the brakes so hard."

"So what are you saying, hon? That you want to look your best when you bring your child into the world?"

"Yes, exactly. It's an important event, don't you think? Some would say it's the most important reception there is. It's certainly not an everyday thing," she said, pausing once again to grit her teeth against another painful contraction.

It wasn't so much a succession of blows this time as it was an alternating sense of fullness and emptiness. It was pure suffering, prolonged and reaching into every corner of her body, raking through her flesh with such intensity that she felt as if she were being torn apart from the inside. She thought she could feel the pain even in her face and eyelids . . . but she could no longer discern specific pains. Even so, she refused to take her hand from her hair, even for a moment. Now, if I think about it—if I take a good, clear look at it—I think I might have to agree with her, even if her behavior seems a bit odd, superficial, or lacking in the proper significance (it was this significance that she was trying to infuse it with). Bringing someone into the world is an exaggerated form of self-torture.

When I hear my mother or father (who wasn't present at my birth—he was at UCLA and couldn't get there until three days later) tell that story, the only thing I can think about is how I came into the world in such a "distinguished" manner. I can't imagine that very many other folks have been born quite like that.

<h1 style="text-align:center">6</h1>

Unhurriedly, the lawyer Rosales crossed Libertad—which runs perpendicular to the sea and the wharf—occasionally waving to his left and right. Everyone knew where he was headed: you could set your watch by his eight o'clock morning stroll. It was a deeply-rooted custom, one that had begun almost a year ago, and he would smile smoothly and wave to the ladies he passed, who responded in kind with good-natured gestures of recognition. At first, it was only once or twice, but then it grew to three and now four visits a week to Inés.

Perhaps—though the lawyer would never have accepted this as a reason—he hadn't stopped to speak to the young writer on the beach simply because he hadn't wanted to deviate from his routine and punctual visit to the Casa de Inés, between Atuneros and Pescadores. Still, the respect the writer had for the mysteries of love was moving. He had, at a young age, discovered an absolute truth, or at least something he believed in. He had distinguished something others either couldn't or thought they couldn't see: the difference between those who know of love, and those who only know of women. While at first glance they might appear to be one and the same, they're actually diametrically opposed, if not mutually exclusive, things (though he thought Jasso, in a frustrated sort of way, might be one of those impossible mixed cases). In other words, he who knows of love usually knows next to nothing of women, or only a few, or even one. These sorts could come to love an ideal woman—an invented woman—though according to Rosales, this wasn't particularly important. What did matter to them was to fall in love, an eternal love, even if it was with a dead girl, as the poet Leopardi had done with his gardener's daughter. Those who know of women, on the other hand, rarely know anything of love. They say that they love, even swear it at times. But no—in reality, the womanizer couldn't know any more of love than could the man who had barely known a single woman all his life.

The womanizer, the expert, had fallen in love before. There could be no doubt whatsoever about that. He had to be more persistent about it every time, but—nevertheless—his stubbornness was proportional to his need, as well as to his inability to love deeply or substantially. As such, love's ill-fated destiny had been a burden to him, but—looking at it carefully—it may not have been as ill-fated as that of the other man, the man who had only loved once in his life: the eternal victim and decoy of love. He could be victimized by women, be both bait and easy prey to them. Rosales had understood this ever since that distant day he'd become a widower, when he knew he would never love again. All the time he'd lost in love he was now regaining—consuming—in his transactions with women. He couldn't have become an expert at that late stage of life, nor could he be in any way an accomplished womanizer. His appearance wasn't exactly an asset in that regard; he wasn't what you'd call a Don Juan. So, rigid, wiry, skinny, with narrow shoulders, and green, oval-shaped glasses, feigning more timidity than he actually felt, Raimundo Rosales had—bit by bit—become a regular customer at the Casa de Inés. At first he was only partaking of the new girls La Gringa sent down every few months; now, however, he was enjoying a bottle of champagne or white wine in the owner's apartment.

Before entering the house, while still standing in the shadows under a broken street lamp—the moon shining on high, serving as something of a spotlight—Raimundo Rosales listened to the clear tones of a bolero being sung. He didn't remember having heard it before, but it fascinated him nonetheless. Rosales paused for a moment before knocking: he couldn't place the voice, but he knew it wasn't Inés, and it sang off-key along with an old record:

> *Porque ya me cansé de estar queriendo*
> *a quien no me quiere a mí.*

> Because I'm just so tired of loving
> Someone who doesn't love me.

He couldn't avoid it: the lawyer felt sadness in his heart as he pictured Elías—a lover, a womanizer, or, who knows? perhaps he's both—lamenting over Roberta, haunted by her constantly. The words to the song even coaxed a couple of tears from his eyes. He felt himself undone by sentimentalism, which was surprising, as he had never thought of himself as being sentimental in the least. With the discipline of a boxer, Rosales managed not only to keep the tide of his tears stemmed, but—just as they were on the verge of spilling over and down his cheeks—he willed them back into their riverbeds, breaking the law of gravity.

He knocked on the door. He heard the record player being switched off (why the hell would they do that? he wondered), and then a bustling commotion, the sound of someone stumbling, a muffled curse (surely in response to the stumble), until at last the door opened to reveal the young singer standing there, rubbing her bruised knee. It was Josefina, in a frilly red dress.

"Did you hurt yourself, Fina? Pardon me," Rosales said as he invited himself in with a wave. It's his house, after all, or just as good as his.

"I did just now, running to answer the door," she replied, trying to hide her smile. "Since we didn't have any customers, I was singing."

"Please, continue. There's no need to stop," the drowsy, half-asleep lawyer said. "But I didn't recognize the song. What was it?"

"Lolita," Josefina replied, quickly and earnestly. "It's beautiful, no? The madam can't stand her voice. They say she hates Spanish women. Especially Andalusians. But as for me, counselor, they drive me crazy. I'm fascinated by them. *Because I'm just so tired of loving / Someone who doesn't love me* . . . who could hate those lyrics?"

"I imagine you've seen the flamenco danced, then?"

"Never."

"You'd like it very much," he said as he watched the madam descending the stairs.

He approached her with a gallant, passionate gesture—bowing deeply until his shoulders were parallel to the floor—and it was obvious that he had no more time for Josefina and her eager questions about Andalusia. He followed Inés up the same stairs, taking the opportunity to adjust his glasses and dry his misty eyes. He was still deep in thought, with the image of that immutable young man imprinted on his mind. He reached the landing, and—just before he was about to enter the master bedroom—he saw Roberta sitting on a chair in the corner. She didn't see him, she wasn't even looking his way: she's turned towards her magazine, with the fine lines of her elegant face, her slinky black stockings, and her lush, red lips—lips that purse together when she finally looked up to meet the lawyer's curious eyes. She has to greet him: he's the town councilman, and the madam's favorite customer; just those two things: nothing less and nothing more. She smiled at him and then returned to her magazine. Rosales inhaled the fair-skinned, almost translucent woman's beauty—and her ample, pouting lips—for just a moment longer before entering Inés's bedroom. It would be impossible not to fall in love with her, he said to himself, whether you're a womanizer or a hopeless lover. I understand Elías perfectly now. Yes, all but impossible, he repeated assuredly as he removed his tie and began to unbutton his shirt.

7

Still plunged in a tranquil darkness between the sudden pains in the pit of my stomach—more prolonged now than when they started—I was visited by someone completely unexpected, someone who triggered my later return to lucidity.

First it was Inés's timid, prudish voice asking if she could enter; then that same flesh-and-bone voice telling me that our neighbor was waiting outside in the entrance hall. I made a face, intrigued and skeptical. I just couldn't believe it. I'm almost certain that Laila wouldn't have found out about my condition if my mother hadn't blabbed about it.

In my sleepy fog, halfway between gastrointestinal distress and fever (I'd begun to enjoy using Lascurain's terms), I felt ashamed to realize that Inés had anticipated my anxiety on hearing this latest news. In other words, I faced two indignities: the first being

Laila, the neighbor's, fault, while the second was thanks to Inés, who had to see my pain for herself and perhaps even took some solace in it. I hadn't set foot in the bathtub in two or three days, nor had I had any desire to. My deep depression had become a secret vice. The dirty bed, the sweat-soaked sheets, an invalid body glistening with perspiration . . . all these things combined to form the sought-after peace: to sink down and inhale it—that calmness, that security—grasp it in my fingers, crumble it up and eat it . . . The only thing that bothered me was the impossibility of continuing to observe the closet ritual, if it hadn't already come to an end. I was even beginning to recognize my own scent: almost physically tangible, almost as strong as the smells of others—that pungent, old man smell that I could never discern before.

Without asking—without even waiting for Inés to leave—Laila came in, young and smiling, with her hair cascading about her face. I couldn't help it that my heart began to race and my breathing quickened. I said it was wonderful to see her, or maybe I only imagined that I did and was exhausted by the thought. I fell silent; I had grown tired very quickly.

"No, no, lay back down," she exclaimed when she saw me trying to sit up with my elbows propped up on the pillow. "You can barely move! Here, Inés gave me this pill for you."

I made a great effort not to drift off. Approaching me with a touch of sadness, she took me by the hand and sat down next to me on the bed, her hips rumpling the sheets. I felt her shift slightly, lifting her ass just enough to smooth out the sheets and cover up what had been exposed of my body. She reached out and placed the pill on my tongue, then offered me a glass.

"How was it? Did it go down smooth?" she asked, not expecting a response. She didn't mind, considering my debilitated state. "You didn't come by the house for more than a month, and my mother was asking about you. We were wondering why. How are you doing with *Bodily Prayers*? Federico reminds me a lot of you . . . did you know that? He was my mother's boyfriend back when they were young. You'll see when you get to the third part. I told you that you'd like that little story. You can just about read it in one sitting, or at least in a few days." She laughed to herself for referencing a part of the story that I hadn't read yet. "You should learn something from this, Ricardo. I've always told you that you're too high-strung."

I stopped paying attention, and even prayed for her to stop talking and occupy herself by covering me up, feeling my forehead, or crossing her legs. She didn't, of course, and continued on, indifferent to my silence and the request it implied. Rather, she talked and talked some more, filling every second. My breathing was still labored and occasionally rattled, and it had begun to exhaust me; again Laila began to caress my forehead and trace her fingers—tipped in long, sharp nails—lightly across my cheeks.

She knew full well that I loved her. True, I exaggerated both my love and her to friends (and possibly even to my mother) but I wasn't bothered by it; no, this simply allowed it to grow, to incubate in my chest and belly, like an oyster laden with a pearl. Deep down—between morbidity and timidity—I wondered what needed to or what could ever happen between us. And it didn't bother me to see her with others, like when she would go out with Carlos, from across the street. Nothing happened between them. I first knew her just by sight, having seen her walking down the street some years back. Later, after hours spent preparing myself in front of a mirror, I summoned all my courage and approached her: she was on her way to Mass, and I asked if I might accompany her. She didn't respond; I felt as if my chest had been cut open. But I followed her, took communion behind her, and prayed whenever I saw her kneeling. Laila didn't say a word; she didn't even peek at me out of the corner of her eye. I kneeled down next to her, and could see the sleek shapes of her legs, the backs of her knees, and her shoes folded beneath her, all of which I wanted to kiss. I also wanted to kiss the tops of her pale, naked feet in ways she couldn't even imagine. That is what I prayed for.

Laila was quite abundant for her age. Sometimes, if she wasn't careful, she would even get a bit thick at Christmas or in the summer. Just ever so slightly plump. Even so, I was quite taken. Seeing her there, her firm and prominent rump splayed on my bed, dressed like a twenty-three-year-old woman though she was only seventeen, made me wonder what she would be like when she was my mother's age, because I still harbored hopes of marrying her.

Finally, after months of pleading and romantic compliments, Laila consented to a kiss. It made me abysmally afraid. But why? What prompted such fear? I couldn't understand or even intuit the reason without coming to accept the truth: the certainty of falling—through our kisses—into a bottomless abyss, a sort of thick and humid tunnel. The tunnel of love? Touching her lips produced in me a feeling of vertigo, comparable—I would think—to what Jimmy Stewart experienced up in Hitchcock's bell tower. I'd seen the film some months ago, and now—in my feverish state—remembering those aerial shots disturbed me almost to the point where I felt like I was plunging down to the ground in those same camera shots.

I had only written letters to her, along with a few, all but insufferable, poems. Usually I destroyed them without showing her, but I kept the later ones, which I always put off reread-ing, distracted by my rushing around the house all day, tired from revising manuscript pages from *Las Rémoras* and watch-ing television all through that rainy and monotonous summer. I mulled them over in silence; in other words, I listened to myself reading them in my head, imagining her reaction. It was like an experiment where you set out to repeat a chemical reaction ad infinitum: after an hour or so, you can pretty much predict what the effects will be. Then I'd get bored, and decide to burn what was left. It was always the same. There was something indefinable and yet rather like terror in the simple act of throwing them out, tearing them up, or hoping that they would dissolve when I flushed them down the toilet. Fear that they might endure, I suppose. The poems must become smoke and ashes after a few short weeks. The same with the letters.

This time I changed my mind.

"Laila," I murmured.

"Yes? Does something hurt?" she asked quickly and with an exaggerated concern.

"No, no," I replied. Her poor acting bothered me. "Open the closet."

At first she looked dubious, but then she stood up, walked across the room to the closet door and paused, turning to look at me, excited yet hesitant.

"Go on, open it," I insisted, feeding her excitement with mystery. "Now look in the bottom drawer. Do you see it?"

"This notebook? You want me to bring it over?" she asked, smiling as she opened it. "*Las Rémoras*?"

"No, no. Leave that alone!" I exclaimed through the dim fever-haze. "I'm sorry; my mistake. They should be off to the side somewhere."

"What should?" Laila asked. "It'll be easier if you just tell me what you want."

"They're not for me, they're for you," I said.

"What? These letters?" she asked in her honeyed voice, enthralled, since she was beginning to realize that they were destined for her—as, ultimately, was I.

"Yes, they're yours. I mean, they're for you," I repeated wearily. She asked:

"Can I read them? Right here, right now?" She knew I would say yes; she tore open the first envelope before I had a chance to respond.

Deep down, I liked the idea. I don't know why, but I liked to imagine her reading those same lines I knew by heart. To trace what she was feeling, her excitement and apprehension or lack thereof, her joy, the nakedness I might make her feel when I hit upon just the right turn of phrase. Who knows?

As she read, I felt a new sort of anxiousness: I had to go to the bathroom. A dull, underlying, almost latent sensation. In other words, it's possible that I was mistaken and didn't really need to go; that I just had a vague feeling of distress. At the same time, I realized that I couldn't get up: there was nowhere to prop myself up with a hand or an elbow. Impossible. Laila's body was blocking the empty side of the bed, and the other was flush up against the cork-laid wall. But I couldn't say a thing. She was reading, resolute and impervious to any request or favor. I didn't move; I spied on her, but couldn't bring myself to follow along as she moved to the second letter. She fell silent, smiled slightly, and I could see a touch of dismay in the corners of her lips: she feels sorry for me.

Again, the anxious feeling in my gut: the desire to shit, smooth and liquid, like a handful of sand streaming out between the fingers, a true sense of lightness and relief. But it left just as quick as it came when I heard her say:

"That's so nice! I don't understand why you didn't show these to me before!" She raised a flushed hand to her temple. "You weren't going to give them to me, were you? Don't you know they don't belong to you anymore? Once you write them, they're no longer yours. There's a law—I don't know if it's British or they have it all over the world—which says that letters become the property of the recipient. Always. That's right. These are for me, and nobody else."

She laughed. I'm afraid: once again I'm walking into the shadow, the dark depository of fright over which she reigns. The one who receives them is the one who owns the letters. Does "always" mean until eternity, where everything ceases to be finite and expires? But she never actually did receive them, either from me or from anybody else. They certainly weren't postmarked; her name wasn't even written across the flap of the envelope. I can no longer control the urge to shit; I'm going to call Inés for help, to hint to Laila that she should leave . . . perhaps because I'm not feeling well, and that it's absolutely imperative I take my antacid now. Anything. I couldn't move a muscle, I couldn't respond at all, couldn't even smile. I wanted to get up, but I was barred by her body, her hand resting upon my shoulder while she continued reading, content and unmoved, reading and crumpling up my ridiculous love letters, my cheap, affected letters.

Finally, calmer after my anxiety had subsided (along with the desire to shit and my subtle, desperate need to escape), I felt a kiss graze the corner of my lips. It was like a prize, yes; it was as if the *cabrona* had awarded me a prize. Afterwards, she left: broad, young, content, the arch of her prominent hips swaying as she walked.

8

When Rosales entered Inés's room, Roberta composed herself, tossed her magazine aside, and exposed something that had been hidden between its pages: the poem that Elías had written her a few days before. She didn't understand much of it, but she enjoyed it, and reread her favorite passages when she had the time. The madam had loaned her a dictionary, and with that in hand she set about deciphering it. She focused all her attention on the words, but ultimately it was impossible not to tire. Her interest began to wane after only a few minutes.

There was no doubt whatsoever that the young man—a year younger than herself—was intelligent and had a way with words. The architect Iginio and Rosales himself had praised Elías as such. Did she love him? She still wasn't sure. What she did know was that she hadn't wanted him to fall for her—anything but that. Why? Perhaps because she did love him, though this would be a contradiction. She wanted to love him, but he had insisted on loving her more, on loving her first. She mulled it over time and again in her head, but she still didn't know how to respond. Again, she did love him, but not like Elías wanted: he wanted to impose his love upon her, to be admired and adored because of the love he gave and not for who he was. He had suffered a lot; that much he'd admitted to her. He'd endured her attitude, which in turn was brought on by his advances. Elías didn't seem to be picking up her subtler hints, so Roberta laid it out in colder, less uncertain terms: "It's how I am, and that's that," she said, cruelly and without remorse. "I'm not going to change my attitude for anybody, and if that bothers you, then too bad." And that was it. Roberta knew it: it was the greatest hurt she'd caused him since they'd known each other, and he hated her for it. It was into the midst of all this that he had cast the strange poem he'd given her. Still sitting there, in the corner of the landing, she picked her magazine back up and began clandestinely to read it:

The Sign

I

I do not love the people I love
Naturally
As a sense of tepid uncaring, dark and daily,
Blooms forth from my body.

I do not love anybody and do not fear
Without ceasing to love the flesh
More than what I do not love now.
I have an unloving sign in my blood
A ghoulishness that rages and shames me.
To love you, Roberta, believe me,
Is to cast off my love for you forever.
To kiss you is to taste the hatred in your unread lips.
Love is discredited if I love you
Which is why I do not love you, Roberta. I hate you.

II

In empty flesh is sunk
That unnatural fire, obsessed with love,
That scald of death,
The efforts to endure you
In order to love you,
Flooding me with pain
For neither loving nor detesting you.
Far from you I fear no one,
There is a painful taste of life alone. Do you see?
I do not love the people I love
Natural and tepid.
There is nobody, Roberta, whom I love and hate
    more than you
Which is to say
That I love your heart so, and drink of it without
    thirst.

Clearly it was an odd thing, obscure and filled with contradic-
tions. Still, in spite of it all, she felt a sense of understanding, or at
least intuition. And she did like everything else he'd given to her
up to that point: the other poems, the letters, the flowers. And a

turtle he'd found on the beach, which—he said—might have been looking to commit suicide. She released it into their backyard pond, but it died within a couple of days. How? Was it suicide after all? Nobody knew, so Ruth, Fina, and the other girls cooked it over a slow flame, and they had broth for soup all week.

The two had met there, at the brothel, late one afternoon, so hot and suffocating that an iguana drowned in that same backyard pond, hoping that a dip would bring relief. She had only recently arrived in Las Rémoras, and it was one of the first times that Roberta had slept with a local. He was twenty-three; she was twenty-four. From that first encounter, the future—unknowable, according to the madam's incorrect assumptions—was forecast. It was well-known that Elías had a certain fondness for single mothers—as he also did for fatherless boys, which is a similar if not parallel appreciation. This time, both fondnesses were united for the sake of his goodwill—and ill-will—because Roberta's son lived in a room separated from the main house. The boy spent his days in the upstairs hallway or in the living room where the other women relaxed, smoking and drinking, when they weren't off swimming in the sea with men or killing jellyfish. He was six years old, and his father was either dead or didn't exist; nobody was sure which. Roberta had kept a long-lasting silence on that subject.

After their second and third meetings—that same week—the dark seed was planted, growing within them, drawing them together with the same power of attraction that our bodies feel for the sea. But this attraction also threatened to tear them apart—an impossible paradox: they wanted each other so badly that they hated themselves for not loving more. Six or seven weeks passed and nothing changed. It was as if things were suspended—as they invariably are in the town of Las Rémoras—with Elías thinking about Roberta from his rough stone perch at the end of the beach, and Roberta thinking about Elías while she contemplated this or that indifferent body on top of her. The small city's atmosphere kept them in place, stagnant and redundant, each one pondering the best way to forget and flee from the other. But the more time that passed without them seeing each other—without them sleeping with each other—the more they came to love each other, and the more inseparable they felt. On certain afternoons, the passion was all but exhausting: it was like a riptide. Roberta at least could diminish love's pain or at least delay it some by embracing her son and taking him for morning walks by the wharf. They ate together, they talked, they embraced. On Sundays, she took him to Father Roldán's mass, with Josefina and Inés at their side. She eased his pain, she prayed to the Virgin, and it helped her steady her attitude towards Elías.

Another fact of the matter—their matter—was that there was no solution in sight; no guarantee that could convince the other. But convince them of what? Of the need to distance themselves? To flee? No, it wasn't about guarantees, nor was it about trying to convince yourself of something after the fact—they didn't understand each other, they didn't complement each other, they suffered terribly, she was a mother while he was a womanizer (or that's what she thought or wanted him to be); he refused to concede, as did she, etcetera, etcetera—it all boiled down to one imperative: wait. Yes, wait and hope, as if it were some sort of password. And, at the same time, the only thing that they could wait and hope for was that love might disappear and leave them in peace. One—or perhaps both—of them was going to have to suffer the consequences. The consequences of love, of course.

Elías, who felt free and unbound, was also fully aware of the towering obstacles facing him. The freest of men is also always the one with the greatest burden. And the most foolish, they said, sitting there mindlessly on the rocks. Why the most foolish? The answer was clear: because you're always on the verge of falling in love again. The same thing happened to Roberta. There was a bond—a chain, really—that one day and without any apparent reason, snared and seduced her. Now there they were, each one sick of hating and loving the other. Every time they lay together in bed, they felt a numbness that eventually gave way to tense irritation, because they could see what was happening with absolute clarity: their love was tinged with a sense of desperation, an insatiable hunger. It was perhaps the worst of all combinations: a whore and a whoremonger. There was also a good deal of fear involved, for an excess of love can cause great waves of panic to come crashing down on you. Eventually, even Inés opted to keep quiet and swallow her anger, to neither interfere nor offer advice, to remain static in the face of love's mystery—as did Rosales, who revered the event intimately—and to leave the two of them in bed for two or three hours, kissing themselves sweaty in front of a fan that struggled to dry the worn-out fibers of their bodies.

9

A very tenuous, opaline light settled in my eyes, and I scribbled out a poem. A bit later—a few hours perhaps—the little light disappeared.

This particular August, each morning dawned cold. As soon as the sun ventured over the horizon, it wrapped itself up in a great gray coat: a swatch of sky, milky and mottled and wrought with a single, long cloud. It's as if a great mass of spray were hovering over the city like a giant cauliflower, ready to burst open and dowse all manner of men and beasts.

Starting around nine or ten in the morning, I could hear the rhythmic drumming of the water: an ozone-and-monoxide drizzle, a typical rain that with gentle regularity was always ready to come down on passersby, who lowered their heads and furrowed their eyebrows in disgust. Mexico City became a hazy, torrid marsh that—instead of getting infested with insects—glazed the sidewalks with thick gobbets and sad drops falling on foreheads, mingling with sweat. Before noon—before the first meal of the day, actually—faces were dull and gestures halfhearted, indistinct, and damp. By four o'clock, the sky looked a frozen, mysterious turquoise. The hours passed in the darkness of the house, without change.

Until now, the fever and the pain had been somewhat deadened, or that's what I believed. Looming over me was the memory of Laila in my bedroom, sitting there at my side, and the two or three things that she'd said to me and which still seem rather strange and imprecise. It also seemed odd that she would have come to my house in the first place. It didn't quite fit with what I expected of her, her customs (though, admittedly, I didn't know much about those), or her detached and reticent character. And yet it was clear: she had been there, chatting away, by my side in my bed, smiling. How had she found out about my illness? My mother? Maybe Inés? I remembered at once; I ran to my closet, opened the door, and looked in the bottom drawer for the letters: gone. Only my notebook was waiting for me, with pages ripped out; *Las Rémoras* would be at a standstill for some time. But if I had burned all those trite, idiotic, ridiculous little letters? No, definitely not! I was sure that I'd pulled out the last three or four just last week. Then . . . it was true! Laila had them, damn it! She'd come over because I was sick, and I gave them to her. *There's a law—I don't know if it's British . . .* and *Letters become the property of the recipient. Always.* Again, out of place, like something I would say, or like one of the lines I write when I'm alone. Yes, maybe I was feverish and said it to myself, repeated it to myself like a litany. I'd read or heard it before (though now I don't remember where), and constructed a fitful though more or less congruent soliloquy that—in my delirious state—was wholly convincing.

And Federico Ross? When the hell did she loan me that little Federico Ross book, *Bodily Prayers*? Or did I steal it from the library a long time ago? And even worse: she'd had the gall to claim that the author had known her mother, or had been her lover. Impossible! I first became interested in the novella when someone told me that it took place in La Paz, which led me to believe that it might serve as a useful model as I wrote my own story set in Las Rémoras. So it was impossible for her to have given it to me. And Carlos, from across the street? That was also a lie: I'd never been jealous of him, since he's never even gone out with her! I'd never seen them together, at least. But I still had to consult my mother, so I decided to wait until later to verify my theories. Yes, I waited for quite a long time, or at least it seemed that way to me. Soon, however, a new question was hanging over me: Inés? Why hadn't I consulted her if she was the one who orchestrated the visit? I called her. She came right up, knocked, and asked carefully:

"Can I get you something?"

"Did you let Laila in to see me yesterday?" I asked. I didn't want to give her time to think. I wanted to catch her.

"The neighbor, you mean? It wasn't yesterday, it was the day before," she said, melancholic and flat.

"Why did she come? How did she find out?"

"I don't know. I have no idea."

"Could my mother have called her up? To tell her that I was sick? Laila's mother, I mean." I was not in a good mood.

"I'm not sure. I don't think your mother's spoken with the señora recently. When she gets in, I'll ask her . . . if you want."

"No, Inés. It'll be better if you don't say anything." I paused, suspicious. "When did she come?"

"Around noon, she stayed until one o'clock maybe. Your mother wasn't around. I made her wait at first, but then I let her in. I mentioned it . . ." Inés, candid Inés.

"You mentioned it," I asked, "to my mother?"

"Yes."

"And what did she say?"

"She didn't say anything; she just laughed."

This was embarrassing to hear. My mother laughing at the fact that Laila had come over to the house to visit me. There was nothing else worth asking; it was all over now. Inés showed herself out without saying goodbye. I took off my pajamas and went into the bathroom. A thick, dark beard hid my smile from view, as well as my lips, which I made mouth the word *Laila*. I rubbed a bit of lather into my whiskers and began to shave, feeling almost content there, watching myself in the mirror. Steaming water ran from the faucet, gradually fogging the mirror up until I couldn't even see the hand wielding the razor.

But just then—standing there in front of myself—I understood everything and realized that the little laugh Inés and my mother had shared was due to Laila smelling my soiled pajamas. That's what it was. Did she really notice it? How could I find out? I certainly wasn't going to ask my mother, since she knew about Laila and had probably made that ridiculous invitation in the first place. The fever had made me delirious, confused, and I still wasn't quite clear about things.

Which might be why another idea came to me on the heels of the first one. It arrived like a flash of lightning through my mind when I noticed the small nick on my chin and the drops of blood in the sink. Why hadn't I thought of it before? The smile I put on my mother's face like a mask was none other than Inés's incipient, macabre laughter. She'd tricked me into blaming her; that was the only possible explanation. My mother didn't invite Laila . . . Laila hadn't even come. I just hadn't realized it in the midst of my delirium and bone-rattling shivers: the "timid, prudish voice" that had asked permission to come in belonged to the same person who had stolen the letters. Inés was Laila.

But Elías still hadn't come out of his torpor: half meditative, half love-struck.

Nobody knows quite where they stand until the day when they have to move. Such is the nature of love. We don't know how much we truly love someone until that infamous day on which we stop or try to stop loving them. Before that, everything is cloudy and confused, like an endless freefall. A man comes to know a woman: yes, quite easily, it doesn't matter who. In other words, every man ends up doing it. It's a fact. People are, by nature, promiscuous. It can't be any other way. Crusoe can spend his life on a desert island without ever knowing another woman, true, but it's all relative, since he'll still be thinking about someone, drawing pictures of her, dreaming, or masturbating to her memory. Day to day he loved, and he survived. The question, then, becomes quite simple. Ultimately, nobody knows for sure what their relationship with another person actually means, what the essence of their communion is, what type of situation they're building and living through. And the uncertainty and ambiguity is even worse when the relationship is a patently romantic one. In that case, nobody knows quite how deeply they're sunk into love's shitty abyss until they try to leave . . .

Let's take E, for example. One afternoon, he meets R, and they sleep together. It's all very neat and clean for him: he pays, and that resolves the situation. It's been depersonalized, and it makes the question of love one of asepsis. Then he goes about his business and forgets about it, or at least he thinks he does. The same goes for R. She takes the money, undresses quickly, and waits for him sans modesty. If there were any modesty or other defense mechanism, she knows she might develop feelings for this stranger whom she hadn't met before, whom she's never even looked in the eye. But what happens during the interlude—during all the interludes of life—when the man is alone and knows it? Remember, the aloneness and the knowing are two

*different things, and they can unite either for or against that man.
Those interstices can be woeful, and they can also dredge up a lot
of ideas that you'd thought were more or less settled—more or less at
peace—in the soul.*

*For example, what happens during that bit of time when E undresses
in front of R—or maybe he turns his back or does it in profile—while
she waits for him without much caring which way he's turned? Usually
neither of them thinks anything of it. They're treating this as a simulation, going through the motions of love. Neither would intentionally
ruin this performance. Everything is set; everything happens with such
ease, and the connection is so facile, that it's easy to feel something
strange taking root deep inside your heart. Everything points to this:
the heat that their bodies give off once they've been seen—or, rather,
since E and R saw each other's eyes. They understood each other without saying a word . . . he approaches, she's waiting, expectant, yes,
waiting there anxiously at the top of the stairs, and still she doesn't
know it. R waits to feel his body on top of hers, and she could swear
on all the Bibles of the world that she's not expecting anything from
that body, that there's nothing on earth that body could offer her. We
see there, in that time, in that interstice—that abyss opened up in
time—love's worthy accomplice, desire, which invariably draws two
souls down unexpectedly into love's shitty abyss.*

*Nevertheless, things might not turn out that way exactly. Perhaps
R and E don't fall during that first encounter, but something important
continues to smolder until the second or third. A closer look shows
that this can't be true, because the third encounter invariably leads
back into the second, which leads to the first. All encounters (even
unforeseen, unwanted, or chance encounters) lead back into previous
ones remembered by both individuals. Lovers insist on deciphering and
reconstructing memories, on looking for signs with their obsessive and
lonely nostalgia. But is all this really worth anything? Of course not.
It's purely a lover's superstition, just as it is when someone curses the day
they first met someone else, first talked to them, first laid eyes on them*

or kissed them. But, paradoxically, this part is true: there are *certain cursed days in life. Even between two elderly people who have enjoyed seventy-three years together, filled with love, marriage, continuous sex, and faithfulness . . . even they will curse the day they met when one of them is dying while the other can only sit by and watch, or when the moribund contemplates how his or her partner will continue to live after he or she is gone: alone. Love begins to wither from the moment it takes root. And, nevertheless, there are those who opt to label this an egotism or sophism equivalent to that which states, "each year you live is one fewer you have left." But if you look at things clearly, without lying to yourself, you'll see that the worst part about it is that it's true. That's how love works.*

Sitting in Tony's Lonchería one day, Iginio Jasso said to me, Elías, do you know what I like best about love? In the beginning, he replied, it's pure joy. The early stages are the easiest to remember. Blessed are those who begin again or renew their love often. He told me that what follows is something routine, and the desire to fill yourself with that which you once felt, even though it no longer exists. Believe me, muchacho, it's worth it to start over in love as often as possible. The more the merrier! It's the sweetest thing, but it's also the most difficult. But why does it have to be difficult, I asked some three or four years ago. An astonished Iginio responded, Because it's insufferable. It's pretty damn insufferable. And who the hell wants to go through that, I ask you. Who? Nobody I know, that's who. It's the price you have to pay, Elías, and it's a fair one if you're used to it and can look at it all very carefully. Yes, believe me, you can get used to the suffering after a while, maybe a few years. It all depends on how shrewd you are. He continued: Even pain can harbor something good, and—just as love can sometimes last for many years—so can you get used to pain and lose a bit of respect for it. It's true: the pain of love becomes a habit. But you have to know how to remedy it in time—concluded the architect Jasso—and start searching for a new love soon.

I didn't know it then—I was only eighteen at the time—but what Iginio was recommending was that I become a womanizer. Maybe that was the solution. He was a rather frustrated womanizer himself, as everyone in Las Rémoras knew. Still, from that point on something had been cleared up for me: women unequivocally believe that men do not suffer. It's a sort of consensus, an uninformed superstition that convinces them that we either don't suffer or that we're at least better able to endure love's pain. Since it's in a woman's nature to endure childbirth, it's quite easy for them to imagine that it's in a man's nature—our virility—to endure the difficulties of love. And it's because of that ridiculous belief that women become bitches. Yes, it's a miscalculation or an error in judgment, I'm sure. I don't blame them; there's no perfidy in this treachery of theirs, in their coldness. There's only the ancestral, atavistic misunderstanding between men and women: what each party hopes and expects of the other, because they trust in each other's powers of immunity. But how the hell do we make them see that this faith is misplaced? For example, one day, Inés told me, Womanizers—or those who are well on their way to becoming womanizers—learn not to love. Remember that. And many years later—loving Roberta as I love her now (and she knows it better than anybody)—I'd like to answer Inés, to tell her that she was wrong, that, indeed, they are the ones most likely to succumb to love. This isn't blackmail, self-righteousness, or a display of melodramatic sentimentality. No, Inés. I'm telling you that even though you're sleeping with the town councilman right now and can't hear me from this rocky crag I'm sitting on, you are completely mistaken. And there's a very simple proof to demonstrate it. It's them, Inés, the womanizers, big and young (you prefer them that way), who're most susceptible to falling in love and—therefore—to suffering. It's them, the womanizers, who open themselves up, who are proportionally closer to risking their necks, because they are the ones who risk more. Don't you understand? I'm telling you, Inés—since you seem to think you know so many things, so many men, because of running the brothel that I curse out of love—that there are only two laws. The first is that the greater the exposure to love, the greater the pain—but also the greater the pleasure (confirming Iginio Jasso's theory). The second is the same, just in reverse: the lesser the exposure, the lesser the pain, but also the lesser the enjoyment.

Getting back to R and E . . . but what a euphemism, Elías, avoiding the names that are too difficult for you to write, to not admit that you yourself are the poor fool in love with Roberta! Yes, yes, but again: getting back to R and E . . .

It's precisely in those early, short but intense interludes, and then in the longer ones—where one waits impatiently for the other's arrival— where love gestates and grows like a polyp. Its tentacles quickly unfurl. And neither of the participants perceives a thing, they don't realize what's happening: the desire they've been afflicted with is like Hydra or Medusa, and the sea is like an abyss filled with nothing but detritus, and they sink, hopelessly, without knowing when, how, or why. Also, love is like a stingray. You step on one, and at first you feel no pain; just a light itching sensation. But when you step out of the water and notice the puncture, you simply can't believe it. The sting is barbaric but the wound is worse! And it's during that time—between when you feel the itching and when you actually step out of the water—that love's suffering gets going. You've sunk without your consent or approval. It's particularly interesting to see, because neither of the participants is wearing any diving gear, so to speak. What's more, they even seem to enjoy love's shitty smell and the corrosive flavors washing over them. At the very least, it doesn't take them too long to get used to it. And if one day they get asked whether it was true that they did in fact enjoy that shit, they would respond that they—the lovers—were in no way a couple of disgusting coprophiliacs. They detest shit (in other words, love) as much as anybody. But there they are, without their diving gear, because they've grown oblivious to the shit surrounding and inundating them each and every day. That's what passion is when you live—suffer—through the voluntary-involuntary process of submersion.

But why isn't it possible to maintain a pure and uncorrupted heart?
To preserve it as if in formaldehyde? The answer is that if R and E kiss
each other time and again, like a secret vice being fermented between
them, then clearly it's because there was something there in that first
kiss—behind its depersonalized appearance—which led to a second
and third, ad infinitum. It's what's called "the predestination of love."
There would have only been one way to avoid it, and that's if R and E
never actually kissed at all. If the two of them hadn't slept together one
afternoon at the Casa de Inés, if they hadn't seen each other at all, if
Josefina had been waiting there at the door instead, if R hadn't gone
to Las Rémoras to live with her son, if the boy's father hadn't died, if
E didn't have any money that day and just decided to stay home and
masturbate, happy not to be bothering anybody, ejaculating cleanly
and peacefully . . . in other words, if all of that had happened, then
other things would have happened differently across the world and in
Las Rémoras in particular. Of course, it's lazy and simply superstitious
to think in those terms: if the tragedy didn't exist, then of course the
tragedy wouldn't exist. But it's true, Elías: love can reduce you to a
most imbecilic and undignified state. That's what lovers are wrapped
up in. If they weren't, then obviously they'd be caught up in other mis-
eries anyway, and their unhappiness would be a whole other story.

Anyway, Elías, you're now smack in the process of ascending from
that shitty abyss, which is why you're only now starting to recognize
the depths to which you've sunk these past few months. Sometimes it's
a violent assent, yes, and if you're not careful you can succumb to the
bends. The best thing is to do it calmly, slowly—almost impercepti-
bly—so your body won't have to undergo too much strain. You've gotten
out of worse situations than this. Try to look up: you still have a long
way to go. The shitty abyss is always deeper than any star-struck lover
(sarcastic or not, womanizer or not, wise man or not, warm or cold)
thinks it is. Even those who have the foresight to anticipate a submersion
and bring their diving gear along are deceiving themselves, because it's
well known that anybody who submerges with the same person more

than once—no matter who you are, no matter what you do—does so
either with faulty equipment or without any equipment at all.

Elías continued to sit there on the rocks at the edge of the beach. The moonlight reflected off the waves about to break and danced in his face. He remained motionless deep into the hours of the night, when the lawyer Rosales saw his stony figure out in the dark. Still, he didn't try and say anything to him, and simply made his way back past the narrow wharf. He wasn't thinking about the boy, or Roberta, whom he'd seen earlier on his way out of the bedroom, sleeping like a log, sprawled out in a sagging chair in the corner of the dining room, while in the background Lolita sang the Andalusian. Raimundo Rosales was thinking only about the sex with Inés, wondering how the hell he'd fallen in love with her . . . and yes, this time he realized it.

II

Lascurain doesn't realize it, but gastritis can be caused by love. It's possible, even, to speculate that all cases of gastritis and degenerative ulcers are caused either by love or the lack of it. Which is to say, the madness of love. Neither he nor my mother can understand this, can see the connection between the gastritis and the fever, between the fever and love, between love and the gastritis.

12

That morning, after having said goodbye to Santa, the lawyer Rosales—ever punctual in his appointments—adjusted his glasses and headed towards Tony's Lonchería. Three times a week he had an eight o'clock breakfast with the architect Iginio Jasso. There, seated under the beach umbrellas that the owner had put up to proffer shade to the few tables he'd set out early, they could talk for two or three hours without even thinking about it. Anybody who worked for the city council knew when and on what days the lawyer could be found there talking with the architect. On the four mornings that he didn't have breakfast there, Santa made him huevos rancheros—with turtle meat, if there was any—her own special refried beans, and fresh-squeezed orange juice. Which is why Raimundo, unlike Iginio, never ordered eggs at Tony's Lonchería. Instead, he'd have fruit or chocolata clams.

He didn't walk past the wharf this morning, which is why he wasn't sure whether or not Elías was still at his usual post, without having gone to sleep or slipping away when nobody was watching. It was a mystery that everyone in Las Rémoras had wondered about for days, but which nevertheless was soon put to rest, given that nobody was interested enough to actually set up surveillance. That morning, Rosales took another route, a block away from the street that overlooked the wharf. It wasn't something he normally did, because he thought it important to have a look at the sea before breakfast. Yes: when he looked at his watch, it read 7:57, and he wouldn't arrive at 8:00 or even 8:05 if he swung by the beach to watch the roiling, feathery waves.

On his way he slowed down to offer a couple of amiable nods—which cost him a few seconds that, when taken in sum, could translate into a delay of minutes—then turned onto Libertad (with its semblance of a proper promenade), where, finally, he saw the hairless back of Jasso's neck shining under the morning sun. 8:02. Almost perfect, he said to himself. They didn't even wave to each other, such was the assiduousness between them. Rosales simply sat down next to him under the umbrella, where not a single ray of sun could get at him. He absolutely did not share the architect's affinity for sunbathing, which he said did him immeasurable good every morning. The sun doesn't burn in the early morning hours, he'd say, and the skin does not perspire. In fact, an early morning bask is all one needs to last the day.

It was just as he drew his chair up to the table's edge that Rosales noticed he'd stepped on a small, sleeping lizard.

"*Carajo!*" he swore. "Don't look, Iginio."

"At what?" the architect asked, not seeing the animal guts at his feet.

"I squashed a lizard, señor. Son of a bitch! What the hell was it doing there . . . At least I wasn't wearing the shoes I had on yesterday."

"Which shoes?"

"Which shoes? The ones you've seen a million times, Iginio! The ones I brought back from Los Angeles. The Italian leather ones I wear whenever I go see Inés. Those beautiful brown moccasins I polish myself. By the way," he interrupted himself with a wink to his friend, "that Inés is one hell of a woman! My God, she is fucking great."

"I know, I know. Remember, I knew her before you did. But be careful, Raimundo," he said half-seriously. "Inés's pussy can eat men alive. Back in the good old days, they used to call it the Bermuda Triangle, since so many people either disappeared or perished there."

"Now it's more like the Baja California Triangle," the lawyer said joyously, his eyes partly closed, as if he were trying to recall a distinctive yet unnamable scent. "You know, nobody would ever guess that she's at least forty already. I swear, Iginio, she seems more like thirty. Yes sir, there's no doubt about it: that woman's got a hell of an appetite!"

"It's true, she never tires, Raimundo. But we do."

"Why argue if it's the truth?" asked the lawyer rhetorically. Just then, the jovial Tony emerged from the kitchen, waved respectfully, extremely tall and incredibly queer, and set their breakfasts on the table.

After he'd left, Jasso wasted no time in asking the lawyer in a low voice:

"And what can you tell me about Roberta?"

"To be honest, I haven't slept with her. Sharing a bed with Inés for over a year doesn't quite facilitate that sort of thing, believe me. Besides, you know, the poor thing is lost in thought, dumbstruck even, over that boy—whom you also know. Frankly, I just couldn't go to bed with someone like that. I need a little more life, a little more zest . . . who knows? I want to think that they want me, that their mind isn't occupied with other things. You know what I'm talking about, Iginio. Maybe it's that Inés actually enjoys her work . . . And I might even be falling in love."

"Maybe they want to win you over," Iginio laughed as he slurped his orange juice. "Think about it: town councilman, widower, no children, a little bit of money, a house, and a maid. Everyone respects you . . . the old, the young—even the fishermen. What more can you ask for?"

"A woman like Inés, for one. That's what I'm missing."

"That's true, Raimundo, but you need to dedicate yourself to other pursuits. Not pussy, okay? Because that stuff will just burn you out."

"Why bother saying no? Anyway, what are you going to do about it?" Rosales asked, hacking at the slice of cinnamon pineapple sitting on his plate. "People have to maintain their dignity . . ."

"Their appearances . . ."

"Whatever you want to call it. Anyway, you haven't answered my question: what are you going to do about it?"

"Fine. Run off and get married. Or just shack up with her," Ignio said, smiling.

"Mark my words: the day *that* happens will be the day all the ladies of Las Rémoras send telegrams to the Capital bidding me farewell. No more president, hell, no more nothing! It sounds easy, but it's tougher than you think," he said just as Tony interrupted them. The words seemed to be coming directly from his well-groomed moustache. He asked whether the architect and the lawyer would like another cup of coffee. They did. Tony poured fresh cups. They sipped in unison and burned their tongues in unison, but it was Iginio who asked:

"Have you seen Elías sitting there on the rocks? He's absolutely immutable. It's just not possible."

"Yes, I know. Nobody's seen him move. It's like he's dead or a statue. I almost went up to him yesterday, Iginio, but now I'm glad I didn't. You know what that boy is like . . . he'll just furrow his brow and look right through you. He won't even nod. He's a hard case, all right. You just can't help those matters of the heart."

"You might not be able to help, but you can keep someone company, señor," Jasso suggested dunking his bread in his egg yolk.

"And how are you supposed to do that, Iginio? He doesn't want any company. He just wants to sit there, like he's getting ready to jump."

"I don't think it's quite that bad."

"But I do," Raimundo said, taking another swig. "I bumped into Roberta yesterday, you know, she doesn't even make the minimum with her clients, she doesn't get into it, she doesn't greet anybody, doesn't smile—though it's certainly true that there isn't much going on at Casa de Inés during the week, and the madam lets them relax a little bit."

"Well you certainly keep things quiet, Raimundo. What were you doing with her yesterday? Isn't once a week enough? I'd say you're pushing your luck. And if you ask me, she'll eat you alive."

"Don't kid yourself. A widower has the strength of ten men."

"And now you'll tell me that widowers have nothing to lose," the architect said as he shoveled a forkful of eggs and beans into his mouth.

"Believe it or not," Rosales affirmed. "Tell me, for example, do you really think that Roberta, for instance, has anything to lose? What can you lose, when you've already lost everything by the age of twenty-four: a husband, your parents, your home, your land. All she's got left is her son, and she lives for him. She has nothing to lose with Elías, but he—on the other hand—is losing in spades."

"That's not true. She lives for her son, sure, but she also lives for herself. She's not stupid. And let me tell you: she's hungrier for love than he is. At the very least, she needs it more. The boy is losing heart—I don't doubt that for a moment—but Roberta stands to lose someone who truly loves her. That's a rare thing these days, and she could live to regret it."

"So then why doesn't she accept the boy? Why be so reluctant and resigned to loss? I don't understand. What sense is there in such capricious suffering?"

"I don't know, Raimundo, I really don't. It might be that they don't accept each other for who they are. Nobody wants a son, and nobody wants to fall in love with a whore, Raimundo, but sometimes—despite all efforts to the contrary—it happens. And when it does—and when the love happens to be reciprocated—then *poof*! There's nowhere to run to, nowhere to flee. But look at Roberta. She knows better than anybody that the writer isn't worth it."

"Why the hell not?"

"Well, to begin with, he wants to be lady-killer. He's twenty-three years old, and he's a convicted son of a bitch—or a son-of-a-bitch convict—who still hasn't learned how not to suffer. I told him as much myself. But instead of getting him out of his funk, he just kept on sitting there, crestfallen, lamenting and spitting—yes, spitting!—his stupid verses at the sea. Roberta never even paid them the slightest heed. If someone sets about being a

Don Juan, then they can't let themselves be waylaid by love. Or don't you agree?" Here he paused to take a swig of coffee, and the town councilman took advantage of the chance to do so as well. "Secondly, Rosales, he was the first one to complain about her not being suitable. Can you believe it? He said so himself. Just flung it in her face. And the more stern she is to him, the more it hurts. He's saying, 'I don't love you, Roberta, I swear I don't,' but at the same time they're making love all afternoon long. And words, señor, can only convince for so long. Actions are something else altogether. Elías walks around simply dying for her, and everyone in Las Rémoras knows it. And she isn't far behind. But you said it best: she doesn't have nearly as much to lose as him. But she does stand to lose someone who truly loves her. Okay, besides getting fed up with his insistence on an amorous skepticism, a sort of cynicism that would wear on and discourage anyone, you have to admit that Elías doesn't have a cent to his name, and the reason why La Gringa sent Roberta to Las Rémoras was to make some money. Believe me, I understand her motives there. I'll even agree with them. Man can't live on poetry alone—women even less so—and poetry is the only thing that boy knows how to do."

"But if, as you say, Elías flung it in her face, at least he's being honest," said the lawyer, putting on his contrite and supportive face.

"But there's no room for honesty in love. He's not going to win her over with honesty, and he's not going to get anywhere with his poetry."

"I'm not sure I believe that, Jasso," said Rosales. "Take what I found yesterday: a poem hidden somewhere in the pages of a women's magazine. So you see, even whores can be moved by poetry."

Raimundo Rosales took a slip of paper from his jacket pocket and handed it to the architect. The lines of poetry were straight and neat and written in a measured hand, and Jasso began to read them under the sun that so annoyed the lawyer. He finished reading, surprisingly moved, and looked off into the distance, where he saw the town councilman's secretary, Rosinda, and one of the local officers hurrying up the street. Just before they arrived at the Lonchería, Tony emerged with a coffee of his own, and so the three of them—Raimundo, Iginio, and Tony—strained to overhear what Rosinda was saying to the officer, who nodded dumbly and sleepily as he listened in turn.

13

I was thinking about Laila's idea again . . . my memory did nothing but revisit the moments that I'd spent with her. Perhaps that's why I understood that to accept Laila being in the house, seated on my bed, kissing me and reading her letters—my letters—was to accept Inés's innocence. I couldn't believe that Laila hadn't come, and yet—paradoxically—I also wasn't able to accept that Inés was innocent of tricking me. To search for Laila, to find myself faced with the absolute, would have broken the enchantment. So I withdrew into my delirious consciousness and sustained myself with my thoughts.

Sometimes I wondered if Laila had any idea about how much I suffered for her. When a person loves—whether he realizes it or not—he invariably imagines that the object of his affection approves of him. That's the law, and it's impossible to contradict it. The other person doesn't know what's happening, what it's about—or maybe they do—but the lover never realizes this. That, then, is love: a dizzying descent into the pure silt of hell . . . where everything hurts, where everything burns, everything is suggested but never realized, where everything is false, possible, ambivalent. Love is at once a falling and paralysis. The soul is stopped and the body is paralyzed. Sores open up and spread themselves. Lovers' bodies are flayed until they're left with nothing but their hide, shivering and happy. Love, then, is an obscenity, an affront to everyone, a filthy mess that you concoct for others, hoping to make them cry or be scandalized. But it's worth adding that this baseness is only one part of loving; the other is refined in an equal yet opposite manner, growing and expanding. Loved ones are precious; those who love are pigs. San Francisco was mistaken, as was Pablo de Tarso, and many others besides. Laila still didn't know it. Unconsciously, involuntarily, she was refining herself, her tastes, her ego. It wasn't so much that she was loved as it was that I loved her right then. And that's something no woman can ignore. Or better yet: no loved one could not know it; otherwise, they wouldn't be loved. Loved ones are designed for that, not for descending towards Erebus. Those who love . . . they descend, they are humiliated for love, they are buried in a world of cold fury, masturbation, in a hell that's just insane enough to live with and thereby soil themselves, to relish their paralysis and to revel in their filth, all for their infinite and loathsome love. Those who love drink their own filth; they consume it. They simply cannot abstain; they know no other thing than to love. It's where their pleasure lies, as well as their sin. But even so, I repeat, this doesn't matter to them: they take pleasure in suffering and love, it's an eternal joy, perhaps even more powerful than that other thing: actually being there, being desired and loved, and knowing it. The loved one is magnificent and sublime, while the one who loves is vile and coarse. Laila was loved, while I—Ricardo Urrutia, Ricardo the Pig—was the one who loves.

14

"Inés was found dead this morning, sir. She was killed in her room."

Those were the words of Rosinda, the secretary. She stammered them out between tears, horrified, while the officer struggled to maintain his composure as he nodded, corroborating the litany that the girl, staked to her spot, spouted indefatigably at Rosales, Iginio, and Tony in her incredibly shrill, fairy-like voice.

"Inés was found dead this morning, sir. He killed her."

The architect was perplexed. The town councilman of Las Rémoras stood up with a wince. Then, for the first time since the officer and the secretary had come running up to the Lonchería, Rosales's met Iginio Jasso's eyes. Something indescribable was just visible in them . . . something that said, "It was you, Mister Lawyer. You killed her. That's what you came here to tell me this morning, even though you didn't have the guts, and it had to come out like this."

In the offing, hurrying down the street off of Pescadores, were Josefina, Roberta, and two other girls. They were running and waving their hands wildly, shouting something unintelligible. Nevertheless, Rosales had no chance to see them, or the two constables and the man accompanying them, his glasses completely fogged over from the haze permeating the air.

15

The Presumed Death of Inés

I am going to tell the tale—though I don't really want to—of the presumed death of Inés, of the death she so desired.

Two days after the shaving accident when I nicked myself upon realizing the truth, I called her into my room.

Nobody was home.

Papá had been dead for some months now.

I didn't plan to choke Inés, and I didn't reflect on the best way to do it. I only recognized my method in a filial, almost brotherly sort of way, just like what happens in Hitchcock's *Frenzy*. It was something of an augury, of a tragic necessity: Inés would be killed by Laila, which is to say by nobody, which is to say, by me. In those two days, she had understood—finally—the meaning of love, and its profound significance to her. Without Laila, she never would have known.

During those days, I sank down into the most silken entrails of my consciousness, into the softest parts of my body. I had fallen into love's net. Laila had brought me there without my knowledge, and without even knowing it herself.

Though I'm sure of one thing: love is irreversible.

As much so as death.

And so we have the death of Inés.

After asking me if she could come in, Inés said:

"Your mamá asked me to tell you . . ."

"It's not important," I said.

I asked her to sit, there, on the edge of my unmade bed. I could see the consternation in her eyes and mouth. What was the boy going to ask? Panting, troubled, she resisted the temptation to ask me. She waited silently, waiting for me to pick up the pillow.

"It's to suffocate you," I said.

She didn't show any outward signs of discomfort. She didn't even blink: not a fiber of her being had been disturbed. I knew instantly that she was not afraid. She knew that she was going to die, which is why she didn't feel the slightest twinge of fear. I, on the other hand, felt a certain respect on seeing her there, without any intention of defending herself. When I approached her with the pillow, she lay back and allowed me to place it over her face.

Inés gasped for breath. I pushed down with greater and greater force. She gasped again. Then and only then did she put up a bit of a fight: perhaps from belated fear, or some other subtle, animal impulse. Nevertheless, she showed great restraint in not dramatizing her death.

I leaned over her prone, stretched-out, blue-lipped body as if to kiss her. I didn't of course; I just wanted to check if she was breathing. Inés was no longer looking at me . . . she was observing something deep within herself: inquiring, assaying her own death. And then there was only one labored breath in that room. My own.

I picked her up and carried her into the bathroom. I laid her out in the tub and began to undress her with quiet care. At last I saw her naked. On seeing her there, as white as the bathtub molding, I changed my mind: I picked her back up and took her back to my bed. I lifted up the baseboard and hid her underneath it.

How quickly life can change, suddenly compromised with death.

I felt no regret about Inés, nor did I feel sorry for myself. No clouds came to cast a shadow over my face. Life went on: unchanged, seamless, mild. I understood: death and life are ultimately interchangeable, both natural and distinct ways of living, even if most people don't know it.

Inés's death had helped me. I knew that immediately. It had helped me bear the weight of my terrible love for Laila; it had saved me from dying in the sepulchre of that immensity. Now I could cease to love her without fear and without pity.

Did Inés suffer? I don't know, though I don't think so. I do know that she felt pity. Nevertheless, I would like to say—to explain—that I, like she, now understood the full significance of death: Nothing. It has no significance. It was lost in some other part of the world. In other words, I'd like to make it clear that there's no such thing as tragedy. It becomes negated when death loses its significance. I would like to repeat this a thousand times over.

Death is identical to life, Inés.

Only love has meaning, a center. And that is why it is filthy, crawling, conniving.

Because also, remember, people love to love, and perhaps that is our disgrace. My relationship with Inés was always free of such dirt. Between us there was nothing but life and death: one and the same. Two sides of a single coin.

But with Laila, there was love. Is love. There was never any life, and there was never any death.

That is why I did not and do not kill Laila.

That is why I love her or do not love her.

Laila. Am I delirious?

16

Immediately after the prostitutes and other folks arrived, the competitors could see the number-two elected official of Las Rémoras—who worked immediately beneath the town council-man himself—approaching. Without beating around the bush, Francisco Sigüenza asked:

"Señor Councilman, these girls here tell me that you were with the madam yesterday. Is that true?"

Still not quite believing his ears, the councilman stood up so quickly that he knocked over his chair, without concern for either the sun or for any basking lizards. The official, flanked by two more policemen, repeated the question. Finally Rosales responded, surrounded by the confused, astonished looks of the assembled company: Tony, who hung back inside the Lonchería, the architect Iginio (who was scrutinizing him head to toe), the flush-faced secretary, and the others:

"What are you talking about, Sigüenza? Tell me one more time," Raimundo Rosales said, with his eyeglasses still fogged up and his face growing more and more pale despite the incandescent heat.

"I'm talking about placing you under arrest, sir. I've already spoken with the governor; I'm sorry, but he's the one who gave the order. They're coming from La Paz tomorrow to interrogate you. In the meantime, I'm to gather evidence."

"I can't believe what I'm hearing," Rosales said, dazzled. The others watched with the same sense of skepticism as he himself did, contemplating his trembling hands. Suddenly, he blurted: "This is a joke, right? Some sort of practical joke? I swear: I'll have you all sent off to the prison in Mulegé just for trying to trick me. I will."

"We saw you leaving there, sir," Roberta said with aplomb. Her eye makeup from the previous night was still fresh.

"You were the only customer in the house last night," Josefina immediately added, "and anyway the last to leave"—confirming Roberta's story right there in front of everyone. "We never thought to check on the madam in the middle of the night. We thought she was sleeping, and anyway since there hadn't been any clients coming to the house that day, we didn't see any reason to disturb her. You seemed very cool and collected when you left, even though it was past midnight."

"I saw you when you came down," Roberta added. "I'm sure you thought that I was already asleep on my chair on the landing. You knew that my room would be empty."

"I don't deny that, muchacha, I don't. I was there, yes, until very late, and maybe I was the last—the only—one there, as you say. But I didn't kill her. Why the hell would I?" asked a desperate Raimundo. A couple of tears edged out of the steely riverbeds of his eyes, usually so adept at quashing any signs of sadness. This time, however, they all saw it: he didn't know how to stem the flood. And though everyone thought he was crying out of anger, he was crying because of Inés. He knew—

he realized—that he had always loved her . . . no doubts now: he'd loved her.

"I'm sorry, sir," said Francisco Sigüenza as he gave the sign for the two officers to handcuff him.

Which they did, and in full view of those assembled—some women who happened to be passing by at the time, a couple of traveling salesmen, a fisherman, Tony, the speechless architect Jasso, the stupefied Rosinda, the made-up Roberta with her three coworkers, the first officer who had escorted the retinue, et cetera—councilman Rosales was led away by the officers without incident. They walked down Libertad towards the wharf. The sun was raging on high, without a single cloud to hinder it.

Before reaching the sea and bearing left, Rosales could see clear across to the other side of the beach, where the young librarian was still perched up on his rocky crag. He looked as if he was counting the waves. Who knew? It seemed like no amount of sun—however strong—could drive him from his perch; that he would spend the rest of his days there, alone, thinking about Roberta.

Before going through the main doors of the city council building, which stood at the edge of a basketball court, Rosales asked Sigüenza:

"How the hell did she die, muchacho?"

"You're really something, sir!" he scoffed, showing a smirk that seemed to say, *I'm in charge now, and please don't be so cynical. Don't be asking me things that you yourself know better than anybody.*

"How the hell was she killed, Sigüenza? Tell me, goddamn it!" Rosales insisted, trembling, as he wrenched free from one of his captors, who immediately took an even stronger grip on him.

"She was strangled and hidden under the bed." Then Sigüenza sucked in his breath and asked, "If it's not too much of an imposition, Rosales, I'd like to know what was going through your mind when you did it. Why did you hide the body under Roberta's bed, of all places? What good could that do you? No matter how many times I go over that part in my head, I just can't figure it out."

Rosales didn't answer; he was hit with a wave of nausea that he just managed to quash in time. Then his thoughts turned to one thing alone: if Jasso showed the stolen poem to Roberta or otherwise allowed it to reach her hands, things would get decidedly worse for him, and any opportunity to save himself would shrink to nothing. In other words, there would be palpable proof of his guilt: a poem from Elías that everyone would assume he—Rosales—had taken from Roberta's room.

New tears of love began to appear on his cheeks.

17

6:00. I woke up from *The Presumed Death of Inés*, or whatever it was. I watched the sun sinking slowly and wonder how my bedroom window manages to filter out the pale shades of light but not its bloodier hues. My soul emerges from the saddest depths and encounters the things that surround me, taking them on, fusing with them.

The sun lit up the carpet and then winked out. The same happens with the room: it lit it up, then shut itself off. Something antique and inexpressible begins to invade the bedroom, reaching as far as the hallway. Something I didn't know how to describe or what name to give it other than a simple "yellow." The rarified, stagnant air—caused either by the filtering window or by the barely perceptible odor of Inés's body—was itself yellow. But not the yellow of the sunlight; it was another sort of color. More opaline, sad, and sickly. I'm not sure how to explain it. I also don't know how my soul emerged, nor quite where it came from.

In clouds of mist, perhaps? No: it simply passed from one place to another on hearing her, when I asked who had buzzed the intercom and heard her voice answer, Laila.

The presumed death of Inés had a place now, had a proper significance: it allowed things to take their natural course and not stagnate. It was the sluice needed to allow my soul to flow naturally and not be obstructed.

Laila greeted me as affably as always when I opened the door. I lost the timidity that had taken me over whenever I'd thought about her, and invited her in.

I dragged my feet for no reason at all as I followed her into the foyer. Nothing was said about my health. It must have been obvious that I wouldn't have let her in if my fever hadn't broken or at least gone down. The same with the pains in my belly.

She went into the living room, sat down without so much as a glance at the kitchen, gathered her skirt, and smiled. But not at me, I knew. It was a vacant, lost smile. Taking a seat near her— quite near, I should say—I observed her coldly and without fear. Laila fixed her eyes on mine, and this time the smile that came was for me, beaming at my face. I thanked her not with a gesture, or another smile, which would have been the proper response. On the contrary, my face showed nothing at all. I wanted to express nothingness, the non-smile. I'm not sure whether Laila was disconcerted or simply didn't notice. Perhaps she attributed it to my sickness, its embers still burning. Then she asked:

"Did you know that I came?"

At first I didn't hear, or rather I didn't understand, what she was asking. Then I answered intuitively, picturing the smiling inquiry in her lips.

"Actually, I wasn't sure if you had. But I asked Inés, and she told me that you had. Then I remembered."

"What about her?"

"She's not here."

There was a pause, and I saw her reflect for a moment before continuing.

"You were really quite sick. Maybe I shouldn't have come."

"No! On the contrary, it was good that you came."

"I bumped into your mother on the street, and she told me."

"She told you to come?"

"No, that was my idea."

I didn't say anything.

"And where is she?" Laila asked.

"I don't know. I suppose she'll be back later."

I could hear her short breaths: the same sound a bird's wing makes against a window. I smiled at the sound. Outside, a bird fell dead.

"Thank you for the letters; I read them all. But actually, I came to tell you that I never imagined . . ." She broke off, hesitated for a second, and then said: "I mean, what is *Las Rémoras*, Ricardo? I promise I won't tell anybody."

I didn't blush. I remained impassive, unresponsive, absorbed in her movements, in her friendly gestures, in the lines of her body and the space that it invaded when she moved or spoke. It's as if they were two distinct creatures: Laila and her body. The representation of Laila and the incursion she made in space. Now I simply beheld her body, contemplating it without haste or hysteria. I remained absent, listening to her, spying on her out of the sides of my eyes. But then I saw through her: her lips began to tremble when she spoke, when she wanted to explain to me how she'd felt when she read those stupid letters, how she'd never imagined . . . I could see her darkening cheeks, her ears withdrawing from the cold they felt. I probed deeply into her body with my intuition (like a weapon): there was so much pillaging going on inside of her, and she didn't even realize it. I cast myself into her skin, as if my consciousness were leaving its own body behind. I took her by the hand, squeezed it tightly, and she fell silent. She didn't pull away. I saw my body near her, first leading her across the living room, down the hall past the first bedroom, and finally into mine. I saw her speechless . . . I still remember her as she was before she entered the room. I understood everything before anything happened. I heard the shortness of her breath come and go. Then I forgot that she was breathing; I forgot that there was a living soul in her. Laila was a body, and yet somehow I forgot this for a few precious seconds. I immediately made an effort to think about it, and I remembered who she was. I beheld the various parts of her body with certainty, and had them there, at my side, together. I concentrate on the memory. I am also a body, a body that emerged from Laila, that surfaced just before our love in order to enter into it. And so I did. We did. Laila and Ricardo went over to my bed without so much as a word. Laila and I stretched out between the sheets, next to a dead woman's body. We undressed, or I undressed her, sharing the bed with a lifeless body. A man and a woman, both very young, lay down with a woman whose death had made this passion possible. Ricardo and Laila made love. Ricardo and Laila would cease to love. It's that they wouldn't love forever . . . because love isn't forever.

18

It was twelve on the dot, and the Las Rémoras firmament seemed like an immense skylight letting in all the light of the world, the full, disturbing presence of God. The tenuous, monotonous waves didn't slacken in their pursuit, battering at the rocky, valve-shaped beach, its promontories, and the enormous crag where the son of the town, Elías, caviled his love:

Now that I've done it, I have no remedy; I can't change the facts either in my mind or anybody else's. What I did, I did for Roberta, in order to save our love. Of course I didn't tell anyone. They'd call me crazy, ostracize me. Nor would they understand that Inés, in her stubborn dedication to keeping us apart, had to die. That Inés, like the true whore that she is, didn't believe in our love—didn't believe in love at all—and ultimately disapproved of it: she lied when she allowed us to devote entire afternoons solely to our pleasure. She only wanted us to get tired of each other. That's why she didn't order you to see other clients when I was around. And you know what, Roberta? You're mistaken if you think that she held me in any sort of regard, or that she loved you. All that was important to her was taking over the brothel—driving out the real owner, La Gringa—and leaving you, Ruth, and Fina for the lawyer. She wanted to take over Las Rémoras . . . our entire sleepy little town. That's what Inés was all about.

Last night, I heard the lawyer passing by here. I thought that he was going to stop, but no, thank God, he didn't . . . something compelled him to continue on to the Casa de Inés. Not a soul was about at that hour: it might have been 12:30 or 1:00. I got down from the rocks, crossed the wharf, and headed up towards Libertad. For a brief moment, I thought that I saw someone at the Lonchería—maybe it was Tony—because I saw what I thought was a light on. But my eyes were playing tricks on me: it was just the moonlight reflecting off the shop window, not a light inside. I continued on, passing first Atuneros and then Pescadores. Both streets were completely deserted. I didn't see so much as a dog, nor hear a single bark. I stopped outside the Casa, where I heard music: a woman—perhaps Andalusian—was singing a tune I couldn't quite place. Instead of jumping the gate right there in front, I went around to the back. There's a little knoll in the undeveloped land there. Do you know it? In the lot next door, which was abandoned by a family way back when. In any case, it's easier to get back in there.

I wanted to see you, Roberta. I couldn't stand not being able to look at you anymore. I'd spent the last few nights coddling myself in my cocoon, the most conceited of all men reduced to licking his wounds like a dog. I couldn't stand my body any more. I couldn't take my smell, my presence . . . I couldn't stand myself, see? Sitting on that stone, crestfallen, waiting for nothing, because—as both you and I know—there is nothing to wait for. That's why I had to find you, to make love to you even though I was scared, even though I had promised myself that I wouldn't touch you again, even though I would die. I wanted to feel consumed at your side one final time. To consume myself, I mean, and not our passion, which is the only thing that Inés really wanted, after all. Our love wasn't going to wane, Roberta, even if we did. That's why I went into your room. When I saw that you weren't there, and when I more clearly heard the song being played downstairs in the living room, I understood that you would be there, alone and pensive, smoking a cigarette even though you almost never do. So I stole into Inés's room, which is right next to yours. I thought that she would be sleeping . . . but from the stuffy darkness of the room, I heard her caring, mellifluous voice ask: "Is that you, Raimundo? Did you come back?" At first I didn't respond; only after taking a couple of soft steps towards her body—lying prone, with her back to me—did I let out a whisper, as if to say, "Yes, now be quiet, I'm right here at your side. Shhh." I took the time to sit down on the edge of the bed. Then I picked up the pillow that Rosales had surely lay on himself not an hour before, and began to smother Inés. She resisted, thrashing about with her entire body, and so I got on top of her, straddling her with my legs, pinning her down. My arms didn't let up for an instant. She gave one last push to try and escape, then collapsed, at which point I knew she was dead. Poor thing, she died thinking that it was Rosales who had suffocated her. I felt neither pain nor joy. I did it without hesitation, fear, or feeling; without having to overcome any of the obstacles I might have expected. I just saw myself doing it . . . yes, I could picture myself in the act of suffocation. All for our love, Roberta. To save it.

After I stood up over her inert body, I went over to the bedroom door and opened it a crack. The Andalusian Lolita's song continued

. . . I could still hear it wafting up from downstairs. I turned back to the bed and picked up Inés's body: she didn't seem to weigh anything at all. There was no soul inside her; only her body remained, vulnerable and exposed. Everything happened so fast that I can barely tell you, Roberta, what thoughts were flying through my head: that I should hide her there under your bed, as if in sacrifice to our love. I understood everything instantly. It was our last resort. Perhaps her death could pull us from this quagmire, from our paralysis . . . maybe something would happen. I don't know, I just don't know. Perhaps I could sit down and write again, Roberta. Perhaps I could go to the Lonchería and pick up the threads of my story. Continue with it. And love you without this sorrow, without this solitude.

Here at the beach, some boys sitting near me are building a sand-castle with a wall like the one that used to surround Loreto. They're sunbathing, either unaware of or oblivious to my stony solitude, and content to pay me no mind. They don't know, and I appreciate—even esteem—their disinterest, their obliviousness more than ever. I haven't moved, as if camouflaged, so as not to attract anybody's attention. Yes, especially now that I've seen the officers carting Rosales off. They think he's the guilty party . . . what a development!

You know the rest, Roberta. You were the last one awake that night; you went up the stairs a half hour later, after shutting off the record player, opened the door to your room, and found me lying there in your bed, naked, face up, waiting for you though you weren't expecting me. You startled me. You were startled too, I know. How would your skin react after this brief interlude? Would it be a bad idea to try again? you wondered. Where would passion take us? And the overwhelming desire to unite death and sex? We had to make love over Inés's body. We had to, to save ourselves. It might have been our last chance. You couldn't have imagined it, could you, Roberta? You couldn't have known that we were sleeping just above a smothered body. And no, there was no light on, Roberta. Not a single bit of illumination save for the moon filtering in throughout the bedchamber.

Now I'll try to go home and resuscitate the novel I'm writing. The one that has been in stasis for so long now. The story that you, Roberta, were preventing me from finishing, because of love and its shackles, which you may not know. The story that was imprisoned for so long because of passion or desire, lost in a mountain of files and documents. Roberta: at last I will be able to decide what to do with Ricardo, with his life. It's urgent. Like saving my own life.

A few minutes later, the boys were stunned to see Elías climb down from his rocky perch and set off walking past the wharf. And not only that: Iginio Jasso was able to discern his blurry silhouette in the breeze that blew in off the sea, taking the edge off the radiant sun. Less than an hour later, others observed him crossing Sardineros and then Encaladores, heading towards his house, and then returning to the wharf with a notebook in hand. It had once been a common thing to see him with his notebook every morning at Tony's Lonchería, but this time he skipped Libertad. Instead, he went down to the beach where the boys—along with a couple of women and an officer—paused, perplexed, to watch as he climbed back up to his perch and—with the sea and burning sky in his face—sat down to write about love's life:

19

It's well known that love's life—its duration—is a short one when two seventeen-year olds are involved. Which is why we can lay out two undeniable truths here: first, that Laila and Ricardo are in love. Second, that soon their love will come to an abrupt and permanent end. They're two truths, or two halves of a whole truth, and are not at all contradictory. They are perfectly reconcilable. If someone were to ask her, Laila would respond that yes, it was true, she did love Ricardo that afternoon. And if someone were to ask him, he would also say that yes, he loved

Laila that afternoon when they lay on a mattress over Inés's lifeless body.

At night, when Helena returned with Lascurain, and a captivated Laila had gone home, Ricardo had everything ready with which to begin his journey, the pilgrimage. Discreetly hunkered down in his closet, Ricardo watched through his peephole, and discovered that it was not, in fact, Lascurain who had entered the house with his mother. It was someone else: a tall, broad-shouldered man who dropped his trousers down around his ankles before urinating.

He saw his shape in the mirror, the sink, the showerhead, and the toilet. Ricardo wasn't interested in what was about to happen; rather, it was the fact that this man—his face, his frowning lips, and thick eyebrows—looked quite familiar. Like his father, in fact. The resemblance was quite striking.

What happened next wasn't certain, since the next thing Ricardo Urrutia knew was that he woke up surrounded by shoes and hanging clothes. He snuck another quick peek, but couldn't see either his mother or this new man. He could have nodded off for a couple of minutes, or for an hour or more. With practiced stealth, he carefully stood up and made his way to the bathroom. He lifted the toilet seat and began to urinate while at the same time contemplating the odd, ruddy, velvety semicircle of hair on his chest. He gave his eyes a good rub, and finally, without a second thought, ended up packing the last few things he would need. He looked at the clock on his nightstand: it was 3:30 in the morning, which told him that he'd dozed off for several hours, and he wasn't about to try and fall back asleep before morning—before he left. Instead, he'd begin the book that Laila had loaned him—or, depending on how he remembered it, the book he'd taken from the library—and then he'd leave. Finally, his pilgrimage was about to begin. The last thing he did before settling down to read was to stow the bills he'd taken from his mother in his pocket, open the bottom drawer, and take out the notebook in which he'd been writing the story of Las Rémoras, which he'd been inventing during his idle afternoons. He stowed that away too. Then he lay back against his pillow to begin again with that little Federico Ross novella, and this time he read the entire first section in one sitting:

BODILY PRAYERS
(DAY ONE)

They took me away that night. I didn't realize that I'd been stripped of my primary sensation: having a body. Then, without noticing, I had lost it . . . though perhaps only to recover it again. From that day forward, I keep the sensation locked in my memory, to maintain it, for it to remain alive.

I write.

They took me away that night, many years ago, in La Paz. It doesn't matter what night it was; it could have been any. Darkness is the same everywhere. In outer space, I'm sure, there is only one, maternal night. Sometimes we're aware of it; we know that it's one and the same, while it's we who are different. She, on the other hand, is eternal and majestic in contemplating us.

"Federico, today's your lucky day," says Cecilio, laughing. Everyone else in the car laughs as well.

"Such a pure, saintly little virgin . . . how sweet!" Hugo says sarcastically. "The whores are going to love you—you know that, Fede?"

The others celebrate. They celebrate me. The night is close, and the blue Ford's dirty windows make it seem darker still. The darkness seeps among us, as if keeping watch. Was I bound to them in the route, in the celebration, which was ultimately mine as well? Did I feel even the slightest hint of the ardent joy that they felt? In any case, it was all about a unanimous celebration, since I was being divested of my remaining innocence. In the end, however, in a place separated from both my consciousness and my soul, I doubted whether I had anything in common with their diverse and confident bodies. Maybe I did, or maybe I was only similar in our collective, unique memory. I don't know. But *now* I know I feel the painful weight of desire pulling me down, and I realize that it's the deliberate weight of illusions that are interrogating me, since *then*, in just a few hours, they'll cease to be what they have been for so long: pure desire.

"If your father finds out, we're dead, Fede," says Cecilio. "We're obviously doing this for you . . . or do any of you other guys want to dip your sticks tonight too?"

Everyone laughed. If I were to listen to it *today*, after so many years, I might discover in my laughter a certain anguished note, short and sweet, like the fatigue that's born out of the pain of desire itself.

"Listen, *cabrones*, it's still pretty damn far," says Hugo. "This shitty road makes me nervous . . . there aren't any signs or anything. People who go there always end up getting very drunk. So be careful, Cecilio, just don't make an ass of yourself. Listen, you guys, keep on talking to him, otherwise he's going to fall asleep. Damn, Fede, try and have a good time, OK? Let your balls hang out a little bit."

"The poor guy is hung like a radish," says Cecilio, letting go of the steering wheel.

"Just drive, don't mess around," says Solón, his more quiet and reserved brother.

"Yeah, just drive, you fucker," Hugo repeats, mimicking Solón rather effeminately.

Now Hugo is dead. It happened a couple of years ago. My cousin Cecilio was the one who told me about it. I didn't believe him at first . . . over the phone, it was almost impossible to believe. His death, however it happened, was an anguishing plunge into the abyss. It was true—it is true—because many years have passed since then, since Hugo disappeared. And when someone disappears, it means that they're dead. When you think about it, he dies twice: soon comes the confirmation, with a permanence in it. Hugo, our beloved and *evidently dead* friend whose protruding belly and nervous loquaciousness we will never see again. He will never *be* again. It was the first real loss I'd ever really noticed. The first I had ever truly experienced. Before, I hadn't really felt death to be real; it only existed in movies. All this happened—I remember it well—two years after that night I learned, once and forever, to accept the loss of that feeling. My body.

Now I know full well that death and love are what give us life. How? By diminishing it, by snuffing it out. Death and love grant us perdurable memories of life. You'll realize it if you just close your eyes for a moment and *see*. See and think. Then *remember*. To think is to remember, or to create variations on memory. Life wanes while memory remains. It's as natural as love and death can be, and I think only children do not understand this.

Not everything is worthy of memory. I'm still not sure how to describe it. *Now* I'm only able to glimpse three long and narrow taverns along one side of the highway, out in the open air and the night. From the shoulder, I can just hear the murmur of music; no louder than a baby's cooing. I notice how the lights of the taverns stab at the air, the thick darkness, the suspended time that, *now*, I try to penetrate, try to lose myself in. The blue Ford skitters over a band of loose gravel by the brothel. I feel a certain unidentifiable malaise deep in my stomach. There is the bumpy ride, the tight confines, the oppressive heat of the night and the laughter, the music that—bit by bit—grows in our ears and dampens them entirely. But this malaise I feel is due more to my anxiousness at losing my body, my innocence. *Now* I understand: all men try to recover it, at least those who understand that we survive because of our body and our innocence. A Portuguese poet and a Greek poet both knew this. The former went about denying himself any other body, while the latter lived by conserving the memory of his own. Two very different things, to be sure, and yet each survived in his own way. Both were right, though one of them was afraid. Pessoa writes:

> With what gesture of the soul
> Do I take the step from myself towards the possession
> Of another's body, horribly
> Alive, conscious, aware of myself, as much he
> As I am I.

The other, Cavafy, writes:

> Body, remember not only how much you were loved,
> not only the beds in which you lay,
> but also those desires for which your
> eyes openly glowed,
> and voice trembled—and some
> chance obstacle made them futile.

Now I will try to silence those voices as best I can, to quell the tumult of my friends. I will hear the sounds of things that have no sound: the defenseless landscape, the vulnerable creatures and their shadows. I will understand the sound and its silence, and—on contemplating, on remembering the sight—I will establish the language of sensations. I will remember desires that not even they, my friends, know they had. I will speak here the words that do not speak, those that mean nothing and are understood *naturally*: the sort of language we hear in a silent film, entranced, understanding or just *knowing* what isn't said aloud. I will mortify my senses only to remember them yet again and create something that lives and only barely dies; I will erase meaning and strip the names from things. The language I conjure up will be seen, desired, engendering nostalgia.

We get out of the blue Ford. Right away, someone embraces me. I'm not sure which of my friends it is, I can't see them. I'm afraid: *now* I don't want to want to go on or go back. I'd much rather that the moment of truth never come. I understand that I will never have another chance to be born again, but—for just an instant—I forget this and sink again into desperation. I can see that nobody feels sorry for me in the least. How could you forget that, Federico? I reproach myself.

We go in the first of the taverns. Up above the door, a cracked neon sign spells out the name of the place: El Ranchito. A gaunt, drunk, dull-looking man brushes past me. He doesn't even notice; he is unaware of both his skin and of his body. *Now* I am unimaginably fragile and sensitive. But when is *now*? This is unimportant: it is any *now* in which it's possible for me to feel fragile. For example, *at this exact moment, as I write these words, I am remembering* what it was like to enter my first brothel, where a nauseous, staggering man bumps into me.

I listen to the music. The band plays tirelessly on a dais off to one side of the dance floor. Couples dance: there are some perfumed women rather vulgarly adorned with green and blue lilacs, and others wearing black velvet gloves despite the heat and who embrace any man who comes their way. They are one and the same, as are the men. It doesn't matter whether or not they embrace there on the brothel's dance floor, or even if they've ever seen each other before, whether they love each other and haven't slept together yet, or if, some time, to their disgrace, they do sleep together and then think that they're in love. Everything is diffuse, and everyone irredeemably condemned to being themselves. I listen attentively to the cumbias, and *now I know* that these musicians will never tire of playing there in the El Ranchito dance hall. It gives me a feeling of Eternity, or at least some simulacrum of it.

The women let themselves be groped . . . not too much, though, for fear of "losing their self-respect." We watch them. I cautiously watch (for fear of being seen myself) Solón, the shyest of the group, Cecilio, Fat Hugo, and Octavio. I know they're afraid, but they smile, trying to dispel their nervousness. At the same time we watch how a woman embraces a man and is afraid herself. The man is intimidated, despite the embrace, as am I, because I can discern the effects of that fear. It's shared equally, so that perhaps it wanes as it spreads among the crowd. Yes, I discover this universal fear, and immediately find myself infected . . . and I pass it on to others with the greatest of ease.

We begin to make our way around the room, walking slowly and together. We're different: these men know it, as do we. Nobody says anything because there's nothing to be said, nobody speaks because we are not to be spoken to, nobody has so much as a rude or derogatory word for us. I think, shouldn't someone come up to us and ask what were we doing, what the hell were we looking for there among the whores?

We work our way around the split tables, tacking (as if we were a boat negotiating a shallow reef) until we reach the opposite edge of the room. We set up at one end of the bar, something of a refuge from the ominous darkness and oppressive noise. Here, people seem to pay less attention to us. Waiters run back and forth, yelling out orders to the bartenders. Nobody gives us a second look, as the hustle and bustle of work to be done offers us something akin to camouflage. Cecilio approaches one of the waiters and—in a hesitant, pusillanimous voice—orders a round of beers. The man ignores him and walks off. I take a moment to survey my friends, but they simply make dismissive faces.

Octavio says we should leave. The air in here is foul, stifling and staining. Defeated and ridiculous, we file towards the exit, in a state difficult to define: when bodies take their seats and space is drawn out like a blade. I feel everyone watching me. My cousins, Solón and Cecilio, are seventeen and eighteen, respectively; Hugo is nineteen, Octavio only fifteen, while I am fourteen. I'm not tall and I'm not going to get much taller. I gather that others can see this, which is why they notice my small frame, even when hidden it's amongst my circle of friends. I follow them until, finally, exhausted, we find the door we came in through. Standing there, a woman dressed in blue makes eye contact. I look back at her and blink. Inevitably, I tear my eyes from hers; now—without intending to—I contemplate her legs running up against the wall. I look up again and find myself faced with Octavio's broad back. I rest my eyes there, as if it were a last redoubt, a bastion fear has yet to reach. I detest eyes and eye contact . . . they are another part of me, strange and external: they don't belong to me, and always end up bringing me towards the *other*. My eyelids flutter: I try and rub them, but inevitably I cry. It might have been from the cigarette smoke or the heat. Shame rains down everywhere, exhausting me. We leave.

Several people are walking around outside. A drunk grabs a woman roughly from behind. The August heat is approaching body temperature, corrupting and consuming everything in the brothel. Her facetious protests are clearly audible, and we laugh amongst ourselves. It was all we could do. Octavio insists that we try the next brothel over, no more than twenty yards away. We walk up to the door, which—just like the previous one—is crowned by a neon sign. This one reads El Ferry, and I remember it well: it's the place where she found me, where she caught me watching her, thinking—mistakenly—that *I* had found *her*. It's always the woman who finds a man. There's a congenital, ancestral error in thinking that it's all the man's doing, that he catches her watching him. It's just not true: she notices him before he even realizes it, lifts her veil, and then waits for him to notice her. Nothing is true in a woman's eyes.

She—the prostitute—leans lightly on the bar, chatting with the bartender. The place is mostly empty. Nobody is dancing. All we hear is the muted sound of a jukebox tucked away in some corner: a soft, unobtrusive melody that respects the peace in this little house of love. Without looking away from the bar, I can hear the few couples talking. They drink a little, smoke, they talk and don't understand, they breathe and answer. The woman is a mulatto, very thin, with the willowy body of an undeveloped thirteen- or fourteen-year-old boy. She is almost a reflection of myself. She is narrow in the hips and lean through the chest, and the fine lines of her face are cast into relief by the light. Her cheekbones give her a sort of warm, sleepless look. She pauses, her mouth opens into a smile, and I can see her teeth. Her eyes shine intensely. What's more, *they're shining right now.* She understands what I want in a way that no other woman has before, the desperation in this rigid, unexpressive mouth; she understands things that I'm not even able to grasp, and she amazes me across the centuries, like a poison. She knows the body—each hope and hidden, sinister desire—of every man. She laughs, and I am caught in the gesture. She is moved, or simply trying to move me.

She is wearing a loose-fitting, violet dress decorated with sequins and fringe and straps crisscross her bare shoulders. Looking at her fills me with a kind of tenderness; I don't know if it's her or her eyes or her face or what. Her arms move easily through the night air of the room, and a breeze flows around them, encircling her legs, one of which is propped up on the bar rail, which also supports the inebriated bodies of the patrons.

I move to stand next to Octavio and Cecilio, who are talking nearby. I can barely stammer out, *It's her,* she's the one I've been dreaming about for years. They're surprised, they laugh ecstatically . . . I have no idea what they're thinking or what they find so funny. I simply repeat, *It's her.* Hugo comes over and asks me if I'm sure. I know full well: her, there in the El Ferry barroom one August day. It's hot, her eyes shine—flicker like flames—and *now I know that it's her risqué, resplendent earrings that have struck me,* that are reflected in her lustrous eyes, mesmerizing the souls of the naïve. Still, however, I believe it was love that moved me, though *now I know* that I am mistaken; only now after so many years do I ask myself if love has anything to do with tenderness, and if my body has anything to do with the love of the woman standing right in front of me. After all these years, I realize that no, tenderness and love are nothing more than a morbid pleasure, a sort of disease that dulls the senses, overcoming them.

Hugo walks confidently over to her, and from that moment on everything becomes absurd and slow. Time lengthens. Hugo's tall and poised, and we watch as he winds a long and circuitous route around the tables. He reaches the bar and sidles over to her, but at no moment does she take her eyes off me. Then, for the first time, as they smile at each other, I discover another human response, which is perhaps its worst allergy: jealousy. I am jealous. Jealous of Hugo talking to the whore. He winks at me and makes a sign with his hand. But *right now* I can only watch things unfold in time and space. Solón taps me on the shoulder and gives me a slight nudge. I think that I'll never be able to cross the threshold of this moment . . . I wonder if it's still possible to desire something else, but I don't have the will to make it happen. I try to figure out just what part of my body is producing this anxiousness. I hear the others muttering behind me. With no small effort, I urge my legs into motion and walk over towards the bar, driven by a great uneasiness. I recognize it: fear pulls at my thighs and knees, and my arms become dead weight. From that moment on, *I know* that my body has begun to age. My hands grow numb, and I can feel torpor and fatigue knitting in my neck. I cannot revolt; I can't contradict my destiny. I feel her lay her hand on mine. Hugo offers me another conciliatory wink that, now that I think about it, dissolves into a simple gesture without meaning. The woman leads me off, never letting go of my hand. We go out the barroom's back door, and yet I'm still thinking about my friends and cousins, as if doing so will infuse me with some new strength and courage. I see a narrow concrete passage. We walk towards an open area flanked by contiguous booth-like rooms. I ask if I can undress her when we enter ours. Of course, she says. She nods but she can't understand that flagrant desire, which—for the first time—I'm daring to voice in front of someone. And I don't regret having said it. I've dreamt about undressing a woman, not penetrating her.

We stop at a booth, and a large man inspects me closely. The woman tells me I have to pay for the room up front. I take out a bill. She nods at the fat man, and he in turn smiles at me. I don't know if it's ridicule or sympathy or if he's taking pity on my young body. Doubtless he endures desire just like everybody else. *Now I know.* I pay him. He produces two bills from underneath his desk and lays them quietly in front of me. I weigh the apathy of my hands, the torpor of my body, and I submit even more, hoping to prolong my date with this prostitute and draw this time out indefinitely. The fat man laughs. I try to keep my distance as I reach to pick up my change. I tuck it away in my pocket and immediately the woman takes me by the hand again. We walk off, and in the deepest reaches of my soul, I wish that she were my wife.

We go up to the door to our room: there's no lock, and it yields with a push. *Today* brings the idea that, all things considered, I'm following an Order, and it pains me to be a part of it. Its preestablished will—in other words, having to do with this Vocation which overtakes us all from time to time—gives me pause. But *I understand now,* as I watch how the door gives way at this woman's touch. The Order watches us like a tiger ready to pounce. I'm afraid of losing my balance and falling into the abyss if I stumble, if my voice falters, or if I give too much away. She recognizes this, assuring me that my body will soon feel at ease and that I mustn't be afraid.

The door has already closed behind us. The light has grown dim and stains every corner of the room. And the woman hasn't waited for me; she's undressing herself. I give her a look, but of course she doesn't understand my reproach. She hasn't taken off her heels, and the only other thing she's wearing is a pair of panties. Her breasts are small and pointed, and her silver-dollar nipples grow erect as she moves to touch me. She caresses me softly, carefully: almost motherly.

I kneel down and examine her: the corners of her intriguing lips, and her wide eyes. I begin methodically to pull down her panties with my hands, though without letting so much as a finger linger on her hips. I lean towards her face. When I've got the panties down to her knees, she interrupts me for a moment to lift one of her legs and discard them completely. She leans on one of my shoulders. She takes me by the arm and leads me over to the bed. She undresses me, lays down with me in front of her, and *now I know* that this body here next to me, waiting for me, does not belong to me. It only purports to be mine—or a reflection of mine. Her body will never belong to me, regardless of whether I sleep with her or not. It's a fleeting specter, nothing more. Nobody has ever had a body of his own; nobody has ever owned the body of someone else. I did not know it then.

She smiles at me, and again I contemplate the delicate lines of her mouth and the feeling of tenderness that she provokes in men. She asks me to move, not with or beside her, but on top of her. And then I'm there, though I don't remember how it happened. I don't say a thing; I simply bend down to smell her, with my face in close, restraining myself, taking her in my mouth. I pull back from her, rise up, and bring my face towards hers, looking into the whore's eyes. Her face is nonexistent, unintelligible. I can feel her hand maneuvering my cock, at first down and then up inside her. I want to understand a little bit more, but soon it becomes impossible. I begin to kiss her shoulders, but I've lost control of my mouth, and my saliva covers her skin. She moves beneath me, lightly, as if she didn't have my body on top of hers. I had no idea that she could be so agile beneath the terrible weight of my body. I move with her, following her lead. There's nothing for me to brace myself against—no handhold or footrest—and the only thing I find at hand is to just be there, moving my body over hers. I think I'm about to faint.

It was over. The soul and the body will never again be of one substance. From now on, desolation will be a part of them both. The soul and the body (which in the beginning are the one and the same) are now no more than *soul* and *body,* irredeemably separated. All that remains is the struggle to learn this again in each and every body: to wish, to obtain, and then to lose. It is thus, until the end.

"Muchacho, get up. You drooled on my shoulder," she says, pushing me off to the side.

Solón and Octavio bounce around, sweaty, one on either side of me, as the blue Ford navigates the road back towards the city, towards the coast. It's the same road either way—the same road that will take you anywhere and nowhere at all—but the world is different now, narrower. They're trading nonstop insults and cunning repartee. First one calls the other a tasteless slob, then the other insults him back, and pretty soon the whole car is caught up in wild laughter. I—Federico—feel dwarfed between them there in the back seat, and yet I can't stop listening to their cursing and shouting. It seems that, for a moment, they've forgotten about me . . . no, I'm wrong, it's just that they feel safe now that I'm one of them, and they're unanimously celebrating the dispossession of my body, the act that finally affirms my link with the world. They are happy, and *now* I can imagine their arrogant, flashing eyes that night. I watch the road, and Cecilio's hands locked around the steering wheel. A warm, thick darkness blankets our bodies that—with the gentle bouncing of the car—bump and graze against each other. I don't want anyone to look at me. Fortunately, my position in the middle of the back seat keeps this from happening. I can't think of any other way to shrink myself down and vanish, other than to keep my eyes focused on the road ahead and the steering wheel gripped by Cecilio, who—bluntly and out of the blue—asks me:

"You didn't go down on her, did you?"

The whole car erupts in laughter, almost shaking it right off the road. *Now* I wouldn't feel any shame in telling them the truth.

"What do you think? Do I look crazy to you?"

I tell them and they believe me: only a madman would do that. Immediately I feel bad about lying. (The highway is almost a straight shot to the La Paz coast, its beloved wharf, and—at this time of day—is mostly deserted. Only a few sets of isolated headlights break up the darkness and the thick feeling of time.) I give myself over to exhaustion, and I lack the will to fight off a sort of noble sadness. I begin to drift off. I sleep.

I sleep. It's night. There's a blinding sort of clarity in the kitchen. I wait with my sister and my father for *her* to serve us dinner. We're drinking milk. I contemplate the fine hairs on my sister's lip, drenched in white. I see Selma caught for a moment under the ceiling light, heaping spoonfuls of sugar into her glass, and I make fun of her. My father scolds me, and I fall silent. I hear the spitting and sputtering of the sausages, which *she* has put into the skillet. Now she turns to look at me. Her look is the warmest I will see for many years. I will not find it anywhere else. Then, kindly, her eyes stunning, bathed by the overhead light, she says something to me, and from that moment on the world grows small, and I'm aware of nothing but that voice: it's only my mother there, observing me, her skin dissolving as she does the dishes, my father who admonishes us, and the sizzling frying pan on the stove. Her contours are delicate, almost breakable. At any moment, she can escape, she can flee. *I know this now.* I did not know it then. It pains me, not having known it that night, or the previous or following ones. We have our supper. My mother eases herself carefully into her chair. She's expecting another child; her belly is just beginning to show, so I can ready myself for having a new little being around the house. *Now* I know that it will never come, and I am ashamed.

The ceiling light is blinding and casts shadows on the wall. We're all talking at once. We each want to say something important, to impose our voices and our wills. Chewing, gesticulating, waving theatrically, and suddenly, to me, everything is reduced to this overhead light and the dark depths of night just outside the window. Each one wants to get his words in without understanding what everyone else also wants to affirm in front of *the other.* Everyone doubts themselves, and, for that reason, blinded, they speak in ever-louder tones. I watch my mother as if she were just one more sibling, interrupting, taking charge of the conversation or ceding it to us, moving and scraping at space like we do without knowing that we're copying her, the way I see my sister Selma doing it, or the way I contemplate myself in the round mirror of some dressing-room, even my parents' when they're not around. We talk, and nobody pays any attention. My father speaks the least of anyone; even if one of us interrupts him, he doesn't mind. He understands. Yes, understands: all of us—even him—are just like my mother in that regard. We finish, and my sister and I know that it is time to go to bed. The clock strikes nine. I kiss my parents and tell my mother that I will wait for her. We won't fall asleep if she doesn't come upstairs to tuck us in.

Selma and I, each in our own room, hear her climbing the stairs. We toss and turn in bed, mussing the covers in an attempt to prolong these fleeting moments. We focus on the rhythm of her steps in the hall. She goes into my sister's room to tuck her in first. I can hear both women's voices: a prayer I know and which begins, *Barukh atah Adonai* . . . I understand that my sister doesn't want to let her go; she wants to hold her there as long as possible. Finally, though, I hear our mother kiss her goodnight and walk towards my room. It's dark; the only light is what filters in through the half-opened door. It expands. She comes in, and I can just make out her body, her arms. After covering me up, she sits down on the corner of the bed. I can feel her hand stroking my chest through the smoothed-out quilt. I'm cold: I curl up and tuck my hands in close to my body. My mother squeezes me through the blankets, and I feel a bit warmer. I am uneasy. She recites the prayer in a voice scarcely above a whisper: *Barukh atah Adonai* . . . Each of her words is like a salve, and also (though she doesn't know it) like a jab. Yes, the unfortunate conclusion to her nightly visits to my bedroom. I'm only interested in the words that can keep her there a little longer; nevertheless, I fail to find them. The prayer is coming to an end, the words falling sadly away like grain. Then I hear the unfortunate "goodnight"; my mother gets up, and the space which she occupied has once again become *an island safe from time*, a great warmth radiates right from that spot, a wave of heat that I myself could never generate in sleep. I take advantage of that space of hers, nestling down in it. My mother bends down and kisses me on the cheek. I haven't found anybody who resembles her in quite some time. It's not a question of tenderness or caring, and it doesn't have to do with the pleasant corruption of the kiss I received. It's heat. The things that I keep tucked away in my memory are her indelible kisses—which repeat themselves if I remember them—converted into warmth. I hold onto the sensation even after I ask her to leave the door open, that I want to be able to hear them—her and my father—as I fall asleep.

I sleep. I lift up my head, and I find that I've nodded off on Solón's shoulder. Octavio, my friend from Mexico City, shakes me awake. I'm a bit more aware now. I hear Hugo's cheerful voice say, We're there, man, and I realize that it's one person who sleeps, wrapped up in a dream about his mother, and it's someone else entirely who writes it all down years later. There's a strange feeling in all of this; that is, in the act of discovering that we might once have been one and the same. And no, these are only my likenesses, though I remember them, and we always wake up among them, which is to say, among *ourselves*. And while they do not write, they might remember me. It hurts me to know that I'm not him, that I'm not the one who dreams, and it shames me to know that *now I am the one who writes*, the one whose sole function is to record it all . . . but I understand at once that nobody else lives and remembers at the same time either. I have decided on the memory that absolves, that saves us from fleeting time. But who will save me when I myself am only a memory or a piece of writing? I live, and the nine-year-old boy who sleeps in the warm hollow left by his mother understands it; I live, and the young teenager forever stripped of his innocence—who, at this moment, is waking up in a car somewhere in La Paz—understands it; I live and at long last they understand it, though it's true they still don't remember. Only I understand it now, and remember it down to the last, tiny detail . . . I understand and still I can't manage to live in it and ponder it at once, in a single, perfect moment.

Octavio and I get out of the Ford. It's late; the streetlights cast their resplendent stain on the side of the house and the nearby wharf. I don't remember saying goodbye to them. The car just takes off, and I watch until it's nothing more than a spot of blue in the night. The wind blowing in off the sea breathes a bit of life into my legs, and the pounding surf drowns out the fading sounds of the Ford's engine. Ours is the only house in sight, and the streetlights are barely able to illuminate the broken, mossy planks of the pier. I breathe in, and hear Octavio's voice. He's stopped on the loose dirt driveway that my father and uncle park their cars in. He's waiting for me; his call is more of a hiss, so that he doesn't wake anybody up at this late hour. I ignore him, quietly watching the yachts and sailboats moored there along the pier. The sea breathes in deeply, exhales like a great whale, and then gathers itself for another powerful breath. The tiny little palms sway along the street, their fronds clashing lightly. The world comes to a halt—suspended in the night—and as I contemplate myself standing there, my body feels as though it's been supplanted by something foreign. For a few seconds, everything around me—the rising wave laced with foam, the invisible yet tenacious breeze, the sky pierced by a sailboat's mast, the sleeping yachts, the dry knocking of the wild palms, and the insistent hissing of my friend—are newly born, as if they have never been before. I discover a preternatural order in everything around me. Then I feel a hand . . . Octavio, tired of waiting for me to respond, is tugging at my shirt. He's annoyed, but what of his reproaches? Yes, I know that's what they are *now*. But does it make sense for someone to reproach or reprimand somebody who doesn't understand them? How can it be that words insist on having meanings when they've never made sense? If they ever did have meanings, they've long since worn away; words have lost their power to harass us. How, then, can one friend reclaim those powers, and get his meaning across to another? I don't understand what it is that Octavio is trying to tell me, and I'm not even sure I want to find out. For a moment, I feel a resplendent silence inside of me that is so alive, so resonant, that no voice could ever disturb it. There can be no talk, because there is simply nothing to say; there's nothing worth listening to. Dialogue is a farce, a simplistic superstition invented anew whenever someone feels the need to communicate. Monologues are what they really want. The whole world is talking to itself—itself and nobody else.

Octavio opens the front door and mutters that I've gone insane. His mutterings make no sense because they have no meaning. I follow him inside, I get undressed. I lie down in bed, I close my eyes. I sleep.

I do not sleep. My eyes are wide open. I can hardly breathe. My temples are throbbing with pain. Nobody is home besides my sister and I, though the maid is always around when my parents are gone. I can picture her long lashes and her eyes focused on the shimmering, deceitful television. Epifania has such excessive lashes, they light up her face along with the flickering light of the TV coming from the kitchen. Even lying in my room, I can still see her long, almost triangular chin, and her cheekbones, just a bit too prominent for the brown narrowness of her face. I imagine—from my vantage point in bed—her jubilant body settled securely in the easy chair. She's watching attentively even though she knows that soon I will come calling. She waits. We both wait. For my sister to fall asleep. My parents have been gone for just over half an hour. Despite the cold, I can feel a strange rush of warmth in my cheeks. My eyes are wide open, and they've adjusted to the darkness of the room. Epifania's have not. She's been focused on the TV, her lashes collecting light from the lamp like pollen, her simmering eyes fixed on the screen. They deceive her easily. I deceive her. I don't quite know how, but one day I dared to tell her I loved her, and she believed me. That may have been the first lie I ever told in the name of love. Then again, perhaps I didn't deceive her at all; perhaps she was only pretending. In any case, it was a warm, taciturn Sunday; there was no breeze to rustle the tejocote and pear trees in the garden, and the sole eucalyptus was silent and scentless. That Sunday, I saw her returning to the house absorbed in thought. I said something to her, and she didn't respond. She was noticeably upset about something. I asked her what was going on, but she paid no attention to me, turning away without so much as a glance. I was taken with the sorrow in her bent shoulders. The affliction that was weighing so heavily on them was, at the same time, a pleasure, a deep source of attraction for me. I followed her to the laundry room; I often went along to watch as she washed and dried our clothes. It was a sweet and languid refuge, just like my mother's warm embrace and bedtime prayer. We watched the wind in the treetops, dozing quietly, and the silent garden mottled by the superfluous grays of the afternoon. The corner where we spoke was steeped in the smell of starch. The shirts in the basket, the balled-up socks, the smooth, bright-white underwear, my father's enormous pants hung up to dry . . . everything on display there was sacred and blessed by Epifania's aspergillum. She presided over that warm, memorable, embalmed space. It was there that she told me, in a fit of pain, that her boyfriend never wanted to see her again. She didn't know why, and it made her feel ill and on the verge of fainting. I thought she might be feverish. She came to me, and I embraced her. Very slowly and cautiously, I brought my hands to her neck, and *I whispered it in her ear*, though I had no idea why. I don't even know if it was the truth; whether I really did harbor some feeling for her in some recondite corner of my being. But I said it, and then I felt her body nestle against my own. That was all she did. And ever since then, we would look at each other and understand, without the need for words.

She had given me an unknown man's name that afternoon. I forget it now. Nevertheless, I loved her, or I believed and said so enough to deceive myself, or her, or perhaps after all it was she who wanted to deceive me. I still haven't been able to find an answer after all these years. You can't share the pain of a woman you do not know. Our pain (or *her* pain, I should say, which she subtly meted out to me) was transformed—without our knowledge—into pure desire. Deep down, we shared a concern that it would eventually wane, that displeasure would creep into our eyes and leave our bodies listless, forgetting their own weight for hours on end, engendering empty spasms and false comforts.

My eyes are wide open, as they are on so many nights when my parents go out and my sister, Selma, sleeps soundly for hours. It's nine o'clock. My room is dark, save for a tiny thread of light that enters in through the half-open door. I can hear the TV on all the way down in the kitchen. She waits for my voice. My pulse beats in my temples, and a wave of heat slowly blankets my body up to my cheeks. At long last, I call her. It's a moan—almost a plea—for her to come quick. My parents aren't around, and our ruse is that I wait for them to pull up my covers, tuck me in, and leave the door open a crack on their way out. Soon I hear the distant humming of the TV switched off. I imagine her long-fingered hands smoothing her apron and adjusting her close-fitting rose dress so that it accents the ample curves of her barely twenty-year old body. Her eyes are no longer lit up, but her lashes are still quite noticeable: they look almost like the shadow of some bird flying past the face of the sun, and her eyebrows are like the canopy of a tree. Epifania starts to climb the carpeted stairs; I can make out her muffled steps and picture her svelte body moving clean and clear towards her desire. She can feel her blood coursing beneath her skin, but first she checks my sister's room. She peeks in and whispers her name softly, and the peaceful silence coming from the bed lets her know that Selma is asleep. *Now* I can picture her pulling the door shut before hurrying—excited, on tiptoes, silent, not even blinking—down the dimly lit hall towards my room. She opens the door. I watch: my eyes are still accustomed to the shadows. Hers aren't, and she has to grope her way wordlessly across the room. She is the sun that knows no shadow, and yet here she must feel for my bed in thick darkness. I have been waiting impatiently for months. She sits down on the edge of the bed, leans back against the wall, and I hear her inviting voice: *Here I am.*

I slide over a bit. She has just enough room to swing her legs up onto the bed. They smell like browned bread: slightly bitter and yet smooth. They also somehow remind me somehow of the scents of *melapia* or pears. She has covered our bodies with the quilt, and I lightly trace her calves. They are bare and fresh there in the bedroom penumbra. Now I settle over her hands, and she does not speak. She never speaks; she simply waits anxiously to feel my skin against her long and lustrous legs. I acquaint myself with her knee. A country girl doesn't have such smooth knees. Right there I can feel the smooth hem of her dress; it reminds me of the soaring eaves of a church. I sculpt her hidden skin, and the backs of her knees—under those same, darkened eaves— yield the forms that I am shaping: cherubs, saints, and devils in eternal struggle. Under the quilt, the Parish of San Jerónimo (where I take communion on Sundays) slowly appears. The padre watches me, questioning. There is a sheen—or a sparkle, at least—which moistens my fingers, and there is another sheen in my eyes when I look upon the priest. Nevertheless, the bitter embers of Epifania's skin douse me. I find the corners of her flesh exuding the bitter wine of consecration. The whole world compels bodies to rise up and to come together, just as it hinders them—in the opaque darkness—from knowing one another. We are born, then, just in time to know how our bodies are reviewed in the night, how they are touched, how they rise like bread, how they grow moist, and—at last—grow unacquainted again in the dark.

My hands can't be the same warm hands I had before. I've ventured past the edge of her dress, and have now reached her slip. Epifania doesn't offer so much as a sound in protest. Darkness proffers silence and elicits concessions without our having to ask for them in words. I trace my hands over her thighs as if it were an act of praise. I find that the outside world is not smooth; it's not at all like Epifania's sleek, warm thighs. Her flesh gleams, yielding, welcoming each subtle movement closer and closer to her. My head dives beneath the quilt, and now I lift up her dress as far as her waist; for her part, she maintains her intimate and beautiful silence. She gives in both to my body and her unfulfilled desires. I kiss her cautiously; I cover my parched lips with the scent and wetness of her taut skin. I moisten her inner thighs with saliva; now she opens them invitingly, bountifully, so that I can dab at them with my tongue. I lay my hand on her panties just over her mound. My hands burn at the touch. I bring my face in close, she squirms while I brush my innocent lips over her panties and she feels a burning of her own; she exhales a low moan, presses into me, and—at the same time—I remember her eyes watching the door, hoping that it would remain shut and that the world would never find out. I sense that her lashes are damp, as if she's been crying, as are the downy hairs on the nape of her shadowy neck. She is wet; I can smell it. I don't know how this could be. I moistened her with my tongue, but this isn't saliva: it's a different sort of bitterness, a distinct, cloistered freshness, an ancient dampness whose scent I'm soon enamored of.

Epifania is from a small town. Her naked legs show the heartiness and luster of the fields. She's gone now. I no longer watch the women from the towns—often with unpronounceable names—who come to the house to wash and iron the laundry. I don't see them, and *now*, after so many years, I don't even recognize them. At night, I wait up for my mother to return and come upstairs to kiss us goodnight before going to sleep. When she still hasn't gone out with my father, I toss and turn in bed, calling her, waiting for the prayer which I have yet to learn: *Barukh atah Adonai* . . . It's nine o'clock. I can hear the television in the distance, and I picture the faltering lashes of that new woman who finds it so easy to believe in the false men and women who strut and move across that box's brilliant screen.

Epifania was sad that Sunday, true, and both of us (without speaking, without discussing it) decided to deceive our bodies for a time. To lie to our destinies. *Now* I understand it, and I remember it fondly. But it wasn't too long ago that I found these verses, and memorized them just to be able to remind myself of her whenever I wanted:

> Epifania returned one afternoon
> and I chased her through the garden
> pleading with her to tell me what that man had done
> because my room was there
> like an empty gift box.
> Epifania laughed and ran
> and at last she opened the gate
> and let the street into the garden.

20

Ricardo simply has to get out of that place. He doesn't have anything to do, shut up in there like that. Mexico City is like a cage infested with vermin and Neanderthals. He killed Inés, and that's enough. If someone were to ask about it, I could respond for him. I could say from my own experience that it was, in fact, for love. He embraced it, even at the cost of losing it. Nevertheless, even though he's abandoned her, he does still have something that even she can't give away: something indescribable, something that everyone—mortal or immortal—dreams about. Ricardo can step outside at dawn without a sound, leaving behind him the stiff, cold bodies of his mother, the unknown man, and Inés, hidden under the bed, and carry on with the memory of Laila, his neighbor and first love.

Sitting there, dejected on the crags, Elías—apparently unconcerned about sunburn—wrote monotonously, frenetically, without so much as a glance this way or that, and without any concern for the inquisitive eyes of the people walking along the wharf. Every once in awhile he would stop, chew on his pen, and ponder something, some obscure detail that nobody else in Las Rémoras could see, and which only had to do with that novel he was continuing now at long last, free from the burden of love. Though he continued to sit there, his passion now flowed naturally and effortlessly. He loved Roberta, but now without any shackles. He'd managed to dispense with the death that had pervaded everything. Yes, the two of them—he and Roberta—had forever done away with Inés, and, therefore, had done away with death as well.

He, Ricardo, will come to visit us here in Las Rémoras. He has nowhere else to go. Here he'll be able to get a job, and maybe even a place to live. If not, he'll stay with me at the library. At long last, I'll be able to meet him, to see him as he truly is. I, on the other hand, am incapable of leaving this place. I must stay here to write his story, to set it down in black and white, so he doesn't disappear off the face of the earth. I must, despite feeling smothered here in this forgotten, unremarkable city in Baja California. Ricardo has to get out of there soon. He has to get out of Mexico City and come to my town, on the sun-drenched and sultry coast of Las Rémoras.

Elías stopped chewing on his pen and once again set himself to putting words down on paper. Just then, a sweet Southern breeze scudded in off the water, cleaning and clearing his head.

No, there was no way Ricardo would destroy *Las Rémoras*. It would be a crime. Like suicide. He would have to take it with him. It was one of the last things he had left, apart from the memory of Laila's love and that of his mother. If he hadn't completely forgotten his father, then all that remained was a faint glimmer or fraction of him. He was dead.

He packed his things—Federico Ross's novella *Bodily Prayers*, and the *Las Rémoras* notebook with its missing pages—and left the house bundled up in a black sweater. It was five o'clock in the morning. There was no traffic on his street just yet, but two blocks up was Libertad; the dawn's incipient sounds were coming from there. He strolled easily, unhurriedly, engrossed in thought. A car he hadn't noticed honked at him to get out of the road. He jumped aside and—for a moment at least—emerged from his trance; but this wasn't to last, and soon he'd fallen back into that semiconscious state, walking robotically down the street, rubbing his hands together in an attempt to stave off the biting morning cold.

Eventually he arrived at the avenue, the source of the noise that had occasionally reminded him of something very small, very contained, hearing it from his bedroom: he had at least to get out of there, out of his house and out of the infinite Mexico City—that subterranean rat-infested hostel—mirrored in the face of its every inhabitant. It isn't possible to say that Ricardo was either sad or happy. He just wasn't thinking about anything at all. Things had happened in quick succession: the death of his father four months ago (which now seems relatively remote), the *Las Rémoras* project put on hold and then taken up again, the sickness, Lascurain, Laila's strange visit while he was still taken with fever, the presumed death of Inés, the unknown man who his mother had kissed yesterday, and now today . . .

It couldn't quite be called night, even though a sliver of pale, yellowish moon was visible on the horizon. Even though the sky was dark, a dim, uncertain brilliance, come perhaps from the very bowels of the earth itself, spilled over the street and brought a touch of light to the air. Ricardo could just make out the silhouette of a man hurrying to work. A moment later he saw a woman standing on a street corner hailing a taxi. Another pair of workers—each sporting identical blue or dark green uniforms—crossed near him; one even brushed past his arm without realizing it. The morning bustle was beginning. The stirrings of the city melded smoothly and imperceptibly with the soft and slow August dawn: they went, reservedly, hand-in-hand. The darkness and the cold dissipated just as people began to emerge from here or there, scattering, coming out of the sewers, the walls, or the electric streetlamps. He checked the time: it was 5:08. Shadows still lay crisscrossed all around, cloaking objects and hiding them from view. The thick sloe-like color made it difficult, for example, to see where you were stepping. You would see the shiny tips of your shoes twinkle, and then suddenly you put your foot down and hit pavement . . . but the sound was perfectly synchronized to the shine, not the impact. Feet step when it's necessary that they do so.

At long last, Ricardo stopped and boarded a bus. A couple of minibuses had passed him earlier, heading down the avenue, but he had let them go on by. At that time of day, he wouldn't have been able to get a seat anyhow, and he'd decided he was comfortable walking. Now, a nauseating, sulfurous odor assailed him. The nostrils just might be the most vulnerable spot on the body, he thought. He remembered seeing his mother sniffing his father's old suits—the closet ritual. Now he, Ricardo, had to endure this new, debilitating stench. Where was it coming from? It was the people, their clothing and shoes, packaged food, bad breath, mud and lime stuck to the cuffs of trousers, underwear turned inside-out and worn again, earwax, the sweat from bodies coming into contact with the cold morning air, and the grime caked under their fingernails. It was the smells of Mexico City: hidden corruption and decay, satisfied sexual appetites, dreams, bleary-eyed old ladies, a lack of sanitary napkins, phlegm on the ground, teeming, gnawing rats, the shortage of potable water and clean clothes, yesterday's socks, open wounds, babies in arms . . .

Ricardo hated all of this. He hated it.

Such a feeling came as a surprise, and immediately he said that it wasn't possible for him to hate, that hatred didn't exist, that such a thing was sheer lunacy. But then again, how could he not believe in hate? Why not that close and wonderful feeling which comes from detesting one's neighbor when it's proper and necessary? Couldn't it come from contemplating those weak-willed men, sitting there with their terrible *cuatlicues*, and those women with their two harelip children, others muzzled with scarves, all of them dirty, withered, indistinguishable, brown-haired, popping up or settling down on every corner, touching his shoulder (which wasn't a sign of humanity—of any humanity at all), packed together there, vulnerable to hatred, to curses, to intimate disdain, and even—if it were possible—to being squashed like a worm?

And almost immediately, something else occurred to him: it was possible to love them. In fact, he did.

Ricardo badly wanted to give the harelip boy a kiss, to smooth out the toothless old woman's stockings, to embrace the man who had just spat at his feet, to share that pregnant woman's food, to peel that boy's tangerine, to caress that blind man's hair, to smile at that driver. He loved them all. He loved the jam-packed humanity of the busses at that hour, wavering between darkness and the smooth, nascent light of dawn. And suddenly he wanted people to stop getting off at their stops . . . he wanted more people to get on, actually; he wanted everyone to be jumbled together, bodies and clothes all touching, smells commingling, growing used to the smell of sweat, to the gray morning, lukewarm food brought from home, everyone happy, content, and loving one another for all eternity, just as God does and will do . . .

When at long last he emerged from his thoughts, Ricardo discovered something as immense and clear as the sun—now peeking around the edge of a building and lighting up their sunken, expressionless faces—namely, that all feelings are always relative to other feelings. In fact, they're never more important than you want them to be. To hate, to love, to whatever . . . these things do not exist. You could even patent them, get the exclusive rights to new feelings and new ways of feeling. You could make them fashionable, communicate them to others, sell them, auction them off, explain to others how they feel, how they're used, what they go with, et cetera, et cetera. It's incredible—Ricardo thought just as the bus came to a sudden stop, throwing him into a stranger's broad back—to realize this now. Hopefully it will always be this way, this easy, with no need to kill anyone in order to survive, no need to hate anybody, and with the knowledge that while you might have feelings, you never truly *feel*. Feeling is deplorable.

As the day forms itself in the streets and moldy avenues, while it gathers dust both in and outside the bus, thoughts emerge, impalpable and winding. Finally, at Insurgentes (the longest avenue in Mexico City, and quite possibly the longest one on earth), Ricardo got off the bus, gripping his bag tightly. Between ten and six there wasn't much traffic, though some cars were beginning to appear on the streets by magic. People massed at crosswalks, waited for the light to change, and then hurried across to the other side. From one island to another. From one group of tall, thoughtless buildings in the sun to another, equally inconsiderate group. Mexico City is a block of asphalt that is born, grows, reproduces, and dies anew each and every day. Yes, it's the most beautiful thing to contemplate it dying—or better yet, to see it dead—to flow through its arteries, its unburied body, every night when you can see a car stopped at an intersection, a dog mounting another, a bored prostitute, or a drunk pissing on a wall. The sleepwalkers and the solitary, obsessive freaks are eyesores, true, but they're also the ones who best appreciate their beloved city's body. The best time to contemplate—to love—this city is between 2:30 and 4:30 in the morning, in the solitude of night. Outside of that, it's a different city, a different thing entirely. After 5:00 or 5:30, Mexico City prepares itself, gets dressed, waits for the light of day to show itself in what it mistakenly believes is all its splendor. Pity those who are enchanted by the morning's orgy of twenty-something million people: the tumult of gloomy children, the clean-shaven widows and grandfathers, the conceited men in ties, the blind with their seeing-eye dogs, the diurnal fire eaters, the Jehovah's Witnesses, the schoolgirls in their busses, the cautious beggars, the bodyguards and newspaper vendors, the well-dressed ladies in their late-model cars, the seven- and eight-year old children hawking Chiclets, the police searching for an unsuspecting criminal who isn't around today, the Mormons with their cheeses, unsatisfied divorcees, the vegetable vendors at their little stalls, the squeegee men washing car windshields with their own saliva, the PRI bureaucrats, the bilingual secretaries, the wrinkled old maids, the rich, lazy kids from the Universidad Anáhuac, the leftists from UNAM, the starving professors, the factory workers, the campesinos planted at the doors of the Procu, the tireless milkmen, the motorcyclists, the plumbers, the thousands of bloodsucking attorneys, the solitary men at the Sanborns Cafés, the thousands of bored readers, and the lovesick virgins. They're all there, busy little bees, living that orgy from sun to sun, twenty consecutive hours.

Ricardo boarded a minibus. Crowds of them follow pedestrians around, pursuing them. Cars honk behind them, drivers smile, people take advantage of the opportunity to run across the street, and the sun continues to come out, though the overcast and hazy sky won't quite allow it yet. Finally Ricardo found a seat. It's a stroke of luck; nobody ever gives up their seat for anybody. If a woman gets on the bus carrying her child, someone will say to himself, emphatically and convincingly, *Why the hell did she have a baby? And why the hell am I supposed to help her?* And if an elderly woman with two large shopping bags were to board, your average Mexico City denizen would say, even more convincingly, *Why isn't she dead yet? It's not my fault; she's not my grandmother.* That's just how it is. You have to see it, live it, breathe the eternal cigarette smoke and exhaust fumes, the incense burned by the Coyoacán hippies, the starving dogs taking shits in the streets, and the overflowing sewers. You have to understand and adjust yourself to the detritus of an eccentric and ungrateful city, under threat of death, at every avenue or intersection.

Ricardo hasn't moved from his spot; his hands are propped up on his bag, which is resting on his lap. He was no longer cold. At the stop before the viaduct, a man with bags of flour-covered peanuts got on board and began shouting out the prices: five pesos per bag, or three for ten. But the most incredible thing, thought Ricardo, was that six people bought twelve bags off him. Is it that their teeth were so fidgety that they couldn't resist a pile of peanuts at six in the morning? Or is that what poor people eat for breakfast in this city? Then a man appeared in the back with a handheld case full of chips and candy and seeds; he also sold a good amount. When the first man got off the bus at the viaduct, Ricardo saw a girl of about ten get on. She had nothing to sell; she simply sang along to the strains of a harmonica that Ricardo couldn't locate at first. Then he saw it: a boy, perhaps her younger brother, was huffing away at the instrument. And it sounded rather nice; he accompanied his sister well. Ricardo gave him a coin while his sister made her way up and down the aisle of that enormous bus, her hand held out for alms.

He didn't know if it was the girl's voice, the monotony of the people appearing and disappearing along the streets as if they were on sale, or just the swaying of the minibus as it made its way down Insurgentes, but something put Ricardo to sleep for a few minutes. The bus was past Reforma when he woke up: there wasn't much time! His watch showed 6:42. But what was the rush? There really isn't any, he told himself. Or was there? Yes, something was urging him on. It had to be something, perhaps an encounter waiting for him down the line. Just then he became aware of just how hungry he was. And it wasn't just his ulcer acting up; he really needed to eat something. He looked around at what some of the other passengers were eating: an orange, a quesadilla, blue corn chips. At least some floured peanuts would be able to tide him over for a bit. Five minutes passed, and then ten . . . he grew frustrated with each car that blocked the minibus's path, and impatient with every stoplight that further delayed his breakfast. Finally, he saw the train station looming long and tall and bluish in the distance. A multitude of people, dogs, and street vendors were gathered on the sidewalk surrounding it. Before the bus reached it, Ricardo observed—right there on Insurgentes—a bicyclist carrying a stack of bread loaves on his head, an ambulance making an illegal turn, and a crash between a Volkswagen and a Ford, resulting in two women trying to out shout one another, a serious and—to be expected—ineffectual policeman standing between them, and a small crowd of people who were now impeding traffic.

Ricardo decided to get off two stops before the train station to avoid the bottleneck. His stomach was rumbling desperately. There, a few steps away on the sidewalk, a group of people were surrounding a very fat woman. She was taking orders: pulling tamales out of a steaming tin and unwrapping them before sandwiching them between slices of fresh bread which she kept in a separate bag, wrapping them up in a napkin for her hungry customers. She repeated this task at an incredible speed, never seeming to tire. At her side, her daughter—also quite solidly built—offered hot *champurrado* or *atole* to drink. Ricardo watched all this, sizing up his hunger.

"I'll take a sweet one," he said.

Before the woman could respond, he found himself holding a plastic cup with cinnamon spiced *atole* in hand. Although he hadn't asked for one—at least he didn't remember asking for one—he decided to drink it anyway. He burned his tongue just as some barbarian in a rush bumped into him from behind. He whipped around but couldn't see who it was, as a winding line of people was forcing its way along the sidewalk. It began to drizzle as he took another, more cautious sip of the *atole*. Still, the sun hung in there, making a sincere effort to warm up that small group of humans. A few tiny drops spattered on his forehead.

"Here you go, one sweet," said the woman, but Ricardo was still looking off behind him. She repeated: "Sonny, sonny . . . one sweet."

Finally Urrutia heard her; he took the sweet tamale and bit into it. As he wolfed it down, the pleasure he experienced was infinite. The drizzle had all but stopped. Maybe it was just a quick shower, he said to himself. As he was chewing his last mouthful and fishing around in his pocket for a few coins, he decided to order another one. An intense sense of satisfaction came over him. He paid the girl, got his change, and walked off without counting it, sipping his atole. Life and the world came together nicely, collaborating perfectly despite that barbarian who had pushed him. He slung his bag over his shoulder with his left hand, while in his right he held his second tasty tamale. As he bit and chewed, he avoided obstacles: people, dogs, muddy water, lampposts, and kiosks. He took long strides across the rain-spattered sidewalk—weaving up and down as needed—until he finally reached the entrance to the station: a crumbling old building caked in dust with stairs running every which way and a large glass front that allowed you to see what was happening inside.

Everyone—from frantic individuals to large families—was bustling in and out of the doors, and porters and vendors were rushing after them. Ricardo scanned the train information boards from across the room, looking for Mazatlán. Finally, after what seemed like an interminable search, he found it. He went up to the ticket office, where there were six people waiting ahead of him. The woman behind the window, however, was lazily sipping her coffee and chewing with some sort of taciturn pleasure on a donut from a plate filled with pastries; she wasn't about to help anybody until she felt like it. Every few minutes, as if regaining consciousness or returning from some imbecile dream, she would help a customer or answer a question half-heartedly. Ricardo saw all this clearly; nevertheless, he felt no particular rush, his stomach was pleasantly full, and he could form little opinions about the people around and in front of him in line. Some of them he hated, others he loved, while still others he couldn't care about one way or another. He was indifferent; it was as if for him they didn't even exist. That's what they call equilibrium, he thought.

Eventually, it was his turn at the window. He asked:

"One for Mazatlán . . ."

"For today?" the young woman asked. "Wait one moment."

It looked as if she were checking something on a clipboard she had at her side. Ricardo hadn't even said Yes, today's the day, I have to leave the city. The woman either didn't understand or didn't care.

"Excuse me, what time does the train leave?" He asked, interrupting the young woman's search. She was wearing a good deal of eye shadow.

"At 8:30 this evening," the other attendant called from the safety of her office.

"There's nothing at all leaving this morning?" Ricardo pressed them.

"8:30 P.M. Do you want it or not? Don't waste my time; there are people waiting."

"How much is the ticket?"

"Five-hundred-forty-seven pesos and fifty-five centavos."

"I'll take it."

He took out his wallet and carefully counted out the bills in front of her, which might be why she took her own sweet time giving him his ticket and change. Finally, the transaction was completed. The woman took advantage of this to take another bite of her donut. Ricardo was about to walk away, but then he turned around and asked:

"Excuse me, but how long is the ride?"

Choking down a mouthful and making a utterly disagreeable face, she answered, her lips covered with powdered sugar:

"It arrives tomorrow at 6:30 P.M."

"Thank you." He paused for a second before, full of bile, he ventured one last question: "Your name doesn't happen to be Éclair, does it?" he asked, referring to her mound of pastries.

The woman didn't catch on at first, but eventually, when she noticed a young boy and a woman in the back of the line snickering, she lashed out with some lame obscenity. Ricardo, however, was far away by that time, paying it no mind and with no desire to turn around.

He'd have to wait twelve hours there at the station, plus almost another day on the train. Although he really wasn't in any hurry, he was starting to feel a nagging sense of urgency, as if—yes—there was someone waiting for him . . . and that someone wasn't Elías. Before he could see his character, another important encounter had to take place. Ricardo could foresee this.

He walked around the station for a couple of hours, his satchel still slung across his shoulder. He killed some more time by leafing through magazines at a newsstand until the owner told him to either buy something or leave. He got in a three-person line at a shoeshine station, and when it was his turn, he simply walked away, leaving the shoeshine man with a bewildered expression on his chubby face. Finally, after having gone outside for a few minutes to watch the commotion that was Insurgentes (cars blocking traffic, a truck belching black smoke into the air, the food stands, and an old man with a limp selling lottery tickets at stoplights), he went back inside and—with a certain calm patience—he sat down in one of the long rows of yellow plastic seats. After a sweeping, bored look around the circumference of the station, he opened his satchel and took out Federico Ross's *Bodily Prayers*. He started in on the second part ravenously, without pause, sometimes even forgetting to breathe:

(DAY TWO)

The body makes charity for the soul. This is its labor when it has failed and resigned itself to being nothing but substance. Then it only looks to perpetuate and prolong itself. The man who lives charitably will receive charity only from his own body and from the comfort he gives to others.

In the meantime, the flesh is worn away, and it looks to restore, to repeat itself, that lost state in which the spirit can rest upon the waters, floating, primordial. I lost this ability when I was fourteen. If before that (at nine years of age, shall we say) I had rested peacefully on Epifania's shoulders, then just the other night at El Ferry, I had misled my body entirely, I had sunk it irretrievably in the waters. I had subverted my innocence. If before, my body and soul were able to live together—if ultimately I was both of them—then yesterday I had condemned myself (forever) to be a single, unified substance, and I was perhaps anxious at this change. Looking ahead, I know that they ought to be two distinct things, the soul and the body—recovering in one another, ingratiating themselves to each other, in an endless state of coming and going. In the history of everything and everyone, I was able to divine it that morning: the history of love. But, how can all the histories of love be as men and the world tell them? How could they be so deplorable and senseless? Summed up in stories, histories of love become one absurd, abject tale that Someone drew up and repeated, forgettable and detestable: loss and recovery, sinking and floating, over and again. So it is true that it's all but unbearable.

I was thinking about these things—or at least *today* I go over them—lying in bed, tense, my eyes shut stubbornly despite the light filtering into the room. I heard the whisper of the ceiling fan. I could make out footsteps in the hallway, and the voices of my aunt and uncle, my parents, my sister Selma, my cousins Emilio and Aarón, all of them engaged in the hustle and bustle of making summer breakfast. Soon (I still hear it *now*, I can distinguish it after the passing of so many years, and even *today* it makes me tremble) a call from out of nowhere strikes at the heart of my exhaustion: my grandmother is calling me. I paid no attention. Yes, I stayed there under the sheets without acknowledging the sound and the contact with the outside world that, at that moment, it represented. To dream . . . to continue dreaming throughout the entire morning without having to yield up my bed. To avoid the light and the difficult, harsh contours of the day. To remain there, shrunken and bashful, until at long last the night makes love to the earth and darkness hovers over the world—deep down, that was all I wished for. To stubbornly maintain the silence: my grandmother's voice silent, forever silent. But she did not oblige—she wouldn't have obliged—determined as she was to wake my body up. Instead of silence, I heard the squeak of the door opening. Octavio stirred in his bed. I knew that I had to wrap myself up, obstinate and disobedient, in sleep; to maintain my sneering paralysis under the sheets. I didn't even dare to blink. I begged the world to let me keep sleeping. My grandmother wanted to separate me from time, from something long ago . . . perhaps from Epifania lying there, sleeping at my side, back when I was only ten. I meditated, feigning fatigue, innocence. But that wasn't it. Innocence was long gone, and actually I was completely alert.

"That's enough, Grandma," I said, trying not to sound rude.

"Breakfast is ready," she replied in a satisfied, tinplated voice. "We're not going to wait all morning, Federico. It's late; you have to get up and face the day."

"We're not hungry, señora." It was Octavio, his voice daubed with dream, speaking from beneath the sheets.

"You know your mother and your aunt are getting annoyed, Fede," she replied, a bit more sternly.

"We're coming," I answered curtly.

My body responded every time she poked me through the sheets, forcing me awake. An effective tactic, and one for which I had no defense. There was something else too that morning, something she didn't know about, and something that she had no way of finding out. A hidden *other.*

"All right then, I'll let you get ready," she said as she left. "But don't dawdle!"

"Yes, señora . . ." Octavio muttered, smoothing out his bitterness with a touch of forced courtesy that I couldn't help but laugh at. His voice—something of a groan, actually—filtered through the sheets enveloping him. One more word, and—try as he might—he wouldn't be able to go on concentrating and preserving his dream. I understood completely. I couldn't hold it in anymore, and let out with a laugh.

"What's so damn funny?" he said.

"Grandmother," I answered.

"Yeah? Why her?"

"Well, it's her, and it's you too."

"How am I funny to you?"

"It's nothing. Just that you were asleep. I was faking it. I've been awake for about an hour already. Just thinking."

"About what?"

"Nothing in particular. About last night, I guess."

"You woke up thinking about last night? You sure didn't say too much about it on the way home, Fede."

"I fell asleep."

"Yeah, I know. But how was it? Was it worth it?"

"Of course." There was nothing else I could say. It was the obligatory response.

The serious thing was not really knowing whether it had been worth it or not. I had to say yes, of course, but I wasn't sure. I thought about it for a few moments, wanting to remember. The mind blank, the memory of my feelings like a pit. I would have to wait for some time to remember, and even then my feelings might be barely identifiable. Maybe I'll write them down one day as a form of recuperation. I didn't know, and I didn't dare answer Octavio's question truthfully. I just gave him the obvious answer. I must uncover my doubts, delve into the most intimate of things, and my answer even *now* is ambiguous: a fistful of handwritten pages that only I can decipher, and which turn out wrong before my eyes.

The house my father and Uncle David rented was an old, two-story office building. The walls were chipped and peeling everywhere. Its paint had been thoroughly rinsed out by the rain, and it maintained something of an ancient, maritime effect. It's the kind of house that comes to mind when reading about Havana. There are times when the imagination superimposes itself over reality, when we repaint or recast it according to something similar that we've read or seen: a small connection that manages to make what we've actually experienced mysterious. It happened to me with that enormous, two-story house in La Paz. I can't manage to separate it from something I read a few years later: *The Happy Summer of Miss Forbes*. In that story, two kids are convinced that they've killed their tutor in a summerhouse. I don't remember any of the plot beyond that, and I've never wanted to revisit it. I'm afraid; I don't want to strip the memory of my house from what's superimposed over it. I'm not worried about any of the details, and I have no desire to discover my errors. For me, that house next to the wharf is the same—ancient and maritime—as that which the author described in some spellbinding passage of his novel (if, in fact, he did).

There could be a strip of bare ground near the entrance for parking cars; I see them all caked in dust. Perhaps a broad patio with some folding chairs and a table out front that nobody uses. You can look out over the sea from there. To the left, the wharf runs uninterrupted until it reaches the dock, devoid of people. There's never any work there; you can find folks drinking beer along the wharf, but they're the year-rounders—the captains and fishermen—never the dockworkers. A few American yachts are moored there peacefully, as are a few brand-new sailboats that I've watched tacking back and forth during the few Christmases we've spent here in La Paz. (My family prefers summer vacations.) To the right lies a heap of stones: the remains of a store or factory whose construction was never completed. Out in the middle of the water sits a jumble of vertical wooden pillars, serving as something of a diving platform. The pilings are lashed together with white, nautical-grade rope that won't disintegrate in the saltwater. It looks as if they're capped with a light dusting of snow, but actually it's a layer of droppings from the gulls who perch there throughout the year. Maybe that's what it's there for; I don't know. The platform lends a certain amount of unintentional grandeur to the sea. Once, many years before, while some friends and cousins and I were taking turns diving off it, I discovered that the droppings had no smell, and that the whitened caps were as smooth as snow. For years I've longed to return there and lay the palms of my hands upon those pilings again. I can't remember why I haven't.

The house sits a short drive away from downtown La Paz. It's reachable via a long, deserted, untraveled street that stems from the wharf. There are no electric lights, and the asphalt is filled with unavoidable potholes. All you'll see is the occasional weekday truck making a run to the factory or the dock. My aunt, uncle, and their two children live on the second floor, which consists of two large bedrooms linked by a common bathroom. There's also a long exterior walkway with a view of the sea and a veranda at one end, and a set of stairs that lead down to a sort of indoor patio or glorified landing protected by a door with mosquito netting. That's the back entrance to our floor, which includes the kitchen, the living room with its ancient television turned on every night, and a hallway leading to the bedrooms, two of which have their own bathrooms.

I don't quite know how we managed to share that space during those long summers by the sea. It was customary to go to La Paz with my father, my Uncle David, and his family. Between the two of them they had been able to purchase a rather old yacht that was nevertheless well-equipped for three- or four-day excursions to Nopoló, Bahía Concepción, or—nearer by—to the Isla del Espíritu Santo. Some of these beaches were virgin territory, their sand intact, full of a splendor that wounds you with the absence of humanity. We didn't even differentiate between islands and beaches; coastlines and geography were unimportant to us. Those spots are unreachable by car, and very few ships dropped anchor there, perhaps opting for more distant shores.

We believed Veracruz when he said that there was a new, deserted, undiscovered island nearby. Excited, we dove in before my father and uncle even had a chance to anchor, and raced each other to the shore. Then we set off exploring. We heard the curly-haired Veracruz christen the place something clever, we pondered his wit and his wonderful inventions, but the name was already there, printed on some nautical chart of the region's littoral. We were awed by the long dunes, which we spent the day tumbling down, by the transparency of the waters which were knee-deep and perfect for wading across long distances, until an eel would suddenly swim across your path and force you to stand stock-still until it passed, until the perfect yet fleeting leap of a manta ray which we hadn't seen until it broke the surface, until a turquoise-blue jellyfish that blended in with the color of the water, the pure, cloudless sky, and the sun dancing on our shoulders.

At night—if Veracruz agreed to join us—we would all camp out on the beach. We prepared for a night out of doors. Veracruz built us a huge bonfire, and I pictured my mother back on the yacht watching the flames, and perhaps complaining about the danger to my father or to my aunt Frida. It was a shame watching night fall, taking the sea with it; from eight o'clock onward, we couldn't see anything at all. We wouldn't even have been able to see each others' faces at arm's length if it weren't for the bonfire. We'd gathered the wood earlier in the day, and Veracruz stacked and lit it. It burned so long into the night that we couldn't remember hearing it flicker and die out.

We sat there on the smooth sand and told pirate stories. Veracruz always told the best ones, and we were easily captivated while the sea murmured in the background and the waves crept up the beach. The world ground to a halt while we, assembled there on the beach, tried to make out the lines of the sleeping yacht, and I examined my friends' faces among the flames with the same feeling you have standing on the edge of the abyss and staring down.

The next thing I knew, I was being tackled by Octavio. I hadn't even noticed him getting up, but his move had shattered the late night calm.

"Wake up already!" he said, ripping the sheets off me. "We have to get ready for breakfast before they come back up here and get really pissed off." He looked at the clock hanging on the wall over my bed, and then bent down to yell in my ear: "Cabrón, it's already past eleven."

I looked blankly at his face.

"I'm not hungry. Stop fucking around," I answered, unmoved.

"I don't care; I *am* hungry. Get up before your grandmother has to come up again."

I yawned and with a belated effort, I stretched my limbs. Octavio picked himself up off me. The back of my neck was incredibly sore . . . I couldn't tell if it was from the tackle or because I'd slept on it awkwardly. We pulled on some shorts and t-shirts and headed out of the room. We could already hear the commotion being caused by my cousins, Aarón and Emilio, down in the kitchen. I watched my mother preparing something next to the stove.

"Another all-nighter?" she asked.

"Not quite, mama," I responded.

"Not quite, señora," Octavio echoed.

"When did you guys get in?" my sister asked, inopportunely.

"Early," I answered, and then I regreted responding to someone who, because of her age, didn't warrant such respect.

"Early, early . . ." I hear my father repeat, upset.

I said nothing. I preferred not to answer. Uncle David chewed contentedly. Everyone else was starting to make plans for the day. It's unanimous: everyone wanted to go downtown for bootlegs and knockoff merchandise. My father turned back to his paper. Then my aunt Frida's voice:

"Sit down and have something to eat. There's huevos a la mexicana, quesadillas, frijolitos, fruti . . . what would you like?"

"Nothing for me, thanks," I said as I sat down next to Emilio who—at eleven—was his oldest child.

"Thanks, I'll help myself," Octavio said.

We both knew that Frida liked us, and she was also quite fond of Hugo and my cousin Cecilio. She was only thirty-five, and carried herself quite well. It's the same thing every summer, us watching while she conscientiously rubbed suntan oil into her skin. It's almost as if she knew that we're watching. Perhaps she did. My cousins—her children, both of them younger than me—and Selma could never imagine our hungry eyes, our comments. Until the previous summer, I'd only looked at Frida in an affectionate, caring sort of way; she was my mother's sister, after all, and she looked quite a bit like her, albeit younger, more attractive, better put together. But that was before I'd started listening to Cecilio's lewd remarks. I'd never thought about just how erotic her presence could be until one afternoon when I was left alone with her, trembling.

It was during the last few days of the past summer. At around five or six, a pleasant sort of lassitude settled down, bringing sleep. A haze was rolling in from the sea and the wharf as I was coming home. I didn't hear anybody in the house. I walked through the first floor rooms before going up to the second floor, which is where I found my aunt, lying in bed with a fan blowing over her. She was dressed in a short nightgown, and was doing something to her toenails. My attitude was unchanged, natural, and serene: she was the flip side of my mother's coin, and I didn't even notice her body, or how different mine was in light of hers. She asked me to help her; I sat down on the bed and began to file her nails. She stretched and laid her arms back on her pillow as if to say she was tired. She watched me for a few moments, or I imagined or felt that she did. She seemed to be enjoying it when, without warning, I felt myself growing erect. I don't know if she would have noticed. I became nervous in front of this woman who, nevertheless, was still my aunt. So I kept on with my task, unperturbed; for moments at a time I saw her naked legs, her calves, her loose nightgown. The afternoon heat was beginning to constrict the bedroom. Despite the best efforts of the fan, I felt my pores dilating, and sweat poured from my forehead and soaked my shirt. I had one hand under her ankle, supporting it in the air, like a fine, rough gem that needed to be polished but not dropped. Perhaps she became embarrassed, and I heard her say, *Thank you, that's enough, Federico.* I said goodbye as best I could without daring to look at her, covering the protuberance in my shorts with my hand. I jumped down the stairs two at a time until I reached the landing and saw that nobody had come home yet. I ran down the hall and went into the bathroom. Sitting in the tub, soaked in sweat, I masturbated. It was then that I understood Cecilio and everyone's comments, but I wouldn't tell them a thing. Back in Mexico City, I dedicated myself to the practice while thinking about Frida, recalling every lucid detail in that room while filing her nails: each step of a terrible and violent voluptuousness. It wounded me, and I abounded in that pleasure to the point of exhaustion. I had fallen into a foot fetish with Frida, and the only feeling I harbored in my heart was impatience for the next summer in La Paz.

This time, my attention was overshadowed by my friends and by Cecilio's absurd fantasies. He shared his burning desire for my aunt with us. When she wasn't looking, our eyes passed over her body. I would spy on her at length as she walked along the waterfront, and excursions on the yacht took on new meaning for me, anxiously waiting for her to sunbathe next to my mother, for her movements as she rubbed suntan oil into her skin or spoke to someone, for the kisses she would give Uncle David, for when she emerged from the berth to towel off Aarón's little body. For the last few weeks, I stayed in the house whenever I could. I would come home early from the beach, hoping to find her alone.

Catching her alone in her bedroom became a fight to the death between us.

Octavio shoveled food into his mouth. Everyone else had gotten up from the table, leaving my grandmother sitting there across from us.

"You're not going to eat anything, Federico?" she asked.

"No, thanks," I repeated for the umpteenth time that morning.

My mother and my aunt were washing themselves. We could hear them talking and laughing. I didn't take my eyes off them as I picked a glass of juice from the table and sipped at it. Outside the door, I heard my father and uncle calling:

"Let's go, ladies! We're waiting in the car."

"I'm not going to go out today; I didn't sleep much last night," said my aunt. Then, to my mother: "I think I'm going to go to bed, Elvira."

"Didn't you hear, boys?" asked my grandmother, getting up from her seat. "You'd better hurry, or you'll get left behind."

"I'd better go to the waterfront instead. Veracruz said he'd be around there."

"If you're not going, then I'm not going either," Octavio said from behind me.

I felt a tremor run down my spine. But I put on a false calm, and said, "No, you go ahead. You wanted to buy a snorkel, right?"

That left only Frida and my grandmother in the house. I headed towards the waterfront in time to see the family off; maybe I'd see Veracruz there fishing or taking a siesta. Through the clouds of dust, I could see Octavio through the window; he waved at me and flashed a toothy grin. I don't know what he might have been trying to say. Something about the previous night, the secret we shared with Solón, Hugo, and Cecilio? Or maybe he knew the real reason I wanted to stay at the house? Would he ever think about saying something to the others?

I hadn't yet reached the waterfront when I decided to turn back. I'd lost sight of the car. I walked across the dusty parking lot and then across the patio. I paused there, as yet undecided. Finally, I went up to my cousins' room in search of some little thing I'd invent if I were caught.

It's been only a couple months since Epifania left. Her man came back for her one day and carried her off forever when I was still only nine years old. Today there's nobody home, just a nameless woman from some town with an unpronounceable name who washes our clothes. I know that she's there in the washroom, engrossed in her work. Completely forgotten by the world and everything else that exists and revolves around the sun. She works tenaciously, blindly, unconsciously. I watch her closely, but I can't stand to be at her side for more than a minute. I move away. I walk around the garden. The space is immeasurable if I stay silent, if I keep still. Again I go up to the room where Epifania used to celebrate the heat . . . through windows laced with condensation from the iron, I contemplate the new woman, standing with her back to me. She doesn't even hear me. I am standing right outside, on the other side of the steamed-up window, and she doesn't know, she couldn't guess. This woman is alone, she is older, and she cannot share in my solitude the way that Epifania did. The afternoon wanes, and a strange sort of lassitude takes over my body. There is only pleasure there, in the strange sort of pain invading me. I want to cry and I don't know how to do it, to cry for someone else, as I would years later when Hugo died.

I open the door and enter the house. The furniture, the tables, the pictures on the wall . . . everything is in order and still. I grow impatient. I go up the stairs, I hear the telephone ringing. I pick up: nobody is there. I can't stave off the solitude, creeping in through deep fractures. Epifania is gone, and she is the obsession that has been consuming me. She didn't leave only the house; she knows that. She left me, laying there in bed every night, waiting for her touch. She preferred that man who she told me about one time and one time only. And I never asked about him. I simply waited every night, waited to hear footsteps on the stairs. I hear them, someone is coming up, opens the door to my room, and prays: *Barukh atah Adonai* . . . It's my mother; it's not you. She doesn't know that it's supposed to be you—not her—who comes up to my room at night. I cling to her body, I plead with her, I don't let her leave. Finally she does, and it's as if you were leaving. Each of you is leaving me for another man. Once again, the space is immeasurable if I stay silent, if I keep still. But I walk to my parents' bedroom and go inside. I go up to the closet. I've closed both doors. It's right next to the bathroom with its giant vanity mirror that reflects the entire room. I walk up to that: I am almost ten years old. I examine myself carefully, and I'm stunned, absorbed in my image. It's definitely not me. It looks like a caricature, an exaggerated simulation, an excess of artifice . . . thinking that I am the image in the mirror and then, yes, I start to succumb—a bit livid—since I am not, in fact, the one in there, in the mirror. There is, on my part, a certain sense of morbidity; the person I'm looking at doesn't know that such morbidity and sadness exists beneath the surface of every body. I have barely discovered it; I've only begun to reveal myself, this body that the others all see, that I only know through other people's eyes. They tell me what I need to know when I want to decipher it. My hand finds a lipstick on the sink. I can feel it but I do not look. Long, cylindrical, metallic. I open the cap between my fingers. The pure intuition that I should try it (yes, try it) comes to light. I raise my hand and begin to paint my lips. The one doing the painting is someone else . . . a girl. She makes herself up in order to please me. She does so carefully, delicately; I don't want to smear myself. Another hand guides me; it's the one I see now, more audacious. I observe her red lips, how they fill out. Her mouth is beautiful, fragile, and—like mine—slightly moist. I am completely absorbed in what I'm doing, in her white and delicate hands. It's as if she's doing her lips for the first time: she's still young, no older than me. There is tenderness in her eyes, compassion and a reserved solitude. Like me, she's very alone; she doesn't know what to do with her body, and only wants it to please me. That's why she's painting her lips. I see myself: how lovely she is. I lean over and for a moment turn my eyes away from hers; I no longer know if she's looking at me. I take a mascara brush between my fingers, uncap it, and bring it up in front of my eyes. I watch, she waits. She extends the black bristles and begins to comb my drooping lashes in a spiraling, out-and-up manner. I do it a bit awkwardly; she fixes it. Carefully repeats the movements. I see her, now even prettier. Again I make eye contact, and she demurely looks away. I rummage through more of my mother's sticks and compacts. I find some red eye shadow. She knows I like that color dusted over my eyelids, and she passes the sponge fastidiously across them. My eyes are not accustomed to this, however, and I can feel them burning; I learn that it irritates her eyes as well. She dusts my cheeks; I breathe in without meaning to and cough. She coughs. I pack everything up and stow it in the cold, shiny medicine cabinet. I can feel the tension and impatience in my hands. Will she notice? Will she be suspicious of my haste, or does she also feel it, intimate and amorous, without daring to say so?

I lean forward again, and she does the same: our eyes meet, and all I can think of is that she's even more beautiful than before. Her face shines, and I cannot for a moment tear my eyes away from the hidden filigree of her teeth. I begin to undress: I unhook my belt and kick off my shoes. I pull off my dirty pants, shirt, and socks. I make my way to the closet . . . I don't want her to get impatient, to notice my absence, or realize that I'm doing things any differently from usual. She still doesn't understand that I'm doing it all for her. I open my mother's dresser and pick out a few things that she hasn't seen before. A silk corset, a pair of stockings, a scarf, a black bra, and a pair of panties. Then I go over to the closet where she hangs her dresses. I leaf through them, almost without looking. I know which one she has to wear: it's the dress I most enjoy seeing on my mother. I find it, and take it down off the hook. It's very dark violet, decorated with sequins and fringe, and should go quite well with the blush and eye shadow.

The two of us are alone. I put on the black corset and tie up the sides; it fits snugly, and I'm surprised at how cool the fabric is against my skin. I don't turn around; I don't allow her to see me, and I wouldn't want to know if she did happen to be peeking. When she finishes getting dressed herself, she'll call me, and then I'll go to see her. I pull on the stockings, and stumble while doing so. It doesn't matter. We are alone, she and I, in the closet in my parents' bedroom. I learn, and repeat: the space is immeasurable if I stay silent, if I keep still. For that reason alone, I don't want to become distracted. Next I put the brassiere on over the corset and adjust it; I pick my own socks up off the ground where I tossed them, ball them up, and stuff them in the cups. I pick the dress up off the floor, smooth it out, and slip it on over my head. I look around for a pair of heels, and sit down on the floor to put them on as well. I look at the scarf at my side and try to gather it up, but since I don't know how to wear such a thing properly, it falls all over me, and I decide to leave it there in the closet with the other articles of clothing. I take a deep breath, trying to calm down. I need air. I am nervous and there's no reason, or at least there shouldn't be; she waits, yes, I turn around and see her at a distance, tiny, watching me from the depths. At this distance, her eyes are even more beautiful than before. I approach her and stumble. I want to impress her, but don't know how to do it; I smile at her, and she smiles back at me. She's gotten dressed up just for me; when I wasn't looking, she got all decked out just so I would be happy, contemplating her nubile body, desiring her. She wants me, she desires me, she searches for ways to save me. More than anybody, she understands my frustration, my ruination on account of being alone. She knows my solitude and my vehemence, my nightmare the past few months and its cause: Epifania's flight. It makes me sad to know that she understands; she loves me, and for the first time I feel nostalgia for something . . . maybe for someone else who loved me, and maybe because they never did. Her desire and what she has done here are for me, and she wants me to be her first. But I don't know how to do it; I don't know any body other than that of Epifania, whom I loved, though without ever entering her.

My eyes are fixed and overwhelmed, I understand that she's waiting, that she waited for my parents and sister to leave me alone in the house. Nobody wants me, only her, my friend, my twin. I know it now, and she is finally here, facing me, my small body. I go up to the medicine cabinet and push some things around. They fall, I hear them, it doesn't matter. Now I watch her at the medicine cabinet too; I watch her legs, like a girl's. I crouch down, as she does. The blush is on her cheeks, which are flushed even more now, and she hasn't stopped watching me as I contemplate her, how I await her lean and tremulous body. I lift up her dress to reveal her thin, hairless legs, which can be discerned beneath her stockings. I take the edge of her dress in my mouth; I bite it. I press my body against hers, and immediately pull back: she's quite cold, and I prefer not to touch her. I move closer, though without contact. *Now* I know: what I feel is the pain of love. Ever since I'd recognized her there in the closet, my tiny little member had been hard.

Like my mother, she's gotten dressed and made up for me, to make me happy. Now she awaits my movements, awaits my body's instructions. I rub my hand against my penis, I knead it slowly,

I try to move a bit closer to her, to bring my body almost but not quite in contact with hers. Our eyes find each other's: there is true love and sweetness there, she knows me, I know that she loves me, and my excitement is beyond words. There is profound desire in her face, and in her lashes, which she has lengthened for me. I feel their stiff thickness. I can't bear it anymore: I loosen the dress she is holding in her teeth, and—at the same time—I place my mouth on her lips. I don't know how to kiss, and the contact is a frigid one. She sustains my lips, which are thin and, like hers, moist. I continue rubbing my penis, and I know that I'm close to the end, I can tell from my quickened breathing. My body resists for a few seconds, I pant and gasp, I don't know why, and I look at her: she is suffering, it's as though we're hurting each other. She grimaces, I groan. There is a perfectly rhythmic murmur. Suddenly I hear footsteps resounding on the stairs: a formidable noise. I watch her, astonished. I'm coming, yes, over her, over the sink, on the mirror. I hear knocking on the door. I pump myself out a few final times, look up, and find her still there as our eyes meet. I hear the unmistakable voices of my parents, who are knocking more loudly now. I hear my name being called through the wood, while she, lifeless, in front of me, says: *I'm coming, I'll open up.* She knows full well that I want her, that I love her. I back down as best I can from the sink and turn towards the door. She has vanished.

I grasp the doorknob; I'm about to open . . .

Reaching the second floor landing, I feel weak, sick throughout my whole body, too weak to lift my feet. I go up to the dirty window shades of my aunt's room. I peek out furtively, and I see her reclining. She's wearing the same clothes that she had on earlier in the kitchen. I can make out the mortal lethargy of her body, stirred only by her breathing. She's fallen asleep quite quickly. The fan is pointed at her face, and her long hair is fluttering slightly; for a moment, the breeze even stirs her lashes. She is sleeping, or at least she appears to be.

I make my way carefully back down the stairs; I go in the kitchen and help myself to a slice of cheese from the table. I'd prefer to leave. My aunt is sleeping in some bedroom, leaving an acute silence and only one breath in the house. It's enormous, the emptiness here. I can hear it: the silence of someone who occupies this place and yet is nowhere to be found. It's a terrible sort of muteness, then, that then inhabits the house. This silence is, I think, similar to the hollow made by the wounded, the sick. They are simultaneously alive and yet absent from the world. Their presence is that of a dream—that of a ghost in a dream—and they don't share our mortality, forgetting about life for hours on end. They exist yes, but in some other place, separated. They do not occupy your space; they live the bodily dream, that's all.

In the midst of the La Paz lethargy, without any sense of haste (the dog days of July and August tend to provoke a certain sort of muscular dystrophy), I head out towards the waterfront. First I pass by the forgotten dockyards, sunk in another time and on the verge of dissolving in the noonday heat. But soon I've reached the waterfront. I walk across the rotting boardwalk to where the boats lie at moor. I go up to the last slip, ours. The yacht is quiet. I call to Veracruz . . . no answer; he must be sleeping. I haul in the rope with all my strength and jump down into the stern. The doors to the sleeping berths are closed. I tap on the windows; no answer. I search the ship bow to stern and—finding nothing—lie down in the shade of the gunwales for a nap.

I awake to the festive sounds of Veracruz's voice and the fishing tackle in his hands. I talk with him: he asks why I haven't gone downtown with the rest of the family, and just then I remember the reason I've been waiting, killing time, not driving into the city with everyone else. I should head back to the house so I can watch her before it's too late. That was it. The days near the sea were nearing their end, the summer was winding down, and soon I would be left with months of irritation at not having taken advantage of opportunities such as this. Veracruz laughed then, showing me his chipped teeth and shaking his dirty-haired head.

Walking back across the boardwalk, I slip on a wet, moldy spot and fall, hurting myself. I pass the docks again, and this time I find a pair of fishermen drinking quart bottles of Carta Blanca beer. I keep on walking until I've reached the dusty parking lot outside the house. In the back, standing on the patio, I hesitate for a moment. What if she were downstairs, talking with my grandmother or helping her with some obligatory chore? Plus, what if she were still sleeping? I cautiously put my face up to the kitchen window and peer inside: I can't make anybody out. The house seems unchanged in its lethargy: sluggish and abandoned. I breathe in deeply; my lungs feel shrunken, tender. The dry dust catches in my throat, and for a moment I feel like coughing. But I manage to choke it back, not wanting to make the slightest noise. It's terribly hot; the sun's dynamo has capped off the summer by baking the scant few shrubs and fruit-trees out by the patio. Once again I start to climb the stairs. I'm just over halfway up when I hear the distant rushing of the shower. My legs begin to tremble, and it's with no small effort that I continue to climb quietly. Nobody can hear me, though, and my caution seems rather absurd. My grandmother wouldn't come upstairs; she would still be asleep, and even if she woke up she would get right back to her sewing. So I continue on down the hall, past my uncle's room, until I reach the terrace. I look all around and see no cars on the road; I can just make out the drunk fishermen at the dock, as well as Veracruz, who had apparently joined in their fun. Suddenly, he turns around, and I think I see a wink of consent in his eyes. Had I been found out? Did he know of my urgent, impatient desire? Would he be telling the other boatmen about it, and sharing a good laugh at my stubborn devotion to Frida? *Now,* after all these years, I am sure that he also took pleasure in watching my aunt's body as she lay sunbathing on the bow of the ship, and—perhaps—he looked at my mother the same way.

I turn back and slip into my cousin's room. I hear the falling water clearly; I imagine it breaking on my aunt's naked shoulders. I shut the door behind me, and in the sullen silence broken only by the shower, I go up to the bathroom door. I know what I have to do down to the last detail. I have learned the steps and the signals. My temples are pulsing—I notice how their throbbing alternates with that of the veins in my neck—and there's a bold, insistent tingling sensation in my chest. The world happens . . . it's about to happen, right in front of my eyes, and I wait. I hear the faucet knobs turning and the water shut off, cease hitting her shoulders, and I catch my breath. I'm hunkered down next to the door, my knees are burning, and my eye is pressed up against a tiny crack that someone must have knocked in the door. She towels off in the confines of the shower stall, so part of her doesn't come into view . . . only later am I able to contemplate her fully, when she steps out and her body is vividly illuminated, and I know that *you shall not uncover the nakedness of your mother's sister, for she is your mother's flesh.* But I am seeing it, despite the tight space, and her skin appears almost to brush against the edges of the wood. She is only inches away; I can almost touch her. A hot steam is still coming off the bath, and I can smell it: the pleasant scent of her body. Frida is there, right in front of me, and the room grows cloudy. I lift my eyes just a bit so as to catch the extraordinary roundness of her breasts. The nipples are rounder still: perfect, pink circumferences that tighten delicately (as if they could come) at the touch. I see them, erect and pointed. Only *now* do I dare to think that she *knew* I was watching her, that her body was anxious for the certainty of my eyes, to have the eyes of her nephew upon it, and that she was excited without ever managing to accept it. Under my shorts, I feel my turgid penis. Her back to me, I watch as she props one leg up on the toilet seat and dries herself. The steam condenses, softening her skin, and tiny drops roll down her vigorous, bronzed back. I contemplate her hips, her flanks moving . . . perhaps they are calling to me, or they can feel my eyes on them, and on her firm buttocks, a shade whiter than the rest of her body. She continues to dry herself, slowly or with theatrical delight, for my benefit. I watch as she pauses between her legs and bows her head . . . now she dries the closed, dark mound of her pubis. Then she discards the towel, bends down a little more, and examines something I can't quite make out. For a few seconds, she holds her hand there in space, and I think of the infinite beating of a hummingbird's wings. Under the intense light of the heat lamp which dissipates the lingering steam, I contemplate her, and she is real. She picks up the towel again, and now—with her arms stretched above her head—she runs it through her wet hair. She closes her eyes, and there is pleasure in her face. I'm sure of it. She continues to dry herself calmly, and I do not look away from her body, complete and pure and gilded: the event that is my seeing it, almost being able to feel the flesh of her breasts, and be able to squeeze it. I barely breathe; I must be careful not to dispel this enchantment. I reach down again and find my shorts are wet. I pull back from the crack in the door. Silently and with great caution, I stand up. Nevertheless, without wanting to, my hand reaches to the doorknob for support . . .

. . . I open the door; my mother is there, watching me.

When Ricardo woke up, his copy of *Bodily Prayers* was lying facedown on his belly, and one of his legs was propped up on his satchel. He was exhausted from reading. The simultaneous layering of stories—that of Federico, the confused eroticism (the fetishism and voyeurism), the confounding of characters in the mirror, the converging timelines, the concentric forms, the jumbled chronology and juxtaposition . . . in a word, everything—had left him feeling overwhelmed and delirious. Who was this woman, this "she" in the book who would pop up everywhere, and yet always be inaccessible? Where was that "*now*" really coming from, the one that kept interrupting the narrative? Where was the story being written from, and—by the same token—what was its true center? Did it even have one? After turning these and other questions over in his head, Ricardo fell into a deep sleep. When he finally awoke and checked his watch, it was a quarter to one. He felt hunger rumbling in his stomach again. He tucked the book in his satchel and exited the station. On Insurgentes, two blocks down, he saw enormous orange letters that spelled out *Vips*. He headed off in that direction, and—after being perfumed with several clouds of carbon monoxide—he entered the air-conditioned establishment. In a corner of the restaurant (perfect for observing other people without being seen yourself) he sat down to eat some enchiladas verdes with a large Coke—extra ice—and a slice of date pie for dessert. Just when the waitress was about to bring the coffee, he opened his satchel and took out the notebook with the torn-out pages. He asked to borrow a pen, and the girl—friendly and flirtatious—gave him one.

On the page of *Las Rémoras* where he'd left off several days ago, he took up the pen and wrote down the recent developments in that village by the sea:

22

That morning, the three of them were sitting there at Tony's Lonchería on Libertad: Iginio Jasso, Elías, and Tony himself.

At a separate table, alone and distant, Doctor Díaz Gros read a magazine that came, monthly and late, from Mexico City. Tony and the writer sheltered themselves from the heat under the beach umbrellas that the owner had set up to offer a bit of shade. The architect, however, welcomed the sun's benign rays, letting them set fire to his bald head. It wasn't yet eleven o'clock in the morning, and—aside from the doctor—there were only a pair of midwives there drinking coffee off to the side, on the sidewalk.

The Lonchería formed part of that row of buildings that ran up Libertad towards the other, unpaved streets, and gradually moved away from the sea and the little waterfront. The sidewalk, perhaps six feet across, lay alongside the road—the only paved road in town—which had a sort of boulevard running down its center where Tony had set up five or six tables and umbrellas with permission from the city council. Very early every morning, he would bring them out from inside the Lonchería where they spent their nights. It was no small task, for while the tables and chairs were made of plastic, the umbrellas had steel stems that he'd rooted in cement blocks that took almost superhuman efforts to drag into place.

Tony occasionally got up from his seat to see if the doctor or the midwives needed anything else, hurrying across the street in case a car was coming (though that was exceedingly rare in Las Rémoras) to deal with something back behind the counter, eventually returning to the table and the conversation that had got the three of them so worked up, especially now that Elías had come down off his crags at the end of the beach. That morning, and to the amazement of all, he'd even started writing at the lonchería again instead of keeping to the beach or his home, the library. Eventually, though, he joined in—as he would often do before Roberta—the old, ongoing conversations between the architect and Tony.

Elías kept his notebook close at hand, tucked under his arm and topped with his pen. He seemed to have been interrupted in the middle of something important. Jasso swilled his coffee without so much as a passing thought for his intestines. Each new sip made him eager and gave him the strength to speak. Tony listened to him, absorbed and effeminate, shading himself from the sun. The pace was leisurely, as it always was in Las Rémoras.

"So now that she's gone, what do you think? What are you going to do?" the architect asked flat-out.

Tony was dying to know. That may well have been the only question that he (or anybody in town) cared about. They had discussed love, love's lies, love's jealousies—in other words, love in all its varieties—but it was always in the abstract, without reference to reality, simply for the pleasure of talking and feeling the friction between words that allude to everybody, yet never name a thing. Finally, Jasso had mustered the courage; he'd gone all in with his chips, trying not to lose his composure at the age of thirty-six.

Contrary to what he and Tony would have thought, Elías did not seem upset at the question. He smiled instead, looked pensive, and then spun his notebook on the table as he answered:

"I don't know. I imagine I'll keep on writing."

The others fell silent. This wasn't the response they'd been looking for. Or rather, it wasn't the point of the question. They didn't want to know what the twenty-three-year-old librarian was going to do with his *life*. They wanted to know what he was going to do with his *love*. That was what bothered them. Ultimately, everything else was of lesser import. The topic of love concerned them all. And who else besides an accomplice—a patient recently released from that hospital—could say what he thought? It was almost like speaking with someone who had been imprisoned for years in a concentration camp.

"Writing, of course," the architect insisted. "But what are you going to do about your love? That's what I was referring to."

Without a moment's hesitation, Elías answered: Nothing. Nothing at all. But then, after thinking it over, he decided to qualify his statement, saying, "I knew in advance that she was going to leave. She didn't say anything or telegraph it in any way. But I knew. It didn't bother me. Well, I suppose it did, but at the same time I needed to learn to live without her, needed to see what it was like. Understand? Of course I loved her, if that's what you're asking. But it's also true that you can't stop loving someone overnight."

"But how can you say that you loved her, Elías, if it was only a matter of a few months?" interrupted Tony. "You're so much more at ease now, and that makes me think that you didn't love her. At least, not as much as you may think."

"Maybe something's to be learned from all of this. I don't know . . ." Elías replied with perfect serenity.

"What?" Jasso asked, voice like an arrow, the sun bouncing off the lines of his face.

"Well, that love is like a weapon, Iginio. A delicate weapon. Its use requires a great deal of care. Plus, it's not just about love. Every emotion in the world is just as delicate, just as capable of completely going to shit. I don't know how to explain it, but I know it now. I recognize it."

"No, Elías, I understand you perfectly," said Jasso, taking another sip of his tongue-loosening coffee.

"I agree," said Tony, making it unanimous.

"For example," Elías continued, "I think quite highly of you, Mr. Architect. Really. You too, Tony. Sometimes I could even say I love you both. It's just a matter of getting a bit drunk or melancholic and there you have it: I love you guys. After so many years, it would be hard for that to be turned into farce, but—if you think about it—any one of a number of little things could potentially put an end to a centuries-old friendship, no? Emotions are not deceptive, but they are quite fragile."

Elías paused. Without meaning to, his words—carelessly tossed out—put the architect Iginio's longstanding friendship with the lawyer Rosales into a different light. The bond between those two old friends was broken. But Elías preferred to take no notice of this, and continued:

"Now let's take love. What sustains it? What guarantees it? Nothing. If you replay this little drama a few times, you'll see it. I feel bad for people who've spent a quarter of a century in love and still barely realize it! Too late! Like Black Santa and Joaquín, you know . . . Now she's alone, and he is too, always out fishing so that he doesn't die from the pain. And the worst thing about it is that neither one of them can see it. So I ask myself, how—after twenty-five years of sleeping together—can such a thing be? Well sure, you just have to see it to believe it."

"And if not, look at this: it's also the same with Rosales. Now he's been widowed twice," Tony interrupted.

The joke (the allusion to Inés) didn't make anybody laugh. On the contrary, everyone was struck silent, and Tony—a bit embarrassed—left to freshen the midwives' cups of coffee. He came back a short while later and asked the architect if he'd like some more himself.

"Thanks," Iginio replied, lost in thought.

Then Elías said:

"Feelings are a very fragile thing, Igino. Fragile like a weapon. Any little thing can destroy something important. It's horrible. You can't live that way, letting things happen as if nothing matters. Afraid that something might happen at any place, at any time."

"It's just that nobody really knows how to handle a weapon. It can go off at any time, just when you think you've got it under control," said Tony in his high-pitched, mellifluous voice. He seemed a bit shrunken, down from his usual, well-built, mustachioed self.

"Nobody can control it," agreed Elías. "You take it in your hand, you clean it, you oil it. But maybe, out of habit, you forget that it's loaded, or you forget that it's even a weapon: a double-barreled weapon. With one barrel, you can desire someone, you can love them, and with the other you can scorn them, destroy them . . . and even destroy yourself in the process. With love, emotions are so delicate and transparent that sometimes I doubt they even exist. You can ask yourself, do I ever feel them? Before the whole Roberta thing, I'd already seen how people drown themselves when their passion comes to an end. They don't know what to do, or where to turn. Why? Precisely because they put all their effort, all their will into one emotion . . . they become dependent on it, subjugate themselves to it, and they do so willingly, closing their eyes to the fact that they're risking everything. You shouldn't do this. I was on the verge of going there with Roberta . . . yes, I was ready to. About a month ago. Even knowing full well that it was a bad idea. And I think she nipped it in the bud. Once I asked her if she loved me, and she didn't respond . . . she flatly refused to answer me. Because of that one little remark, we didn't see each other for days. Ridiculous, you will say, but I don't think so. She might have been right. I can tell you this: Roberta is more astute than I ever imagined. Let me explain how difficult it can be to love someone who resists being loved. Yes, more than the person who loves them, it has to do with being loved at all. There are people like that. They feel responsible for the care of others, and for love that they wear like an expensive dress. Mainly because it's not quite about the love being offered. No, not at all. When you feel it, Tony (just as I did during those few passionate months with Roberta), I swear, nothing else will matter. You'll go to the bottom of the sea for your love."

"But it's also true that not wanting to be responsible—for anybody's love—is an act of supreme egoism," Jasso affirmed.

"Yes, an enormously egoistic act," agreed Elías. "But what can be done? A lot of women feel this way, especially those who've suffered the most. They don't want to feel compromised, and there's nothing on earth that they'd take in exchange for being responsible for somebody."

"Or, rather, they're afraid of ever hurting someone. That's why they avoid the issue. That's the nature of their egoism. It's a charitable, humanitarian egoism," said Tony.

"Yes, but before that fear—before that charitable concern for other people's feelings—lies the egoism. It's as clear as water. That's the problem. A lot of women don't like getting their hands dirty. Am I wrong, Tony, or is love anything but charitable? No, they prefer charity and philanthropy to love. Whatever the cost, whatever the price, they want to die with their hands clean. I'm not talking about virgins and saints here . . . they just don't want to dirty themselves, even with the love of a husband. And it's impossible to live that way. Really impossible."

"And that's what Roberta was like?" Tony asked, making his rounds.

"I think so. Deep down she believed that, since she got dirty once, that day when she loved a man (maybe the father of her child, I don't know), she was vaccinated against it ever happening again."

"In other words, Roberta had what you might say was an over-flowing sense of self-respect," the architect interrupted. He also asked for a splash more coffee. "And haven't you ever considered that what actually happened was that she loved you so much that she had to leave, to flee, to forget about you before she began to feel dependent on your love? Or, at least, she could have been becoming dependent on her desire to love you, which—according to what you've said—is fatal? That would also explain things, right? Have you considered it?"

"I doubt it. I think that Roberta was proud of her lack of affection, of not being attached to anybody. Not in terms of her attitude, because I don't want to imply that she didn't have a great heart. But that's just it: pity the dope who falls for her! She would put a stop to it, and pour all her scorn out on him."

"So that's what happened to you," concluded Jasso, more for the purposes of their debate than sincerely.

"I believe so. I believe so now," Elías answered without a moment's hesitation. Nevertheless, his "now" hinted at a good deal of past thought. "Eventually that's what happened, especially when she opened her eyes one afternoon and realized that she'd already fallen a bit in love with me. Understand? That was the straw that broke the camel's back. And it didn't just violate the 'not feeling responsible for the love of another' clause—which, if you look at it, becomes quite a burden itself—but it also corresponded (whether or not she realized it) to that other's love. In other words, she wanted that love, wanted to give it to someone, someone like me, for example. That, I suppose, is where she began to feel betrayed . . . first by herself, by her own deficiency or inability, and then betrayed by me, by the love that I felt for her. It was so much more than her simply not loving me in return and then flying off the handle, like when nothing's going your way."

"That could be; besides her son, she can't seem to love anybody on earth," ventured Tony, sitting there astonished, taller than the others.

"Yes, but that's a pretext, an excuse that she makes to herself so that she's able to separate herself from any other loves. Because her son's love is the be-all, the end-all. She accepts that. So why not use him for protection, right? She holds him close and fills him with everything: her aspirations to love, her desire to love, to love somebody, and also to feel cured of love forever."

"In other words," the architect said, "you consider women who love their children that much to be a burden?"

"Yes, when the child doesn't force them into it by being too needy."

"You might be right, Elías," Iginio punctuated again, taking a sip of his now quite lukewarm coffee. "No son loves his father as much as his father loves him. It's an unalterable law of life. Actually, I think that if that wasn't the case, it would be unnatural. So Roberta's son has to bear the full brunt of his mother's love, the love that she declines to give to anybody else. Everyone has to have their heart well-grounded, don't you think? But don't make your son into your husband. Because sooner or later, he's going to leave you. And vice-versa. Anyway, tell me, Elías, where the hell do you think that woman went?"

"I have no idea," he lied. "She didn't even say goodbye. She left yesterday. But that's the least of it. She knew full well that, when it came time for her to leave, she wasn't going to say goodbye. So, on the other hand, at least she turned out to be predictable."

"All women—according to your experiences, at least—are predictable. Or didn't you see that?" the womanizing architect said.

"I beg to differ . . ." joked Tony, feigning offense.

"Yes, you're right, not all of them," Iginio corrected himself, making amends with a smile. Then he turned back to Elías and asked: "So do you think that she's going to keep breaking that same old ground, or is she ever going to look for a husband?"

"A husband?" Elías laughed. "She'd rather die, though she swore a thousand times over that she would get married some day. She wouldn't be able to bear it. And think about this, Iginio . . . just because you marry someone, it doesn't make them your husband."

"I don't understand," he interrupted.

"Like I said, she doesn't want to love anybody, but on the other hand she did say that she wants to get married. More for her son than for herself. Roberta would be just fine dying alone and unmourned. A martyr to love. Whore to all but never to one. Her sense of pride demands it. She has to do it as part of her destiny. Understand?"

"This whole husband thing reminds me of the Parable of the Good Samaritan," said Tony, his moustache quivering with excitement. "Her fifth husband or whatever he was . . . According to Padre Augusto, he wasn't her husband anymore, right?"

The architect didn't understand, but Elías nodded: that was it exactly. They took advantage of that opportunity to fall silent for a spell. Eventually, Jasso spoke up:

"Elías, what *I* think is that, up until now, you've lived in a black-and-white world. For example, you've made love an absolute. More than anybody else, a womanizer is highly dubious of absolutes. Believe me, things are not that clear. Love—like any other feeling, any other thing—is relative. You decide to love someone, or you decide not to. You put the absolute in God, or your mother, or Roberta, and the result is the same, but if you know how to distance yourself just a bit and think about the act itself of loving someone or hating someone, you'll see how it's all relative, how in the end it doesn't matter what you feel or don't feel. Love them or hate them, who cares? It's all the same in the end. So with regard to the proverbial delicate weapon, it's those feelings you've turned into absolutes that have become delicate, not others. You say, for example, *I love her*, and when you hear yourself say that, you hear an absolute intended to convince yourself that this feeling will last. And that's a lie. It's a hole, an unfathomable gap between what you say you feel and what you actually do feel. Believe me, Elías, in reality you don't feel it at all, you're only trying to convince yourself when you say you love. But ultimately none of this is important, nothing is as important as it seems at first, especially what you feel or stop feeling." Here he paused for a few moments before continuing. "What happens is that soon you lose this notion of the hole—that space with absolutely nothing in it—and you try to fill it, to justify it. But you know, if you put yourself in that hole, you would realize clear as day that you only feel what you want to feel. You don't feel emotions as if they were something external, predestined. This is an illusion, a mirage. If you picture yourself there, Elías—if you can set yourself in that hole without panic, without nausea—then you'll see that everything is just a craving of yours, and susceptible to change . . ." He paused again, and then said: "Do you know why feelings change? Why the gun goes off, as you say, and all of a sudden you no longer love people whom you've loved for so long? It's nothing extraordinary, I assure you. The feeling changes or simply comes to an end because that's what you decide, whether you realize it at the time or not. But, on the other hand, yes, the feeling can endure if that is what you decide, Elías. As the years go by, you ingeniously construct certain absolutes. Falling in love, for example, is to place everything into an absolute that does not exist, that you simply invented."

"I suppose you're right," Elías responded, lost in thought, having only half-grasped the architect's words. There was one conclusion, at least, one thing that was left absolutely clear: he was not, for the past month—while he loved Roberta—in that hole, walled in, where there's nothing for you to do except invent what you want, make it absolute and immediate, according to your pleasure, your whims, or whatever you need at that moment.

"Nevertheless," Iginio finished, "I grant you that sooner or later we have to create certain sets of absolutes in order to continue to live. Why? That's something I don't have the answer to, yet. Where the hell does this need come from, when you know that everything in the world is completely relative?"

Tony listened without saying a word. They all fell silent, actually, each one preferring to mull things over on his own. Elías, for example, meditated on the insignificance of feelings, and the delicate, loaded weapon which goes off after years of sure-handed care. The architect Jasso pondered the impossibility of telling the truth to Elías, for it was an unnecessary truth, and a relative one at that: he'd slept with Roberta a couple of times himself, and he wasn't going to soon forget them. If he mentioned it, the weapon would go off, and the gentle affection that they shared between them despite their difference in age would vanish in a puff of gunsmoke.

Just then, the midwives called for Tony, who got up, and—still completely distracted—stepped on a small lizard. At the other table, Doctor Díaz Gros, looking up from his reading, started giggling.

23

When Ricardo looked at the clock, it was 8:06. He had spent over seven hours there in the corner booth at Vips. Alone and submerged in the pages of his novel. He slipped his notebook into his satchel and called it quits, almost out of disgust. He paid the check, and—although he wanted to return the young lady's pen—her shift had ended hours ago. He stuck it in his pocket under his sweater; who knew, maybe he would want to write something that night, on the train.

Through the window, he could see a darkness identical to that of the dawn: not uniform, darker in some places, lighter in others, perhaps where people were hurrying, where the soles of their shoes hit the ground, or where the warm twilight air mixed with exhaust fumes. He ducked into the station, ran over an old disabled woman, bumped into an employee, and finally reached Platform Four. A switchman showed him the way, and—quite anxious, since he still couldn't believe it was happening—he took his seat. The train was no more than a third full, so he discovered (with an unhealthy sort of joy) that he would be alone on this trip. As alone as he wanted to be. He could sprawl out on the seat, look out the window or down the aisle, and sleep comfortably. He was going at last . . . he knew when he heard the train whistle that there was no mistaking it. The train left right on time: 8:30, just like the officious and ridiculous donut-girl had said. Ricardo laughed.

He spent nearly four hours checking out his fellow passengers, feeling the warm night air as he walked from car to car, ordering a sandwich in the restaurant coach (which he quickly abandoned after two bites), and—finally—truly hungry to know what would happen, he sat down to read the third section of the Ross book, which had him completely captivated:

(DAY THREE)

The summers in La Paz have ended. Time flew by without so much as a breeze. I close my eyes and find myself in the middle, living days at random. Time is an infinite task. If I stop for even a moment, fear takes root in my body, and so I prefer to continue writing without understanding too much. I just want to continue without looking at that chasm which has suddenly been opened. I still can't fathom where it comes from or what actually happened. Time or some breach thereof has been widened into a definitive space. I am here, alone—in some form, outside of time—writing, as I must. I have a mindless impatience that I can't quite control or cure. It's absurd for me to stop and observe. God or the world or time, I don't know—I don't want to know—they're leaving us, teasing us and laughing among themselves, laughing at this despicable act. What is it to live? Where does it occur? Or better yet, when does it occur? In what moment? Nevertheless, I suddenly intuit it again: we can't be sure of living at all. In fact, it has to do with an illusion that we all share equally. If someone were to truly do it—in other words, were really to *live*—they wouldn't even realize it, since nobody can live in the passage of time. Nobody that I know is *remembering that they live*, while they're actually living. What maintains us is memory, the shifting forms that we create with it. We spend our lives in them. Or in the unconsciousness. Only we deceive ourselves, we give ourselves excitedly to any bit of convenient nostalgia. And so we live for the future or the past, for the before or the after, according to what pleases us, and nothing, after all is said and done, is certain: neither of the two exists. They both happen simultaneously, though we don't realize it. Therefore, only *what lives*—what is living—will come to be true. And who does it? Who knows that they are doing it while they're doing, and—more—that they will remember it? In other words, that the moment of living has already become a recollection? That, even as it occurs, it is only fuel for future memories?

In this way, then, we give ourselves candidly to pleasure and suffering without memory, as if life were (and sometimes it seems as if it is) an art of prestidigitation or amnesia. Nobody recognizes it because nobody knows it. I, on the other hand, do know it, and irrevocably sink into the illusion that is my body. Therefore I cannot explain how it can be honest or chaste to touch oneself, to hear your viscera swell at night, to fortify yourself, to feel the pulsing veins in your neck, when it would be better to do away with the body completely. How can one not give up in the face of so much disorder, such an ill-starred and putrid body, such presumptuous flesh, the injustice that is contemplating the body, to live, to hurt, to enjoy? How can one not be frightened at their immensity, their fatality, their luring us into the abyss?

And perhaps even art doesn't transcend it? I don't know; I don't want it to matter to me. And desire, does it transcend? Again, I don't know, although I recognize desire always, I live subject to it, and I imagine that I am there, in eternal unfulfillment. Together, desire and art. Without touching, one just barely in front of the other, recognizing, waiting. But for what? They take life thus, in its nonsense, its discontent. They have simply to wait, as do I. In the meantime, to be dying very smoothly: devoted to it, softly and without objection.

I recognize them (desire and art), they can be close at hand, touching. They can even be in my own body, and in the soul of all things simultaneously. It is my desire: impregnating the profound soul of things, the *anima mundis*, identifying with them if only for a moment. Then I discover, in the blink of an eye, that art is quite close indeed and even shows itself from time to time. Art, I say, lies in the soul of things, but does not appear. It is the artist, then, who must yield to it, and only thus be able to overcome it, reveal it. Desire also appears in this way: I see it, I have it, it is within me: there, over things, under them, perhaps even in them. But first, the dark premonition that the world is eternally unfulfilled continues to pervade me. It must be so, and art as well: I detect it in the body, in objects, in forms.

I watch, I contemplate men: they do not live, they simply do not live, because *they do not know*. I also contemplate myself: I don't even dare say that I truly live. I remember. I do nothing more than remember, which is something very different from living. I look only to save my life, that other life, the one from before and that is yet to come. I look to save any one of my lives: even those I no longer have, not remembering them in time. Nevertheless, I close my eyes, I am there, remembering in the future—February 2008, for example—that *now* in which I write, in which I imagine and remember. If I close my eyes and think about it, I can be there again, I will be there again. Only if I want it. *Now* I understand it easily: I can be transported. *Now*? When is *now*? I respond that I do not know, I do not know when *now* is. I may be lying if I say that *now* is when I write. Which is why I repeat: I do not know. But if I open my eyes, where am I? I don't cling to anyone; I don't see or feel my body. I am nowhere. I already desire nothing. I am not obstinate, I do not think and do not even believe that it—I—remember or imagine. I write. I only write. I lost the route in the deepest sea: there is nothing above and nothing below, and I don't see so much as a bubble. I write. Perhaps memory is dead. Dead for quite some time, and yet I don't know it. There's no reason to be obstinate or to desire something. What would it be? And what for? I write and nothing else matters to me. The world is dead. I am also dead. Dead for quite some time.

I have never been in love. It's just the same as saying that I was in love once, in some place, at some time. Which is why it's better to say that I have never been in love. Just seeing it written fills me with a miserable sort of tenderness: these words have the capacity to corrupt. If loving or falling in love moves me to tenderness (that most harmful and falsely warm of all emotions), then it is clear: the essence of my body—the fragile equilibrium of its four humors—has become corrupted. In love, the secret mineral might dissolve even further. Thus I hear the vertigo of my viscera wandering and folding, and the pores of my skin softening. I disturb myself, and the world intimidates me. I am apprehensive about feeling fear or pain in front of others, so I shy away from them and pity myself. Disturbing myself, terrifying myself, the hidden organism rotting. *Now* I know that everyone, in some way, is burdened by such suffering, that their viscera also rots as mercilessly. In their foolish lethargy, men dilute themselves and forget. Above all, the latter: they forget.

If there was at that time a foreign emotion for me, like a slap or some sort of imaginary sickness—call it love—I had yet to discover it. I found it several years later; its name was Laila. Those torrid summers in La Paz and Los Cabos were left far behind. The yacht was sold, the house on the waterfront was abandoned, Veracruz disappeared. The years went by, warm and imperceptible; and in the meantime, I submerged myself in the devastating current of the body.

Since then, I have known that two antagonistic beings live together in memory, destroying everything they can: pleasure and pain. Memory is always pleasurable or painful; there is nothing else. The two maintain and support each other, vulnerable, like volatile liquids fermenting in their separate stills—like hatred and love. Sometimes, however, the balance is upset: pain is the one that prevails, upsetting pleasure and stability. I repeat: this time, the pain has one name, one owner: Laila. Yes, just yesterday I found an old letter with her name written across the flap. There it was, quiet, and I felt that since it was written—perhaps even before it was written—it had known its final destination: to be included among these lines, this pathetic little passage in my book.

The letter was written, peacefully and silently, solely in order to tear down my pleasure. I know it. I had no choice but to open it and read it again after all these years; in spite of myself. But first, I will tell you what happened. From the beginning:

In those days, when I was seventeen, I was preparing to stage a play, Edward Albee's *A Delicate Balance*. The school principal supported us. The year before, my colleagues and I had produced, with limited success, a version of Benavente's *The Bonds of Interest*. Actually, it was more of an outright failure—months of hard work for nothing. The actors (my colleagues) and the actresses (their sisters and friends) didn't want to give me another shot at directing. He might not be a bad actor, they'd say behind my back, but as a director he leaves much to be desired. The problem was, they couldn't find anyone else who wanted to do it. I want to remember: in the days leading up to its first performance, *The Bonds of Interest* was advertised all over the school with advertisements and invitations posted in the classrooms. Some scenes weren't finished, while others were deteriorating without hope of rescue, and one of the students' voices was magically going hoarse just as opening night was approaching. The rehearsals were a disaster when we heard her monologues . . . slurring constantly, chewing up the words, soaking them with saliva, ruminating them, forcing them out, and the result was a voice that sounded at once muffled,

Pythian, and clipped. A friend of hers was similarly unable to get things right; it was almost as if they were trying intentionally to annoy us and force us to start the whole production from scratch. We spent long hours sequestered in the (sometimes closed) auditorium, often lasting well into the night, when the watchman came and asked us to leave. Silvia could never stand where she was supposed to. Which is why, in the middle of one of those afternoons, after everyone had debated whether a particular scene should be cut, I got up on the stage and shouted that if she couldn't take direction, she would have to leave. And then, in front of everybody, foaming at the mouth like a dog, I spat on the stage, right on the spot where Silvia was supposed to stand.

The others, I remember *now*, were stunned. To be honest, I was as well. I never thought myself capable of such a thing. Silvia ran off the stage, crying, with her friend at her heels. A disaster . . . everything that afternoon was a disaster. We cancelled rehearsals for one, two, three, and then several days, so I hardly need tell you how the three actual performances of *The Bonds of Interest* went. There was a good deal of booing, laughter, and general mayhem among the dozens of students who'd come to see our production. It would have been humiliating if it weren't—as we knew—a comedy, and so intended to provoke a *little* hilarity. Nevertheless, we soon saw—without the slightest doubt—this reaction for what it really was: rude sarcasm and mocking laughter. For several months, all of us—actors, actresses, lighting technicians, prompters, musicians, and stage managers—were afraid to show our faces. Probably none of them wanted to see their disgraced pseudo-director either, the clown who'd also had the gall to play the character of Harlequin in his own production.

As I said, it was several months later, at one of the first performances of *A Delicate Balance*, where Laila came in with Silvia. I had regained the support of the school principal, as I've said, and I had reserved the auditorium for our rehearsals and performances.

I was broke, apart from what I'd earned promising not to represent Sartre or Genet on the stage under any circumstances. (The Marists weren't familiar with Albee, which is why they approved him.) From wardrobe to props, everything came out of our own pockets, and we were prohibited from charging admission. The principal and teachers didn't offer us anything other than approval and a touch of skepticism: a sort of curious sympathy for the naïve theatre group and its director. There were a few students that year who harbored some talent or interest in becoming actors (though, of course, *they hadn't met me yet*), along with myself, a stubborn, inexperienced director.

Only Octavio, my lifelong friend, was at all interested in Albee's work. He read it, and—as could be expected—loved it, though he did point out that it would be difficult to adapt for the stage in our impoverished condition. Right from the start, he wanted to be what we rather presumptuously called the casting director, and he decided on Silvia, whom I hadn't seen in eight or nine months, and a few friends. She was the only holdover from the previous year's cast who dared to return. The other "Benaventes" sent their apologies; at least, that's what Octavio told me. It was on the third day of rehearsals that a slightly less resentful Silvia arrived with her friend. Immediately, and to my dismay, I was struck once and forever (even *today*, as I remember it) by her loveliness, which was so incredibly rare. Out of this world, really, is the only way to describe her and her pleasing scent, reminiscent of Frida. They approached us and, in less than a minute, I knew: I was completely taken with the ambiance or mysterious atmosphere of her body. If some memory of Laila still remains with clarity, it is her air (I don't know whether to call it fresh, hot, or warm) that makes her feel ever near. Even though she isn't. On the other hand, it seemed as though Silvia had given up on her deep-seated antagonism towards me. Rehearsals began to improve and the whole routine was quite superb. Everyone was completely wrapped up in their roles—just as I wanted—infected with them, really, and our enjoyment of the piece did not wane as our preparations continued. Still, Octavio and I knew from experience that the worst was yet to come, as we approached the final dress rehearsal and spirits became agitated under the threat of opening night. Nerves were frazzled, and everyone would eventually take out their frustrations and quarrels squarely on me. Me, who for months has been their director and psychoanalyst. And it works both ways: as I said, it really is a form of therapy.

I've also said that I had no directorial experience, no serious equipment or methodology to support the extravagant ideas that I had then about theater. It all boiled down to a thin little Stanislavsky book and one by the German director Carl Gustav Grüber, which my cast presented me with one day. Nevertheless, things happened as if by magic, and I only imagined my role to be that of someone always compelled to impose his will on all the others. I wanted to think that was how it worked; *now* I know that I was mistaken.

That particular afternoon, Laila dedicated herself to watching from the auditorium seats, maintaining an absolute, reverential silence. I was hardly able to keep my mind off her, her presence, her calm and measured breathing behind me. I felt restrained, imagining her watching me, and I couldn't approach the actors as I normally would. I don't think, though, that they suspected anything . . . my changed voice and the false ease with which I gestured were only apparent to me. I implored the angels on high to end the rehearsal early; they must have been listening, since my prayer was answered. Just before saying goodnight, I asked Silvia about her old friend, the girl who'd always mangled her lines. Eavesdropping, Laila knew exactly who I was talking about, and laughed: her voice was almost a trill. The flat, round whiteness of her face was vividly accentuated, and fixed in my pupils like a camera's flash.

"I haven't seen *her* in quite some time," Silvia said to me. "Looks like you're out of luck yet again, Federico."

"Looks like it," I replied dryly.

Even Laila had to know (she would have found out) about my despicable habit—spitting on the floor—even though I'd only done it once. With time, such things become stigmas, and soon you're known everywhere as *the director who spits on the stage*. In any case, it didn't seem to bother her; rather, it was me who was bothered. Without taking her attention away from us and our conversation, Laila seemed to be searching for some hint in my face: who I was, what I was like, and why I did such odd things. I would have had to explain to her that in the theater, everything is played out in terms of outburst and apology, but I didn't say a thing.

When they left, I went over to Octavio, who asked, "Hey, pretty hot, don't you think?"

"Who?" I asked with incredible shamelessness.

"Her," he answered. "Silvia's friend."

He left me stunned when, two or three days later, right before rehearsal started, he said, "Federico, guess what?" His grin a mile wide. "I called her."

I shrugged my shoulders as if I had no idea who the hell he'd called, or why he was so excited to tell me. But deep down I knew it; I could tell from the moment he opened his mouth and said my name.

I answered, calm and ferocious:

"Who the hell are you talking about?"

"Laila, who else?" he replied, delighted. "I asked Silvia for her number, and I called. Gorgeous, don't you think? And no complaints. She said yes, that she'd go out with me."

"That's great!" I said.

I felt doubly bad, being dishonest with him as well as being unable to deflect my jealousy. Once again, it had taken hold of me, sudden and senseless. I hated myself for it, and didn't say a word more. The rehearsal went badly, which was my fault, and at one point I unloaded my frustrations on Octavio, as though it was all his fault.

A week later, however, I learned from a quite frustrated Octavio that they still hadn't gone out. It was, I have to admit, a pleasant feeling. She had called to cancel; he called back and left a message with her mother, but according to Octavio she seemed determined not to return the call. He just couldn't stand girls that made you wait. Octavio, you see, was incredibly proud. Which is why, deep down, I cherished the hope that he wouldn't *really* pursue her.

At long last, I mustered the courage to ask Silvia for her number. I did it like a child, behind Octavio's back, a month later. Silvia didn't say anything, but I could tell that she was honestly surprised. I wrote Laila's number down on a slip of paper and tucked it, clumsily and hastily, in my shirt pocket. Silvia seemed preoccupied at rehearsal. I didn't say anything to her; this time, I opted for the caring, amiable approach to directing. Silvia was watching Octavio out of the corner of her eye, scrutinizing him before getting back into character. It was obvious that Silvia was going to call her that night to let her know, which is to say, *to warn her*. Nevertheless, as soon as I got home, I dialed Laila's number; perhaps I would get her before Silvia did. She answered herself: Laila, the girl in full bloom with a hot, sweet, ancient musk about her body. Once again, her voice was a melodious trill . . . even from my vantage point on the other end of the line, I could picture her throat, her breasts. She didn't have to think very hard to figure out who was calling, and that—I must admit—was quite flattering indeed.

Our date went splendidly. I dropped by her house, we went out for coffee, and spent the entire afternoon talking. Whenever she spoke or smiled, I couldn't take my eyes off the tautness of her skin, the deepness of her eyes, and the darkness of her lashes, flapping tirelessly in her round face. Once again I felt myself awash in the mysterious air of her skin, without any desire to take shelter from it: something indescribable about her, a true question mark *to this day*. Without a moment's thought, I took her hand in mine, and she didn't protest. We remained there, holding hands for hours, and just then—just before the check came, still seated there, our knees touching lightly—was when I discovered it, found the solution to an enigma, though only for a moment, a flash. (This, however, was a new enigma, an enigma that had been born in the moment of its being solved.) Yes, it was in one of those almost involuntary movements of her hand, tossing her hair back over her shoulder, that I realized it: just behind her smooth, flat temple, one of her ears was missing.

It is already very late when they return from downtown. I find out from Emilio that we'll be going sailing the next day. My uncle David wants to go to some beach on Isla del Espíritu Santo, his favorite place. I've spent the rest of my afternoon at the waterfront, talking about women with Veracruz. He's had several, he told me, and in my curiosity and desire I wanted nothing more than to be older and to have had—like him—many women.

Later that night, when everyone is asleep, I hear Octavio's clear, inquiring voice ask the question I'd been waiting for:

"So what did you do all day, Federico?"

In the opaque blackness of the bedroom, I can't quite make out the gesture with which my friend is trying to convey or express something to me. He can't see me either. So, unable to discern each other's faces despite being alone in the same room, I answer:

"Don't fuck around. I was down at the waterfront with Veracruz. I'm tired; I want to sleep. You know we've got an early start tomorrow, right?"

"What about Frida?" he insists.

"Didn't you hear me? I want to sleep!"

Have I deceived him, or have I—ingeniously—deceived myself? *Today*, after all these years, I am still not sure, I still do not know. We fall silent. All of La Paz does as well.

Nevertheless, I enjoy imagining the city there, waiting for me to arrive one day, for us to meet. I think of La Paz as the Barcelona poet thinks of his place of birth:

> City
> Already so distant!
>
> Distant by the sea: afternoons in port
> And the wandering neglect of the waterfront.
> The tides stubbornly grow
> Across the hours there.
>
> And there will be a sound,
> A deep rumbling bearing sleep,
> When the nighttime lights appear
> Over the sea.
>
> Deeper, ever deeper
> You go with me, City,
> Like a sunken, irretrievable
> Love.
>
> An occasional wave and silence again.

We weigh anchor early. Excursions always begin at eight o'clock sharp. My father and my uncle attend to the last few details: replacing a lost lifejacket, the boxes and bags of food, sausages, and other usual victuals, the enormous coolers with beers and sodas, the Zodiac with its outboard motor, the rods and reels.

We never go too far the first day, because the yacht must drop anchor before sunset.

Suddenly, in the midst of jokes and wild laughter, Veracruz says that tomorrow we'll be heading for new, completely unknown shores. When? In the morning, after spending the night in La Partida, he says. What's it called, ask Selma, Aarón, and I. Las Rémoras, he answers, laughing. *Now* I know that he invented it, that Las Rémoras has never existed, that no such town appears on any map of Baja California Sur. Nevertheless, we all believed it then. Perhaps some day it'll appear somewhere, appear in some book, and I won't even know it.

I can't sleep at all; I am consumed by memories of the past two days in Las Paz: the living, carnal memories of Frida, my aunt, and of the prostitute at *El Ferry*. I don't want a single detail to escape, and I have no doubt that Octavio's extraordinary snoring will help me keep them safe.

It's nine o'clock by the time we're finally ready to shove off; soon, to starboard, we make out La Paz and its long waterfront before sailing onward. I spend a couple of warm hours seated in the bow, and I watch with anticipation to see whether each successive wave will break across it. I watch them, count them, waiting to see if my predictions come true. If not, I simply make an adjustment, and sure enough the next wave doesn't disappoint. That's how it works. It's my little game, and I take a daydreamer's delight in it. If I look out over the stern, I watch, perplexed (like Ishmael in *Moby-Dick*), as the gulls and the occasional white albatross hang there, almost stationary in the sky, following the track of our foamy wake. It seems that it's the yacht that's stopped to watch them there, etched against the smooth morning sky: static, without so much as a flap of the wings. I watch in suspense, not letting them out of my sight for a moment. Eventually, however, the giant birds grow tired of the game and peel off, just as we're leaving the bay and heading out to open water.

We pass some beaches: Coromuel first, replete with vacationers, followed by Pichilingue shortly thereafter, where the ferries from Mazatlán and Topolobampo are arriving and departing. We eat there; some of us order plates of chocolata clams and giant oysters prepared with vegetables and wrapped in aluminum foil. Others are having grilled *mojarra* or *bonito* (which also comes wrapped in foil), while the rest opt for enormous abalone or tripe cocktails or *seviche*. Everyone, however, polishes off the meal with heaping plates of whiting or shrimp with rice and fried plantains. Sometimes Veracruz drops anchor and swims out to eat with us; other times he hangs back, and from the beach packed with sunburned tourists, we contemplate his curly mane of hair, his doughy but bronzed body, and his long, bare feet propped up on the tiller. He seems like an immense black prophet out there, eyes lost in the blue offing he knows so well.

We finally make for La Partida, which is one of those coves that cuts into Isla del Espíritu Santo. It's not more than two hours from Pichilingue, but nevertheless, to those of us on board—Selma, Octavio, Emilio, Aarón, and I—it seems like an eternity away. It's impossible to compare those smooth, nautical distances with travels on land; over sea, we move in an imperceptible, almost aerial manner. Our bodies seek the ephemeral breaths of wind at the broadsides of the yacht, or else apply suntan oil and lay out on deck, while my father and uncle spend the majority of the trip in the stern with their fishing lines out to sea. They chat, they drink, and they wait with the steadfast apprehension of men hoping to catch their dinner. My mother and my aunt talk below decks. We hover around foredecks, gripping the handrail, dying of laughter, horsing around or looking for dolphins in the bow wave. We see them quite often, their blue or gray or silvery shapes darting in and out of sight, following us like an escort until they tire and return to their own business like the albatrosses before them. Unlike the albatrosses, however, the dolphins always come in groups of five or six, and are fast and sleek in their synchronized zigzagging. We begin to shout, a general commotion onboard: we wave, they frolic, twisting in the sea. Then they disappear into the depths, gone forever. We call for them, beg them to return, but to no avail.

Finally we reach Isla del Espíritu Santo. There, among many others, lies a beach: La Partida. Emilio and I hit the water almost before the anchor does, swimming for shore without waiting for the Zodiac to inflate, which Veracruz is doing with an electric pump. We run desperately over the clean, burning sand, dip into the surf to cool off, and then get back to chasing each other around again. Our lean bodies dry in the sun, but minutes later we repeat our exhausting game of swim-and-run. The sun seems to chase us too, eager to evaporate the beads of water clinging to our skin.

My sister burns easily, and is allergic to sand fleas. After a while we hear my mother calling her back to the yacht, and with a concentrated scowl of annoyance, she shouts back that she's not coming. The rest of us laugh, tell her to go, saying that it's too bad she's a girl. Selma remains resolute and mutters something that the others can't make out. I can, however, as she intended it for my ears alone. I don't know why Eden is so suddenly shattered. La Partida disappears, Puerto Balandra vanishes, and Pichilingue, Nopoló, even La Paz evaporate in puffs of smoke. My sister comes up to me, tells me once again, and then takes off running. It isn't hers, however; this repentance or revision is my body's own discontented search, a yearning from the deepest roots of my being. I go after her, rancor swells in us both beneath the barrage of sun on our backs, and without knowing why or how, I give myself over to instinct. I dive, hitting her, and our bodies are instantly spattered with sand. Each of us cries—*I hear them still, suffocating me*—rends the calmness of this little world, its pristine, ancient order: an affront to nature itself. The blood on her head doesn't even bother me. I feel the others swarming around me, pulling me off of her—I wouldn't have had the will to do it myself. I hear Selma's shouts and cries again: impurities staining the endless tranquility of the sky.

We finally staged *A Delicate Balance*. Everything went incredibly well; nobody forgot their lines, and our errors were all but unnoticed. Everyone was patently happy, satisfied with their work of the past few months. Afterwards, when the theatre group wanted to celebrate, we all went out to Garibaldi Plaza. Octavio, Silvia, and Laila all rode with me in my car. In the midst of the general tumult of the plaza, the mariachis and guitars, after having a few drinks at a nearby cantina and a stroll along the street, Laila and I split off from the group without so much as a word. Then, in one of those narrow and dirty side streets, I kissed her. Perhaps I imagined, as we all do sooner or later—weak and lazy—that this particular woman who is with you . . . you suppose, for a moment, that she is yours (yours?), and so you decide on some frigid night—decide without so much as a thought—to share your life with her, decide that you will certainly, invariably, be in love with her forever. You think that everything you feel is immortal. But it is, on the contrary, a sad, ill-fated bit of ignorance to believe this: you are mortal, your feelings (like hers) are transitory, and will change. We live in the daily oblivion of things, Federico, remember that. All of a sudden, a cold wind sweeps across the sidewalk, and you see her pale face, her thick eyebrows, her profound eyes, her neck, her throat. Everything is immortal, you repeat over and over again as you embrace her, and then—without realizing it—you let go. Those days die.

It's worthwhile to point out that, after that night, Laila and I shared a time that was pronounced in both its brevity and its beauty, during which everything was—as Albee would have said, ironically enough—delicate and balanced. From the beginning,

Laila told me that she would be going away to live with her parents and brother; they were Cuban and for some months they had been hoping for visas to go and live in Miami. Imperceptibly, the days of youth abandoned us, and before I even realized it, they had gone. Laila couldn't stay, nor could she delay her departure. A new life was waiting for her in Key Biscayne, and—unfortunately for me—I wasn't a part of it. Nonetheless, I was stubborn, as Laila was in the beginning, and we waited. For what? Time, I told myself, some indefinite and absurd time. That illusion with which we defraud life, sweeten the palate, and learn to pay attention. Several years passed that *now* I have to force myself to remember; years of writing letters I no longer wish to read, years of brief and desperate visits, years that culminated in this final letter of hers, in which she wrote something that—*forgive me—you don't want to know* . . . *Federico, I'm getting married.*

Afterwards, you have no idea when or how time went by so smoothly, as if borne by a river. One afternoon you open the drawer of your writing desk and find a letter next to Laila's . . . this one from Octavio (as you recall, the last one he ever wrote to you), in which he tells you even more things you never wanted to know, things you never asked him about, things you never thought could have happened back then (*when he went out with her*), and now it happens all over again, and anyone who reads that letter knows exactly what it was.

Overwhelmed by this surprise ending, Ricardo could hardly remember his own Laila. He went back over her words: her mother had actually been the author's mistress, and Octavio, her father, had been the man who he robbed? What a shitty friend. Ricardo shut the book, deciding to leave the final chapter for a better time. At this particular moment, he was struck with the urgent desire to write a poem—whether it was prompted by something in Ross's writing, he didn't know. He spent a few minutes formulating his words. He reached under his black sweater and took the young waitress's pen out from his shirt pocket and then pulled his notebook from his satchel. He got up and moved to the very back of the coach. A cool breeze flowed in from the front door and exited out the other end of the car. He took a seat after having taken a look at the stars; the train was traveling through a field—barely distinguishable in the night—melding seamlessly into the dark, deep sky. Yes, he had to write (it almost felt like taking dictation) about what—many centuries ago—another writer had started writing about that same night, at that same time, in some perfectly isolated corner of the world . . . as isolated as it was real, if anything can be said to be real in this world.

And Ricardo, in something of a fit, titled one page of his *Las Rémoras* notebook "Poem of the Inconstant Young Lover in the Middle of the Night":

24

I am the Inconstant Lover, the Only Probable Inconstant
Impudent in his joy,
In his deplorable, repeated pleasure. The night the ancient young man watches
Is the same irrepressible Shadow which I watch. The night that looks upon the ancient young man
—alone, in the midst of Nobody—
Is the pulse that, identical, inhabits this night. Beneath the eternal Obscurity of the sky
I am the eternal, lustful Lord of bodies in pain.
I am that same adolescent who writes, prolix, invariable, since before,

Since before: ever writing. The ancient and young nocturnal
man
  Who—knowingly—opens Time into Darkness; the Probable,
sterile lover
  Of all possible and future worlds,
  The final and primal Adam. I lift my eyes: there is the Night,
the constant Night
  And I am pure and those men encouraged (they write, they
write this
  And in my ecumenical chest they dream while I dream in
theirs)
  And every Inconstant Lover knows now what I know
  Then.

When Elías finished writing his poem, he knew that others like
him—both after and before—also knew it "Then"; yes, there were
many like him, an indefinable number of Inconstant Lovers, nocturnal youths of antiquity and adolescents of the future. He even
perceived that, although it was decided—calculated, really—that
Ricardo would write this poem as part of *his* story, the story that
he was being made to live at that moment (on a train heading
for Mazatlán, as we already know), Ricardo would have thought
exactly the same thing about him, Elías, there in that mysterious
notebook he carried with him always.

It was 1:30 in the morning when Councilman Francisco
Sigüenza, on his way home from his girlfriend Pilar's house,
found the writer there on the beach: alone, absorbed, scribbling
in his notebook. They made eye contact and greeted one another
from a distance with an almost undetectable wave. It couldn't
be said that they were on good terms; rather, they simply put up
with each other. For Francisco Sigüenza, Elías was an impossible
case, a real peculiarity: he had no boss, no job, his writing made
no sense, he was always pensive, and he owned the keys to the

library, which he had gradually settled into to live and which nobody else ever visited. And that whole thing about going after a whore—falling in love with one—he just couldn't understand it, couldn't accept it. In his own way, Sigüenza was stubbornly conservative and formal. A Puritan. The councilman continued on his way past the waterfront under a night sky laden with stars that did not shine. Even the moon wasn't able to fully illumine the high-water mark on that broken, valve-shaped beach.

25

It was 6:30 in the evening; in other words, the time his train was supposed to have arrived in Mazatlán (according to that rather unhelpful, donut-loving ticket agent). But of course, he wasn't there yet. He asked a conductor, and found out that the Guadalajara stop had been longer than anticipated, owing to a mob of people who swarmed the cars all at once. They would be arriving in Mazatlán at 7:30 or 8:00 instead.

The atmosphere had become unbearable. The earlier tranquility had disappeared. The new passengers shuffled around insistently, changed seats, fanned themselves theatrically, crammed the aisles, snacked incessantly (and more to kill time than because they were hungry), propped their feet up on the seats in front of them, threw orange peels on the ground, and pontificated over every triviality. It was like they were in a cage, weakened, withered, sweaty, irritable, stealing breaths of fresh air from their neighbors, smiling. Ricardo reread the poem he had written there the previous night. He saw it just the same in his notebook, interpolated within the story of *Las Rémoras*. He could imagine him—Elías, that is—perched on the crags overlooking the beach, writing. Captured to perfection. Right there, with Sigüenza's greeting. But, he asked himself, why the hell had he named the girlfriend "Pilar"? What was that about? It might have been enough to say that Francisco had left his girlfriend's house; the name didn't matter. Such a devotion to creating characters! Deplorable indulgence. Nevertheless—he justified himself—she was just a random, tangential character, not worth criticizing. All novels have that sort of thing in them somewhere. Forster loved *War and Peace*, and what other novel features so many random characters, so many men and women who, after an epic journey—a couple of chapters—disappear without a trace? Even characters who aren't random—characters who are actually quite important—pivotal characters, incredible heroes—can disappear suddenly, as Galileo Gall did in *The War of the End of the World*.

It didn't matter to Ricardo if they criticized him. There she was, Pilar, and soon she'd take her leave. Maybe. You could never know for sure. Even storytellers themselves sometimes don't know the real importance of their characters; they just go around whining and making demands, that's all. Only the narrator respects them. They grow, they develop, and that's the most important part of understanding and accepting them, of considering these creatures who consider you in turn. Although irredeemably written, they *lived*, and many people forget that. Better yet: they *live* irredeemably, in spite of being written. Yes: in those terms, the importance of Pili—that arbitrary girlfriend—became apparent.

Francisco Sigüenza was really pleased—almost euphoric—though rather annoyed that he could still make out Elías despite the intricate darkness of that night, making it difficult to identify (or even see) the people around you. Still, he didn't know why he was so happy, or where the emotion could have come from. Ricardo did, though: after asking permission of her mother, Sigüenza was going to propose to Pili. Also, for the first time—after years of waiting—he had stayed at her house quite late. The only thing that Urrutia was sure of about Pili was the young girl's beauty and her age: eighteen years. Inevitably, he felt jealous of Francisco.

Finally he heard the metallic squealing of the train's wheels braking on the rails. The passengers, festive and ominous, began to stretch their limbs and pack their belongings away: thousands of insignificant things had been strewn about the coach, making it look like they'd been camped out there for a week. Ricardo gradually made his way through the human fortification that forms in planes and trains at the end of a long journey. Finally he was able to jump down onto the platform, which was crowned with skylights. He slung his satchel over his shoulder, lightening his load. A sultry warmth pervaded every molecule of the atmosphere. It caught in his nostrils, permeated his skin, and immediately made him break out in a bitter, tropical sweat. Ricardo's underwear, pants, and socks were soon damp. At an information kiosk, he asked for the schedule of the ferry that would take him to La Paz. It would be leaving at ten, ten o'clock that night, said the attendant. Without so much as a thanks, Ricardo took off running through the station, through the crowd—hurdling the occasional homeless person who lay on a broken-down cardboard box, covered with a bedspread despite the oven-like heat—until he reached the street. There, he hailed a taxi, and nonchalantly asked to be taken to the waterfront. The crosstown ride takes no more than fifteen minutes, and by 9:05 he was looking out over the Sea of Cortéz with a ticket for that night's ferry in hand. Dawn would find him on the other side of the gulf.

He spent another half-hour watching cars being loaded onto the ferry before going up to a hot dog vendor and ordering three. Then he drank a bottle of tamarind juice and finally boarded and took a seat inside. An unbearable noise rumbled deep within the bowels of the ship: the motor perhaps. The dog days of August are always bolstered by the sea, he thought; they drain expression from the face, they wash you in humidity, dim the eyes, and swell the body. Anyway, that was how he felt after the trip to Mazatlán—which he didn't remember at all—after this long voyage that was not yet at an end, wherever that end might be. Ultimately, though, one place was as good as another, and—that being so—he knew he wanted to learn more about Las Rémoras.

Sitting there in his seat, submerged in his uncertain future, Ricardo was assaulted by a sense of doubt that had little if anything to do with himself: what would become of the lawyer, Raimundo Rosales? Had he forgotten about him? He really ought to decide what to do with him; to put it off would be risking the verisimilitude of *Las Rémoras*. After mulling it over a while, he came to an answer that truly pained him. He felt sadness for one of his most dearly loved characters. Still, it was logical. There was nothing else for it; no way to save him. After the interrogation, it was only natural. And just when Elías was wondering whether he should turn himself in to the authorities. Elías looked up to Raimundo, and Raimundo looked up to him . . . yes, it wasn't a grudge. Elías would never have wanted Raimundo to get blamed for his crime. But he no longer had a purpose, couldn't become anything. It was too late. The appearance or disappearance of a character in a book is always allegorical. It even happens in reality, especially when nobody desires it. So, almost without their wanting it, love does things for them, gives them form.

26

"Enough!" they heard Elías call out.

He was at Tony's that morning, sitting off to the side at one of the farthest flung tables, under the shade of an umbrella. He had gone to bed late the night before, rambling again along the beach. At first light, with his notebook in hand, he went to the lonchería, took a seat, and without a word to anyone, began to write like a madman.

It was eleven o'clock, and the sun rained down hard, burning the skin of any Libertad pedestrians. Inside and out, Elías could hear the happy din of people ordering beer or coffee; it was still relatively calm, but he noticed it.

That's what weekends were like in Las Rémoras, especially during August—the month of rest for any true *californiano*. People were beginning to arrive from Mulegé, Loreto, Santa Rosalía, or El Dorado. But above all, people were coming from the U.S., hitchhiking and RVing their way down the peninsula. Even the folks from neighboring towns like Loreto or Punta Chivato were accustomed to spending the day in Las Rémoras and returning home at night. You could say that August was both the hottest and busiest month for that little costal town. Many locals knew that Las Rémoras and a nearby beach known as Bahía Concepción were the best places to spend a weekend. A bit on the boring side, certainly, if you aren't sure how to make use of your time (which is to say, how to waste it), but ultimately it's a decent, cheap place to get some sun and splash around in the sea for a couple of days.

The problem being where to stay: there weren't very many rooms available, which is why some people preferred to stay in Mulegé. Others, though, opted for those faded Las Rémoras shacks that were transformed for the season into guest cottages rented by regular visitors, usually old acquaintances or recommendations. August found the people of Las Rémoras either working or celebrating their Saints—neither of which they bothered to do the rest of the year.

Off to one side, Jasso and Josefina sat at a table; they were both drinking Irish coffee and chatting away. The former, as always, was letting the sun beat down on his poor bald head, while the latter just talked and talked. From time to time Tony would join them until his other customers needed attending to. When they heard Elías's exclamation, they all turned to see what was going on. He had looked up from his notebook, bleary-eyed and exhausted, and said:

"This can't be. Why the hell are they taking so long to meet? Mexico City, Guadalajara, Mazatlán, and now—as if that weren't enough—a fucking ferry to La Paz. That's it! God, how many stops do you need? And now, of course, we'll have to find out what happens on the ferry. Enough already! Let's get to the point."

"What are you talking about?" Josefina asked, intrigued, from her seat.

"Nothing," was the librarian's curt response. He turned his eyes back to his notebook.

Josefina pressed, sensing that she was on the verge of hooking him: "I'm sorry to bother you, but if you'd tell me . . ."

"It's nothing. I can't tell you right now," Elías replied. Then, without any preamble, he went back to his work, muttering, "Get to the point! Get to the fucking point!"

Like a Russian ballerina, Tony tiptoed up to him and refilled the writer's coffee cup. But Elías didn't stir, not even when a tiny lizard invaded his tabletop, approaching his cup as if the foolish thing wanted to take a dip in coffee. Tony brushed it aside in the nick of time, and it scurried off, probably to die of panic.

Again, Elías was too resolute even to thank him. He ignored his coffee and didn't even blink (himself like a Mexican salamander with no eyelids)—continuing to write, tiny and undecipherable, in his mysterious notebook. Tony immediately returned to his friends' table, filled their cups to their brims, and said in a low voice:

"What's going on with that muchacho?"

"That's what I'd like to know," said Josefina, exasperated, spying on Elías out of the corner of her eye.

"I suppose he's working on one of those newspaper serials he likes to write," the architect offered. "But your guess is as good as mine, right Tony?"

"That's true," Tony confirmed.

"I'm sure Roberta would know what's up . . . she never said anything to you, Josefina?" Iginio lowered his voice so Elías wouldn't hear him.

"No, she never said a word to me . . ." Josefina whispered. "You gave his poem to Sigüenza, right Jasso?"

"Yes," he said, looking at the ground, apologetic. "I had to do it, Fina, it was my duty." The others nodded in agreement, looked away, and fell silent. Elías muttered something to himself. Tony froze; they were calling him from the kitchen. He hopped across the street and ducked inside. Both Jasso and Josefina could see him saying something to Pilar. They sipped their coffee. Then Fina chimed back in, saying:

"I've been thinking, Jasso, maybe the poem could have saved him. If I'm not mistaken, they're taking the lawyer to La Paz as we speak."

"Yes, to indict him, and then he goes to the jail in Mulegé, I suppose."

"They say he hasn't said a word in his own defense."

"Do you really think that it was him, Fina?" the architect asked, sadly.

"Yes," she answered without hesitation. "Don't you?"

"I did the day they hauled him out of here—beyond any doubt. Also when I took the poem to show Sigüenza," he said. "But not now. I really don't think it could have been him. What sense does it make to kill someone you love so much? Maybe that's why I'm having second thoughts."

He interrupted himself. Perhaps he had been trying to delve into that recondite corner of his heart in which he'd sequestered the whole matter, and couldn't find his way. Then he said, "By the way, Fina, do you know anything about the madam? I mean, the one who owns the brothel? The one they call La Gringa."

"I heard she used to come back here once and a while in the old days. Who knows? Truth be told, I've never met her," Josefina said, exhausted. "What I want to know is what the hell is going to happen to us now that Inés isn't around."

Just then, Tony emerged from the kitchen and rejoined them at their table. He said, "Pili finally agreed."

"What?" asked the architect.

"She agreed to stay and work with me this month," he explained, beaming, as if a great weight had been lifted off his shoulders. "She says she could use the money, since she's getting married to Sigüenza. The son of a bitch proposed yesterday. Incredible!"

"That asshole of a worthless councilman?" exclaimed Jasso, patently upset.

"That's what she says. And you know, they've been together for years. But at least she'll be around to help me out this August. The Gringos are coming, and nobody around here wants to do any work. Rémoranos don't much care about money . . . they can't stand earning the stuff. It makes it impossible to find good help, especially this time of year. They just don't get it. The rest of the year I can take care of myself, you know?"

"Yes," Josefina agreed. "I know you can, but I'm still amazed that you can keep this place afloat on your own. August is the cruelest month of the year."

"As far as the restaurant goes, it's all thanks to God, sweetie."

"But if it's so hard, how come you haven't looked for some permanent help?" countered the architect. He took a sip of coffee; this cup was much more bitter than the first. He spit it back out. "Tony, something's off here!"

"What?" Tony looked as though he might faint.

Any mistake—however slight—with the coffee or food drove Tony crazy. He expected his lonchería to be perfect at all times; when things went wrong, he felt like pulling out his hair. And everyone knew it was no act: Tony only had a few tufts left on top. Just at that moment, Santa—Joaquín's old lady, who'd worked as a maid for Rosales and Roldán the priest—appeared on Libertad, dragging her feet, awash in tears. Everyone turned to look, and a few of those seated at the counter inside the lonchería came out to see what was going on. Even Elías was jolted from his funk: he put down his pen and turned to look. He and everyone else there heard her say, between sobs:

"He died! The lawyer died this morning!"

The architect stood up sharply and—incredulous, staggering (he didn't know whether it was sunstroke or the shock of the news)—made his way over to the woman.

"Are you sure? How do you know?" he asked. When Santa didn't reply, still too choked up to explain, he pressed: "Who told you this, Santa? Who?"

The black woman said, "I saw him with my own eyes, señor. I was bringing him a change of clothes and some food too. Nobody was there, no guards or anything. I thought he was still asleep, but no . . . he was dead!"

Elías felt faint himself. His feet or the ground beneath them seemed to pitch and roll at Santa's devastating news. Yes, Raimundo Rosales had died, and there was nothing unusual about it at all.

27

He'd died because of love. There was no other way to put it, Ricardo thought as he was disembarking from the ferry in Pichilingue, on the giant wharf in La Paz. Died because of love. It was eight in the morning by the time the boat had put into port, and he was still feeling a bit seasick from the rough crossing. He'd felt a surge of nausea during the trip, and now he felt a vague, indescribable sadness for the lawyer Rosales, but it was more than that; after all, Rosales was dead, just like Inés. He also felt sorry for Santa, who had loved him so much, for his friend Jasso the architect, and especially for Elías. He—Ricardo Urrutia—was the only one who knew how close the writer had been to turning himself in. But he didn't. Not in time, anyway. But what does that mean, "in time"? In time for what, if the lawyer was destined for death ever since they found his mistress Inés smothered? Such are the trials of life, Ricardo said to himself sadly as he stepped down off the gangplank with his satchel in his hand. Love is always to blame. And we're all susceptible.

A very heavy woman pushed him, and without so much as an "excuse me" she bustled on her way. But this shove was enough to knock Ricardo out of his cheerless musings about the lawyer's fate, and he hailed a taxi. He didn't know where he was going, so he asked the driver:

"How far is downtown?"

"No more than half an hour."

"Take me there, please."

Ricardo was exhausted and only thought about sleeping: the trip had been a thunderous one. He took one last look at the gigantic ferry, then he saw her standing there next to a kiosk on the pier, motionless, almost in front of him. Roberta took her son by the hand. Ricardo recognized her instantly, and panicked for fear of not being able to stop the taxi in time. But he quickly composed himself, grabbed the driver by the shoulder, and asked him to pull over.

Ricardo opened the door, grabbed his satchel, and jumped to the ground. He took a few steps towards her. Just before he opened his mouth—to say what?—she looked him coldly in the eyes, scrutinizing him with an aggressive green stare that stood out against her smooth, spectacular cheekbones. Her nostrils flared for a moment and caught a vague whiff of the sea as he came closer and silently reaffirmed his recognition. Roberta looked as though she was rifling through her memory, trying to place him. He looked quite familiar, though Roberta finally decided that she had never laid eyes on him before. Maybe that was why his agate eyes seemed to shine as they did, twinkling while his nose searched for something indistinct in the air. It wasn't there. She heard him say:

"Roberta? You're Roberta, right?" She was dumbstruck. He continued: "You don't know me, but I know you. Forgive me. I've just arrived from Mexico City."

After a long silence, she heard herself respond in a dry yet affable voice:

"Yes, I go there quite often."

"I should have known. I apologize."

Although she didn't understand—and he only partially so— their eyes, especially hers, had become gentle. Her little boy broke the silence:

"Mamá, you said we were going to the beach."

"Be patient," she replied. "We have to go buy tickets first. We have the whole day to spend there if you want."

"When do you leave?" Ricardo asked.

"We hope to be on our way tomorrow," she said, smiling. "Right now we have to go see what we can find."

It was the first time Roberta had smiled. She had a wide, ruby-red mouth, and the corners of her lips turned downward whenever she spoke or laughed. Elías had understood intuitively; presuming that she loved him, despite the fact that she'd never let him feel loved—despite the fact that Ricardo, writing about them, had never been sure what she really felt. Roberta felt sorry for Elías. And to stop loving someone with that voice, in perfect time with the rhythm of his mouth and the sounds it emitted, was going to be very hard indeed. Roberta's eyes were languid and green, her forehead was broad and clear, her face was round and feline, as was her prominent yet feminine nose. Her skin was quite pale, which made her emerald-green eyes stand out all the more. Her temples, hands, and shoulders were all especially white, but her teeth were the color of tea. Yes, she was just as Ricardo had imagined her, and seeing here standing in the light of the sun, speaking to her son in a sweet yet measured tone, inspired an ominous, possessive sense of affection in him.

He followed her—sometimes at her side, sometimes behind her—to the ticket office, which was located on the other side of the wharf, near a small restaurant. He waited off to the side while she stood in line. She bought two passes and returned, hand-in-hand with her son, who was tugging excitedly at her dress, urging her along.

"We need to talk," Ricardo said.

"About what?" she replied, eyes on the bay.

"Elías."

She looked disconcerted, but quickly composed herself . . . she had finally reconstructed him in her memory. She knew who he, Ricardo Urrutia, was. Then she said, rather offhandedly:

"Do you know him?"

"No," Ricardo said at first, before quickly correcting himself. "Well, actually I do."

"It doesn't matter either way. You realize he knows who *you* are, right?" And perhaps Ricardo didn't hear this last bit clearly, because Roberta continued walking over towards where a line of taxis was waiting.

"I know you, Roberta," he muttered behind her in last attempt to stop her. "Even if you don't know me. Please, it would mean a lot to me if we could talk. There are things you don't yet know about. Things about Elías. I'm the only one who knows about them, and I'm the only one who can tell you."

She turned around and, with an irritated, almost cruel look in her eyes, responded, "Believe me, I know things too, Ricardo.

Things that you don't. Important things, things that he told me about you."

Ricardo could've expected any number of things, but not this . . . not this answer that contained nothing but emptiness itself. He felt his whole life falling headlong into this emptiness, this uncertainty. And what about his name? How did Roberta know who he was? What else did she know about him? And how could she have found out?

She continued walking, and—just as she opened the taxi door—she turned one last time and said:

"Are you coming with us? We're going to spend some time at the beach."

28

When Santa and a tearful Jasso had both gone down Libertad towards the city council building, Josefina—who alone had stayed at the table with Elías—said:

"I lied to them, you know."

He didn't understand what the prostitute was trying to tell him, and he coldly asked, "To whom? About what?"

"To Tony and the architect, Elías."

"About what? What the hell are you talking about, Fina?" he asked, as he continued to tap his pen pensively on the point of his chin.

"They wanted to know what you're writing about. I told them that I had no idea. But I know exactly what it is." Josefina smiled, halfway between hiding and showing her cards, though she knew perfectly well that she wasn't about to give up her secret.

Elías didn't appreciate the implication; he could feel his rancor building to a crescendo inside him. At first he tried to dismiss it, not at all sure that Josefina knew what she was talking about. But then, after sipping his coffee, he looked at her again and—with a slight frown on his lips—said:

"Who told you? Roberta?"

"Yes," she replied matter-of-factly, and happy too at thus having confirmed what her friend had told her.

Elías couldn't respond: Tony was making his way back to the table, skillfully avoiding the basking lizards at his feet. He'd brought them a shrimp cocktail. The writer lowered his pen from his chin, and—still shaking, whether from the news of Rosales's death or from regret over his carelessness in letting Roberta read about Ricardo's first few adventures—continued to write.

29

"Love is a string of probabilities."

Roberta sat there pensively, apparently mulling over Ricardo's words. Obviously, he was talking about Laila. That was her point of reference; if not the only one, at least the closest. She knew from having read a passage or two from Elías's notebook. Meanwhile, propped up on her elbow in the sand, Roberta watched the sun diving and playing in Coromuel's light, prickly surf. The only thing to worry about was jellyfish, which would sting at the slightest touch. Although they appeared in their greatest numbers during the winter, they were also treacherous in the washed-out indigo waters of the summer sea.

"Look at it this way," Ricardo continued. "A young man calls up a girl and asks her out. He saw her at a party, asked a friend for her number, and called her up. She accepts, delighted, because she thinks it's someone else entirely asking her out. In fact, she doesn't even remember the guy who actually called her. On the day of their date, he goes to pick her up, and when she comes to the door, he discovers that she isn't the one he thought he was meeting either. Whoever gave him the number was either mistaken or playing a practical joke. But in any case, as soon as he sees this girl, he goes quiet, same as her. What I'm trying to say, Roberta, is that they're both mistaken, both smiling, and both lying to each other at the same time. They keep quiet, out of respect or whatever you want to call it. Still, though, neither of them considers that they might be in for a wonderful evening. And that's just what happens. They fall in love, and—in time—they marry. Then, maybe a year later, they go out to a restaurant, and notice another couple sitting at a nearby table. She recognizes the man: it's the one she was expecting to go out with the year before. And her husband recognizes the girl too: she's the one he thought he was calling up for a date. They end up engaging in a bit of good-natured small talk. They laugh, if a bit nervously. But tell me, do you think that their relationship is over and done with? Of course not! Quite the opposite. Do you really think that—whether they're in love or not—they would confess all of a sudden to their mistaken expectations and offer to switch couples? What I'm trying to say is that love is a string of probabilities, either for or against. A can be with B, but also with C. It's all about the circumstances. It's about chance. True, attraction has a lot to do with it, but it's not the be-all and end-all. And why is that?" Ricardo paused for a second in case Roberta was drifting off, but she was still listening, even if with half-closed eyes. "Because you can be attracted to more than one person. Many people, in fact. Not everyone, of course, and not everyone will be attracted to you, but nevertheless it's a great big sea out there, and there are quite a lot of fish in it, Roberta. I realized that when I left Laila. There's no such thing as a soulmate, as a "better half." It's a fallacy: the grumblings of someone deeply wounded by love, or—on the other hand—someone on the verge of getting married. Love is not exclusive; in other words, loving someone doesn't rule out the possibility of loving someone else, however much the one in love might want to believe it. Love disintegrates, vacillates, and is—unfortunately—the most relative thing on earth. Perhaps A and B will never be in love with me, or I with them, but this in no way means that C is the only one put on this earth to love me. It may well be true that I'm not much taken with A or B, given that they don't love me, or perhaps I'm simply not attracted to them anyway. But that doesn't matter, because we've got D, E, F, G, H, and many others to consider. It's just that they haven't happened to cross my path yet. If that's the case, who's to say that I can't fall in love with one of them? For example, say I'm walking back from C's house after breaking up with her. On the way home, I bump into D, and—without planning to—we hit it off. Of course, it's also equally probable that I would have bumped into E or F. Who knows? Maybe none of this would have happened without C's help; maybe I owe her a debt of gratitude. And here's another example: say I'm on my way to meet F for the first time, but—two blocks before I get to her house—you and I have a little fender-bender and end up shouting insults at each other. Half an hour later, I'm knocking on her door, still unaware of the coincidence I'm about to run into. Maybe we're embarrassed or we apologize to each other or whatever . . . but the point is that any potential love there could have been shattered by the earlier events. Understand? So it's possible that F and I fall in love, but it's also possible that we don't. It's all the same, Roberta: one long string of probabilities, either for or against . . . that's all. And I can understand if you find what I'm telling you unpleasant or if it makes you skeptical of love as something worthy of our attention as rational creatures. But whether you believe it or not, this much is true: love is pure animalistic coexistence: fortuitous, ephemeral, and circumstantial. I learned that after leaving Laila."

After that, both were silent for a long while. When he heard her question, it sounded like the kind of excuse or apology that Ricardo would have made to himself:

"So what happened with her?"

Contrary to what he'd intended—which was to respond by asking her about Elías—he found himself examining the origins of his love, its inexplicable reasons for being, and its eventual disintegration.

Meanwhile, the boy kept eagerly on with his task of catching and diving through the small green waves. Two other children had joined in the game, and the sun was beginning to bring some color into their faces. At last Roberta said, a bit pensive and dubious:

"Could be . . . could be. I agree that love can act—as you say—through merely fortuitous avenues. But there's something else that's more important."

"What's that?" He sat up in the sand and turned to look at her directly.

"The quality of love. Yes, the quality of the love that's given, and the quality of love that's received." She stopped to think for a moment, choosing just the right words, and then continued, "With the passage of time—and with the passage of bodies, Ricardo—you come to realize something. You discover a quality that some people can provide, and that others cannot. I really don't know what it consists of, or how exactly it happens. But look at it this way: ten years pass, and then you happen to bump into Laila . . . maybe then you'd see how what you feel for her is—despite everything else—more intimate than what you could feel for someone, say, that you've only just met. This new encounter—you'll see—verifies something in you: a sort of affection or esteem for earlier days, now lost. And that's when you realize something else: that anybody who knows her or meets her will seem insignificant when compared with the feelings she harbors for you. You have nothing to fear from anybody you have the advantage. You both share a very intimate and personal bond, something that nobody else has. Maybe it's something that I'll share with Elías one day. Who knows."

"So then why did you leave him?"

Roberta looked out into the offing, well beyond where her son was splashing around with the other boys. Her only answer was:

"There are some things that simply must be."

"I don't understand, Roberta," he said. " 'Things that must be?' Why?"

"There aren't any reasons . . . that's why I say things simply must be that way. You can't ask questions or read into it. You just know and accept your fate; you don't question your will, your spirit, or your soul. You just do what's necessary."

"Even if it makes things worse?"

"It's not a question of better or worse. In this case, the result doesn't matter. The question goes beyond that. I might be worse off for leaving him, but I had to do it. Either way, the decision is the same."

"It must be tough," Ricardo said, almost to himself, without looking at Roberta, "to be that way with yourself. To not pay any heed at all to cause and effect or even free will. You're torturing yourself because you've convinced yourself that you need that sort of thing—'must be'—whether you do or not."

"You're beginning to understand," Roberta said, turning to smile at him.

The sun was full in their faces. Only a scant few other people had found their way to Coromuel beach before continuing on to downtown La Paz. The taxi had brought them there after their initial encounter in Pichilingue. During the ride, Roberta hadn't said a thing; she was more interested in enjoying the rush of wind blowing through the open window and her hair. Ricardo stole occasional glances at her: she looked recovered, less sad, less sullen than he expected. The only thing she said before they reached Coromuel was: *If you want, you can stay with us.* Ricardo accepted the invitation silently. At the beach, Roberta shared a corner of her towel with him while her son made off for the water, which—from the looks of it—he was quite familiar with. Before Ricardo could begin to question her, she'd looked at him and asked, out of the blue:

"Why did you leave Laila? I didn't know that part. If you cared for her so much—if you were so desperately in love—then why did you break it off all of a sudden? I never would have imagined you could leave her, or that I'd find you here in La Paz. At the very least, I expected to find her here with you. I believe your love was sincere. I can tell when someone is in love, and you, Ricardo, most definitely are." She paused to take a breath, and then asked with renewed vigor: "Did you sleep with her?"

"We slept together once, at my house." Ricardo stopped to think for a moment before continuing: "It was my first time."

"Hers too?"

"Yes."

"So what happened? I don't understand you, Ricardo. Did you just up and vanish without a word? Why, if you loved . . . ?" Roberta trailed off, but it was just as well, because it was at that point that Ricardo began his *Love is a string of probabilities* litany. He'd wanted to explain—though he wasn't sure how—why he stopped feeling what he had always said he'd felt for Laila.

The hours passed, warm and restless. Some gannets flew along the line of the breakers, while just past them a pair of pelicans dove for fish in the gray, shimmering water. A few groups of beachgoers set up in a thatched-roof hut or picnicked under the palms; they walked along the water, they swam, they sunbathed. Sitting there among them, Ricardo and Roberta seemed to be old acquaintances. The boy came back to interrupt them for a moment, and flicked a few drops of water at Ricardo. The writer flung some sand in return, and the two new friends took off running towards the water. Roberta also took advantage of the opportunity to take a quick dip. The sun was riding at its peak, and the sky held only a few thin clouds that offered little protection against the radiant summer heat. It was as if some celestial spotlight had been lit unnecessarily and focused on the noontime beach. Roberta emerged from the water and within a few minutes was already dry from the sweltering morning air. Salt was crystallizing on her body, and her brown hair, now wet, had taken on a darker chestnut color. She looked fixedly at Ricardo, and said:

"You know, you look like Elías . . ." She paused to chuckle before continuing: "Only several years younger."

"Or maybe that's just how you remember him now."

"Of course I remember," she replied, taking a seat next to him. She seemed caught a bit off guard. "But that's not it. I really do think you look like him. Quite a bit, actually. It's disconcerting . . ."

"All right then, what do you want to do now?" he asked, a bit uneasy.

"Work, the same as always. Is there ever anything else to do on God's green earth?" She shrugged, and then answered her own question: "I think that there is, actually. Yes, you're right, there are other things to do."

"Like what?"

"Don't go falling in love with me if you really want to find out." Then, without waiting for a response, she went on: "And you? What are your plans?"

"I don't know. Continue with my travels."

"To where?"

"I suppose it's Las Rémoras. Anyway, I'm going to have to scrape together some money first. I'm about to run out."

"You should look for a job," Roberta suggested. Then she thought for a second, adding: "I have a friend who might be able to help you out. Not here though . . . in Las Rémoras."

"Who's that?"

"His name is Tony. He owns a small restaurant . . . well, it's more of a bar-slash-lonchería. It's usually very busy in August; people come from all over. I'm sure he'd be happy to have an extra set of hands. He's all by himself there. I'll give you a message to give to him, and we'll see if he can't find you some work. I think he'll be able to pay you pretty well. How old are you?"

"Seventeen. Almost eighteen, really," Ricardo replied. He already knew a few things about Tony, but had no idea that Roberta was friends with him. It was a nice surprise.

"You should know that he's a fag," Roberta added. "But he's very respectful."

"I imagine he must basically have your character," Ricardo ventured, even though he was sure he was right.

"He does, but that's not important. I'm sure you'll get along well with him, he'll pay you well, and after that you'll be able to get wherever it is that you've got to go."

"But I don't know where that is, Roberta. It all depends on how things develop. But in any case, thank you."

With just a touch of contrition and curiosity, she asked:

"You haven't thought about going back to your mother?"

"I'm not sure. Not yet, anyway." It was all the response he could muster.

Just then, Roberta's son returned carrying a stick with which he'd impaled a pale, turquoise jellyfish. The poor thing looked like a melting Popsicle. The other two boys ran up next to him and watched as he dribbled its runny flesh over the sand. With patent satisfaction, he marveled at the power the sun held over this shapeless blob that was losing any trace of its natural form, bit by bit. Ricardo and Roberta watched as well.

"Don't tell me why you left Laila if she was your first love," Roberta said suddenly, brushing the dried salt off of her shoulders.

"I think it was necessary. Something was broken, and I'm still not sure what it is . . ."

"Exactly," Roberta replied. "Something was also broken inside of me when I loved Elías the most. You can ask me all you want, but I didn't know what it was. I just couldn't put my finger on it. Maybe it was the need to do it, to get the break-up out of the way, even if it hurt him . . . the same way you hurt Laila, Ricardo."

"I don't think she was hurt. Not her. She's a strong one."

"You're wrong. You stopped loving her the day she fell in love with you. I'll swear to that. The break inside of you, Ricardo, happened on that very day the two of you spent together. The only one. You should ask yourself what it was: maybe your affection and your sexuality are separate. I know mine are. I can also swear that I'm not sure what happens to me in that sense. Maybe you do; maybe you'll be able to figure it out. You'll have to let me know."

"You might be right," Ricardo said to himself. "It *was* that day, and I didn't even realize it . . ."

"And you should know that it mattered to her. It most certainly did," continued Roberta. "The way a relationship ends is always important to a woman. If a woman leaves a man, he doesn't suffer nearly as much as a woman does in that situation. Infidelity might hurt him, but not being abandoned. So I don't think that Elías will suffer too much."

"Let me assure you, Roberta, that you are mistaken. Elías is going to be very hurt by the fact that you've left him. He already is. And there are some men who put up with infidelity. They'll put up with it if they're convinced that they love the woman, or at least if they know that someone else does. He would have endured infidelity from you, but not your abandonment. Not a retraction of love."

"But if I haven't stopped loving him, then all I know is that something is broken inside of me, and I have no idea what the hell it could be . . ."

"Abandonment could be the worst of all infidelties, Roberta. Believe me. And whether you want to admit it or not, you abandoned him."

They had sucked dry the meanings of the words that define— if they define anything at all—feelings. What's more, those feelings never really existed; they were invented by people who spoke those words, who believed they could feel, and who—nervously, and blinded by their naming the world—talked and talked and pretended to understand one another.

Ricardo got up and headed back towards the sea without so much as a word. He'd had enough of the water, he was done with the foamy sawmill of the breakers, he was fed up with its destructive force. On lean legs, he walked slowly over to where the boys were. He horsed around with them for a while while Roberta remained behind, propped up on her elbows in the sand, watching him wade out into neck-deep water and ride out the heavy green, blue, and white waves. That's how the day was passed. Later in the afternoon, they ate some rice and fish grilled in aluminum foil, which vendors (the closest things to restaurants in Coromuel) were hawking on the beach. At long last, they found themselves satisfied, exhausted, and truly removed from their pasts and any semblance of feeling, and they hailed a taxi.

The salt and the calming *chicha* beer that the heat propitiated, the indivisible sand, and maybe the effect of time itself, marching slowly and gradually and imperceptibly and without direction— winding its way no more—were the reasons that they, Roberta and Ricardo, became diluted, at last mingling with everything else, with the simple outside world, with things that can actually be seen moving, gesticulating, searching for something that had nothing to do with conscience. Enough with them. Enough with words that try only to name. Enough with contemplating—morbidly, slow as molasses—the act of living. How pleasing, how comforting it was! To exist for no more than a day, an hour, a minute at most!

On reaching the hotel, Ricardo said goodnight to Roberta and her son, who were both ready for sleep. He left via Los Arcos, passed a wooded jetty, and sat down on a small patch of sand to finish reading the story of Federico and all the surprises and developments that he had come to rely on from it. Under the cool shade of a palm—for the fourth and final time and in one fell swoop—he read the last chapter of *Bodily Prayers*:

(FINAL DAY)

I write in the future. I begin it now: February 23, 2008. I close my eyes and verify that it is absolutely true. That I am there, writing, at this very moment. Then—that February 23, 2008—I close my eyes and I'm back here, writing, and it is absolutely true again, absolutely real. Both things are true; it is enough that I wish them to be so. *Now I am going to write in the future* and it is not that it is *beyond*, because *beyond* is the here and now, where I write: February of 2008. I cannot glimpse the future, nor divine it. I can say nothing more than that I remember. I long for it because I have lived it already, because I am living it.

For the past six or seven years, I have been renting a modest apartment on Rue Monge. It consists of an eat-in kitchen, an empty pantry that I built myself, a bathroom with shower, and a tiny bedroom that becomes the living room when the few friends I have pay visits. Why I left Mexico City is a long story indeed. Let me say simply that I was offered a position as a lecturer at the Sorbonne, and for some months now I have been dedicating myself to the unhealthy task of drawing up a long essay that I'm sure no one will ever read. The stipend is barely enough for me to live on; certainly I wouldn't be able to support anyone. I claimed my autonomy a year after arriving in Paris. By that time I'd had quite enough of sharing apartments with visiting foreign professors and local students. Only with time and a bit of savings was I able to get this place. The street is not bad, and it affords easy access to the Cardenal Lemoine metro, which will take me swiftly to Pompidou or the University. And since they repaired the sewers some years ago, you can even endure the platforms and enormous tunnels without the aid of a surgical mask.

It's already late. I have just finished a light lunch with my two friends Volpi and Nedim Gürsel. The former is an Italian hoping to have his novels translated into French; the latter, a somewhat older Turk, is also a novelist and a professor of Comparative Literature at the Sorbonne, with a book published on Hikmet and Aragon. As soon as I arrive back at my apartment, I sit down at the computer to write, just as I did before: in moments of inspiration. Right from the start, I feel something like an enormous flash of lightning or a stroke: it's as if I've lived all this before. I close my eyes, and immediately I want to find that slim volume that I published back when I was young; twenty-one years old I believe. I set about searching through my books, stacked together in boxes and bookcases, until finally it turns up: *Bodily Prayers*. I flip desperately through the pages until I come to the fourth chapter, "Final Day," and I begin to read: "I write in the future. I begin it now: February 23, 2008. I close my eyes and verify that it is absolutely true. That I am there, writing, at this very moment. Then—that February 23, 2008—I close my eyes and I'm back here, writing, and it is absolutely true again, absolutely real. Both things are true; it is enough that I wish them to be so. *Now I am going to write in the future* and it is not that it is *beyond*, because *beyond* is the here and now, where I write: February of 2008. I cannot glimpse the future, nor divine it. I can say nothing more than that I remember. I long for it because I have lived it already, because I am living it."

So it was true.

I immediately toss the book aside and rush back to my computer to see what I wrote when I first came in, inspired, and it's identical word for word. I repeat: I wrote what I had already written. Or did I only write it once? In a sort of eternal present? Or outside of that present? I compare the two passages again, and they are the same. How could I have written that passage before, if I have only just finished it now, in reality?

I finished *Prayers* over the last few days of February, 1975, when I was twenty-one years old, and yet somehow *I am writing it now*. It's also true that I detested my book before finishing it, and I thought even less of it when I saw it published by the old company Siglo XXI. Sometimes (I must admit) it seems rather like a bad poem, or an attempt at one. I even saved the review by a critic, Armando Pereira, who cared enough about it to write, "*Bodily Prayers* is written in a frankly adolescent voice: hurried, careless, jumping from one vicissitude to another, and whose characters—all of them adolescents themselves—struggle between a pretentiously philosophical speech and a confused sexuality, one more imaginary than real" (*Unomásuno*, Saturday, November 28, 1975). I scroll the document down to the bottom. I truly thought that I was sick—delirious even—when I stopped and glanced at a copy of *Le Monde* that was lying on the floor. The headline reads, *AUJOURD'HUI, 23 DU FÉVRIER, 2008*. I sit down again and hastily leaf through my book, that tale of love (or, I should say, those many tales of love), which went unread and lived quite an anonymous life. How could I have written there what I write here? How could I know the future, remember it? I didn't want to predict it, I simply wanted it to come to pass.

I set myself about the act of remembering, and now I see it written just so: February 23, 2008. Yes, I will leaf slowly through the pages; I will dedicate myself to reading that Final Day of the story. My story. Or perhaps I will take a break and set *Bodily Prayers* aside. Yes: I return to the computer and set about the act of writing. I will work through this icy night until I come to a proper conclusion. Then I'll be able to get some sleep.

Volpi and Nedim have supported me since I set my plan in motion, and from time to time they're able to help solve pieces of the puzzle. The investigation has been going on for three months now: first I did a preliminary rereading of certain books, I made notes, I wrote down dates, and still I wasn't sure how to start. Starting is usually, at least for me, the hardest part. I've been searching for the proper theme, of course—it's occupied me for years now—but I also have my departmental obligations, which are just as vast and obscure as the forms taken by the minor prophet Hosea in nineteenth- and twentieth-century novels. There was nothing to focus my investigation, which made things all the more difficult and tiring. To start with, I scattered across my desk books as variegated and yet similar as *The Idiot, Crime and Punishment, Santa, Nana, The Green House, The Obstacles, The Honorary Consul, The Place Without Limits, The Razor's Edge, Of Human Bondage, A Sentimental Education,* the "Circe" chapter of *Ulysses,* the third chapter of *Portrait, Swann's Way,* et cetera, et cetera. But the list keeps on growing exponentially with each new suggestion that Gürsel and Volpi make and with each new discovery, which is why I feel that the task could quickly get out of hand if I don't stay on top of things. Most recently I added one of Nedim's own novels, *The First Woman,* to the list, and—as I just told myself today, as a matter of fact—other works by Moravia, Jan Valtin, Sue, Lajos Zilahy, Amado, and Onetti. Would these writers have read Hosea before embarking on their own books? What kind of an influence would it have had on them?

Would it even be possible to detect? Is there a chance that it would manifest itself—overtly or otherwise—in the work of a Samaritan prophet, a Nazarene, or—for example—an Orthodox Russian? How is it possible to understand a man—a madman, really—who in the throes of political agitation leaves his family and starts shouting in the streets (just as the prophet Jeremiah did), to whom God offered a prostitute one night, and who then decided to write a book that the Church, centuries later, would declare a sacred text? There are so many questions to answer, so many puzzles to break down, that it sometimes seems impossible, especially without a solid foundation on which to support the project. It's true, very little is written about Hosea. I might need another pair of hands to help me with my work, but thus far the Department has declined to offer me a research assistant. I still don't know if the project will hold up to its finish, or if it'll end up with the fatal flaw of being deadly boring. In any case, I'm supposed to finish in just over two years. During these February days, any attempt to leave the house and track down a new book feels like being wounded: the biting wind lances through me and knocks violently at my windows and door. My electric heater is over ten years old, and is barely able to keep even the bedroom warm. The area around Rue Monge is nice enough, even with the occasional dilapidated block of flats—like mine—that somehow escaped any and all renovations through the years.

It's late; I have just finished dinner with Volpi and Nedim. They have, I suspect, become somewhat complacent with regard to my work, not identifying as many connections as I think they should. These types of critics and friends are, unfortunately, often rather indulgent. I should look for someone else, since I sometimes find that I'm losing perspective and forgetting the true purpose of the project (today, for example, I don't know what it is). I'm risking too much. We had a decent enough supper at a Chinese restaurant where the owner, Fushia, waited on us attentively. We usually meet there during the week, though the increasingly cold weather is making that more and more difficult. Afterwards, we said goodnight with the promise of getting together again very soon. I take the metro, and sprawl out in a corner seat. There's only one other person on the train, an elderly woman. Eventually, I get off at Cardenal Lemoine and—without so much as a word—I head towards my apartment. A few cars pass. It's woefully cold. I open the building's outer door, thinking only of diving under the covers of my bed and going to sleep. Rather than wait for the elevator, I take the stairs two at a time to my landing. I unlock my door; I step inside and kick it shut behind me with a resounding slam. I look at the lamp sitting on my writing desk, next to the computer and surrounded by books, and without knowing how or why, I find myself involuntarily bellying up to the desk and writing these words that still have no clear meaning and which I barely even recognize. Perhaps instinct has once again yanked me out of my somnolence, struck me like an enormous flash of lightning or a stroke of consciousness. Nevertheless, eventually my eyes close, and it vanishes into thin air.

Everything is dark, and the cold is cavernous and eerie . . . or, at least, this is how one might imagine cold would feel in the afterlife. I walk down that gloomy hallway, devoid of any flicker of light. *It is only me*, Federico, but at the same time I can picture myself at a distance, walking there. I'm afraid, and I wrap myself tightly in my arms. Perhaps that will help to quell my fear. But it does not. *I feel myself*, it is you, Federico, though you seem remote, though you seem to be another. I can't, however, move in any other direction than that *where my steps are taking you*, Federico, like a magnet: drawing, guiding, driving down that infernal, black corridor. Suddenly you find yourself outside; the hallway has given way to a broad, isolated street, just as dark, and devoid of a single soul or breath of life. You—which is to say, I—continue on, and you don't know why you haven't stopped, why you haven't come to a halt. And if you did, where would you turn to? Would you turn back? But where? If you don't know where you've come from, Federico—if you're suddenly walking here, alone, through a hall that dumps you out onto a dirty, icy, cobblestone street? You continue; you hear nothing except your own footsteps; the echoes resound clearly in your ears, and the street is damp and black and murky. You can't see past your outstretched hand, which feels only an emptiness, a sort of horrifying abyss into which you would plunge if you were to stumble. You shouldn't torment yourself, Federicio. You know that. There will be a light, some crack in the dark, some sound calling you, guiding you, directing you to where you need to go. You press on, groping your way, solitary, *it is me, Federico, but it is you*, the same one who feels a gust of wind biting into you, painful, unavoidable. It's deplorable. Soon, in the distance, you find a spot of light, something which illuminates the end of the as yet undefined street. It could be a floodlight. Your pace quickens, your breathing is labored, and you blink furiously against the wind in your face. You struggle to continue. At long last, you're able to make out a few faint sounds in the distance; they seem to be coming from that light—you know they are—from the same location as that glowing bell-shaped glass. You approach without hesitation. As you do, the light expands and the sounds become clearer and more discernable: you find that there is a sense of continuity to them, something harmonious, even—with affinities between sound and sound—and eventually you see that it's music, Federico, that you now hear, which you finally recognize. You feel a bit more at ease; you catch your breath and contemplate the milky vapor rising off the street, and then take off running through the inclemency. You no longer care, your arms have released their grip on your body and your fear has begun to wane, to fade, and with every step you feel more and more relieved of that monstrous, earlier weight. Finally you're there, you've reached the light, and find yourself standing on someone's front step. You open the door. You are awash in the music of a band and a loose crowd of weary people. An enormous cake sits on a table in the middle of the room; it must be a birthday party, you tell yourself. There are young hipsters, older folks, lovely women, men in suits, some of them drunk, others smoking, and everyone decked out in their best clothes. They've noticed you, they watch you, and you can tell that you don't fit in, that they suspect you weren't invited. Nevertheless, you pay them no heed, feigning ignorance . . . Instead, Federico, you go right on in, among the bumping people, dancing, drinking, chatting. Like a magnet, *I impel you*, Federico, *I push you* through the mass of unknown bodies, and you weather the mild jostling. You remember perfectly where you must go, where your steps are leading you. You've known it all your life, and you remember it *now*: you perceive a compact mass, and you move towards it. A path through the crowd slowly opens up to you, and there—in the back, by a group standing at the bar—you see her. Solitary, ornate, and right next to the bartender . . . you know him, remember him well. You make your way over. Since you were walking down the hallway, or perhaps even before, your body has been moving towards her, drawn by instinct, impelled by the soul, as though from a fatal premonition. As you near her, you contemplate her violet dress decorated with sequins and fringe; you note the way it falls over her fragile, erect body, ending just above the ankles. As you get near, she turns her body so that you're not able to make out her face, her features, or even the glint in her eye. Only her dark, sloe-colored hair, shining in the light of the party, Federico. Nevertheless, you're quite taken with the sight, and for her appearance, her pure characteristics, to be fully revealed seems almost unimaginable. You muster all your will, and yet can't make contact. Which proves it: what you have here, close at hand, is a woman more beautiful than any you've ever seen. But haven't you seen her before? How could you know it, how could it be proved? It's something that you just know, *right Federico*? And not something you can explain. You embrace with nary a word, your arm about her waist, and you begin to dance out on the floor, surrounded by umpteen couples. You hold her tightly, and she does the same to you. Your hands are at the small of her back; hers about your shoulders. You feel, at long last, a sense of safety, and the fear you felt earlier seems to have faded, melted away. You've almost forgotten it, or at least you think you have. You are each resting your head on the other's shoulder, which makes it rather difficult to see the room freely. *I close my eyes*, Federico, *and now I know*, because you remember it deep in your soul, Federico, *that I love her*, that you have only ever loved her, and that now you have her in your arms. You don't want to let her go, and you understand that she's been waiting a long time for you to arrive. You don't have the slightest idea of who she could be; nevertheless, you want to know her face, to picture it, to have something concrete in order to love her as you've never loved anybody before, and—as you know—as you will never love anybody ever again. You see the future, and it pervades you with a wave of unutterable nostalgia, a pain you cannot comprehend. You are stricken at not having loved before, or at least at not remembering it as such. Suddenly the music stops and the other couples vacate the dance floor. You don't want to let her go, but nevertheless, you must. It is then, Federico, that you finally realize the reason for everything: it is a dream. You discover that *you have been living within my dream*, and it is there that you remember it, it is there that everything is revealed to you like a wonderful giftwrapped package or a cargo crate impossible to load. You can't bear (it's too painful) the deceit that you've been subjected to, but then again, who's responsible? *Perhaps I?* You fill with anxiousness and regret, your breath runs short, you desperately ask for her to give you her name. Yes, her name . . . you beg her. You'll come for her later, you say, after you wake. She doesn't seem to understand, and smiles skeptically. You examine her fixedly; you do not want to forget her lines, her evenly lined teeth, her manner, the mysterious scent of her body, her dark and profound eyes . . . you'd like to hold onto them forever, no? You contemplate her hair: it sparkles under the light from a disco ball, framing her face. You still have no idea who this woman could be, and only for an instant do you think you recognize her, do you hazard a guess, a hesitant stutter, you've looked upon her always, though you still don't remember where, don't remember who she is. She moves her lips; she wants to say something to you. But you can't hear; you move in close to her, you want to embrace her, you can't lose her like this, so easily and for all eternity. Bit by bit, you feel that same, cavernous, wraithlike cold creeping over you as before. This time you lean your ear in close, brushing up against her lips, and yet you still can't hear: you can't make out what she's trying to tell you. Once again she pronounces something, and you watch as she moves away, disappears, or rather it's you, Federico, it's you who is going, despite your embrace, despite your best efforts to hold her tight against you. You contemplate her from a greater and greater distance, as though through the fog. She, your true love, your life, is dispelled. Disappears. Or you do. You beg for her name, you call out to her, shouting that you'll come for her, that you'll find her wherever she may be, wherever she asks you to go, wherever she waits for you, if only she'll give you her name . . .

I open my eyes and slowly realize . . . I try to keep them closed, I concentrate all my will on the dream which has already gone, I try to recapture it, I make a concerted if wasted effort. I can't even glimpse the place I'd found myself in. My mind resists the urge to wake up, though my body stretches, seeking that very thing. I feel an oppressiveness in my chest, the full weight of the world's gravity, like insistent heartburn. My breathing is labored. I peel back the covers, and immediately the cold invades every corner of my body. My eyes feel liquefied, and a strange sense of warmth floods from my cheeks down into my lips and salts them. I don't remember a thing, and for a long while I remain there, motionless, breathing deeply and trying to quell the suffering of that nightmare, which was like an ancient pain, both unknown and irreparable. I'm covered in a light sweat. I get up from the seat where I'd fallen asleep and stumble around the room like a madman in search of help until finally I find the edge of the bed. From there, through the frosted-over glass, I contemplate a harsh grayness that looks more like a filthy shroud than a sky. My watch reads 4:35 in the morning. I get up again and walk over to my writing desk. I do it automatically. I pull back the chair and sit down. The tears stop; my lips no longer taste of salt. Paris is still asleep, resting, oblivious to the suffering of all of us who have left their own countries to come and live with her. I switch on the small desk lamp, adjust it, look for a pen and paper. I begin to write; I don't quite know if I have a good reason for doing so, or if it's just instinct again that drives me to it. I scratch away with the pen, quick and agile, forming letters so small that I can barely make them out. Yes, I make a more or less detailed description of that otherworldly dream. I finish. I look at my watch again: 5:05. At last, I put down my pen, fold up the paper, and file it away.

That night they took me off for the second time. Once before I'd seen myself as being stripped of an ancient sensation: having a body. Then, without knowing it, I wanted to recover it. I knew it just as I was stripped of it, and *now* I keep that body alive in memory alone. I have kept it there for many years now. And that is why I write.

It was some days after that excursion to La Partida—I don't remember for certain—maybe the night before our last summer night in La Paz. Could be. In any case, that night was identical to the one before it, as is any night during our lives. The nights are the same; it is we who are different.

We're packed into the blue Ford just as we always were: me in the back, with Octavio and Solón on either side, Cecilio behind the wheel, while Hugo—laughing, and not yet dead—rides shotgun. It's terribly hot, and the air is thick with haze. The car jumps and jolts its way down the road; suddenly a set of headlights in front of us momentarily break the monotony of the night before disappearing. Like them, I no longer have substance, now that we've celebrated—or rather, the others have celebrated for me—unanimously jubilant. We're all happy that hot and humid summer night: we are equals, brothers—men, perhaps; I don't know—but we're the same, our bodies together, defeated, exempting us from our splintered innocence. Cecilio concentrates on the road, focusing on the faded white dividing-line while I focus on his hands wrapped firmly around the wheel; I hear laughter, the vulgar nicknames we throw at each other, the consensual lies . . . everyone's talking at once, and I laugh right along with them. The car bucks. We drive over a grating; we've arrived. Off to the side of the road we see the rows of shacks, their multicolored lights crisscrossing the landscape and the music of a band stretching out across the horizon and its thick darkness. Cecilio stops the car; Hugo and his paunch get out first, followed by Solón and then me. Not many cars are parked there—it must be a Monday or a Tuesday—and the vociferous chatter of men is notably missing. With considerably more confidence than on our first visit, we enter *El Ranchito*. Inside, band music blares, people quaff beers and play cards, and a few couples grope each other out on the dance floor. We notice several women, each off in her own little corner of the room, looking at once exquisitely bored and invitingly open, waiting for *her* man. Their legs are sheathed in black fishnets and garter belts; they smile at you one second and turn their back on you the next, they act aloof, checking out other men, and taking contemptuous drags of their cigarettes. Hugo, being both lewd and shrewd, doesn't give us any indication of his plans; we simply see him go up to one of the women. He says something; she nods at first but then quickly shakes her head no. They talk, they kick terms back and forth, negotiating. Finally, we see them make their way out the back door of *El Ranchito* . . . he turns to smile back at us as the woman leads him by the hand. He's happy, this dead man is happy for the time being, and is oblivious to the fact that he'll soon find himself in the grave. We turn to look at each other. I see Octavio, incredulous, his brow furrowed, shrugging his shoulders as if he doesn't know what to think. Cecilio sidles over to me and asks, slyly:

"What about you? Are you going to play another round or what, Fede?"

"Not here," I answer with false seriousness, blasé in the way that only fourteen-year olds can be.

And with that, I turn away from him and begin to make my way back to the front door. I can imagine the looks of skepticism on their faces, with Cecilio making some snide comment while Octavio praises the stunt. I walk outside, and cross the mostly empty parking lot. I touch my shirt, and find that it has become stuck to my body and smells of tar. Up above me are the big, neon letters proclaiming: *El Ferry*. I know the place well; it hasn't been too long—only a few days, in fact—since I've been there. I remember the empty dance floor and I hear the same piano music cooing softly in the distance, enhancing the sense of peace in that little house of love. There are only a few whores, sophisticated and bored, chatting amongst themselves. Nobody pays attention to one teenager who folds his arms across his chest and draws himself up straight in an attempt to look older than he is. I ask for a beer; the bartender serves one up immediately. I toss out a bill, wait for the change, and nonchalantly stow it in my pocket.

I wipe the mouth of the bottle off on my sleeve, and immediately make a mistake: I tip bottoms up, and somehow force down half the bottle in a single gulp. Terrible nausea churns in my stomach, and I hold onto the bar for support while I wait for the burning bitterness to leave the back of my throat. A moment later I turn to the left, and *there she is, it's her again,* watching me with her dark, shadowy, long-lashed eyes, and laughing. She takes the bottle from my hand, and, wordlessly, I begin to drink of her instead. We both know why we're there and who we are waiting for. She smiles, and this time I feel full of confidence. With her at my side, this place is like home. On seeing her again in that violet dress decorated with sequins and fringe, straps crisscrossing her bare shoulders, the heels of her shoes elongating her slight, graceful, and svelte figure, her supremely straight, white teeth, her skin the color of fresh-baked bread, her eyes gleaming *even here*—cutting through the thick cords of time—the bottle suspended in the air, I feel protected by this woman who I'm on the verge of loving, as if our two souls have known and understood one another since time immemorial.

I pull the bottle back from her hand and take a sip. The bartender still pays me no mind; he goes about his work, or simply goes through the motions. She takes me by the left hand, and I let myself be led off, knowing what lies in store for me. My body burns. We walk down that narrow concrete corridor that leads to the row of rooms. We don't speak; not a single word. We stop once again at the cubicle. The fat man isn't there this time; rather, it's an older woman with too much make-up and a giant mole on one cheek. She takes the bill from my hand without even looking at me, but I can't take my eyes off of the horrible hairs sprouting from her blemish. I gather my change and once again follow the prostitute down the hall. Our pace has quickened. Before I know it, she's opened a door; perhaps it's the same one in which the Order—like a tiger ready to pounce—is waiting for us. She waves me in first, and then enters herself, this time without hesitation. No sooner has she closed the door behind her than do I feel the soft touch of her hand on my shoulder. She brings her mouth to my neck. In the middle of the room she begins to undress me, and the ceiling light falls over our bodies, making them unmistakable. We are completely naked; we've tossed our clothes on the ground and know each other once again.

I watch her recline on the bed, languid and lovely and waiting for me. She smiles, lips revealing the whiteness of her teeth, as well as her moist, scarlet tongue. She makes a face, and her cheeks bunch up underneath her eyes. I move towards her, place one knee up on the edge of the bed, and then—very slowly—I mount her. I feel her entire body trembling slightly beneath me as I enter. Situated thus, our bodies infected with their nearness, like reflections in a mirror, we burn slowly, carving at each other's skin like flint. The heat brings beads of sweat to the parts of our bodies still dry, dampening the skin, lubricating it. She moves, and I follow her lead, marking the rhythm of her back, her hips, and the muscles of her thighs. She grabs me by the ass, and my arms clutch at her shoulders. I squeeze her, she digs in with her nails, hard, and the slight pain that I feel spurs a distinct pleasure in me, a distinct impetus. Suddenly, still inside of her, I feel her spreading my ass, clawing; she lets go with one hand and then, without warning, without any other bodily movement, I feel a finger penetrating me, sinking into me. My muscles clench, but she holds on and holds tight, and I can't help but let out a moan. She doesn't stop to rest, though; she keeps our bodies moving. I lose my concentration, lose the friction and rhythm of our bodies; I just can't take my mind off what she is doing with me back there. Finally I take her shoulder in my teeth and forget myself, lost in the pain and pleasure inside my body, quite literally in my guts. A moment later, I feel her draw the finger carefully out; it is no longer there, but I find a void that remains, a *memory* of warm and sleepy days long ago when my mother would introduce a thermometer to check for a fever before withdrawing it: the feeling was one of perplexity, followed by one of a desolation. A second later, I hear a silent cry cross her lips.

Still inside her—awash in the complete and total lassitude of our embrace—we kiss, her sweet mouth on mine. I look at her for a long time, and finally dare to say:

"What is your name?"

In March of 2008 I received a brief, laconic note from my sister Selma: Mamá died, she said, and then gave the reasons she had for not informing me before. She concluded with a rather austere goodbye on behalf of the family.

Years ago, when I was still living in Mexico City, things didn't go very well between us. Then, after I'd moved to Paris, I lost contact, save for the (occasional, mind you) Christmas card. If Paris seems suffocating now, Mexico City certainly was when I left towards the end of 1998. It was like a dying man who didn't know where to go or what to do with his own corpse. (What will have happened, I wonder, to his sad old bones during the time that I've been gone?)

Of course, that wasn't the only reason for leaving. It also had to do (as in all lives) with love—with its exploits and vicissitudes—and then, later, when things have changed their appearances, you forget the real reasons for everything. Among them, of course, was Laila and Octavio. Since then, I've firmly believed that the world is driven ultimately by love. It is a latent disease; you can feel fine for years, and then suddenly it flares up, and brutally so. Now, I can't even begin to describe the strange and cruel feeling I had when my sister's note arrived at my Rue Monge flat. The pain was all but unbearable for hours on end, and it only began to wane days later; the mark, however, the mark of its bite, was indelibly there. Many years passed, and I got used to not hearing from my family—not one word—as well as to the abstraction that enables us to negate our emotions without fuss. That could very well be why I never saw it fit to return to Mexico. Who would be there waiting for me? "Many things are done in order to remember, however in the end they are revealed to be harbingers of death, and many things that want to be done for death are mere memory, fearful nostalgic memory, anxiously guarded so as to never be lost," writes Broch. What would I do there? Visit her tomb? Hear about her demise or listen to posthumous memories retold by innumerable lips, so anxious to speak with me? I didn't want that; it made no sense. Selma's note was a simple piece of information, a transmission from home, and that's how they—the family—must have felt about having it sent to me. I want to go on now just concentrating on my work, without anybody afflicting me or interfering with my peace, without finding out about any new things or discovering new details. I'd lost track of my mother, and my memory of her was enough; all I'd had for years was the occasional bit of news about her. Or about my father. They were always reticent with me. And now? What do you suppose I should do? What awaits me? Should it matter to me all of a sudden? Should I become taken with grief and go mad? No. But in spite of everything, I have to admit that I felt very bad indeed, incredibly sad and regretful. It was a terrible wave of shame that slapped me in the face. I had the shakes, and then came the fever. The pain of a loved one's death lingers long—years sometimes—festering deep down. Never healing. When they found out about my condition and the state of prostration into which I'd sunk by the end of March, Volpi, Gürsel, and a few other friends sought me out; between them and their wives, I was kept in good company. I appreciated it, yes, but deep down they couldn't understand. It's impossible for others to share your pain when they've only recently come to know what you've known and felt for someone your entire life. How is it that sometimes you lose a loved one to death, and other times you lose them by leaving the country, not knowing you'll never see them again? In any case, it was an irredeemable loss, and my Paris friends would never understand. Places and people that we end up abandoning never return to us, not even with their sudden death. By the same token, thankfully, they never come to wound us again. That, everyone knows, is what death, and our tenacious memory of death, are good for. Everyone waits for it, day in and day out; it's coming anytime, anywhere, and for anyone. And yet, we don't: we don't act as though we're waiting. Even though it's likely that each of us dreams with his sleeping face crawling with death.

I didn't respond to my sister for two months, and even then I said nothing more than thanks, I'd heard. I didn't want to get involved; didn't want to recriminate her for not telling me sooner or to press for details about Mamá's death. Nor did I want to hear about Selma, her children, or my father. If they hadn't mattered to me in years—if I'd managed to forget them (which, at least, is what I believed)—then they wouldn't matter to me now. I hadn't even heard their voices on the phone since I left Mexico, already several years back. And we were right (though for a quite debatable and ambiguous reason) not to speak: it was awkward and potentially counterproductive when you didn't even know what to ask them, without even knowing what to say. It must have happened to them as well. So I didn't send my father so much as a letter of condolence.

Two years later—*I still remember it clearly, in amazing detail*—in the summer of 2010, I finished that dense, cumbersome book for the Sorbonne and, a bit dubious and disenchanted with Paris, I decided to return to Mexico City. The manuscript, *I remember*, was left at the press along with hundreds of corrected proofs and the promise that they would send it to me as soon as it was ready. I had sublet my Rue Monge apartment a month before, during which time I had moved in with Gürsel and his wife. For their troubles, I gave them some furniture that I wasn't going to be taking with me, including a nice set of bookcases and a good refrigerator that I wasn't about to leave for my landlord. Everything else went to Volpi and the students and professors in the department. Luckily, I think, I wasn't under the shadow of love this time. I was leaving France with nothing in tow, and without being owed anything by anybody. Promises were made to each and every friend for a speedy return, but—nevertheless—none of us knew if we would ever see each other again.

Things started rather awkwardly in Mexico City, since—without a job or place to live—I was obliged to stay for a few weeks at a time with friends or relatives whom I hadn't seen in years. Like Ellison's *Invisible Man*, I was a stranger in a strange land; a foreigner in my own country. But six or seven months later I found a small, furnished apartment in the southern part of the city, in the most polluted neighborhood of all, right in the shadow of the Ajusco, and I got a job not far away as a full-time researcher in the Department of Philology at the former Universidad Nacional Autónoma de México, and there I've taken back up with my surly, solitary work. The capital city has been completely transformed into a suffocating, multiracial swarm of dangerous people where time doesn't exist for anybody, having been replaced by habitual haste and stress. It is from that point on that things started to happen, *as I will now describe*:

In September of 2011, fifteen months after having arrived from Paris and feeling rather settled in, my aunt Frida and my uncle David invite me over to celebrate Rosh Hosanna with their family. Their Polanco home is filled with people I haven't seen in many years. Besides Frida, now older, and my uncle, older too, there's Aarón and his awful wife Ruth; also Emilio, who got divorced many years before; my sister, her husband, and their two children; three of my mother's sisters, each of them old and alone; their children and grandchildren, whom I've never seen before in my life. Among them I feel like a middle-aged stranger, cut off from these sorts of dinners, which I'd stopped attending years ago. When my mother died, my father stopped attending too. I remember *now* the moral obligation—for my father, it was always a question of morals—that these dinners consisted of for him. He'd always detested the food, and he didn't like feigning gratitude. He'd also always found it difficult to remain standing (he suffered from a bad back) during that long, unintelligible prayer which preceded dinner and which he never much enjoyed. Selma's children have grown up like typical Jewish kids—her husband is Jewish too; she, however, still celebrates Christmas with my father's family, just as we both did many years ago. Yom Kippur and Rosh Hosanna on the one side, and the Holy Week and New Year on the other. All things considered, though, I think that nothing else matters to us besides reliving a memory (from childhood or adolescence), identifying with it, and then—of course—our nostalgia. That, perhaps, is faith, is true religion.

We eat very late, just before midnight, actually, and right after Aarón and one of the boys have finished the Hebrew prayer. We eat until we're positively bursting, savoring everything the women have carefully prepared: haricot beans, matzo ball soup, a basted chicken known as *yash tayam*, an enormous leg of lamb, flavorful meatballs known as *quipe basha*, and the *meshi meshmor*: exquisite calabashes stuffed with meat and rice and served with apricots, tamarind extract, and plums . . . all in all, a banquet to sweeten the Jewish new year. Finally, after dessert consisting of some incredibly sweet *balawa* and Turkish coffee, we make our way into the living room to pour through some old family albums. With aunts and nephews massing and milling about my feet, I leaf through the stiff pages, meditative in the face of so many brittle yellow photos. Yes, the fruition, the cruelty of time. We go on examining the photos for a long while, flipping the pages with a certain peaceful melancholy. Suddenly and without warning, I come across one in particular that fills my soul with a horror, a painful certainty. I freeze, absorbed in its face. Everyone is watching my hand impatiently, waiting for me to turn the page. The photograph in front of me shows several smiling teenagers standing around a giant birthday cake in the middle of a dance floor. It's quite old and weathered, but at the bottom I can make out the date: *November 1949*. Without turning my eyes from the page, I ask Frida who this woman is, standing there in the middle of all the others, and whom I recognize so painfully.

"It's your mother. At her birthday party."

But I didn't need to hear these words in order to know. This was the face that I had contemplated so many times before, without being able to distinguish it: the young woman I had dreamt about so many times in Paris. There was no doubt about it—it was the same girl—and that face, barely visible, was there: deep eyes, dark hair sparkling under the lights reflected from a disco ball, her warm face, and that graceful body sheathed in a violet dress decorated with sequins and fringe.

It was her that night, yes, in the immense darkness of my dream, and I barely—after so many years—even realized it. I look for my sister among the others gathered around, and find her in the dining room talking to one of my aunts:

"Selma, when did my mother die?"

She looks at me, disconcerted, as if she doesn't understand. Perhaps my words are so absurd that she has to take a moment to decipher them. I call to her again, and—suddenly breaking the serenity of the occasion—demand, with eyes wide:

"Tell me, when did my mother die?"

"What? Wait a second, let me think, Federico. I don't remember exactly," she says as she tries to comb back through her memory.

"It was in February of 2008, if I'm not mistaken," Frida offers, alarmed.

"What's the matter?" my uncle David asks me.

"It was the twenty-third," interrupts my sister. "It was around dawn on the twenty-third. Now calm down, Federico, and tell me what's going on?"

"Nothing, Selma. Nothing . . ." I'm sure for the time being, but later I'll have to go back home to confirm it.

Everyone's eyes are still on me, while mine remain focused on that black and white photograph, fixed on the face of that woman in a dance hall who I dreamed about three years ago and who I now hardly remember. I put down the album, and—without saying goodbye to anybody—I leave. There's been a premonition, and I know what I have to do. My face feels flushed, my pulse pounds in my neck, and I can barely breathe. I run down the stairs without bothering to wait for the elevator, and get in my car to drive from Polanco back to Ajusco. I floor the accelerator with the bitter certainty of knowing what I'm going to find, the answer to my deepest and most inscrutable question. Driving the Periférico seems like an interminable loop around an eternal circuit. Finally I arrive. I park the car, feeling hot and dizzy, and open my apartment door. Nerves and fear paralyze me. Everything is threatening, ready to answer to me, dating back to my own infancy. I feel myself gripped by a familiar feeling: visceral terror. My hands are sweaty, and for a moment I can't contain my excitement.

I open the drawers of my bureau, my writing desk; I knock my books from their shelves, scattering them over the floor; I dig out folders and files that I've had for years. I open a closet and finally find what I'm looking for: folded up in the bottom of a box is that sheet of paper that I never read again and in which I find the pain that a dream produced three years back: a nightmare similar to the suffering one experiences before dying, or the feeling of eternal and irreparable loss having survived another's passing.

In slight, barely legible handwriting, it reads: *23 February 2008. I have just woken up. I finish writing at 5:05 A.M. Paris.*

I know it, like an ad you've memorized: at that exact time—waking from my dream—my mother passed away. I read over the marked-up text: "Everything is dark, and the cold is cavernous and eerie . . . or, at least, this is how one might imagine cold would feel in the afterlife. I walk down that gloomy hallway, devoid of any flicker of light. *It is only me*, Federico, but at the same time I can picture myself at a distance, walking there. I'm afraid, and I wrap myself tightly in my arms. Perhaps that will help to quell my fear. But it does not. *I feel myself*, it is you, Federico, though you seem remote, though you seem to be another. I can't, however, move in any other direction than that *where my steps are taking you*, Federico, like a magnet: drawing, guiding, driving down that infernal, black corridor. Suddenly you find yourself outside; the hallway has given way to a broad, isolated street, just as dark, and devoid of a single soul or breath of life. You—which is to say, I—continue on, and you don't know why you haven't stopped, why you haven't come to a halt. And if you did, where would you turn to? Would you turn back? But where? If you don't know where you've come from, Federico—if you're suddenly . . ."

I stop reading, feeling something like an enormous flash of lightning or a stroke. I close my eyes and I can see myself writing this very passage: *I am doing it right now*, in February of 1975, at 4:53 in the morning, and I am on the verge of finishing the description of a dream that is actually a horrible memory, a sort of future nostalgia. I am finishing *Bodily Prayers*, whose conclusion is, at the same time, the detailed description of the dream that I have woken with, today, February 23, 1975:

"It is then, Federico, that you finally realize the reason for everything: it is a dream. You discover that *you have been living within my dream*, and it is there that you remember it, it is there that everything is revealed to you like a wonderful giftwrapped package or a cargo crate impossible to load. You can't bear (it's too painful) the deceit that you've been subjected to, but then again, who's responsible? *Perhaps I?* You fill with anxiousness and regret, your breath runs short, you desperately ask for her to give you her name. Yes, her name . . . you beg her. You'll come for her later, you say, after you wake. She doesn't seem to understand, and smiles skeptically. You examine her fixedly; you do not want to forget her lines, her evenly lined teeth, her manner, the mysterious scent of her body, her dark and profound eyes . . . you'd like to hold onto them forever, no? You contemplate her hair: it sparkles under the light from a disco ball, framing her face. You still have no idea who this woman could be, and only for an instant do you think you recognize her, do you hazard a guess, a hesitant stutter, you've looked upon her always, though you still don't remember where, don't remember who she is. She moves her lips; she wants to say something to you. But you can't hear; you move in close to her, you want to embrace her, you can't lose her like this, so easily and for all eternity. Bit by bit, you feel that same, cavernous, wraithlike cold creeping over you as before. This time you lean your ear in close, brushing up against her lips, and yet you still can't hear: you can't make out what she's trying to tell you. Once again she pronounces something, and you watch as she moves away, disappears, or rather it's you, Federico, it's you who is going, despite your embrace, despite your best efforts to hold her tight against you. You contemplate her from a greater and greater distance, as though through the fog. She, your true love, your life, is dispelled. Disappears. Or you do. You beg for her name, you call out to her, shouting that you'll come for her, that you'll find her wherever she may be, wherever she asks you to go, wherever she waits for you, if only she'll give you her name . . ."

I feel her embrace me again, harder this time, and she says:

"Magda. Magda Gómez." I look into her eyes, deep and dark

like the night, and they are the warmest and most loving eyes that have ever looked on me in all my life. I understand now why her name is Magda Gómez, and in the deepest reaches of my heart I find that I love her. She says to me, "I am your desire, don't you see? You are my husband, my brother, and my son, and from now on you will no longer be called Federico. You will be known as Yizreel, because I have created you and I love you."

February, 1975

30

When Iginio Jasso, accompanied by Santa, entered the precinct, they saw two police officers and the priest Augusto Roldán attending to the body of the lawyer Raimundo Rosales. When he saw them pull back the shroud, tears came to the architect's eyes. Santa joined him in his sadness, standing close at hand, dumbstruck and incredulous in the face of her employer's death. Rosinda, the secretary, didn't move a muscle.

A group of bowed mourners—old *plañideras*, as they are called in Las Rémoras, people who have nothing better to do than to accompany murder victims to their final destinations—had gathered outside the dilapidated old town hall, fourteen or fifteen of them maybe, all dressed in black, their faces veiled, ready to begin their weeping, their grieving, and their prayers to God. Several carried candles or rosaries, reciting hallelujahs or crying out to the heavens to have mercy on the deceased. It was a morbid spectacle of a choir, and yet it was somehow impressive enough to draw many other Rémoranos to see what was going on. Thus they began their work, just as the councilman Francisco Sigüenza, jowly and reserved, with twenty-nine years and one engagement to Pilar under his belt, stepped out onto the street, his eyes red from the smell of the embalming fluid. Rosales's shrouded body followed next, as did the priest and a number of police officers. At the end of the cortege was Santa, holding a dossier full of papers and leaning on the architect whenever she could for support. An odd group of onlookers was crowding around outside the building, trying to catch a glimpse of the deceased or maybe even touch his hand, though without much success. The carpenter and the coffin waited in the wings. Instead of trying to fit the bulky box through the narrow doors of the town hall, they had decided to bring the body out to the coffin and seal it there before finally bearing it to the cemetery overlooking the sea.

The cemetery was located beyond the waterfront, on the opposite side of town from where the crowd was now gathering. First you pass the basketball court, then the narrow street along the water, towards the jumble of rocks that blemishes the otherwise perfectly shell-shaped beach and forces you to take Encaladores. Eventually you reach the circle of houses that forms the outer edge of the town, you work your way up a rather steep hill, and finally—a third of a mile further on—lies a small knoll overlooking the sea, crowned with a meadow and ringed with trees and palms. It's this very spot where, some years before, Rosales had really taken a liking to a particular French poem, and where he'd gotten his idea.

The cortege began when Sigüenza gave the signal to his constables. Four fishermen served as pallbearers. One of them, Joaquín, was hesitant to take up on the side where Santa was walking, for fear of catching her eye. Continuing the procession (along with the officers who'd first brought out the body) were the *plañideras* with their feeble wax candles. The sun was beginning to drum stubbornly on the architect Jasso's fuzzy, leathery scalp, and although he'd grown to enjoy these sorts of solar baths, he was completely overcome with grief, as was the priest Augusto. There wasn't a whisper of a breeze, and the road to the cemetery was empty. The four fishermen were beginning to sweat profusely, for although Rosales was a small and slight man, the coffin itself was rather ostentatious and well out of proportion to his body. The only other coffin that would have suited him, however, had been used a few days before when Inés had died, and nobody—least of all the carpenter who'd been in charge of such things for as long as anybody in Las Rémoras could remember—could have expected that another important death would occur so soon thereafter.

Tony had even closed up the lonchería for the funeral, and he and Pili had decided to join in the procession that now numbered close to two hundred strong. They bumped into the doctor Díaz Gros, said their good mornings, and joined in the cortege. New onlookers and midwives who still couldn't believe that Rosales was a murderer—as inoffensive and good-natured as he was—took their places at the end. Some of them were sobbing repentantly, though they paused from time to time to wipe away their tears. One turned to her companion, offering her a kerchief while telling her to save her tears and lamentations for the service. The *plañideras*, on the other hand, broke out into cries that drowned out the low murmur of the sea.

It was already almost one o'clock, and at that time of day the waves were no longer breaking; rather, they were thin tongues of water that lapped at the sand and gently moistened it. The concave beach gave Las Rémoras the feeling of a lagoon, and the sea was like a shining, polished mirror. The tranquil sky fed into his iridescent neighbor as though trying to sink down and ensconce himself with her somewhere beyond the horizon, past where the eye could follow. The gulls, dulled by the torrid and sullen August sky and without any gusts of wind to soar on, had already taken advantage of the lethargy to roost on the outskirts of town. A few storks swam in the mercury-like waters, and a pair of pelicans were sunning themselves on the top of the highest crag, where Elías had so often sat to ruminate over his unhappiness and misfortune.

At the moment, however, the writer was over a half-mile away from the long and winding procession. After Tony had closed up shop and his few customers had dispersed, Elías had taken off for the cemetery with his notebook in hand, and there—from his new sunny perch, waiting for the cortege to arrive—he'd written something of an epitaph to the man who'd unintentionally drawn him there to his grave.

It read:

Midday

This Sun that accentuates
Like a long, loving, southern wind
Now suddenly exhausts
Consciousness, soothing it.

It continues rhythmically,
Dancing fragrantly
Among the hollows. Wandering,
Suddenly finding itself

In the eyes, by chance,
Dazzled with gold, and burnt
By a zenith that is an altar

For he who has *seen*
(Like three winged Hermes)
The asp held upright, Christ.

In the meantime, leaving behind the final rocks along the water and bearing towards Encaladores, the priest took up his aspergillum and swung it deliberately in the air, even though the water that was suppose to sprinkle from the amphora had long since evaporated. There were no more holy droplets with which to bless anything.

They were ascending the hill that led to the cemetery when a *plañidera*—exhausted from the effort of grieving while walking uphill—fainted. One of the constables was able to catch her by the shoulders and lower her to the ground like a black bundle of roots. Everyone turned, and the prayers were put on hold for a moment. Nevertheless, Sigüenza, not wanting to delay the burial of his old boss, gave a few quick words of encouragement to the officers, *plañideras*, and the two-hundred-odd Rémoranos in tow, telling them to continue to the burial site. At the same time as he was urging the lead group on, he looked back at Pili, standing beside Tony, Rosinda, and Doctor Díaz Gros, which is why, at that instant—in an authoritarian ecstasy—he sent one of the officers back to fetch her to him, which was no small task considering the confusing multitude that made up the procession. The August heat seemed to be taking quite a toll, especially on children who had to help their parents along, on pregnant women full of curiosity, on the weakening fishermen, and even on the officers in their blue uniforms who were required to carry their patently unnecessary guns.

Inside two hundred yards, Elías could make out first the unmistakably bowed figures of the *plañideras* and then the tall, lean outline of Francisco Sigüenza alongside that of the priest, who—without the help of any acolytes or altarboys—had done Rosales's extreme unction himself that very morning while Santa was searching the town, hoping and praying to find him. Then Elías picked himself up from the shade he'd written his little sonnet for the deceased in, and watched, rather perplexed, as the human stain snaked its way towards where he was standing. He never would have imagined—nor would have Sigüenza, nor

Santa, nor even the architect—how many close friends (and how many women) would come to bury the lawyer. If the councilman had decided to have the funeral so soon (and to do it with the full mayoral trappings) then he'd done so to avoid upsetting the small population (meaning those who knew that Inés had died by his hand), and—above all—so that the people of Las Rémoras wouldn't find out. What he hadn't imagined was how rumors could whistle through a town where things were generally quite slow, and what was even more unexpected was just how sad the people seemed to be as they joined in at the end of the procession.

Finally, Elías's eyes met with the cloudy, reddened eyes of the young interim town councilman, who then took Pilar tightly by the hand. Finally, they were there, face to face, and left with no other option save to greet each other with an awkward gesture and furrowed brows while the priest Augusto—who had finally given up waving his aspergillum around—greeted him affably and effusively, happy to see him there for the burial of his friend.

With the help of two officers, the fishermen lowered the coffin to the ground. In doing so, Joaquín happened to look into the red and glassy eyes of Santa. But they said nothing. Or maybe they did, and it was just that nobody noticed, given the general commotion and the pushing and shoving as people tried to move closer to the priest, who was about to begin the service: his back to the sea and facing the large crowd surrounding the coffin. The grave had been dug beforehand, and a large tarp had been set up, casting a shadow over the enormous hole in the ground that was to be Rosales's final resting place, almost camouflaging it. But when the priest seemed to have finished with his remarks, the sermon, and even the final farewell, several woman forced their way through a breach in the crowd, shouting.

They had just begun to lower the casket into the ground when suddenly Josefina stopped them short, saying:

"Padre, you can't bury that bastard here."

People either couldn't hear, or they couldn't believe what they'd heard. But the priest, intrigued, signaled for them to stop lowering the casket, and asked:

"But what are you talking about, Josefina?"

"What do you mean, what am I talking about?" Here she was interrupted by Ruth, who said in a bellowing voice that everyone could hear:

"It was only a matter of days ago that you yourself laid Inés to rest. And now she has to lie next to the man who murdered her? That's not right. We have to put a stop to it, padre."

Nobody had given any thought to what the prostitutes were saying, but they were right. The madam, or pseudomadam, Inés, was buried in an adjacent plot. Everyone turned and looked: yes, there was the freshly dug ground marked simply with a small cross, as the stonemason hadn't finished engraving the headstone yet. The assembled folks were dumbstruck: the *plañideras* were looking around cautiously; Tony, Rosinda, and Doctor Díaz Gros were close enough to hear, but didn't give much credence to Josefina and Ruth's interjection; Sigüenza, needless to say, was caught *in fraganti*; Pili watched the whores, almost compassionately; everyone was disturbed and perplexed, not knowing what to say or even where to look, when Padre Augusto, inspired just in time by the Holy Spirit, solved the problem:

"Girls, what you say is true. But please, be quiet. We can fix this."

At the padre's directions, two officers and Joaquín filled in as temporary gravediggers and broke ground for a new plot some twenty yards away, where it would be protected from the incessant sun by the boughs of a bountiful tree. Elías—who until then had remained silent and crestfallen next to Santa and Jasso—wanted to speak up and defend the lawyer's right to his original plot, but the architect grabbed him by the arm and held him

back, understanding that his protests would ultimately be in vain
. . . and counterproductive. The Rémoranos gave a low murmur
of agreement, and in any case the padre had already decided on
behalf of everyone. Nothing else could be done, leaving Elías
pensive and annoyed. He turned to Iginio and Santa, who was
fanning herself with the dossier, and said:

"Look at that. These are the obstacles that love faces, even
in death. It's such a shitty thing to do. Leave them the way they
were! Who cares? Can't people see they were in love?"

A man standing behind him asked that he be quiet. The
writer did so grudgingly, though it made him angrier still. At the
same time, Jasso—who had been somewhat blinded by grief and
absorbed in his memories throughout the entire service—finally
noticed Santa fanning herself with a stack of manuscript pages.
He asked her, just to distract himself from the pain he felt and
without any real curiosity, "Santa, what have you got there?"

She was lost, watching Joaquín throw shovels of dirt over
her dead employer, and didn't seem to hear. The architect bent
down, almost to her ear, and repeated it:

"Santa, what are all those papers?"

"Ah, I'd completely forgotten, Iginio. I took them from the
padre's writing desk this morning. I went looking for him this
morning to give him the bad news, and I picked them up while
I was waiting. Being in a hurry to tell you the bad news too, I
just happened to walk off with them. When I told him, he said
it didn't matter, that I could return them later. That's why I've
been carrying them around with me all morning."

"So did you read them?"

"No."

"Why? Aren't you even the least bit curious, Santa?"

"It's not that I'm not curious, Iginio. It's that I can't read."
And then, thinking it over, she continued, "I'd better return them
right now, actually, before I lose them."

But before she could act on her impulse and make her way over to Augusto, both Elías and the architect grabbed her by the shoulders with one thing in mind:

"Give it here!" the writer said, snatching the manuscript away.

"*A Convert's Chronicle* by Augusto Roldán," said Jasso, reading the top sheet.

"Can we borrow this please, Santa?" Elías begged, momentarily forgetting his disgust and frustration in light of this opportunity to read something ostensibly about Las Rémoras's own padre. "We'll read it and return it to you, I promise."

"Tomorrow even, if you want," insisted Jasso.

"Please, just don't say anything to the padre . . . we can't have him finding out."

"But why the hell do the two of you want it?" Santa asked. "What if it's important? He'll blame me, and I'll be excommunicated!"

"That's not going to happen. I swear . . ." said the architect. But he couldn't finish his promises, because making her way through the crowd—which had by that time grown to over four hundred people—was a blond woman of average height and perhaps forty-five years of age. Murmurs of astonishment rustled through the crowd as she worked her way determinedly towards the center of the goings-on. Finally, near to where they were standing yet still behind the padre (who was focused on the digging), Ruth, Josefina, and the other whores looked at her in surprise. One of them said:

"Señora, when did you get here?"

The question and what followed it was a veritable vortex of confused events, bad interpretations, and unfortunate misunderstandings.

First there was the look on the padre's face when he saw her, as if he'd just laid eyes on the Angel of Our Lord herself, and the blonde woman looked back at him as if he were the Sphinx on her plinth. Then, almost immediately, Santa looked to Joaquín and he turned to her, confused; which is also what Pilar did to Sigüenza, scouring the councilman's eyes trying to understand what was going on, but he himself was only able to stand there and look on, mouth open, oblivious to everything else except that woman. At the same time, Elías, Iginio, Rosinda, the doctor, and Tony watched, intrigued, and sought out Ruth and Fina, hoping to pick up even a tiny hint of what it was all about . . . Now the padre, now the blonde woman, surrounded by the feverish and voyeuristic multitude, intrigued by this other, this stranger . . . though they were strangers themselves, looking upon this woman with neither shyness nor sympathy, seeking out any detail, however miniscule it might be . . . It was a motionless *mare magnum* of looks and veiled questions subtly interrupted by a dry, formidable blow that left everyone frozen solid: the padre had collapsed and fallen into the lawyer's grave, on top of the casket, between shovelfuls of dirt.

A deafening silence blanketed the cemetery, and only after two full minutes had passed—stemming from the eager yet hushed multitude—did someone dare to offer a diagnosis:

"Maybe it was the Devil. Or maybe the heat. Who knows?"

"Or maybe it was both," offered someone else.

31

After they left their things in the hotel, Roberta, the boy, and Ricardo headed for downtown La Paz, where they spent the entire afternoon pouring over trinkets, curios, and sundry items on dirty shelves in shop windows. La Paz survives largely on black market businesses—less so on tourism—which is why, during August, it can draw even more visitors than Mexico City.

Fruit, drink, and sno-cone stands alternate with those selling clothing, electronics, or toys. U.S. commerce has overwhelmed Mexican business, and very little remains competitive.

The boy held onto Roberta's skirt when crossing the street or, occasionally, dared to take Ricardo's hand. In his left he held a Popsicle that, before he could suck it, crumbled into a white splotch on the ground. Roberta was struggling with her own, racing the heat, but it gave way beneath her tongue and fell all the same. Ricardo, on the other hand, was slowly sipping a barley water.

From time to time the three of them would laugh at a passerby limping along in a torn sandal or a woman who'd lost her grip on a bag of bread; they waited for the moment when the boy would forget about a toy he'd seen that didn't quite fit into their budget; they haggled over the price of a camcorder just for the fun of pretending; they whiled away the hours on dirty streets and in seafood restaurants; they told each other jokes. They saw street vendors proffering fish tacos and hot dogs wrapped in bacon and topped with avocado; nearby was a cart serving up deep dishes of goat meat with chili sauce and grilled onions, ringed with make-shift seats occupied by hungry clients, each with their own green glass bottle of Coke, a lemon Yoli, or a plastic cup of water. The afternoon heat, however, deadened people's movements and pro-voked exaggerated feelings of hunger and thirst. Like any Baja-californianos, Paceños took life with an easy calm and plenty of relish. When they could, they would buy foreign imitation jewelry or hop over to one of the famous brothels outside of town.

From a smallish plaza, the three of them watched the passenger boats roaming the bay, tiny and untiring. Roberta's son wanted to get closer for a better look. The day waned; beyond the boats, in the offing, the ruddy sun was depositing itself in the cellars of the sea like a bottle of mature wine. The waves were a livid purple, and seemed the product of a protective and benevolent sky.

Finally, around eight o'clock that night, they headed back to Los Arcos, Roberta's hotel, exhausted. She washed up with the boy; afterwards it was Ricardo's turn. He dressed in the bathroom, and then—when all three were ready—they went back down for shrimp and squid cocktails at the Bismarck, the tiny restaurant across the street. Afterwards they walked along the waterfront with nary a word, still too timid to broach the subject that nevertheless concerned them both. At long last—ten o'clock, actually—they returned to Los Arcos. As soon as they entered their room, the boy collapsed, exhausted, on the bed, and nodded off. Roberta undressed him cautiously so as not to disturb him, and left him there to sleep.

"You don't have to sleep on the couch," she said to Ricardo. "There's room for the three of us here."

As soon as she said this, she went into the bathroom. Ricardo could hear her brushing her teeth and gargling; meanwhile, he pulled off his shirt, his shoes, and his pants.

"Go ahead . . ." Roberta said as she emerged, a T-shirt hanging lightly over her body.

Urrutia—naked except for his boxer shorts—entered and repeated the procedure. Then he washed his face with soap, took a washcloth to his shoulders and underarms, and urinated while contemplating the fuzzy arc of his chest in the full wall mirror. The hair seemed thicker, redder somehow. Finally—for the first time in several days—he didn't have to think about what the hell he was going to do with *Las Rémoras*. That afternoon, together with Roberta and her son, he had simply lived: Ricardo as Ricardo had disappeared.

When he exited the bathroom, Roberta was lying alongside her son, shoulders bared, caressing his forehead. The boy sighed deeply; it was almost a snore. He was sweaty. It was pleasant, he thought, to see them together there: the mother and her son, each with the same eyes and the same long, lightly gathered lips.

She brushed back his hair and blew on his forehead. Ricardo stood there, watching them, indecisive. Finally, Roberta looked up and beckoned to him. He tiptoed over and carefully eased under the sheets on the other side of the bed from Roberta, with her son in between them. The ceiling fan made a noble effort to push a proper breeze around the room, but nevertheless the heat continued to cling tenaciously. Roberta had opened a window, leaving the screen exposed to the night air. Switching off the bedside lamp, she said:

"Ricardo, there's something that nobody else knows."

"What?" he asked, his voice fracturing the darkness of the room.

"I left Las Rémoras after Inés died. She was the owner of the place where I worked. Well, not exactly the owner, but . . ."

"Yes, I know. La Gringa."

"No, you don't know," she said. "You always think that you know everything, but you're getting ahead of yourself, Ricardo. They blamed the town councilman . . ."

". . . Raimundo Rosales. He was a good man," Ricardo insisted, jumping ahead again.

"But it wasn't him. It wasn't him!"

"It was Elías," Ricardo said. "I understand . . ."

"No you don't. I'm telling you, you don't understand anything," Roberta said tearfully, under the sheets. "Elías didn't kill her."

"Then who was it?"

"It was me."

Ricardo's mouth—if anyone had been able to see it—had contorted into a horrible shape. There must be some mistake, he said to himself, some misunderstanding. Roberta was mistaken, she'd gotten some crazy idea in her head, or she was saying this in order to redeem herself for abandoning Elías. But before he went any further, he heard Roberta tell him things that he—somehow—didn't know:

"That night, when Rosales left Inés's bedroom, I was down in the living room listening to Lolita. Everyone else was asleep—Josefina, Ruth, and the other girls, even the boy was off sleeping in some other part of the house. When I got to my room (the first one down the hall), Elías was there, naked, face up, on the bed. I wasn't expecting him."

Ricardo kept quiet. The darkness of the room became darker still. Some silent, subterranean presence flashed in her green eyes. Ricardo thought he saw a fugitive tear escape and roll down her cheek. He was right; he reached out with a finger to dry it away. Then he pulled his arm out from under the sheet, reached over the boy, and began to stroke the prostitute's hair while she continued to caress her son's head and blow on him, sad and listless.

"What happened then?" Ricardo whispered, not wanting to upset the moment.

Roberta summoned up her courage, permitted a few more tears to moisten the pillow, and said:

"We looked at each other. Then he turned away. Went out onto the balcony. I went over to him, sat down by his side, and began to stroke his hair. I wasn't sure why, but something inside me made me think twice about sleeping with him, about making love. I wanted to hold him, to apologize, I don't know . . . I wanted him to leave. But I didn't say so. He turned his body—his face—and looked me over closely, absorbing every detail. I realized something, and it scared me: he was sick with love. When he contemplated me and touched my face with the tips of his fingers, he grew weak with love. And I couldn't share that feeling with him . . . I just didn't love him the way he loved me. It made it so difficult. I was scared, Ricardo, so very scared. I wanted to ask him—beg him, really—not to love me so, or at least not to show it so much, not to implore me with his eyes the way he did . . . but I wasn't about to do that. I couldn't ask that of anybody."

"So you didn't love him?"

"Until that moment, I did, I loved him as I hadn't loved anybody in a long time. Perhaps not since I forgot about the father of my child. I don't know. I wanted to explain to him that he was ruining the love that we had (yes, the love) with his overwhelming passion, his earnestness. But how to say it to him? His was a fading passion. He would have given his life for someone, which is exactly what I didn't want, not from anybody. I didn't deserve it . . . perhaps nobody does. They victimize you; yes, the dying and the fading make you their victim, Ricardo. They make you an unwilling assassin, an assassin forced to be a victim. Do you see? Something broke inside of me, something that—as I told you on the beach—has no name. Suddenly you realize that you're never going to recover, that it's lost forever . . ."

"What? What's lost forever, Roberta?"

"The love that you felt. The love you felt for someone. Everything I'd felt for Elías was ruined beyond repair, was unrecoverable . . . I just wouldn't be able to love him as I had before. I wouldn't want to. So . . ."

". . . so you detested him."

"Yes, I detested him, but it's not at all like the hatred you feel for your enemies. It's something else entirely. I detested him because he had ruined—without wanting to, without even knowing—any possibility for a greater love, the possibility for me to love someone some day. It might have been my last opportunity ever, understand? It was as if I were saying, *It's your fault, Elías, that I don't love you. You love me too much*. It was a contradiction, I know . . ."

"Yes, a contradiction, but at the same time, it wasn't . . . I understand you perfectly, Roberta."

"We didn't make love. He was desperate; he wanted to try to recover something by doing it one last time. He insisted that we do it. He wasn't going to leave empty-handed, understand? I knew it. The harder either of us tried to save ourselves, the more impossible it became. I didn't want it anymore . . . or, if I did, I wanted it to remain something distant, something lost in time. Sleeping together one last time would break that spell, that ancient flame, those good memories . . ."

"I understand, Roberta. You wanted Elías to remain a memory. Even though he was sitting right there next to you, he was nothing more than a good memory, a ghost from the past . . ."

"Yes, someone who I'd loved—someone who, at any moment, I was going to love, really love—and still it scared me. The fault was all his. Ever since that day a week or two before when he had the gall to beg me: *Roberta, do you love me or not?*"

"Elías was blackmailing you."

"Exactly. That's how I felt."

"How did you respond?"

"With the truth."

"And what was that?"

"To not say a thing."

"So that was the beginning of the end, no?"

"I think it was."

"He never should have asked . . ."

"He had a right to, I suppose. But that doesn't mean he had to do it. You're right about that."

After a pause, bared by the sheet, Ricardo asked:

"Why did you say you killed Inés?"

She hesitated for a moment, and then answered:

"After Elías had gone—after he'd left the balcony—I heard an insignificant little sound. But it startled me . . . I thought it might be the boy, or that I'd heard Elías . . ."

"Heard him what? What did you think you were hearing?" Urrutia asked, squeezing her hand underneath the sheets, asking for the truth.

"Crying. I thought I heard Elías crying, Ricardo, that's what. I'm sorry; I didn't want to tell you. He didn't ask me anything;

I just understood. And what little I said to him, those few words, he understood too. He didn't want to beg, and for that I thanked him. Nevertheless, poor Elías couln't contain his tears. I embraced him very tight . . ."

"So what was the noise you heard, Roberta?"

"Somebody was knocking at the underside of my bed, with their knees or knuckles or something. It was an uneven, almost imperceptible noise. Finally, trembling, I got out of bed and bent down to look. It was Inés."

"How? She wasn't dead yet?" Ricardo didn't believe his ears. He wished he could reach the light switch so that he could see Roberta clearly and confirm what she was saying. "Didn't Elías smother her? I thought that . . ."

"He'd tried to smother her, but . . ." she interrupted what she had to say in favor of something more important, something necessary. "You have to understand, he hated her. He said that she was to blame, that she was the one preventing me from leaving that place, that it was all her fault that I was a prostitute. He believed that Inés didn't want us to be together. I told him what I always did: that he was wrong about her, and that I'd been in the same business for five years, with Inés and without her."

"Did he get angry with you?"

"No. He never so much as raised his voice to me. I was always grateful to him for that."

"So then what happened?"

"I understood everything, noises and all. It was like I'd been shot. Sensing that our love was over, Elías had tried to kill the woman he thought was responsible for it. He thought that this would be enough to recover my love for him. Do you see how he became weak with love, how he fought to the death to keep it all from being over? And let me tell you something, Ricardo, something that you may not know, but that I've come to know only too well: everything in life comes to an end. Sooner or later, it disappears."

"I know it. Or, at least, I'm coming to realize that."

"Generally, it's for the best. And you should always try and prepare for it, since there's absolutely nothing you can do once something's time is up."

"You choked her, right?" asked Ricardo, his voice growing fainter still, saying things that should probably not have been said so close to her peacefully sleeping son.

"Yes, that's right. The poor thing could hardly breathe. She was turning blue. So I picked up a pillow and saved Elías instead of saving her."

"Maybe you dreamed it. Maybe that's not how it happened," Ricardo said. "Maybe you were just sound asleep . . ."

"Yes," she replied, "I was, and that's why the other day, when Josefina and Ruth came in to wake me up, they saw an arm sticking out from under my bed."

"They woke you up, and you thought they were going to blame you, right?"

"Not quite. Right from the start, Josefina said that Rosales had been the last client of the night. She'd always had something against him. I'd seen it too. Everything made sense. And since he's the town councilman . . ."

". . . You thought that he had some sort of immunity, that nothing would happen to him," concluded Ricardo. He didn't want to point out that Rosales *was* the town councilman, or rather that he *had been* until his untimely death. *Now* it's Sigüenza who's taken his place. But Roberta couldn't have known all that: she disappeared from Las Rémoras the same day she had made her accusation.

"Maybe they've finished the investigation by now; maybe he's free to go," Roberta said to herself. "I understand nobody in town is going to look at him quite the same way again, but . . ."

Ricardo moved his head in a gesture intended not to clarify anything but rather to leave her mistaken assumption intact. She had killed for him—for Elías—as had he for her. They were both in the wrong. Ricardo understood that, and preferred to remain silent. Roberta didn't deserve the pain of the whole truth.

"What I don't understand is why didn't Elías leave her in her own bed?" asked Roberta, suddenly pensive. "Why risk being seen by somebody in the hallway just to hide Inés under my bed? What was he thinking? It's absurd; it makes no sense. I had to do it . . . I had to move the body, but so I wouldn't be found out, and so that he wouldn't be found out either. You see? That's why I'm telling you, Ricardo, that I'm positive I took Inés's body back into her room after suffocating her the second time. What the hell was Elías thinking? I still don't understand."

"I do," Ricardo muttered. He hoped that she hadn't heard him.

"Good night," the woman said.

Ricardo passed his hand over her eyelids in the darkness, and he found that she had stopped crying a good while ago. He felt relieved. But before falling asleep—perhaps just a moment before—he realized something: it wasn't Roberta that he was touching; it was the boy next to him. Ricardo felt a few seconds of happiness, and then he fell asleep.

32

A CONVERT'S CHRONICLE
BY AUGUSTO ROLDÁN

A bottomless mass of people swarmed from place to place under the noonday sun. The noonday star was at its zenith, and it hit our heads like the beak of a buzzard out in the arid Baja

California desert. The crowd (some of whom were massing around a street vendor like horrifying, revolting flies on human excrement, while others were listening to a catchy salsa band paid for by the city) filled the streets adjacent to the La Paz waterfront.

The three of us came down the sidewalk that ran parallel to the sea. Not very chatty, my cousins Solón and Cecilio (with myself, Augusto, behind them) were hustling along despite not being in any rush and not having anywhere to go. Bodies limp, withered, and *agüitados* (as they say along the border) from the insufferable August heat, we'd managed to lose our way. The last few girls we really knew had already flown back to Mexico City. We were fed up and even regretful. A sour sea breeze blew in our faces, though the breakers—already retreating at that time of day—were barely audible in the distance. We walked quickly—needlessly quickly—in what I suppose was the direction of the apartment my father had rented for the summer, when we saw—coming down the sidewalk towards us—an obviously American girl of average height. She had a thin, almost pointed chin, and her eyes showed a different sort of heat than the sun's. That was all I could gather from my fleeting glance.

Almost simultaneously, Cecilio winked at her and tossed out a teasing *adiós*. Solón and I looked at each other, perplexed. For a moment, we thought that Cecilio actually knew her, since she returned the friendly gesture. A bit confused, we asked him if he did know her, and he—dry and cocky, as he always was with regard to women—said no, he had no idea who she was. Solón then turned to us with a challenge: *Let's flip to see who has to go after her. Between you guys.*

Why aren't you in on this, I replied. Solón pretended not to hear me, turned towards his brother to see if he would accept the challenge, and without waiting for anybody to second-guess themselves, flipped a coin in the air. Still terrified—a feeling that gambling and games of chance have always provoked in me—I called out with irrevocable clarity, *Tails*, when the coin was at its apex. I won. Yes, I won. Or I lost, who knows . . . how can I explain it to myself or anybody else after so many years? Looking back on it now with the benefit of experience, only Our Lord knows the grand design of things, what is permitted of men and angels. Here, rejecting any sort of narrative suspense, let me go ahead and say this: that coin toss—or Solón's cowardice—would change my life forever.

What I first confused with random chance was, after all, Divine Providence. What impelled me towards her, towards that girl—and I still didn't know her name—was the Spirit of God, the Spirit of the Flame, the Paraclete. All I can say is that at the time I went after her with a grieving, tremulous soul and a deep-seated fear of looking like a hypocrite in front of my cousins, and not out of any true spirit of conquest. Inside two blocks I'd caught up with her. She was wearing faded, frayed denim shorts; I don't quite remember, but I think that was the style back then. From a few steps behind her, I could appreciate her smooth and slender body; then, walking beside her, I could see her slight and pointed chest, untethered, like a canary or a resplendent angel.

"Oye, hablas español?" I asked, terrified, and more terrified still that she could tell I was afraid from they way I pronounced those words.

"Sí," she replied without turning to look at me, though I was fairly certain she knew who it was walking by her side.

"Where you headed? Want some company?" I asked as smoothly as I could, venturing what—sooner or later—had to be ventured.

"If you want," she said, the way that women from any country on earth are wont to do instead of giving you a simple *yes*.

To what did I owe that kindness? Who knows! It is a mystery that I haven't tried to solve for many years, perhaps not since I became a man of the cloth. But in any case, that was how the chit-chat started, the *tell me's* and the *you don't say's*, which—though always trivial—are also quite fragile, to the point where a single misspoken word can bring down the delicate bridge of conversation. Almost nobody ever remembers these first conversations, such is the nervousness and caution with which we watch for slips and stumbles that could prevent us from forging something lasting, whose final form we don't yet know! But the fact is that one of the people in such a conversation is almost always more concerned with what they're hearing about themselves (and with how to curry the other's favor), or simply with tossing any bit of nonsense that might just be mistaken as great wisdom.

Her name was Jenny, and she lived in San Diego with her aunt on her mother's side. She had already visited La Paz many times, and was quite taken with it, just as she was with Los Cabos and Las Rémoras. It seemed like a peaceful place, devoid of troubles or haste, like all of Baja California. The people were always friendly, always obliging, always ready to lend a hand, and had no qualms with Gringos, whom they had grown accustomed to. While she was telling me all of this, we sat down together on a sort of flared concrete patio that looked out over the waterfront and the sea beyond, our legs bared to the salt air, and we watched the fish teeming and swimming around the stones near the dock, which was simply an extension of the street into the sea. Behind us, cars honked from time to time, though honking was never strictly necessary.

My uncle—Solón and Cecilio's father—had a big, well-kept, sky-blue '64 Ford in those days. When he died, a few years before, it was passed down to Cecilio. From time to time we would take it out to *maleconear*, as we would say, which in La Paz meant to go cruise the waterfront and pick up girls, or at least meet them. They would be hanging out there on the avenue, always in groups of three or four, watching the cars roll past, their eyes open for anybody they knew or just someone they found attractive. One or two would be perched on the hood of a parked car, while the rest would be lounging in the open doors. They spend hours there, giggling and gossiping, waiting for the occasional boy to come up and talk to them. This sort of thing usually took place on Saturdays and Sundays. It was an ongoing conclave of young people seeking conquests that took place on street after street and week after week along the water, from around five in the afternoon to one or two in the morning. That was how Paceños spent the long hours of their weekends, having used up their Friday nights at one of the two main dance clubs in town.

At four o'clock we rented a small paddleboat. Actually, it was she who rented it, since Cecilio was holding my wallet. Jenny also bought us a pair of Popsicles. Later, we took a walk down the waterfront, and after an hour or so the traffic had subsided, as had its orchestra of honking horns. There were no street vendors, no music playing, and no police; just a couple kissing off in a corner. We were alone, with the canvas of the sea spread out at our feet. At one of the lookout points above the beach, we kissed, long and peaceful. I don't know why I didn't go off with her; all I remember is that we said goodnight, and then we went our separate ways.

In the morning, around ten o'clock, I learned that Cecilio and Solón had spent the rest of the previous night dancing at El Rollo. They wanted to know every last detail of what had happened between Jenny and I, though I was more than a little reluctant to tell. Nothing good could come of it. Their persistence was quite annoying, but I managed to make it out of there with my secret intact. I was able to keep it a secret until this very day, on which I confess it, though having sought ecclesiastical permission to do so. But getting back to the subject . . . my cousins (I believe) were convinced that nothing had happened. I showered and washed up as best I could, then headed out for Los Arcos, the hotel where

Jenny was staying, near the water and just a few blocks from the center of town. Normally, I spent my mornings reading *Les Misérables*, but that day was different. I wanted to be punctual.

I got to the hotel and saw her there, sitting on a bench in the lobby. I took a furtive look before approaching her, almost as if such a thing were forbidden. She had one of her arms propped up on the railing of the balustrade, and she was dressed in a white skirt, Oaxacan sandals, and her hair was gathered in two long braids. Before I could reach her, however, a young, dark-skinned boy (whom I knew well) in a car called out to her with some flirtatious remark, and she smiled. She waved when she noticed me, more like she was saying goodbye. We greeted each other, and—much to my surprise—she began asking me a barrage of questions. I bided my time, waiting only for my chance to ask her if she knew that boy. When I did, she told me that she had seen him somewhere before.

"He was following me around a while ago and asked if I wanted to go for a ride, but I said no. You know how foolish men are . . ."

Yes, and Marcelo as much as anybody. I felt an incredible sense of jealousy, I must admit—for the first time in my eighteen years. I didn't understand. I asked—with no small amount of ingenuity, I admit—whether some day, if we stopped seeing each other for whatever reason, she would seek out someone like him. Why? she asked, her curiosity piqued. I had to answer with something I hated to admit: that lots of girls found him attractive, and I just couldn't understand that. Dark-skinned, lean, and fairly tall, with just a hint of seediness in his eyes, aggressive, risqué, even violent at times. And the most incredible thing was the way he behaved around girls. He was a close friend of Cecilio, but Solón, on the other hand, found him obnoxious.

I met him myself one afternoon some years ago when my cousin introduced us. He and Cecilio rode up front in the Volkswagen while I sat in the back, watching through the window. It was Sunday. Groups of females snaked their way along the waterfront. I was three years younger than both of them; as such, I was always following them around, learning from their conquests, their behavior, their experiences, and especially their stories, which they never tired of telling, sordid details and all. Suddenly Marcelo pulled the car over and yelled out the window at two quite flashy-looking girls walking down the sidewalk. At first I thought they were friends of his, but then (and to my surprise) he beckoned to one who came over to the car looking like she'd never seen him before in her life. He said hello, asked what her name was in a proud, almost haughty tone of voice, and then without another word he handed her some money and asked her to go buy a pack of cigarettes for him. I couldn't believe what was happening; Cecilio and I watched while the girl did exactly what Marcelo asked her to do: she and a friend went into a bodega, emerged again, and came over to the car to make sure that what they'd got was the brand that Marcelo wanted. But the real coup de grâce was when Marcelo said that no, she hadn't understood him, and if she didn't know how do a little stinking favor right then she shouldn't do it at all. I saw the expression on the girls' faces change, saw how he had tamed a woman's arrogance and bent it to his will. Marcelo had done this—Cecilio's friend—with a single bitter, perfidious comment. Then he simply opened the door and—as if giving an order—told them to get in. The girls looked at one another, but it wasn't the look of female complicity. It was something else: perhaps a mutual understanding between the two of them in the face of a powerful, rude virility. They got in the back seat with me. I was filled more with fear than with a desire to talk to them. Marcelo calmed them down for a few moments, all the while cruising up and down the waterfront. Finally, without asking anybody anything, he turned off and headed in the direction of Coromuel, a beach on the outskirts of the city, and much further than El Rollo, which was the established boundary. But I could tell that Marcelo had a different, hidden beach in mind, one that I wasn't familiar with . . . he laughed it up with Cecilio, put a rock and roll tape on the car stereo, and paid no attention to either the girls in the back seat or their questions. A few minutes later, however, he took one hand off the steering wheel and reached back to place his hand on the thigh of the prettier of the two, the one right next to me, in the middle. I was at once incredibly confused by and completely immersed in Marcelo's actions. Whatever he did (or did not do) was done with complete confidence. Eventually, one of the girls asked again where he was taking them, and Marcelo still didn't deign to answer, even though he'd obviously heard her clearly. Instead he acted as if he was only going to talk with Cecilio, and that he wasn't going to acknowledge the girls outside of that initial insult. If I said anything at all myself, it was to ask them their names and allay my own anxieties. When the prettier of the two asked again, it was Cecilio who answered—a bit more condescendingly than even Marcelo could have managed—that they were headed to the beach. We want to go back, said the other. Then get out and walk, Marcelo shouted furiously. He slammed on the brakes, opened the door, and gave her a brutal shove. He knew they weren't about to get out there on the outskirts of town, which was a desolate sort of place with a barely-visible road surrounded by nothing but sand and storm drains. Then he continued arrogantly along until reaching the beach, where he finally parked the car. He and Cecilio got out and—without inviting us to get out as well—walked off chatting under the light of the moon. It was an incredibly beautiful place, with an absolute, perfect stillness. The surf lent its murmur to the brightness, sliding up the beach before dissolving in the sand. I could tell that Marcelo took all of his "conquests" here, to use his own primitive, degrading term. Of course, none of us were old enough or had enough money to get a hotel room. Instead, things happened in the backseats of cars parked on overlooks, or wherever else you could find a scrap of privacy. The beaches around La Paz were quite dangerous, however, because corrupt soldiers would occasionally come around, and—instead of maintaining the law—they would rape and steal with impunity. We'd heard of countless cases where couples were robbed and otherwise humiliated.

Finally Marcelo returned to the car where the three of us were waiting. He took the younger girl by the hand and asked in a slightly—only slightly—sweetened falsetto if she would accompany him. She took his hand and walked off; immediately thereafter Cecilio came for the other one. Each pair walked off in different directions down the beach while I waited there with the car, quiet and confused and afraid. Forty minutes later, Marcelo came back with the prettier of the two, hand in hand though with nary a word. But before my cousin could return, about ten minutes later, I heard them start talking about something (I don't know what) out on the beach. But I did see Marcelo take out his anger by throwing a bottle against the rocks. Then, when Cecilio did return, Marcelo literally jumped up and ran to the car. He said that it was time to go, and with that he started up his Volkswagen. *What about the chicks?* I asked. *They're staying,* he replied. The one who'd gone off with Marcelo stood yelling at us, while the other ran after the car throwing rocks. She was sobbing. Marcelo turned on the stereo again and started to laugh. There was something strange—off-key, false—about his voice, his behavior. But I didn't say a thing; I just kept to myself in the back seat. Only later would he say to me, as if preaching:

"Now you see how they like to be treated. Like dogs. Do you really think, Augusto, that they didn't have a choice about getting in the car and coming with us? Yes or no? All women are whores to bad luck. You'll see how they come looking for us later. And not to ask for an explanation, either; they're going to want to get together again. They're pigs."

The most unbelievable thing, I told Jenny as we headed out from Los Arcos, is that from time to time I still saw them getting in that same Volkswagen with Marcelo and Cecilio . . . his prophecy fulfilled. I simply didn't understand women. It was a mystery too complex for me to unravel. Maybe Marcelo was right, and it wasn't in my nature to understand them. What I do know is that ever since then a part of me has been capable of deep hatred: not being able to act, not being able to move like Cecilio and Marcelo did, trying to do so and yet always failing, made me bitter. How to despise and degrade a woman? How to bring out that vileness I found in my own nature?

I had told Jenny exactly what I didn't want to say. I'd even revealed an aspect of Marcelo that she hadn't known about, and which she naturally felt upset by ever since. Without realizing it, I had made a connection between them; I had established a first bond between Jenny and Marcelo. A weak, fragile bond, if you like, but now one knew something substantial about the other. This is in itself a kind of relationship, and we live in a community of them: a sticky, smelly web of relationships. I was much too young to understand then, but nevertheless, we learn through our experiences . . . Jenny, on the other hand, told me—more to put my jealousy to rest and reconcile us—that she had a four-year-old daughter who lived in San Diego with her aunt. She'd been married at sixteen, and divorced a few years later. She was twenty-one-years old, and traveling with an older gentleman—her boss—on his business trips.

We ate early, and at the table I was better able to notice (why hadn't I done it before?) the terrible sadness contained in all of Jenny's gestures. It wasn't the contempt that I'd thought it was yesterday; it was the pain of being forced—unwillingly—to grow up very fast. I could tell this by her crestfallen look, as if she was trying to hide the truth behind her downcast eyes, while at the same time maintaining a sense of strength in her brow and hard-set features. Above all it was obvious how much she loved her little girl, her daughter back home, how much nostalgia she felt in speaking about her. When we'd finished eating, Jenny wanted to take a paddleboat out for another spin. We made our way a good distance from shore, and there—utterly alone—we whiled away the day with kisses and caresses . . . When we finally returned to shore, we'd gone over our allotted time, and I had to pay for an additional hour. We hopped out onto the sand, she rinsed off her knees, and then we walked off along the waterfront as we'd done the previous night. Finally, we parted ways with the promise of getting together again later in the evening. I returned home and tried to read. It wasn't long, though, before I set Hugo's novel aside and picked up a notebook and—without quite knowing what I was doing—began to write out a few lines of nonsense, a series of vehement affronts to God, which were very typical of me at the time. It was a series of insults and denunciations of all the morbid art in the world that purports to represent Him, objects that—I thought—exploit our basest instincts and which fly in the face of life, of nature, of Jenny and I . . . which is to say, in the face of the sublime love and incredible joy that we felt in each other's presence. I spent those hours—I remember—by filling page after page, anatomizing and blaspheming like I'd never done before. Now, however, I can only recall this single verse:

I have been born and they have blamed me,
I have been born and they restrict me
With the belief that a few nails can hold
Feet that I myself have nailed.

Nobody came by the house all afternoon; perhaps they'd all gone to the beach or downtown, I don't know. I went out on the terrace and looked up: the sun in the firmament was no longer a blood-red knob in the sky, but rather something of a dark precipice, a gigantic hole where sea and sky were confounded. I went back to the table and continued writing, corroborating what I'd been contemplating for a long time, ever since I first read Nietzsche: that death is an intrinsic part of Christianity, that in order for Christ to rise, he first had to die. Only so many pranks, O Lord, as You well know, which is why I ask You for forgiveness, now and forever. Blessed and praised be Thy name.

I bathed and shaved off the few whiskers I had before getting dressed in the same exquisite manner as Lucien de Rubempré on his return to Paris in *Lost Illusions* (which was my novel of choice at the time). I hailed a taxi to take me to Jenny, my guardian angel.

"Have you been waiting long?" I asked when I arrived at the hotel and saw her sitting on the very same bench as that morning.

She handed me a paper bag, which I opened.

"You like? They're tacos," she said.

"I love them," I said. "But why bring tacos if we're about to go out to eat?"

"There's been a change of plan," she responded in a voice that she'd intended to be conciliatory, but which nevertheless broke something very fragile inside of me.

"Why? Tell me."

"The man I'm working for asked me to attend a dinner with him. You know. It's my job; I warned you."

"That's fine," I answered, proud and hurt. "So you're on your way out, then?"

"No, we have time for a little walk first," she ordered or suggested. "And then, if you want, you can take me to the dinner."

So there we were, off walking along the waterfront for half an hour or so, and then sitting down on one of the benches set up in the plaza where tropical bands will play salsa and mambo on holidays and festivals. I threw away the paper bag, its contents untouched: I'd lost my appetite. It was just then that a Volkswagen pulled up alongside us; inside was Marcelo and a friend I didn't recognize. He looked at me out the window and yelled, jokingly:

"Hey, cabrón, why don't you introduce us to the lady? Or aren't you speaking to your boys anymore?"

"Hello and goodbye," I replied dryly.

Jenny, however, smiled at them as if to offset my lack of courtesy. They drove off. But not five minutes later, another car pulled up alongside us, and this time—much to my surprise—I was face to face with two hefty blond fellows speaking English. She had to go. I understood. All she said was:

"Some of Mel's friends . . . it's that dinner thing, you know? I'm looking forward to a long and boring night . . ."

She got in the car with them, and I watched them drive off as I crossed to the other side of the street. Soon I heard the whistling whine of the Volkswagen, and once again Marcelo and his friend pulled up to me. They told me to get in. Cecilio's friend was dying with laughter, saying that Jenny had stiffed me, and he talked about my ignorance and clumsiness with women, who were all whores and pigs anyway. I couldn't even say anything in my own defense; it would have been rejected, and I would have looked like even more of a fool for trying it. Suddenly someone suggested we go to El Rollo that night, because there might be some girls there who would put out. I accepted. But first we went to pick up Cecilio and Solón at my house. When we got there, Marcelo asked me to just run up to the door and let them know, and then we would be on our way.

I ran up the steps and told my cousins that we were waiting for them down in the car. My sister wanted to go too, but I put a stop to that with some excuse or other. Of course, my mother intervened on her behalf, saying that if she couldn't go with us, then I wasn't going to go either. Finally, the departing group consisted of myself, Cecilio, and my sister. Solón wanted to stay at home. But I should make this clear: deep down, like him, I didn't have the appetite or the will to go out and party. I was in love, and nothing else made a damn bit of difference.

I don't remember much of anything about that night: only that it flew past. I gather we got home very late, and, exhausted, I curled up in some armchair, ready to sleep and think no more of Jenny, her kisses, the caresses we'd shared out on the water, in our solitude. Dawn came quickly: the sun's unwelcome light streamed in through the open window and vanquished the night. It blinded me, penetrating the disheveled hair covering my eyes. It was ten o'clock when I left the house and set out on a desperate search for Jenny, but I couldn't find her at the hotel, the waterfront, or anywhere downtown. I crisscrossed the town, checked every place we had visited together, and then I did it all again. The clock struck noon, then one, two, three, and four o'clock: I was still scouring La Paz—the beaches, the paddleboat rentals, the shops, restaurants, streets, and hotels. Nothing. It seemed as if Jenny had just vanished.

Finally I returned home, feeling deprived and frustrated. I wanted to die from annoyance, from the bitter foolishness that had overtaken me. I had fallen in love so easily and quickly that I went so far as to curse the very *idea* of love as something primitive and vulgar. I felt rather like a young boy who doesn't want anything to do with little girls. I was more *agüitado* than ever. I dedicated the minutes and hours of the afternoon to forming retrospective images of her, anything that would reconstruct her in my mind: silhouettes, subtle movements . . . Yes, it's the most typical manifestations of love that offer us some consolation. It all happened to me just as I'd been trying to penetrate the intestinal Leviathan of *Les Misérables*, which seemed impossible at first. I preferred instead to take up my notebook and to write, since there wasn't a soul in the house, and the silence was broken only by the rattle of our air conditioner.

Cecilio and my sister woke me up. I had fallen asleep with my notebook over my legs. I remembered everything: the entire day wasted in the fruitless search for my angel. Nevertheless, my cousin soon motivated me enough to go to the disco. We left the house at ten that night, but before we got to El Rollo, I had a change of heart and decided that I had better check for Jenny at the hotel one more time. I split off from Cecilio, got back in the blue Ford, and went in search of her. In vain. I even visited three other downtown hotels though I knew in my heart that I wasn't going to find her at any of them. All told, I lost two hours in running around the city in circles. Disheartened, I went back to El Rollo. It was there—just after entering and before I could work my way out onto the dance floor—that I saw them. Marcelo and Jenny. Dancing, their arms laced around each other. Just then, I felt the pressure of a hand on my shoulder. It was Cecilio.

"Hey, where the hell did you go, Augusto?" he asked angrily. "What an idiot. Don't you see that they're eating your Gringa alive?"

Dauntless, I smiled at him. I remained completely unmoved until a nondescript shadow passed in front of me: a woman, any woman, faceless, who I automatically invited to dance.

I took her to the far corner of the dance floor. Finally—awash in the multicolored lights and the thundering music—there were the four of us, which is to say, three: Marcelo, Jenny, and I. Everyone greeted each other with a camaraderie rife with a mix of hatred and affection.

"Where were you hiding?" asked Marcelo, looking every inch tall, dark, and handsome, angling his thick eyebrows.

"Just hanging out, that's all," I said, literally without missing a beat, dancing amidst the masses and putting on a hypocritical air of indifference.

I chatted a bit with Jenny while the four of us danced there in a cloud of cigarette and smoke-machine smoke. Marcelo, I realized, was not about to let her go, not even to the bathroom. I knew many Paceños who wouldn't risk letting their girls dance with their own mothers, let alone an acquaintance. We moved apart as if nothing had happened between us. Actually, everything already had: Jenny was dancing with the boy of whom I'd asked her *ex profeso* never to speak, and Marcelo was dancing with the girl who he knew I loved. In the meantime, I was with someone whom I did not want to be with: a perfect stranger. So we left the dance floor, and I thanked her and said goodnight. I went off to sit down at Cecilio's empty table while he was off dancing with some foreign girl. I was there for a long while, sleepless, alone, lost between an undrunk bottle of alcohol and the people dancing in the various kinds and colors of smoke, until finally I decided to invite a different girl to sit down with me. She accepted, and we chatted away for over an hour: I feigned a certain pleasantness while being careful to duck down every time I caught a glimpse of Marcelo and Jenny out on the floor (now arm in arm, now chatting away happily) their bodies—soft vessels for emotions—very close indeed.

I don't suppose that anybody was much concerned with me at that moment, but for my part I was watching Cecilio as though—perhaps because of the alcohol and cigarettes—I was looking through some sort of filter. He was talking with a robust, dark-haired girl whose skin was the color of toast. He had met her earlier that night, and I could tell he was looking for the right opportunity to kiss her. Then Marcelo sat down nearby, blatantly caressing one of Jenny's arms while she—serene and secure—pressed up against him. They were touching and teasing each other right in front of me—apologizing, excusing themselves for interrupting my conversation with another woman—until finally their lips met and they began, shamelessly and urgently, to grope at each other through their clothes. Meanwhile—no matter how hard I tried to pass unnoticed, to be invisible—*I couldn't help but watch them,* despite chatting away as if nothing were going on. My eyes—if anyone could make them out in the darkness—were like those of a deranged man. I just couldn't understand her, Jenny, I couldn't penetrate her irrational world. Just two days before, we were kissing on the paddleboat, we were . . . And now this.

It was at that moment when I felt the first chills wash over me. The first symptoms of God. First, a vague image of Christ the Redeemer appeared in my mind, an image of Christ pardoning man. Immediately I wanted to reject it: the face, the almost iridescent eyes, the white sackcloth robe, the leather belt, and the fine, delicate, bluish hands of Our Lord. I had a dark feeling of harassment (coming from above) in my chest. A loving harassment. A moment later a certain innate antipathy towards Christ—who had disappeared only to return—was streaming through my pores. Like a litany, I repeated the verse that I'd written at home a few days before; I repeated all the hundreds of verses and sentences that I'd written in my life up to that point. But it was all for naught, my Lord. I quickly came to understand Your presence, the presence of a benevolent, merciful Christ. Although I was physically there in the club, I—Augusto—had left. I was off in some remote place.

Meanwhile, the lordly Christ went about pardoning men, diligent, serene, and composed. I watched him walking, touching faces, clearing a path with the lightest touch of his slender fingers. I averted my eyes and instead pictured His face, contemplated His chest, where His heart shone like a tiny sun. An incandescent light permeated first His flesh and then His robe, though it did not burn; rather, it illuminated His tired and handsome face. He walked towards me, gazed upon me, and I could no longer look away from His eyes, His pallid lips, murmuring, silently calling my name, indicating something incomprehensible, something that I nevertheless understood intuitively, as though he were branding my skin with a divine, subtle language. Something unnamable took my head in its hands; something that—for an instant—had a name, a title: Christ. Thus He restored His name to me, our ineffable Lord.

The smell, the taste of my own mouth, the sounds in my ears . . . everything was adjudged once and for all in the name of Christ, the word of Christ, and the Verb Incarnate that *is* Christ. It was the advent of the Ineffable upon me, introducing himself within my body, throughout every inch of it, and completely without my permission. A manifestation, radiating an inaudible power. A fire growing ever stronger as it whipped across my back and arms; that fire held me fast, numb and stiff in my seat, as if I were drunk or too lost to venture a step. My face burned, my forehead, and even my eyes. It felt like live coals were burning inside me, constantly being fanned, and I couldn't leave, couldn't flee, couldn't say a single word. I was fixed solidly to my chair by a force that overflowed all the spaces on earth and over-whelmed life, the spirit, and the flesh, expanding them, lifting them upward, stripping them momentarily of their gravity, their weight, their base and earthly humility. Yes, it was the Ineffable, now I know, showing Himself, there with me in time, granting itself a name that even I—the greatest skeptic—could understand and grasp: Christ. The Ineffable One manifested himself, showed Himself to me, so that I might hold Him and seek His protection, so that I might find consolation in His purifying, vivifying spirit, His essence of life.

Lord, it was You who interrupted there the festival of men, the dance, the party, the embracing, the drinking; You, crossing that abode of sin and presenting Yourself to me there as if in a burning bush, as if to Moses. What I experienced there—what was exposed to my unsuspecting eyes—was the Ineffable One, repeating his name: Christ. I didn't loosen my grip on my new woman's shoulder; she was my last human refuge. The burning wouldn't allow me to let go, to budge from that spot. Surely, I imagined, this unknown girl feels the vivifying heat of the Paraclete, the same Comforter who God had sent down to His son—me, Augusto Roldán—the hardened, faithless sinner.

Finally I was able to gather myself enough to stand, and, still in a bit of a haze, I made my way over to Cecilio. I asked that he take me home. Maybe he thought I was completely drunk. He hesitated, I pressed, and finally he agreed to take me. He said something to the girl he was with, as did I—I said goodbye without even looking her in the eyes—and we exited quickly, making our way through the smoke and music of that club, which had seemed impenetrable to all but God Himself. I had forgotten about Jenny, the Angelic cause of my conversion, and I had forgotten about Marcelo. What I hadn't done was make amends before I left. I needed fresh air, a blast of salt-sea air like a slap in the face, clearing my head, stretching the cramped muscles of my body.

We climbed in my uncle's sky-blue Ford; Cecilio drove without so much as a word, though his eyes contained sparks of disgust. I had put a stop to his game, his conquest of the night. We drove the length of the waterfront with the car windows open. I could just make out a tiny group of stars floating out in the offing, cold and elusive. Finally, some fifteen minutes later, we reached the house. Without so much as a glance, Cecilio dropped me off. Only after I was walking up the front steps did I hear his voice yelling after me, *You're completely gone, cabrón.*

I didn't answer; didn't even turn around. I just waited for him to leave, to return to the club, to the place where he belonged and in which I—Augusto Roldán—never could. I had become someone else: yes, Augusto was something else, a new man, born again. So I waited for Cecilio and the sound of the Ford to disappear into the immense night, and then I crossed the street. I walked down the path that led to the boat launch and the enveloping waves, and I sat down on a rock on the only strip of beach to be found.

I was something else, something truly different from what I'd been the day before. And I cried, I cried all night long, like I'd never done before, and without reason, simply because, yes, it felt good, cleansing my soul and my spirit, until at long last I saw the sun rising in the East.

Nihil obstat
Imprimatur

33

When he awoke, still in that absurd state of warm lethargy, Ricardo tried to recover some hint of his ignominious dream. He was able with great difficulty to gather a few glimpses, and, bit by bit, he was able to reconstruct nearly the entire thing. Nevertheless, a moment later he discovered—much to his dismay—that the boy lying next to him was gone, as was Roberta's peaceful breathing. Rubbing his eyes, Ricardo realized and understood: he had lost his character's face. She would never come back into view . . .

He rolled over: there, on his pillow, were two envelopes with handwritten designations. He switched on the bedside lamp, and read what it was scrawled across their flaps: *for Ricardo* and *for Elías*. He knew everything at once, without needing to open them. For him . . . a farewell that did not need to be read; for Elías, a letter (perhaps amiable), a love poem, a final goodbye, a simple and pure lamentation . . . it could have been any of these or none. For a moment he thought about opening it, but he stopped himself. He should go, meet the man, deliver the missive personally. Now, more than ever, he was obliged—compelled, really—to visit Las Rémoras, to get to know that small seaside town that he himself had invented, to contemplate it with his own eyes, never to read about it nor write about it ever again. But . . . first he felt the need to sit down and fiddle with his manuscript. He sat for a few moments, pensive, until finally it came to him . . . *Las Rémoras* ought to contain at least one dream. Of course! It's a part of life. And he would put it in right away, even before continuing the story of Roldán and La Gringa, since that story was coming out so precipitously, and after it was finished, it would be much more difficult to slip the dream in . . .

Without any further delay, he opened the curtains and the wide hotel windows and went over to the simple writing desk next to the unmade bed. He poured himself a glass of water and sat down for a fit of writing, lining up the tiny letters in his notebook with the pages torn out. In about an hour, he'd composed a dream for his fictional writer—giving him his own ominous, vivid nightmare—which Elías the librarian would (of course) forget as soon as he woke up in his humble library-house on Encaladores. When he saw it, when Ricardo showed it to him, maybe he would recognize the description of his own faded dream . . .

34

Elías had taken leave of the architect after the two of them read that tale of conflicted love the padre had called *A Convert's Chronicle*. He'd spent the past few hours of night deep in thought and slightly sad, until finally he succumbed to a profound sense of lethargy, and dreamed the following dream:

UCLA, an imaginary university campus, is inhabited by students and professors. In recent months it's been terrorized by a young man who everyone knew and liked well enough until he underwent a strange transformation: he started killing other students, even dismembering and eating them when it occurred to him. There aren't any reasons for what he does. It all depends on his mood. He can feel melancholy and do no harm, or, on the other hand, feel perfectly content and kill on sight. Everyone is in a state of panic, from the professors to the students and even the custodians. But nobody does a thing to stop him. The reason? They are afraid of the incomprehensible. More: deep down, nobody dares to confront their fear, nor do they want to let it leak out into daily life. To admit to such things would be to look right through this person they've known for so long. They know him so well, in fact, that it seems rather incredible that he's been capable of committing such crimes, which—recently—he seems to do at the drop of a hat. The truth is that the face of campus life has changed quite a bit; things are not the same. Fear has blocked out all the other emotions. This makes Elías—as well as everyone else there—rather dour. He's just as terrified as everyone else. Lately, the trail has cooled: they know that the killer is *somewhere on campus,* in one of the buildings, but that he never comes out unless he's looking for a kill. It's not that he's in hiding; no, he just likes to be alone, resting, away from the resentful looks of others. Killing, they understand, is a simple physiological necessity for him, and not at all an act of revenge, a sign of some kind of discontent, or even his simply being impolite. One night, on one of the most densely populated streets on campus, where couples walk, feeling safe in their numbers, flirting under a streetlight, drinking out of plastic cups, carefree and without worry, the young man appears, and casually carves up one or two . . . He does it right in front of everybody, clear in the street- and starlight, and then he calmly walks away. Nobody dares to move a muscle, to say a word. They've seen everything, and are at once terrified and thankful for not having been the victims themselves. Finally, a few hours later, fed up with having to endure this visceral fear, several of them go out in search of him. Why? Nobody knows. They're simply acting out of a need to overcome this paralyzing fear, not out of any real desire to do away with him. Nevertheless, when they are resolved, nobody tries to stop them. The twenty-three-year-old Elías—along with five other intrepid students and two brave professors—head calmly (though surely on the verge of panic) towards one of the dorms. They walk up the stairs, go down a long, lighted hallway, and sit down to wait—without a hint of impatience—in one of the innumerable bedrooms. They talk, they stifle their fear, they want to get out of there and forget everything. Elías asks how to operate a handgun, he's never fired one before. The others explain it to him, and then he picks up the only pistol between them. Finally, in a nearby room (possibly even the next one down) they hear the sound of a shower being turned on. At that moment, the two professors say goodbye and good luck, say they're heading to another part of campus to search. Elías starts to tremble when they leave, when he sees them disappear down the long hallway, and—above all—when he hears the smooth, muted sound of the shower fall silent. It's him; everyone knows it. A thread of steam floats into the room. For some reason, Elías has put down the pistol. He's not only afraid of his young classmate (they say that the killer is the youngest student on campus), but he harbors a great hatred for him as well. He's clouded now by this hate. What the young man does is certainly atrocious, but that's not what matters to Elías: it's the hatred he's held in for so long. Elías knows, in spite of everything, that the killer would never dare to hurt him. There's an insoluble bond between them. Nor is Elías capable of killing anybody tonight. He feels his fear welling up inside him; fear of the young man who's just appeared, naked but for a towel, in the doorway. The light of the room surrounds him, illuminating the steam and his damp skin. He looks at everyone, smiling; his body pale and surprisingly thin. A red circle is visible just above his nipples, and rivulets of water drip down his back. Everyone assembled in the room knows him well, has known him for years. Even the way they look at him—coupled with the calm, emotionless manner in which the young murderer stares them down—is almost enough to make one suppose that they understand and accept the killer for what he is, endorsing the strange sense of immunity that he's enjoyed since beginning his career as a murderer. His demeanor and their silence seem to indicate that he can kill with impunity whenever he feels that particular, organic need; he's the only one who's allowed to do it, and whenever it becomes convenient, though unfortunately—very much so—it means that all of them assembled there must die, one by one. On entering the room, he drops his towel and opens a dresser drawer in search of underwear. He still hasn't seen the pistol, or perhaps he just doesn't pay it any heed: in any event, *his life is assured and he cannot die, for to do so would be to contradict natural law, even divine law.* He is the sacrificial priest of the holocaust, and all the others are his victims. Nobody can—nor do they want—to interfere with this harmony. And if the party gathered there thought so at first—either out of madness or anger—then now they are certainly repenting of it. The killer knows. Everyone looks at him with fear in their eyes; they want to flee even though their young killer is smiling amiably, greeting them as if nothing was wrong, as if someone else were the killer. But it's just at the moment he leans against the dresser and starts to put on his shorts that Elías picks up the gun and points it at him. At first the young man looks skeptical, bored even, and he yawns as he finishes pulling them up. Elías aims directly at his chest, afraid to miss, though he's standing no more than a yard away. It's a joke, the young man complains, while the others try to imagine what he—the killer—is himself imagining. No, this is no joke; Elías is brutally afraid, but he can't back down. However wrong it may be, however damaging to universal harmony, he must kill the young priest. He clicks off the safety, aims at his chest, and squeezes the trigger . . . but there is no sound, no smell of powder, no bullet. The killer, still yawning, though suddenly alert, reaches for his own pistol, which he'd been hiding in the underwear drawer. He points it at Elías, who (regretting his role in all this, regretting even being there) has already chambered a new round and fired again after having taken aim a second time—with the same slow and deliberate determination not to miss—at the young man's chest. He staggers, trying to stand firm, and for one terrifying moment it looks like he might be able to get off a shot himself, but then the pistol falls from his hand and he falls to the floor, dampening the carpet with blood. Elías looks at the crumpled body there on the ground, and levels the barrel of the pistol at it again. From perhaps six feet away, and with his rage and fear invading his heart—standing there in front of the others, who watch, terrified and incredulous at what he's done—he fires into the fallen body, perforating it, riddling the young flesh with bullets, until one of the company reaches for his hand, stops him, shouting:

"Enough, Elías, that's enough! You don't know who it is! Stop already!"

And it wasn't until just then that Elías was able to see the young assassin clearly: Ricardo, it was Ricardo, the same Ricardo he'd known his entire life. Now he could see the young man clearly, the man he hadn't been able to recognize before. Nor is it until that moment that Ricardo, with his last breath, realizes that he was the campus killer all along.

Elías the dreamer, at this moment, is inseparable from Elías the shooter; together, fused, they contemplate the body on the ground. Elías throws the pistol away and leaves the room, runs down the lighted hallway, and before reaching the outer doors of the building he ducks into an empty room to hide. He leans against a table, hides his face in his hands, and begins to moan and curse. He lets loose with an uncontrollable, hysterical sobbing. He has never suffered so much, never built up so much pain in so short a time. Through clenched teeth, he says:

"How could I forget that it was Ricardo? How could I forget him now, if I never forgot him in life?"

35

Ricardo was shocked, stunned. Writing down the dream had turned out to be more of a revelation for himself than a simple addendum to the story of Elías. On waking, of course, the dream had been nothing: it had been lost from view. It had only begun to take shape when he decided to weave together those threads he'd been keeping inside of him all this time. But then, yes, the disturbing nature of the dream was revealed in all its clarity: it was a nightmare in which the villain, the monster, was none other than himself, and yet he somehow hadn't managed to figure this out until the end, when he read his own name on the page . . .

After a good long while and one cold shower, Ricardo decided he was ready to continue, and he set himself to further developing the link between the padre and La Gringa.

36

As we've already seen, Elías had spent the previous afternoon with Iginio Jasso, the two of them reading *A Convert's Chronicle* until the setting sun took them by surprise. Then the architect went to return the stack of papers to Santa. It must have been around 7:30 or 8:00, since the sky was like a funeral pyre, a hearth where indigo flames struggled with black. Elías took his leave and headed directly home. He'd barely opened his front door when he was overwhelmed by the insufferable haze that had welled up inside him: he fell to the floor without will and without strength, exhausted from the day and the funerals.

When he woke up the next morning he'd forgotten all the details of his dream. He was certain that he'd had it, but now could find no trace of it in his mind—only a certain sad after-taste, something disconsolate, the sense that it had been some-thing that it would've been better not to dream.

He left the house and made his way towards the only place it was worthwhile to visit at that time of day: the rundown Alto-zano, which is what they called the little sacristy where padre Roldán lived, and where he officiated on the weekends. The writer wanted to know more about him—because the padre had, in a way, become a fictional character—and Elías wanted to find out how this character was doing after his fall the previous day. But most of all (though he might not have wanted to admit it), he wanted to find out more about the Gringa from the story, that Angel of Our Lord. So without another thought—and without so much as a bite of breakfast—he was on his way . . .

It was 10:30 in the morning, and the heat of the day was already beginning to soak the skin of the townspeople. Elías turned off Encaladores, passed Sardineros, and was walking along the waterfront when he was taken with a tremendously important thought: something that stopped him in his tracks, something that he hadn't yet considered. He'd just realized that he wouldn't be able to know the contents of his dream until Ricardo arrived in Las Rémoras and let him read it, and for that reason—if noth-ing else—he would have to get him there as soon as possible. He didn't have the slightest idea what Ricardo had written about the dream, because—among other impediments—he, Elías, *hadn't written what Ricardo had, even though he had lived it*. The writer was consumed by the need to read Ricardo's dream. When he finally did, he told himself, he'd be able to recognize it, to know whether it was really his . . . And if it was, then the fear would be that young Urrutia would be—at every moment—writing what he, Elías, was actually living, which (of course!) was patently improbable.

Maybe it was all just riddles and guessing-games, Elías said to himself as he started walking again. Just false suppositions dragged in by the scruff of their necks by that dream. But who the hell am I, he wondered, to think that one person can ever know the dreams of another? Was it only because he'd written earlier that Ricardo, "In about an hour . . . composed a dream for his fictional writer—giving him his own ominous, vivid night-mare—which Elías the librarian would (of course) forget as soon as he woke up in his humble library-house on Encaladores. When he saw it, when Ricardo showed it to him, maybe he would rec-ognize the description of his own faded dream . . ."? Impossible, absolutely impossible, and completely insane to boot. An utter failure. But (he whispered softly to himself) I have to wait, I have to wait and hope . . .

Suddenly, surprisingly, he found himself standing in front of the only house in Las Rémoras with a doorknocker, rapping the door with it mechanically. He'd reached the Altozano. Even more surprisingly, the door was opened by the old doctor Díaz Gros. They greeted each other warmly, with a hug that anyone who didn't know the doctor would have thought was false and exaggerated.

"How have you been, muchacho?" the doctor asked. "Recov-ering?"

Elías understood he was referring to Roberta, and nodded: what else was there to do? He didn't much feel like explaining himself, like unrolling the parchment of his feelings, reading them aloud, and then rolling it all back up again. What a task that would be! And what difference would it make anyway? The sooner he forgot about Roberta, the better. It's what he had to do, though no one else seemed to be helping out in that regard.

"How is the padre?" Elías asked.

"Just a little bit rattled. He has a nasty bump on the back of his head," replied the doctor with a wry grin. "But you can come in. He's awake."

Elías made his way into the house, towards the blue door in the back, while the figure of the doctor—with his white and thinning hair—followed behind. Díaz Gros was taller and wider than the writer, but he was by no means fat. He was barrel-chested and short-armed, and his gait was slow and majestic: the gait of a wise, peaceful, and steady man. He always wore a pair of tortoiseshell glasses, the lenses tinted green and slightly smudged, and he always dressed in a white checkered suit, with cufflinks closing off his shirtsleeves despite the Las Rémoras heat. He was never without a tie—usually red, though sometimes pink—and always carried himself with a sense of carefree old-fashionedness; or better yet, carefree meticulousness.

Elías opened the blue door, walked down a short hallway, and finally—after passing through a thin, empty opening, saw the silent figure of Roldán in repose. He contemplated the padre's old, gray body lying there and holding a towel full of ice to his head. When he saw Elías there, he lowered the ice pack and rested it on the edge of the bed. A crucifix hung on the wall above his headboard. In the wicker chair at his side sat Santa, broad and dark, rocking back and forth, looking even more sorrowful than she had at the funeral. She stood up for just a moment to take the damp towel from the padre and then sat back down.

"How are you, padre?" Elías asked as he made his way over to the edge of the bed.

"Recovering, Elías. I'm recovering . . ." Roldán said, mustering up the strength to speak despite his obvious exhaustion. "But now that you're here, let's set aside the protocol and cut to the chase. Tell me: what do you think? Did you like it or not? Be honest with me; no sugarcoating, no beating around the bush."

The writer stood there, a bit taken aback, more confused than anything. He looked to Santa. She was still rocking slightly and her head was bowed deeply, as if counting the broken floor tiles. There was humility in the old black woman's eyes.

"Santa told me this morning that the two of you—you and the architect, I mean—have read my *Chronicle*," said the padre in a single breath.

"Yes, we read it," Elías said. Out of the corner of his eye he glanced at the doctor, who was standing close by, listening. Surely he must have known about the *Chronicle* too.

"Well, what do you think? You're the expert on these things, after all. And don't think that I can't take criticism, my son. I'm just happy that it was interesting enough for you to read it through . . ."

Elías wasn't sure how to respond. What sort of tone should he use? So that he wouldn't be lying to the padre, but wouldn't be indulging him either?

"I liked it, padre. In general I liked it. It does an excellent job of recreating certain La Paz landscapes. I particularly liked the parts about the paddleboats, the waterfront, and the club. Marcelo is a very well constructed character—perhaps the best of the bunch—a real son of a . . ." He caught himself before finishing the sentence. "He comes across as perverse and cruel, just as he should, but he does so without making him seem like a Manichaean character. Solón and Cecilio, on the other hand, seem rather diffuse to me . . . For one thing, you don't make enough of a distinction between the author and the narrator. They're one and the same; rather, they're both you, the one who lends the story its more or less anachronistic tint, with those quaint little words that you like so much, like in a Galdós novel. Nevertheless, there's something about the ending, padre, something that—for me—just didn't fit . . . It's that I really just don't understand how a man can undergo that kind of transformation overnight. There's something hidden there . . ."

"What?" asked the padre, intrigued.

"Some hidden fact, some scene that isn't there, that you've cut down or thrown out or something. I can't say for sure what or where."

"Something *obscene*? Is what you're trying to say?" Díaz Gros offered playfully.

"Yes," Elías said. "To be more precise, I think that there's some passage—some part of the relationship between you and Jenny—that you don't want to tell us about. Because—if I may—it seems to me a bit overwritten and gratuitous to think that two people can fall in love like that without any sort of history between them. Do you understand, padre?"

"Yes, I understand what you're saying, but what do you think about what's actually *in* the story?"

"I'm just not convinced that a man could change his entire life because of a woman . . ."

"*Thanks* to a woman, Elías, not because of one. That's what you're failing to understand." Rolán went on in a psalmody voice: "And you have to remember, she was an Angel."

"So, thanks to some Gringa (I mean, thanks to the Angel), you say your life was changed, right? But wasn't it actually God who effected the change? And if it wasn't Him, padre, then who?" Elías asked rather tactlessly. "Couldn't it have been the limits of your own frustration that brought about your conversion? Failed love, I mean? Have you tried to take a few steps back and look at things objectively?"

"Do you want to know something really shocking, Elías?" The padre paused to catch his breath. "Many years ago, after I'd already become a priest, I realized that God didn't exist." He paused once more before finishing, "Nevertheless, I believe in Him. And I assure you, this is no contradiction. When I came to this realization, I also discovered that I'd never be able to live without Him. In other words . . ."

". . . in other words, it would be impossible to live life knowing that the very thing you've lived for—that which gives meaning to your life—doesn't exist," finished Elías.

"Exactly," Roldán said. "And in the same vein, don't you think that it pains me more to know that He doesn't exist than it would have terrified me had I simply stopped *believing* in Him?"

"The faith of the coal miner," mused Elías.

"So it's not so much that your faith has died, Augusto," interjected the doctor, "than that God Himself has ceased to exist. Is that it?"

"More or less," the padre responded, fatigued. "And so I say to you both that I'm aware of more things than you can imagine."

Doctor Díaz Gros, and Elías were still not quite ready to believe the padre's confession. After a minute or two of expecting Roldán to go on, the writer asked:

"So now what's going to happen?"

"What's going to happen? I'm afraid I don't understand, Elías," said the padre.

"Now that she's here. Your angel, I mean." He fell silent, and then continued on with a slight wavering in his voice: ". . . right? I never would have imagined that Jenny was the madam of the house, that the Gringa from your *Chronicle* was the same Gringa who ran Inés's brothel. This world isn't small, it's tiny!"

"Well, yes, now you know. That's why she came to Las Rémoras. It certainly wasn't to see me!" he said, and laughed. "Although one might have guessed that she'd come down for Inés's funeral, I must admit it took me completely by surprise. It's the years . . . so many years, you know." He seemed to be emerging from beneath a centuries-old shroud of dust. "It was only quite recently that I found out from Inés herself the true identity of La Gringa. Just as you did. My son, up until then I had no idea. I hope someone closes that rat hole now."

Neither Elías nor Díaz Gros—both of whom had been assiduous clients of Inés—said a word. Instead, they exchanged complicitous looks. But only the doctor spoke, this time to the writer:

"She's on her way. She told Santa and I about an hour ago."

Roldán must have been nervous, then, but he was hiding it well. Yes, despite the implications of Jenny's impending visit, the padre looked quite composed. Santa looked up from the floor a moment and then looked at the doctor. He walked a few steps over to a sofa and sat down: he was waiting for La Gringa's arrival, just like the padre, and now the writer. Everyone at the Altozano was on edge.

"Of course," Elías said suddenly, breaking the almost sepulchral silence that had, until then, been stirred only by the creaking of Santa's chair. "You realize, padre, that your cousins are coming as well?"

"My cousins? Cecilio and Solón?" This time the padre did look surprised. "How do you know? Where did you find this out?"

"That's one of the things I came to tell you. They heard that you were . . . not well, and they decided to take advantage of the occasion to visit you. Has it been long since you've seen them, padre?"

"Years. The same as with Jenny . . ."

"Well, they left La Paz this afternoon. From what I heard, they'll probably stop in Loreto to eat. You'll see them today; that should pick you up a little bit."

There came a knock at the door. Díaz Gros jumped up like a man half his age, scattering his thin white hair across his forehead. Roldán quickly straightened his collar and cuffs, smoothed his bed-sheet, and licked his palm, which he then used to flatten his forelocks. Santa remained unchanged, eyes on the floor, counting the tiles, biding her time, ever faithful and humble. As Díaz Gros made his way down the hall to answer the door, Elías took over his spot on the sofa, feeling rather like he was attending a big film premiere. Of course, he'd never been to such a thing before, because there were no theaters in Las Rémoras.

Despite (or perhaps because of) the excitement and anticipation, everyone went quiet when they heard the doctor's voice greeting their guest. Regardless of the sense of suspense that must have been welling up in all of them—Santa couldn't read, but still she was quite astute enough to know what was going on—the doctor was able to remain composed and immediately invited her in. They heard footsteps in the hall for what seemed like an eternity, until finally they all were met with the image of a thin, blond woman in her mid-to-late forties. She stepped into the room tenuously.

Meanwhile, Elías and the doctor were looking back and forth between Roldán's eyes and Jenny's with the sort of quick horizontal glances usually reserved for tennis matches. Augusto, they realized, had undergone something of a transformation, in his face, in his expression, in his soft, pale cheeks. All the padre's preparations—all the precautions he had taken—turned out to be in vain.

"How do you feel, Augusto?" La Gringa asked in Spanish, without even the hint of an accent. She seemed quite informal—brazen, even—considering that she was speaking to the padre of Las Rémoras.

"Much better, Jenny, thanks," Roldán answered, and the others suddenly realized that they might as well have disappeared.

"It's good to see you again."

"The pleasure is mine," was Rolán's immediate, involuntary, and sincere response. He went on: "I didn't know that you were the owner of that house, Jenny. Inés only told me this past year. But why? Why a brothel? And why here, in Las Rémoras?"

"It's a long story, and that's not why I've come. I just want to wish you well. I hope you recover soon; the doctor has already told me that it's nothing serious, just a bump on the head," she lied. It was obviously a pretty horrible contusion. La Gringa wisely forced a smile to her lips. This mature, intelligent woman who could feign a smile of any kind depending on the requirements of a given situation was exactly as Elías had pictured her. Roldán had described her perfectly too. The padre was a pretty good writer after all.

"How's your little girl?" he asked.

"Little? She's already a woman," La Gringa replied, chuckling, with just a hint of tartness in her voice. "She's expecting her first child."

"I would like to meet her. And . . . ?" Roldán stammered.

"Marcelo?"

"Yes, Marcelo."

"I married him."

"I heard. My cousins told me about it just after the wedding. Remember my cousins?"

"I remember Cecilio well. Solón I only have a vague recollection of. He was rather shy."

"Yes, Cecilio was Marcelo's friend. He followed him everywhere; he was like a little lapdog." Roldán seemed to enjoy the memory.

They fell silent for a moment and just looked at each other. Not even Santa wanted to disturb the moment, and stopped rocking in her chair, as though she could tuck all their words in her lap. Jenny said:

"I got a divorce several years ago, Augusto. The idea for the brothel came shortly thereafter, if that's what you want to know. You weren't here in Las Rémoras at the time. In any case, nobody knew me here (which was important!) except for a few of the girls that Inés sent from Tijuana. She was always in charge of everything. That was the arrangement. As you can see, it worked. Well, it worked up until now. I didn't want to come back, and even less so when I found out you were here."

"Yes. Right after the seminary I was sent to Querétaro, then Los Mochis, and finally I put in for a transfer here. To be near La Paz. I love this place, Jenny."

"I know," she said. "That's why I never came, Augusto. I continued to live in San Diego with my aunt. My mother's sister, remember? She's quite old now. Dying. My mother is too. Besides . . ."

She fell silent, caught on the words she was about to say. Finally she mustered the courage to say, "You, the Altozano, this little church . . . you're all like my enemies. Not literally, of course, but from a certain point of view, yes."

"Enemies of whom?" the padre asked, embarrassed.

"Of my house, my brothel. We're two opposing factions, Augusto. I'm sure you understand."

"I do, Jenny, but you have to know that you're not my enemy, and that your house . . ." He paused, searching for the right words. "Are you thinking of closing it?"

"No, actually I've come here to settle up a few things with the town council. I spoke with an absolutely unbearable young man named Sigüenza, and now I'm on my way back to San Diego. Josefina will be left in charge. She's the new madam of the house, like Inés before her. I've spoken with her and with the girls, and gave them all their instructions. The only thing that hasn't been tied up is that Roberta has taken off without warning . . ." Her voice wavered here, and she stopped to reflect. "I'm sorry; I don't suppose these are things that you want to hear about. I doubt they matter much to you anyhow."

"I beg to differ. Of course they matter to me."

They fell silent again. Perhaps there was nothing else to be said? But there was. In fact, it may have been why they both fell silent at the same time. It was only then that La Gringa looked around the room: she noticed the damp eyes of the doctor, then turned to face the writer for the first time. He looked familiar. Elías, in turn, looked back at her, transfixed.

"You're Elías?" she asked.

He nodded. Where did she know him from? He'd seen her somewhere before too. Jenny wiped away a tear as she turned to Santa next, who—once again—had her eyes fixed on the floor tiles, though she'd long since stopped counting. Finally, La Gringa looked at the crucifix on the wall above the bed, and piously crossed herself. Elías couldn't help but feel triumphant: *just think what the architect would give to have heard what I did here today! Caramba! What luck!* But his train of thought was derailed by a question the padre asked . . . a question intended to break up that burning silence:

"And when is your son due?"

"My daughter, you mean?" asked La Gringa anxiously. "In two months, or maybe a bit sooner."

"And who's the father? Who did she marry?" asked the smiling, crestfallen padre.

Knowing that her answer was bound to shock everyone, Jenny steeled herself before answering:

"Marcelo. And just so you know, Augusto, they're not married. They just live together." Had even that limited description been too explicit for that company? She studied everyone's faces, paused to reflect, and then said: "Adiós, Augusto. I'm glad I was able to come by and see you. Take care of Josefina and the others for me, if you can. But above all take care of *him*: you know it's what I want most in life . . ."

She spun on her heel and walked deliberately down the hall. She didn't say goodbye to anybody, leaving them all with blank, ignorant looks and open mouths, and without the faintest idea of who this mysterious *him* could be. A moment later, they all heard the sound of the front door closing. Everyone was still a bit embarrassed by what they'd heard, so much so in fact that they couldn't manage to hate anybody at all . . . any of the primary players in La Gringa's story. Finally Elías mustered the courage to get up from the couch, and—also without saying goodbye—he walked out of the padre's bedroom and out of the Altozano. He had little time to lose if he wanted to write about the encounter between Ricardo and Roldán's cousins, but first he would have to stop and send out a telegram.

37

By the time Ricardo finished the two chapters he was working on—the one describing Elías's dream, and the one in which all the remaining protagonists of *Las Rémoras* meet at the Altozano—it was already nearly noon. He was starving, but he was also eager to get a bus ticket out of town that same afternoon. He had to get to Las Rémoras as soon as possible, because there were so many things happening there, and all of them were worthy of inclusion in a novel. But in the end, Ricardo surrendered to his stomach and decided to eat something first. He wouldn't make it very far if he was running on fumes. There was a seafood stand at the corner. On ice and under glass lay a selection of abalone, squid, clams, oysters, and shrimp. A man was silently and swiftly filling plastic cups with seafood medleys and topping them off with vegetables, cocktail sauce, and chili before garnishing the whole thing with a slice of lemon. A heaping serving, plucked from the sea that very morning. This was the Paceño's standard breakfast; either that or *camaronillas*, or—the staple—savory fish tacos. Ricardo ordered a squid cocktail with oyster crackers and a large bottle of water, and he ate it all right there, standing on the sidewalk, just like the half-dozen other hungry passersby. This was the very spot where—in *Bodily Prayers*—Federico's family had taken their walks, while Federico himself would spy on his aunt (if indeed he ever truly did so). Ricardo laughed at the memory of that scene. As he chewed thoughtfully, he asked the vendor the way to the bus station. It wasn't far, just four or five blocks. He paid for his food and walked off in the direction the man had indicated. It was getting hotter—blazing even. He hadn't even made it halfway down the block before his underarms were soaked and sticky. Still with his barley water in hand—which he sipped from occasionally—he reached the station, which turned out to be not so much a station as an unpaved plot of ground were busses gathered to pick up passengers. There wasn't even a covered waiting area. The monstrous rumbling of the busses pervaded everything, while all around him people were boarding and disembarking. Now a bit nervous, Ricardo walked towards a booth where two women were dispatching tickets through a window. It was being mobbed by city folks who—like him—were eager to leave the city as soon as possible. Shouting, jostling, with children crying, indignant folks young and old who nobody was attending to, two ladies trying to cut their way into the line, people generally crowding one another, and all the while a bus belching a cloud of exhaust into the faces of everyone gathered there. But the two women in the booth were used to it all by now, and weren't bothered in the least; rather, they showed all the calm in the world—or all the calm that was necessary—and only attended to those people tenacious enough to hold their own against the tumult. Ricardo tossed his empty cup in a trashcan, steeled himself for a moment, and then dived into that thick human jungle. After weathering several jabs and knocks and other absurd tribulations—without flagging for a moment, and with one final shove to clear away a competitor—he found himself in front of the two women blinking behind their window and asked for a seat on the next bus bound for Las Rémoras.

"What?" asked one, smacking her gum. "Las *what*?"

"One ticket to Las Rémoras, please. On the next bus leaving." Ricardo was almost begging.

"We don't have tickets for Las Rémoras, not that I know of, anyway. Wait one moment . . ." Dubious, she turned to her friend in that tiny square of space, double-checking, and then turned back to Ricardo to say: "No, we don't have any tickets to Las Rémoras, because Las Rémoras doesn't exist."

"Of course it does," he insisted, discouraged and still being buffeted by the pushing and shoving of people trying to dislodge him from his coveted place by the glass. "It's after Loreto and Nopoló, less than an hour from Mulegé . . ."

"Look, we don't have it on any of our maps, so we don't have any busses going there," said the woman, getting a bit upset. She furrowed her brow and was working her gum so hard that it had gotten stuck in her teeth. "If you want a ticket for Mulegé, then let me know, because I've got people waiting."

Ricardo was about to say yes, just put him on the bus and he'd figure it out from there—maybe ask the driver to drop him off along the road—when a hulking brute of a man lifted him out of the line, while another large man in a T-shirt took his place in line. Not ready to surrender, and still dazed from the heat, Ricardo prepared himself for another dive into that circle of smog and humanity, but just at that moment he felt a powerful hand grab him by the shoulder. He whipped around to find a blond man in his late forties standing there.

"Excuse me, but aren't you Ricardo? My brother and I understand that you're trying to get to Las Rémoras." Another man with curly blond hair stood at his side: just as muscular, though slightly shorter and perhaps friendlier than the speaker. "That just happens to be where we're going."

Ricardo couldn't speak. He was completely undone. He looked from one to the other, and there could be no doubt about it: he knew them down to the last detail. It was Cecilio and Solón there in front of him, actual characters from the *Chronicle* and from *Bodily Prayers*! Still stunned, he let himself be led by the hand through the crowd towards wherever the two brothers were going. He had only just read (or written, via Elías) *A Convert's Chronicle* and *Bodily Prayers*, and now here they were, in the flesh. All of his pent-up stress and frustration gave way to joy as he beheld at long last the faces of the two brothers, those cousins to Augusto and also to Federico.

"So how is it that you happen to be heading to Las Rémoras?" he finally asked them, though he—more than anyone—could hazard a pretty good guess. To his surprise, the shorter of the two—surely Cecilio—said:

"The padre there is our cousin, and it's been years since we've seen him. Plus, we received a telegram very early this morning informing us that he's in very serious condition."

"But I thought he wasn't so bad? Who sent the telegram? Doctor Díaz Gros?"

"No, it was Elías, the writer," Solón said. "He even asked us to swing by the Los Arcos hotel to pick you up. Somehow he knew you'd be staying there. When we didn't find you in your room, we decided to try the bus depot. But tell me, how do you know our dear Augusto?"

"Actually, I've never met him. I've only heard of him . . ." *and of the two of you*, he was about to say, before deciding that discretion was a better course of action.

"Then you must know Elías," Cecilio said with an air of understanding as he picked his way down the sidewalk (and around the issue at hand).

"Not exactly, but it doesn't matter," Ricardo replied. "When do you think we'll be hitting the road?"

"Right now. Actually we're in a bit of a rush," Solón answered, quickening the pace. "Can we swing by the hotel right away and pick up your bags . . . ?"

"All I have is a satchel with a few knickknacks in it. But thanks, yes. That ticket lady was really unbearable, and standing up to that crowd was quite . . ."

Just then, Ricardo found himself standing in front of the sky-blue Ford. Clearly Ross and Roldán had taken their cues from reality itself, or else (why not?) it was reality being influenced—as some novelists say—by their writing. In any event, Solón opened the door and got in the back seat, leaving Ricardo to take the front next to Cecilio, who from the looks of things was the regular driver.

"And the car?" asked Ricardo.

"A '64 Ford. Good-looking set of wheels, eh?" Cecilio winked. "My father left it to me when he died."

"He didn't leave it to you," countered his brother. "You took it."

"Fine, fine . . ." muttered Cecilio as he pulled out, carelessly, nearly hitting a pedestrian.

Less than three minutes later, they were pulling up to Los Arcos. Ricardo asked them to wait with the car while he entered the lobby—the same lobby where, twenty or twenty-five years ago, Jenny had been waiting for Augusto with a sack of tacos in her hand—ran up the stairs, entered his room, and gathered up his bundle of clothes, his *Las Rémoras* notebook with the missing pages, the slim little Federico Ross novella, and the two letters from Roberta. He ran back downstairs and out to the waiting Ford without so much as a thanks for the manager. His blood was roiling in his veins, but then again, how could it not be? This was his chance: soon he'd be visiting the same town that he himself had invented. He'd already spent a night with Roberta and her son, and now he was in a car with Cecilio and Solón . . . why not Las Rémoras itself? How could it not be real? In his heart he felt like laughing in the face of that ticket lady, like spitting her lack of faith right back in her face.

He got back in the car, slammed the door, and then the three of them were off, driving past the waterfront. After they left town, they would pass the beaches of Coromuel and Pichilingue—places he, Ricardo, had already visited—until they reached Puerto Balandra; there they would pick up the highway that veered from the gulf coast towards the Baja California desert. For a few minutes it seemed as if the day's heat was beginning to wane, but in reality it was just breeze whipping through the car, prompting feelings of relief and well-being. These were also due to the fact that the car was quite cozy: you could reach out your arms and touch the doors on either side, but even so there was more than enough room for the three of them. Delighted, Ricardo contemplated the desert landscape for minutes at a time, lost in the innumerable iridescent lines that rose and fell in time with the incessant rolling of the waves, which were nothing more than mirages, tricks of light. At the same time, to the left of the car, a group of gulls and gannets took to wing, which meant that they'd gotten very near to the water—the Pacific, this time—though it hadn't come into sight yet. A minute or so later, though, and Ricardo caught a glimpse—this was no mirage—of the voluminous ocean, or rather a fragment of it, where at that moment a pelican was describing a bizarre path through the sky. Nevertheless, it wasn't long before he lost sight of the Pacific—of her terribly deep, blue color—as the car angled back to the center of the peninsula and the heart of the desert. Now they were passing Ciudad Constitución; soon they would reach Ciudad Insurgentes. Cecilio stopped there just long enough to fill the Ford with gas, and then they were on their way again, weaving east and west yet always south along the thin strip of land that is Baja California. An hour later, a series of lazy, long-armed albatrosses appeared, embracing the burning, naked sky with their gray or white wings. They even blotted out the sun when they passed haughtily in front of it, never deigning to mingle with the other birds. The car must have been nearing the water again, this time the Gulf, and soon they were joined by more birds, sharp needles pricking the skin of the azure, afternoon sky. Ricardo could even make out—when the highway crested a hill, giving them a clear view of the sea, so close he could almost reach out the window and dip his fingers in it—an immense school of flying fish. He'd never seen anything like it before—never even quite believed they existed, really, until he saw them there, leaping in unison: symmetrical, instinctive. In terms of pure joy, rhythm, and grace of movement, however, they just couldn't compare with the games the dolphins played, jumping clear out of the water in groups of two, ten, twenty, defining the arabesques of the waves with bullet-like bursts of speed: turned in concert, integrating themselves into the very life of the wave, participating in its movements with such unity that they seemed almost to be wearing the wave like a watery coat, imparting a time and a measure, a compass and a sequence, to both the waves and their swimming within it. Men without faith are men who haven't *seen*, Ricardo repeated to himself, and that's why they don't believe. Solón reached out of the window and began to turn pirouettes with his hand, imitating the dolphin's movements. The air rushed through his fingers, spreading them. Ricardo turned around in his seat and watched . . . Solón and he smiled, neither one with a thought in their heads, simply letting themselves be carried along (though Cecilio was always a bit circumspect, taking his driving quite seriously, just as he had in *Bodily Prayers*)—as though on the deck of a clipper ship: wind jamming the silk above them, waves breaking under the bow—following the faded broken centerline of the highway. To the left, Ricardo saw a sign for Puerto Escondido, which was accessible only by an unpaved road. They were past it in the blink of an eye. Shortly afterward came Loreto. They still hadn't seen a single other car out on the vast, bumpy road, which was strange: it was as if they were the last living things at that latitude, the only ones who had any desire to reach Las Rémoras. Not another living soul . . . but why? Nobody else believed, thought Ricardo, as he placed his own hand out the open window, taking the wind, challenging Solón behind him with an aerial display of his own. They passed Loreto—ugly, dirty, and boring—and when they reached the outskirts of Nopoló, Solón asked about stopping for a bite to eat. It was 2:30 in the afternoon. Ricardo agreed wholeheartedly: the huge seafood cocktail he had downed for breakfast wasn't doing him any good so late in the day. They should really stop to eat, Solón repeated, though Cecilio wasn't taken with the idea. He wanted to get to Las Rémoras as soon as possible. Finally they settled on the Estado hotel, since the Isla Negra was closed for repairs (though it was obvious that no repairs were forthcoming). At 3:30, full of fish and wine, clams and abalone, fresh tortillas and refried beans, they returned to the car. Cecilio took his customary seat at the wheel, with Ricardo riding shotgun and Solón sprawled out in the back, resting his lunch. Now that the blue Ford was scudding along between desert and sea—one to their left, the other to their right—some three hours out of La Paz (in other words, one hour and twenty-six minutes outside of Las Rémoras), Ricardo heard a carefree Cecilio ask Solón if he felt up to telling the eccentric story of his love with Zoloaida, since without some form of entertainment they might die of boredom before they arrived. Solón was taken by surprise, and he hesitated for a second with his hand still doing pirouettes out the window before he pulled it back inside and sat up. He seemed ready to ignore the request, as if it had been made in jest—did he really want him to tell that story to a stranger?—but then, relaxing almost at once, and not giving another thought to his brother's strange suggestion, he said:

"If you want, Ricardo, I'll tell it to you. It might not be the most edifying thing you've ever heard, but I think you'll enjoy it. Are you sure you'd like to hear it?"

"Yes," Ricardo answered without a moment's hesitation. He was intrigued.

"And since you're a writer—yes?—maybe you'll appreciate it even more. Maybe one day you'll decide to write it down and make it into a proper story. I always wanted to be a writer myself," Solón said as he gave him another wink of complicity.

Ricardo wasn't surprised: it looked like the telegram they'd received from Elías was quite detailed indeed. But he would welcome a love story—they were absolutely his favorite kind of story—and without any further delay he insisted that Solón get on with it. Ricardo turned around in his seat to face the story-teller, made himself as comfortable as possible, and settled in to listen for the remainder of the trip.

Solón turned things over in his mind, either looking for the proper words or coming to grips with his old feelings, and finally let it roll out:

38

Elías, sitting at one of Tony's covered tables, stopped writing and brought his pen up to his lips. He was deep in thought, looking half asleep and half distressed. He looked at Pili, Sigüenza's fian-cée, with a coffee in her hand, about to cross over to the island in the middle of the street. It wasn't as hot as it usually was at that hour, since the sun was mostly hidden behind some cauliflower-shaped clouds, and a light southerly breeze was cooling the faces of the few people making their way up or down Libertad. A few sleepy lizards were basking at Pili's feet, while there in his seat Elías was pouring over the story that had been hanging over him for years. Yes, now was the time to finish it. Tony made a nervous approach. Elías asked him for the time; it was almost twenty to four, Tony told him. The three travelers—Solón, Cecilio, and Ricardo—would be there in exactly an hour and twenty-three minutes. Exactly 128.1 kilometers to go. Would they be bored on the ride? No, they'd find some way to occupy that short span of time that, for Elías, had already become infinite. What would they talk about for the next hour? There wasn't much they could have to say, he told himself. It would be a silent ride, on the whole: they would be listening patiently to the rushing surf to their right, the songs of the birds, and the terse, hazardous desert to their left. But then again, maybe Ricardo would start asking about Augusto Roldán or La Gringa, Jenny or Marcelo, or—why not?—about the two characters he'd just met, Solón and Cecilio. He'd have to have questions for them, things he'd want to know . . . However—he realized—first Cecilio would have asked his brother to tell that sad story which he—Elías—knew down to the last detail, that story he'd felt obliged to write for years and years and had been putting off in favor of Ricardo. And if they'd be arriving in Las Rémoras in an hour and twenty-one minutes (two minutes had just passed; their speed would be averaging between 85 and 90 kilometers an hour), then the story ought to take exactly that long to tell. In other words, Solón should be wrapping it up just as the three of them—yes, including the long-awaited Ricardo—would be pulling into town. Elías called Tony back over to his table and asked him to loan him his watch; perplexed, Tony unclasped and handed it over. After taking a sip of the coffee Pili had poured him (now ignoring poor Tony, who was dying to have a talk), Elías bent over his notebook like a burro following the ever-elusive carrot dangled in front of it, and, taking into account his characters' arrival time—exactly one hour twenty minutes and fourteen seconds away (in other words, 126.4 kilometers, assuming an average speed between 85 and 90 kilometers an hour)—began to write a story that he entitled:

39

km.126.4 The only thing that I needed at that moment of
(00:03)   my life—though I loved her—was to be alone,
completely alone; and the only thing that she
needed at that moment of her life—probably the
most difficult thing—was to be with me. Without a doubt, those were the hardest, most unfortunate days for both her—my beloved—and me.

km.126 How to save them? How to prevent them from
sinking into a chasm, from disappearing into the
deepest, farthest reaches of nothingness? Nor—
as she knew, as I knew—would we ever return to
our love as we had during that year, those eleven
(00:45)   precious months in which she decided, once
and forever, to leave her Lord, her Lover, Jesus

km.125 Christ. Do you understand? I had taken the
place of God in her life; she told me as much,
she whispered that to me every chance she got,
knelt down before me to repeat—with a tireless
ardor—that I was her Lord, her only god, and
that she was my servant, my slave. And I could
say the same: that Zolaida was my goddess, my
(01:25) km.124 only Lady, that I belonged to her, that I would
be her eternal slave. I never betrayed her, not
even on that one nefarious day when we had to
make a resolution, to face an alternative that—
as far as we could tell—did not exist. In other
words, our love was a form of indecipherable
equation, impossible and unsolvable. Yes, there
was nothing else to it: she *needed to be with me,*

and *I needed to be without her*, though we both
loved each other very much, let me assure you.
No, I did not betray her in any way at all. I did km.123
what I did because I loved her, because I wanted
her with all my heart and soul, and because I was
dying from the madness and the passion she   (02:15)
inspired in me. No, I never betrayed her; on the
contrary, I tried to love her even more. And she,
poor thing, felt at that time, in those wicked
days, that she had to be with me constantly in
order to survive. Maybe I didn't understand her,
although I said I did, said I understood her pain
and anguish. Maybe I didn't quite understand
the depths of her need for me—as unshakeable,
urgent, and bloody as it was. I never thought of km.122
myself as a replacement god, and—though now
we were both irreplaceable for each other, and
we knew this and even enjoyed it—I never imagined that she couldn't live without me. But it was
as if I were her heart, her breath, I don't know.
We had arrived together, with our excessive,
flagging love, at the point of death, the point of
no return, the root of everything that matters,   (03:05)
of everything that prophets both true and false
dream about when they dream about love. Without ever having imagined it, our passion had km.121
become the most painful and impossible thing.
It had to be, for it was the most unfortunate love
ever. I needed to be alone despite the fact that I
loved her—no, no, *because* I loved her!—but she,   (03:32)
on the other hand, needed to be with me because
she loved me. That's the way it was. And it wasn't
just a matter of making concessions, where one

of us could say, in her case, *It's fine, I understand, go, I'll endure this time that you need for yourself, which you need to spend alone* or, in my case, *I'll endure this time at your side, despite the fact that I* km.120 *need to be alone.* Do you understand? It wasn't easy—but I shouldn't even talk about it in terms (04:10) of ease or difficulty. Love had played a dirty trick on us, or maybe it was irate, omnipotent God himself who wanted vindication after having lost her to me, He who put us in that impossible situation, that unendurable place. Yes, God had a grudge against us. Maybe if we'd both known, if we could have seen the future, a year ahead, we would have renounced our love. Yes, because changing our lives or our passion, compromising km.119 . . . no, it was impossible. It was better for us to (04:51) have resigned ourselves to our love, the greatest gift life can bestow, and the gift that was taken away from me after only eleven months. Understand? It's because, yes, we had another, distinct, inescapable obligation to satisfy. But such is life, I suppose. Zolaida was born in Mexico City right around my nineteenth birthday. Perhaps km.118 from that moment on, our lives were going to be inextricably joined, and also—though it might seem paradoxical—completely irreconcilable. We would be inextricably *alone.* She probably turned to religion at such a young age because of her mother. Zoraida, her mother, was a Chil- (05:33) ean woman who'd lost her first love. How? He committed suicide for a very idiotic—perhaps I should say unjust—reason: he had failed his entrance exams, and so took an entire bottle of

his mother's Veronal, and two hours later (by   km.117
then he was regretting his act, they say) he was
stone dead. Zoraida sought refuge in novels, and
she quickly devoured her father's entire library,
as well as everything her friends from Santiago
could loan her. She came to Mexico City when
she was twenty-one. She enrolled at the university and then—the semester before her classes
were to begin—she found herself taken by a new   (06:12)
man. He was a thirty-two-year-old widower with
two children, and she was twenty-three by then.   km.116
They got engaged, and their wedding was the
stuff of Jane Austen novels; in other words, happily ever after. Her parents flew in from Chile,
and though Zoraida's mother didn't approve of
the fact that the groom was a widower, she eventually accepted him, and discreetly joined in the
festivities. So did his children from his previous
marriage: a little girl five or six years old, and a
little three-year-old boy. Zoraida, beautiful and   (06:44)
generous, treated them as if they were her own
children. As time went by, the children ended
up loving her more than their own father. One
fine day, when Zoraida was thirty years old,
she decided she wanted to have a child herself.
She wanted one with all her soul, even though
until that day she'd thought about it fleetingly at
most. Two years later, after a flood of begging
and pleading, her husband grudgingly consented.   km.115
Together they had a girl: my Zolaida, my god-   (07:12)
dess, my Juno, my Venus, my vestal, my canephor, my nymphet, my undine; this creature
who was born the day of my nineteenth birthday,

celebrated at El Ranchito with friends and cousins. It was a Tuesday. During our brief time together—many years after what I'm telling you here—I rifled through my memory and discov-

(07:50) km.114 ered without too much difficulty that when Zolaida was born, a Tuesday at two o'clock in the morning, it was the first night I ever got drunk. Really plastered, you know? It's been years since I've done that, though. I gave it up. Anyway, Zolaida's father wasn't a particularly wealthy man when he married for the first time, and only modestly so when he did the second (which was,

(08:11) of course, to Zolaida's mother). But nevertheless, in the days when my baby, my virgin, was born, we could say that he was a man of some small affluence, at forty-five years of age, and unsure

km.113 of what to do with the remainder of his life aside from attending to (and multiplying) this wealth. But it's interesting, you know? He feared death more than anything; death and old age. He dedicated himself to the stock market, to counting

(08:33) over and again the enormous profits he made from the sale of some refinery. He awoke every morning to read *Excélsior* conscientiously over a breakfast of orange juice, sliced papaya, and

km.112 espresso. He moved on to two eggs, bacon, and toast—monotonously, without pleasure—visited a friend of his who was separated from his wife, played dominos with a few others, and later watched movies on television. Zolaida said once

(08:59) that out of the 30-odd days in any given month, he spent half of them out of the house, or even out of the country. Where? Nobody knows—not even his wife, nor did she much want to find out. If you seek then you shall find, they say, and so sometimes it's better not to put yourself through it. You have to take responsibility for what you km.111 come to know, but also what you *want* to know. Still, my Zolaida was only three years old when her mother found out two unpleasant things back to back, neither of which she'd wanted to know: first, that her husband had at least one mistress, and second, that she didn't love him anymore. (09:40) Simply, without tears or complications, she knew in the depths of her heart that she no longer loved her husband as she had once loved him, and so it didn't even matter that he'd taken on other women. A short while later—as though it were a coincidence—a very average little novella called *Bodily Prayers* turned up. It was at this book's release party, which Zolaida's mother just happened to attend with a friend, that she met km.110 the author—a first cousin on our father's side— Federico Ross, an up-and-coming young novelist from Mexico City who was only twenty-one years (10:20) old when she was thirty-five. Can you imagine that difference in age? Do you know him? Ever heard of him? Yes? No? Not him, you say, but you know the book? So you've read that filthy little thing, huh? Well, apart from the fact that it's set in La Paz and that Cecilio and I appear in it (he claims that we gave him permission—even that we initiated things back with the whores, which, you know, isn't true), there's nothing in km.109 there worth reading. Right? You think it has some merit? It would make for an interesting discussion, I guess. But let me get back to my story here, all right? So my Zolaida said that one day her mother told her (back when she was very young, so it's possible that she imagined it) that from the moment they saw each other—Federico and the scorned wife—they wanted and needed each other. They succumbed to a sort of deep and mutual attraction, a rapture that stems right from the heart. Also—I have to say—it had to do with that always dangerous if dignified attraction that comes from appearing in a novel. At the beginning, he suspected that she only loved him for his books—which I thought were just horrible, you know?—and as a way of getting back at her husband. But then he found out the truth, which was much, much worse (from a certain point of view) than what he'd suspected: she really only loved him *for him*, understand? And it gave him a certain ingenuous satisfaction, at least in the beginning, until he realized that she—the wounded wife—truly loved him, Federico, wanted to devour him, to place her entire life in the hands of one rail-thin novelist. In other words, she loved him solely for the amoral arts of sleeping late and boozing. That obstinate little damsel wanted him selfishly. She was transgressing the most basic rules of the lover's triangle. Just as if Federico were actually her husband! Do you understand? Their roles had been slowly and surreptitiously reversed, as happens in Zola's *Thérèse Raquin*, which Fede was surely unaware of (a writer!), since otherwise none of this would have happened. But now you see! The cruel irony

(10:57)

km.108

(11:22)

km.107

km.106

ELOY URROZ

of it! A damned game. Only later did that hack
of a writer ever realize it, but by then it was too
late. She loved him desperately, with a frenzy;
she tore out her hair for him, she even read
everything that he had read. That was the last (12:43)
straw! Federico—not without reason—felt himself swallowed up, buried alive in the lips of that
woman who was not yet old but no longer young.
Thirty-five years. A perfect woman. Zolaida told
me that she even remembers when her mother
would sneak in phone calls to Fede, six, seven,
and even eight times a day. She, my baby love, (12:59)
was maybe four at the time, and could sense km.105
even then that something strange was happening, or was about to happen. Her two brothers—her two half brothers—didn't even think
much about it, never imagined so much as a
particle of that story of fraudulent adultery. At
the very least, Zoraida acted discreetly in front
of them, her stepchildren, who were on the verge
of adolescence. By that time, Zolaida had heard
the voice of her mother's young lover three or (13:33)
four times over the phone; soon she'd come to
know it well. Zoraida obviously wanted to cam- km.104
ouflage the situation, to confuse the little girl.
But children—especially at that age—understand
everything. Six months later, when the budding
novelist had decided to leave her—although it
was supremely difficult for him to arrive at that
decision, given that he loved her in his own
way—her husband found out, discovered her on
the phone with him *in flagrante*. He berated
her, they fought, and were soon divorced. As for

Federico, it was harder than ever for him to walk away now that she was alone, her parents in Chile; Zoraida lost in his books, in those interminable novels of love. Fear and the desire to leave her spread in him with every passing moment, but he—without the will to abandon km.103 her—didn't dare. When he least expected it, she and her four-year-old daughter had set up shop in his apartment. A short while later, she got herself a job, and they both began a new life; at least, that's what my Zolaida told me. But not (14:42) even six months had passed before the father managed to win the custody battle. Zolaida, who was five then, remembers some disputes, she can visualize her father's lawyer with his dark glasses: tall, blond-haired, with a cruel profile; yes, she remembers it all quite clearly (or else imagined it very well) . . . she even tells me about interminable nights spent dreaming about the man with the flat and livid nose, who would grab her by km.102 the arm and drag her into an office to intimidate her, make her give a statement against her own (15:19) mother. It was a green fly with great, glassy eyes, coming to bite her in her recurring nightmares. That was the end of Zolaida's mother. She lost her daughter forever, and then she lost her mind. Six months later, without that hack writer even noticing, she abandoned him. She didn't love him anymore. She left before he could decide to do it himself. She left him for her native Chile. Nobody knew what had happened to her, and nobody tried to find out. She never went looking km.101 for her daughter, never tried to win her back.

Zolaida's mother had lost her mind, and now, in
the last few months before Zolaida was taken,
her mother didn't even read anymore—she only
reread, but more voraciously than ever, as if pos-   (16:00)
sessed by the characters in the novels themselves.
She could quickly go from Ana Ozores or Anna
Karenina to Ariane D'Auble, Otilio Rauda, Mrs.
Ramsay, Nastasia Filipovna, Tina Modotti, Milly
Theale or the other Mildred, the Maugham one;
Emma Bovary, Azul Larralde, Gervasia (Naná's
mother), Fermina Daza, Renata Guillén, Ursula
Brangwen, La Maga, poor little Justine, the km.100
mulatta Tereza Batista, Molly Bloom, Ada Veen,
Albertine, Aunt Julia herself, the Marquess of
Loira or Jacinta—ah, yes—the one from Galdós.
And my Zolaida? Well, obviously it affected her,
it affected her a lot. Children are more aware of
things than we realize, you know? Especially   (16:44)
when they're as bright as she was. Soon she'd lost
her mother, her two brothers, and herself. I don't
think they actually loved their papá. None of
them. In any case, the gentleman found himself km.99
a governess, a woman less impetuous but more
refined, cultured; educated among the permanent members of Opus Dei. My Zolaida, my
beloved, grew up among those rooks, among
those vultures of ill-omen, those tormentors of
defenseless children. From five years on. How
could she not turn out religious, the poor thing?   (17:30)
She told me that there were weeks she didn't
eat, trying to do penance. A devilish penance. km.98
Why did she feel she needed to do penance? She
never told me, though I suspect that it's because

she felt that she was to blame for everything. It's absurd, of course, but she felt responsible for the divorce—and responsible for her mother—as if her father had assigned her all the blame. And remember that he never actually loved her: she km.97 came into the world a tiny gift that her father was giving his wife. It was something of a reward for having cared for his children for almost ten years. Now, all the caring and love that had been placed in the three children had melted away, had been lost in some hidden corner of (18:21) her madness. And the young writer? Well, he never forgot about her, and even tried to locate her several years later, I've found out. Nobody knew, not even his friends, and nobody thought to write to her parents in Chile. Finally, Federico found out—via a letter from Zoraida's father—that Zolaida's mother had left Santiago km.96 many years before. But she hadn't returned to Mexico, anyway, and the word was she'd passed away in the interim. In any case, Federico told my Zolaida, though he almost never saw her. Yes, he didn't see her again while she was growing up, while she became even more beautiful. After those six months when my beloved had lived with Federico and with her mother in his apartment, they only met on a couple of occa- (19:11) km.95 sions. They were amicable; she even told me that she felt a certain amount of affection for him, since despite everything else, Federico had cared for and even loved her mother for a time. With- out wanting to, anyway, Federico committed an error—or perhaps he just perpetuated it—when

he told my Zolaida that her mother had died. I
don't know; she was thirteen or fourteen at the
time. On one hand, it was her right to know, don't
you think? But then again, the consequences
were terrible. Now I understand the deep-seated
sense of blame that she, my beloved, harbored km.94
and even incubated day by day like a cold and
bitter root inside her. It was no longer just the (19:58)
abandonment and her mother's madness, but
rather that she had survived her own mother, the
death horrifying and stigmatizing her. As you
could probably guess, that revolting governess
had her hand in all this. That magpie, that vul-
ture. From what Zolaida told me, she was a tall,
wide woman, quite large all around. Her fore- (20:19)
head and her face were covered in freckles of the
same awful red color as her hair. She was a
monstrous red beast rambling about the house, km.93
doling out punishment and—above all—shrewd-
ly sowing the malignant seeds of blame. Blame
for everything, understand? The blows to the
chest, the catechesis restored by Kempis, Maciel,
Escrivá de Balaguer, Loyola and his partisans.
Zolaida had to feel the abstract blame of Judge-
ment, and how, therefore, could she avoid feeling
guilt for her mother, for the sins Zoraida had (21:05)
committed? Her father, as always, feigned ignorance and spent all his time outside the house.
On business, or simply "out." The usurping governess carried with her all the advantages that
such cruel people have over quiet five-year-old km.92
girls. Zolaida's half brothers were spared from
her clutches, or at least they'd learned to be wary

of her power. They were ten years older than the girl. Therefore, my Zolaida grew up forgotten, by her grandparents, by her mother, by her father—accumulating guilt. At thirteen, when she found out about her mother's fate—the mother she'd barely known—this guilt multiplied, took on a mind of its own. That's where

km.91 the fasting began, the weeks of praising Christ's name, the blows to the chest that later became

(22:08) lashes on the legs and hands. That's also where the anemia began, which would affect her for the rest of her life. By fifteen, my Zolaida—my virgin, my vestal, my undine, my sylph, my nymph—had already decided that she was going to become a consecrated sister of the Divino Verbo Encarnado, one of the worst and most sordid congregations that the Kingdom of Heaven has ever dumped onto this earth. Though her father was not much enamored of the idea, it was already too late. He didn't try to stop her, because I don't believe it was that important to him. The girl was a perfect model of virtue, and a humble servant of Our Lord. Nevertheless, something very strange happened just before she was about to enter the Order. It might have been what brought us together. It might seem strange or

(23:09) just dull to an atheist, but the fact is that for one reason or another—my Zolaida says that it was the Holy Spirit himself—she entered a church one Wednesday at dusk. There, she found a mul-

km.90 titude of people on their feet, singing and praying and some even holding hands. They were the Misioneros del Espíritu Santo. She says that she suddenly felt her veins flowing with a new sap, something slow and comforting, the Spirit of God. She felt all her guilt and shame lifted away. It was something that didn't recriminate (23:49) her and didn't blame her like the bitter breaths of her governess or the sisters of the Divino Verbo Encarnado invariably did. Why? There were hosannas and beautiful canticles being km.89 sung to the rhythm of guitars and tambourines, and a hospitable joy that was both stubborn and soft. In other words, it was the complete opposite of the Congregación del Divino Verbo Encarnado, which she would be entering very soon and forever. She told me that being there with those charismatic people truly did change her life. But how's that, you may ask, if she only changed her congregation, her Order or whatever it's called? km.88 (24:40) It's much more complicated than that, Ricardo. She wanted to be a cloistered nun, forgotten and alienated, a sort of link to her mad mother. But it was only then, just then, after ten years of ascesis, that she received the Holy Spirit. How the hell was she, my beloved, going to become a nun without having received the Holy Spirit? Sor Juana, you see, happened to her. It's a bit confusing, but since Zolaida told me all this, something became very clear to me: many priests who offi- (25:12) ciate over the sacraments, the transmutation of bread and wine into the flesh and blood of Christ, have yet to receive the Holy Spirit themselves. Obviously, all this reminds me of the singular case of my cousin, the priest Augusto Roldán. I km.87 suppose he went through the same exact thing twenty-five years ago with that Gringa: he found God. He said the Fiery Tongues—or, as he called them, the Paraclete—came to rest on his forehead, to crown him, to bless him, which I don't believe for a second, personally. Anyway, what I'm telling you, Ricardo, is that my Zolaida ended her voluntary stay in that unfortunate congregation, and instead joined the Misioneros del Espíritu Santo. And what exactly did that entail? Well, to a lady of Opus Dei—as was the governess—it must have come as quite a shock. After more than ten years of advising and guiding her pupil, for her to decide to become a missionary instead of a nun . . . and of the Misioneros del Espíritu Santo at that! It's trading one extreme for another, like saying, Viva Erasmus of Rotterdam! Down with José María Escrivá de Balaguer! Well, the fact of the matter is that my Zolaida had long since succumbed to the inquisitorial powers of the governess—or those same Fiery Tongues that Augusto claims took him, thanks to God—and before she'd turned seventeen, she was already an expert in religious devotions, orders, missions, via crucis, convents, ministries, retreats, cloisters, fasting, congregations, et cetera . . . but knew nothing of love. Not one kiss, not one idea, not one flattering comment in all her life. (An exceptional beauty such as her, a virgin, a priestess created not for the priesthood but rather for love itself! Can you imagine it?) And though even the governess and Zolaida's father were against it, the girl was devoted to the unhealthy idea of fasting—adamant.

(25:55)

km.86

(26:54) km.85

ELOY URROZ

Maybe her appetite had waned, or maybe a different sort of appetite had grown, but whatever the cause, her anemia was there for good. It's something irreversible: if you don't eat well by a certain age, it just won't do to start later in life. It does irreparable physical harm. By seventeen, then, my beloved had completed any and all seminars you can imagine, all of which were imposed by the governess. Thin, pale, with tired eyes, always smiling, her hands always moving and her sharpened fingers dancing like those of a concert pianist, my Zolaida would reel off the rosary beads in the air, without realizing it, habitually, while her eyes shone like raw pearls or dewdrops, with the same sort of intensity (if you've ever seen how such things shine). Her body was always erect, flashing through space like lightning, or like a figure in an El Greco painting. The nape of her neck was slight and shone beneath her gathered hair. Zolaida had the tenderness of a canary and the agility of a fish; her movements cleaved the cold north wind of the fields, her footsteps clouded the bounty of the sea. She had the strength of an enraged Amazon, or one of those women from Wagner's *Ring* cycle, only more compassionate and faithful. As you might imagine, any penitence was at this point was quite easy for her, after all the punishments that she'd invented for herself! She was a Misionera del Espíritu Santo through and through; nothing else would have been a challenge. And what did it mean to be a Misionera del Espíritu Santo? Simply put, they go on

(27:33)

km.84

(28:12)

km.83

(28:59)

km.82

missions, excursions, and seek to convert men who have strayed from God's side. Not unlike me! Thus it was that, for nearly four years, my Zolaida crossed land, sea, and air, traveling to inhospitable places throughout the world. She explored the Lacondón jungle, San Luis Potosí, and Durango; she penetrated the Sierras of Oaxaca with the *Mijes*; she went to Guerrero, Michoacán, and Puebla (which wasn't necessary, as they're quite prudish there already); she met the Yaquis from Sonora; she converted young and old alike, alcoholics and drug addicts, lost sheep, the needy, the rich, yuppies, Jehovah's Witnesses (always the toughest nuts to crack), the Mormons, Seventh Day Adventists, and even two whole cults, one hidden deep in the Sierra Tarahumara and the other along the Guatemalan border. She went to Central America on more than one occasion and was met with great success. God was her traveling companion, and she was His servant; together they converted hundreds of people, prayed for them, placed her hands upon their heads, made their pains, afflictions, and troubles disappear, so that they became suddenly rich and magnificent and robust, throwing up their arms and sobbing like children. She visited houses, knocked on doors, insistent until the families invited her inside, where she would speak to them for hours. She enjoyed this work, which was so unlike the immobility of the cloistered life. Until one day Padre Óscar, her superior, had the peregrine idea to send her to Baja California, where—according to him—the hand

(30:01) km.81

km.80

(31:11)

km.79

ELOY URROZ

of Christ was urgently needed. She told me that Padre Óscar had informed her that vice and ignorance had devastated us, the Paceños especially, and yet he'd never set foot in Baja California himself. (This is the way rumors get started: from the viperine tongues of priests.) So there in La Paz, we met one another. I still remember the day I first laid eyes on her. Cecilio wasn't home, neither was my mother, and my father had (thank God) died many, many years before; but I remember her perfectly—sweet, on the verge of melting in the noonday heat, standing in the frame of the km.78 open door. She called to me. I contemplated her slight, restrained, marvelous figure, etched there against the sea. I knew then that I loved her, or at least that I would. Why? I'm not sure how to explain it; maybe I projected my feelings and my love for that place into her—in other words, I (32:33) transferred them—and that's why I can say it was love at first sight. At the very least, yes, I can say that I wanted to love her *a priori*, without the need for reasons or explanations. For the simple pleasure of it. In fact, that might just be what true love is: when you don't have to ask your partner anything, when you simply *do*, km.77 because *yes*, there's no reason other than that it's *right*. I couldn't care less what she was doing (33:00) there or what the hell she saw in me . . . but I did know exactly what I wanted from her: the chance to love, simply and without obstacles. And she'd come—like an Angel descended from Heaven, most blessed among all women—to *my* door: resplendent, warm, demure, my Zolaida.

I ushered her in. I was immediately and completely absorbed in her movements, her delicate, tired features, while she sat in an armchair and began to speak—or croon, I should say—to me.

km.76 Yes, I was immediately and completely absorbed, and I didn't even realize it. Her voice trilled like that of a tiny bird, she pronounced things that I couldn't even hear . . . she spoke and I could do nothing but follow the molding of her lips, their size and width, their ardent, intense red, until—get this!—she caught me staring at her. The most urgent thing about Zolaida was her lips, and she didn't even know it: she hadn't

(34:11)   kissed a soul. But she'd soon find out what it was like. She didn't stop for breath during her Christian harangue, convinced now that I was hang-

km.75 ing on her every word. And actually she wasn't that far off, but what I was hanging on was her. Not God, not our Lord, but Her, my Lady, my Goddess, her pale hands—yellow in that tenuous afternoon light—on her scattered, dampened hair, the beads of sweat on her forehead, on her shining, pearly cheekbones, drenched in her own wonderfully healthy, salty waters. She picked up her Bible, moved it from hand to hand, read from it without opening it, her memory chasing

km.74 down every last verse, repeated and recited a thousand times over, until they burst from those delicate lips like a sweet chorale. She spoke of Job and of Paul, then switched over to John

(35:03)   and then on to the Proverbs, until the moment when—with a mysterious penumbra that seemed to descend from the ceiling, bathing my living room in stillness—the Spirit of God illuminated me, the true light of love was suddenly made vivid and abundant, circling us. She recited the *Song of Songs*. I kept silent, and it was a very different kind of silence that what I'd maintained km.73 earlier. It was quite an odd silence indeed, Ricardo, rooted in her eyes, which were boring into my own, so much so that Zolaida soon fell quiet herself. I waited for another second or two, then asked if she wouldn't read me something else from the *Song of Songs*. She looked disconcerted and made a skeptical face, or at least one that I interpreted as such. But then she smiled, gathered up her courage, opened her Bible, and—like an expert who not only knows the verses by memory but who can also flip through a voluminous tome by touch and find exactly what it is that she wants to read—she began to read one of km.72 the Bride's dreams: *I slept, but my heart was awake. Listen! My beloved is knocking.* (Here I interrupted her, and spoke the Groom's lines.) *"Open to me, my sister, my love, my dove, my perfect one; for my head is wet with dew, my locks with the drops of the night."* I fell into a new, reverential, almost Augustine silence. There would be no more words from the Groom; now it would only be her who continued, speaking the words of the Bride. She hesitated for a moment and km.71 pursed her lips—my poor little beloved, my apprehensive Zolaida—going on falteringly with the words she was perhaps reluctant to admit that (37:07) she knew by heart: *I had put off my garment; how could I put it on again? I had bathed my feet; how*

could I soil them? My beloved thrust his hand into
km.70 *the opening, and my inmost being yearned for him. I*
arose to open to my beloved, and my hands dripped
with myrrh, my fingers with liquid myrrh, on the
handles of the bolt. I opened to my beloved . . . At
that moment, I stood up, walked over to her, and
placed my hand upon her mouth, silencing her,
preventing her from finishing the rest of that sad
verse: *. . . but my beloved had turned and was gone.*
My soul failed me when he spoke. I sought him, but
did not find him; I called him, but he gave no answer.
Zolaida could read the rest—I'd covered her
km.69 mouth, not her eyes—so I simply said to her, *It's*
not true, I have not left you, Zolaida, I am here, at
your side, and I don't ever want to turn and go from
you. And she—the beautiful gazelle who'd come
to conquer me, to convert me to her Lord God—
broke down crying, and embraced me. Then we
both began to cry, at first confused and unsteady
in the face of an immense, irresponsible pain,
but soon it was tender and soft, and we were
content and almost unconscious in each other's
km.68 arms. More than any other person, Zolaida had
taken the world's misfortune and held it against
her chest, and I wanted to help her carry it as she
(38:54) continued on her way. That fragile flower didn't
deserve the crushing fatigue that she'd borne for
so long, to the point of breaking. I wanted to
save that miraculous stem, that heart which, in
spite of everything, had refused to give in. On
the contrary, it survived, it prevailed, shared its
km.67 last few drops of myrrh with the others, her
fellow humans, ominous, thankless, none of whom

had ever repaid her or even bothered to notice
her. Not even Padre Óscar or his arrogant missionary brothers, all of whom were supposedly
conquering souls for the Lord. It was giving and
giving, saving your fellow man, loving him, offering him a hand, while she, meanwhile, was alone,
extinguished, forgotten and forgetting, receding km.66
from the eyes of the world. I wanted to accompany her on her long and humble road. That's
what I saw in her as soon as she set foot in my
house, when I thought that I would love her and
I didn't know why. It was then—the two of us
lost in tears—when we kissed, she not expecting
it, me desiring it, anxious, unsatisfied, mad with
love, mad with wanting to hold onto her forever, km.65
now that I finally had her so close. We kissed
like that for hours, oblivious to the world and its
fatuous inhabitants—the poor, the unfortunate,
the rich, the sad, the faithful, the dirty, the
abominable, the whores, the bewildered Jeho-
vah's Witnesses, the yuppies, the starving, the   (40:22)
apostles and the apostates, the sick and the
healthy, the saints and the wise, the barren and km.64
the foolish, the celibate, the ignorant, even the
other lovers, even the womanizers—facing each
other, exposed, our dampened lips stuck togeth-
er with ignorance, and me adapting to her life   (40:59)
through the language of her saliva, adapting to
her soul under the heat of the noonday sun. Yes,
I kissed her and time and time again I said to her km.63
that she shouldn't be afraid, that I would never
leave her . . . *Here I am, I haven't gone anywhere,*
I'll never leave your side, I would whisper in her

ear as I kissed her, my tongue tracing the perfect line of her lobe. And she believed me. She
believed me *because I also believed it*, for that
reason and that reason alone. But in the end, of
course, I *did* betray her, Ricardo. Well, I couldn't
have known it at the time; I never would have
km.62 imagined myself as part of God's stratagem,
never could have imagined the fury of His vengeance in the wake of my having stolen one of his
daughters—perhaps even his favorite daughter—an authentic Misionera del Espíritu Santo,
devoted to Him in everything. I betrayed her
without even being able to glimpse what would
happen eleven months down the road: my overwhelming need, the binding urgency I felt to
leave despite the fact that I loved her, despite the
fact that I cared for her more than I cared about
myself. You understand? She was my life, and I
walked away from it. Yes, I was able to forget
km.61 about her for a while, in the same way that you
can sometimes lose track of your heartbeat or
your breath, and sometimes—when it became
necessary—I could forget that I even existed,
forget that *I left*. But, in the meantime, from that
kiss on, my life no longer belonged to me. Those
eleven months belonged only to her, just as before
she had herself only belonged to her Lord Christ.
Nevertheless, after eleven months, I couldn't do
it anymore, I had to withdraw myself, to leave
her, to be alone . . . But I'm getting ahead of
km.60 myself again. First you have to know what happened; you have to hear about just how substantial a change I was in Zolaida's life. And it was

The margin markers read: (41:23), km.62, (42:02), km.61, (43:04), km.60

the same for me on that bitter, blessed day we met at my home in La Paz. During that week, the week of her mission, we worked things out so that we could be alone together each and every day. Finally, towards the end of her stay, the things that were bound to happen, happened. First, her fellow missionaries found out about me and tried to convince Zolaida that she was doing wrong; second, the time came for her to make the decision to remain in La Paz with me or to return . . . but return to where? And return to km.59 (43:49) whom, if she no longer belonged to anybody else? Until that point, perhaps, she'd belonged to God, through Padre Óscar's order, of course, and before that to the monstrous redheaded governess, and before that there was her father, and then her mother—most distant of all. But there was nobody else now; she had nobody else but km.58 me. She repeated the words of the Gospel for me, specifically those in which Jesus orders his (44:37) Apostles to never put down the plow, for those that pick it up only to abandon it later are those who will incur the outrage of God, their Heavenly Father, who will cast them out of His kingdom. So the sick seed of guilt was already growing, then, inside of her. Her pain subsided only when she adored me and asked me to be by her side every hour of the day, to breathe her in km.57 wholeheartedly, and to breathe myself in through her. Zolaida endured her loss through the infection of my love, through our pain together. She remained at my side, and I dropped everything for her. The other missionaries left, and Zolaida sent a letter to Óscar along with them. It wasn't until later—and even then at my own insistence—that she wrote to her father. She got no response, though this didn't matter much to her. She was a heretic, and I knew it: she'd strayed from her path, and she had done it for me. Cecilio met her, as did my mother, and they both km.56 liked her. They even began to love her. After a few weeks, we moved out of my house and got a little place together on the outskirts of La Paz. We visited Cecilio and my mother on a few occasions. We lived simply to love, to sustain our pride, to touch the most sacred and also the most forbidden places where love hides. And we reached them, those places; we transgressed. We became our own gods and our own worshippers; we burned incense, we offered sacrifices, we touched God, we summoned demons of fiery love who came to us, became each other, cele- km.55 brated our names, offered up prayers, one after another—lost ourselves entirely. But none of it mattered. Time passed—crawling by, slow as an ant—and nothing exceptional happened; or at least, nothing outside of the exceptional fact of our love. Finally, we were visited one day by the dark angel Abbadon, which is what I like to call that particular nightmare of mine. I remember it perfectly: an old childhood dream, and it came unannounced, nine months into my life with km.54 Zolaida, heavy, soaking the sheets and my vulnerable body with sweat. I woke up, suffocating, next to my Zolaida, filled with my old dream, both marvelous and terrible. And let me tell you

this, Ricardo, when we were younger, Cecilio
and I were almost never granted permission to
go out with friends. Neighborhood kids would
call us up and asked our mother if we could km.53
come out and play, but she—under the orders of
our authoritarian father—never let us out. Sometimes we snuck out and played soccer, kick the
can, or—if it were dark outside—manhunt. Finally we'd slink home, fully aware of the punishment that awaited us. Our father would beat us
like we were a couple of Maccabees, can you
believe it? Eventually the punishments became
so great that they didn't even matter anymore, km.52
but, proportionally, the obstacles put in place to
keep us from sneaking out became greater as
well. According to my father, the streets weren't
for snot-nosed kids, but hardened men. And they
weren't for women either; that's what the home
was for, that was their place, for mending socks,
for doing the cooking. It was an awful litany that   (48:59)
both of us, Cecilio and I—and, by extension, our
mother—were subjected to, and we endured it km.51
stoically. Which is how, for the first time in nine
years, I came to have this dream again: it was
late, perhaps seven or eight in the evening, and
the sun was descending like a piece of fruit
blown from the bough of a tree, down behind
the ruined neighborhood houses, the radio anten- km.50
nas lancing . . . lancing the livid disk of the west.
All of a sudden, I see my father emerge from
the house, belt in hand, frantic and cruel. He   (50:06)
approaches a group of boys, and they say that
we're hiding out, Cecilio and me, as dusk is

approaching and we're playing manhunt again. We watch in a silent jumble of bodies, anxiously waiting to see whether he'll find us. On the opposite horizon, directly across from the setting sun, we see the hesitant moon begin to emerge.

km.49 We watch from our den, our lair. Once I thought I saw the sun and the moon both high in the sky at the same time. Two perfect, incandescent spheres, together in the flesh of the night. I swore to it, but nobody believed me. The heat soaks our clothes as we hide there, listening to the approaching steps, on the verge of breaking and

(50:54) km.48 running for the boat, yelling *ollie ollie oxen free* before the other kids can tag us. Yes, there were more than ten neighborhood kids there, waiting anxiously. Then, all of a sudden, I feel a hand on my back, tagging me, grabbing me, and I look up to find that it's not one of the neighborhood kids, but my father, of course. He's smiling a twisted,

km.47 fiendish grin; he looks like a bearded scorpion. His eyes ask me why I'd disobeyed him, and his lips inform me that as soon as we get home I'm going to suffer the consequences. Then he pulls me from my hideout and drags me off by the ear, all the while whipping my ass with his belt.

(51:30) Absolutely terrifying! I hold back my tears until we get back, and he locks me in my room and forbids me to come out. Not long after I hear his voice, saying *I've told you a hundred times, you just can't fly off like that! But I didn't fly off, I was playing manhunt*, I protest. *Oh you flew off all right.*

km.46 Then, feeling very alone, I turn away from the door and see Cecilio asleep in his bed, sighing

sad and unsatisfied. I begin to cry and sit down (52:12)
in a chair facing a wall on which a single painting hangs: yes, a painting of a meadow full of
flowers, with a pond off to one side, full of water
lilies and spanned by a small footbridge. The
whole scene is sunlit, even though the sun itself
doesn't appear in the picture. Suddenly, without km.45
knowing how or why, I am there, in the painting
itself, strolling through the grass, crossing the (53:00)
footbridge, gazing at the water lilies, resplendent
in the sun and feeling truly happy. From inside
that space I can glimpse—at arm's length—my
sleeping, sighing, solitary brother. This is something of a revelation for me, because if my brother is sleeping, it means that I'm not (because km.44
otherwise I couldn't observe him), and therefore
that what I'm experiencing isn't just a dream
after all. Nevertheless, a minute later, Cecilio (53:43)
wakes up, rubs the sleep from his eyes, eyes still
adjusting to the darkness of the room, and then
comes up to the painting so as to see me better.
He looks at me in there as if it were the most
natural thing on earth. I call out to him, ask him
to escape with me. He shouts back that he's ready
to come; I wait for him. Suddenly, again without km.43
knowing how or why, we both find ourselves in
that painting, and yes, we are flying—just like
my father said—flying off and over that meadow,
hand in hand, gazing down on it. And then we are
no longer a pair of tiny figures inside the bound-
aries of the painting, but find ourselves inside km.42
an actual, physical reality: a field filled with
flowers, a bridge, a pond, water-lilies floating,

and—in the offing—a house, perhaps belonging
to Monet himself, with tiny green glass windows
that block out the light, shredding it. From one
km.41 of those windows, the old painter watches us, his
wonderful whiskers reaching down to his chest.
He reaches a hand up to the sky, bidding us farewell, while Cecilio and I soar ever higher over
km.40 that smooth and endless meadow. Just then I
awake to find my mother reaching out to me. I
realized that I'd never snuck out to play with my
friends, and I hadn't gone flying off through that
painting, which was actually a fairly poor print
that an aunt had given us. Nothing at all had
happened. My brother and I were still prisoners
km.39 in our own room, cut off from the world, ready
to pick up our satchels and head off to school,
waiting impatiently for recess, before returning
home at three to eat without hunger—if for no
other reason than to finish off the afternoon—
before doing our chores and retreating to our
bedroom for lockup. It was like that for years,
Ricardo, watching the other kids playing from
our bedroom window, listening to my mother's
km.38 voice calling to them, saying that we aren't
allowed out of the house just now, but maybe
next week. Believe me, I had that damn dream
a million times, it played itself in my head to the
point where it became heartbreaking. Cecilio
was the only person I told about it, and he
simply laughed; he said that he hoped he'd have
km.37 a dream like that himself some day. Anyway,
like I said, I had that flight-through-the-paint-
ing dream again, nine months into my life with

(54:54)

(55:29)

(56:09)

(56:58)

Zolaida, there on the outskirts of La Paz, where
we lived humbly yet happy to be together, and km.36 (57:31)
overconfident in our love, overconfident before
God. She was the first woman I'd ever loved, you
see, and just then that dream—that youthful
sin of mine—came back to consume me. I was
dumbstruck and felt my breath catch in my throat
when her eyes fixed on my own. *What's happening, Solón? What's happening to you?* she asked
desperately. And I saw her there—my poor sister, km.35 (58:09)
my poor baby—I felt her weightlessness in front
of me, felt her terror in the face of what my eyes
hid from her: the dream that I would never share
with her. I took a moment to recover and collect
myself; she insisted on knowing what it was that
I had dreamt, but I swore to her it was nothing,
nothing at all. Yes, that was the first crack, the
first fissure running through the glass of the
mirror that was our love. Before we'd run together like quicksilver, an unmarred and flawless km.34 (59:19)
pool of mercury without a single speck of dust or
shadow etched on it. There was just our reflection, frozen and unpolluted: nothing that we
didn't both know about each other, not one
single little lie between us. Here, now, was the
Lord's vengeance laid upon me for my double
sin: the sin of my childhood, and now the sin of
having stolen away His favorite daughter, my
Zolaida. I wanted to forget about it, and that's (59:58)
how it went: I managed not to think about the
dream for several days, sweeping away its last km.33
vestiges, and I was even able to fit the broken
pieces of our mirror back together, preserving

our reflection almost spotlessly. That's what I thought, anyway, until a few days later, when the dream struck again. This time I leapt right out

(1.00:49)

km.32 of bed; it was still dark outside—there was nothing but some drunks fighting and some dogs howling over the horizon—and Zolaida grabbed me and asked me once again what was going on inside me, asked me to tell her about the dreams I was having. It was so warm in our bedroom that I was having difficulty breathing. I was

(1.01:33)

hovering between nausea, fever, and shame. I couldn't say what it was—I just couldn't bring myself to tell her—and so I swore yet again that I couldn't remember, that I wasn't sure, that I'd

km.31 never actually flown. She looked at me, stupefied, and said, *what do you mean, you never flew? No*, I replied, *I never said that. Yes you did, Solón, I just heard you. And what does it matter if you're dreaming about flying anyway? But I'm telling you

(1.02:12)

it's not true, Zolaida, I don't remember ever having flown in a dream. Look, it doesn't matter whether you remember it or not—come here*, she said to me,

km.30 taking me in her arms. *Lean back. Go back to sleep.* Shivering though drenched with sweat, I held myself tight against her chest until I finally drifted off again. The following morning, I knew that Zolaida hadn't forgotten about my nocturnal slip of the tongue, when—between making jokes and serving me a frugal breakfast in bed—she said, flat out, that she thought it was wonder-

(1.02:52)

ful that I, her beloved, flew in his dreams, that I must have looked quite handsome up there, floating around next to our Lord Jesus Christ,

that now I was her Christ and she was my Virgin,
my sacred vestal, my prostitute. I ignored this
comment, chewing the slice of toast she'd been km.29
considerate enough to bring me, swilled my
coffee, and turned my eyes to the wall so that I   (1.03:25)
wouldn't have to look at her. She made her exit,
disappearing from the room, and now there was
a new smudge in the corner of the mirror of our
love. Nevertheless, a short while later, desperate,
enough so to break our lazy, homebound, amo- km.28
rous routine—it was noon by that time—I left
the house and went in search of my brother
Cecilio. My mother had already left the house,
so I spoke with him and told him about what had
happened. He remembered that dream from my
youth and which he'd once—at the beginning at
least, the passing of the years helping him to km.27
understand its true import—been hurt by, and
laughed off. Cecilio got engaged fairly young,
only a few months after our father had died of a
heart attack. Father had been the obstacle, and
now that he was dead we could finally emerge—
bit by bit, of course—from the shell he'd kept us
in since childhood. And I couldn't bear it; I
mean, I couldn't bear my brother's clean, genu-   (1.05:00)
ine separation, the quick and easy shelter he km.26
found with that girl. Then came our friendships
with Augusto (yes, our cousin, Augusto Roldán)
and with Marcelo, a real son of a bitch friend
from La Paz who would eventually disappear
from the city. The three of them went out on
drunken sprees, picking up women and then
sleeping with them. But it wasn't quite that easy   (1.05:54)

for me, Ricardo. To put it simply, I didn't want to know a woman. I didn't dare. Sometimes the km.25 guys would force me to, but those things always ended badly, you know? I could be very crude and offensive with girls, but it was only because deep down I'm really just shy. I was afraid of them . . . or I resented them. I was sixteen, and I'd lost my brother forever. Yes, I hated all women; that is, until that day many years later when I met Zolaida. Now, that morning I told (1.06:39) him I was having the dream again, after so many years had passed, sitting there with Cecilio in km.24 our father's house, told him about the wonderful alchemy of escape in the dream that, by implication, was ultimately a horrifying nightmare, a recrimination, a vengeance sent down directly from Heaven, the magnificent wrath of God himself, comparing Zolaida's love with our having been locked away by our father. Cecilio was furious. He insulted me, told me that it had never happened, that I should forget about it once and for all, that he was sick and tired of (1.07:22) listening to me, of hearing me say we'd had a horrible childhood. He told me to get the hell out. I went back home, resolved to forget about that painting once and for all, forget about the km.23 room that had been our redoubt against the attacks of the world and the fury of our own papá. Zolaida met me at the door, looking more beautiful and tender than ever, her arms open, ready to receive me. She pacified me a little. (1.08:49) Maybe it was possible to remake my life, to repair the broken part of our love, that naked

mirror that, since the beginning, had held our
blinding passion. Suddenly, just as we were fin- km.22
ishing up the cream that she'd fixed just the way
I liked it, she said with a horrible and subtle
ingenuity: *You never told me why you knew the
Song of Songs. Where did you learn it, Solón? In
school? Yes,* I answered, full of resentment. I
stuffed another piece of bread between my teeth,
as if that might keep me from having to answer
any more questions. *Yes,* I'd responded, though   (1.09:36)
again this was not quite right: I learned the
verses of the *Song* at my brother's side, during
the most loved and hated days of our childhood.
At night I would say (sing, really) the words of km.21
the Bride; nevertheless, on the day when Zolaida
and I had met, I could easily recite the other
part—the comforting words of the Groom—
which had usually fallen to Cecilio. Zolaida must
have suspected something, and maybe there was
even some sort of female intuition that told her
that our quicksilver love was dimming, and that
I wasn't giving her the whole truth. Our passion   (1.10:02)
was like a fountain then, I swear. I didn't say
another word, and she didn't try and find anything else out. But I know she started to feel km.20
afraid. From that day on, the dream visited me
each and every night, keeping me from sleep,
driving itself between my beloved and myself
like the nails of the Cross. *What's happening?
What's happening to me?* I began to ask myself.
Meanwhile, Zolaida—recognizing that some- km.19
thing was happening, tearing me apart from the
inside—clung to me more forcefully than ever.

She needed me, begged me for kisses, for even a single glance. She would flatter me for hours, not wanting to lose me. I don't know; maybe she km.18 hadn't changed a bit, and maybe the one who (1.10:56) was seeing things differently—as more distant, more nebulous—was just me. I can't say, Ricardo. But yes, I did love her more than ever. In the face of that cold, intimate, hyperborean solitude which consumed me all hours of the day—and which I couldn't share with her under any circumstances—I loved her with even more km.17 energy, even more force, as though I was the tide flowing proportionally (inversely proportional, I should say) away. I was an ebb tide, the high-water mark of love demanding (for want of energy) the subsequent low tide. That's how it (1.11:50) was. I had to leave her, at least for a while. That's what my dream was compelling me to do. If I loved her then, it was more essential than ever that I leave. I couldn't possibly harm that girl, my baby, my Zolaida, my sister, my prosti-km.16 tute, my sweet canephor, my little love who surrendered to me one day, kneeling like a guardian angel, that supremely sacred virgin who had (1.12:39) given me the gift of her blessed soul, which had in turn—and without my knowing or even imagining it—rescued my own. I couldn't stay by her side any longer without her discovering what was inside of me, who I was, who the hell Solón km.15 really was. I could no longer deceive my faithful woman, the girl I'd given myself over to, with whom I'd been linked in daily, scandalous prayer. We had created our own religion, and we were

its only acolytes, its only initiates, and—at the
same time—we felt ourselves immolated by our
delight. I had to leave, and I couldn't put it off
any longer. I had to recover my life, to remake
my childhood, to discover whom I really loved,
to learn whether I could share the rest of my   (1.13:13)
days and nights with Zolaida. She, on the other
hand, sought to envelop me even more, to cling
to me like a mother or the abandoned, isolated
daughter she'd been. Without knowing how or km.14
why, the very thing I told you back at the beginning of all this began to happen: the only thing
that I needed at that moment of my life—though
I loved her—was to be alone, completely alone;
and the only thing that she needed at that
moment of her life—probably the most difficult km.13
thing—was to be with me every hour of the day.
So one day I left, Ricardo: I begged her to leave
me alone for a time, and she begged just the
opposite of me; rather, she begged me to stay,
because *she would quite literally die without me.*
But I paid her no mind. The dreams continued, km.12   (1.14:08)
coming night after night to interrogate me, to
bring me to the sins of my youth and my fail-
ures as a man. I needed to resolve my destiny,
my life, before I could dare return to Zolaida.
It was a question incumbent upon nobody but
myself to answer. I fled, I refused to hear her
pleas, I didn't tell her where I was going, didn't km.11
want her to come looking for me. Nor did I warn
my brother or our mother. I swore to Zolaida
that I would return, and I did exactly that, I
returned, but much much later . . . I lived and

worked in Tijuana for five months; I did it,

(1.14:50)
Ricardo, but only to survive. I didn't meet anybody there, and I didn't want to see anyone. I
hated people, I hated all of humanity, the com-
placencies and segregations that united it, its
peculiarities, its pains, its quarrels and its messes

(1.15:38) km.10 of love. At the beginning, almost every day as a
matter of fact, I wrote to Zolaida without using
a return address. I told her to wait for me, that
everything was going to turn out all right, that I
had to piece my life back together: now, before
it was too late. I loved her, but first I had to wash
away the stigma that I'd borne for so many
years. And the dreams began to calm down,
Ricardo, they dissolved just a little bit with every
km.9 morning sunrise, losing themselves in the deepest reaches of oblivion, in the most ignominious
shit-hills, right back to where they'd come from.
Yes, one single dream, multiplied time and
again, accusing me of something, and seeding
the soul with doubt. The day of reckoning was

(1.16:10)
at hand, and with it came the absolute dissolu-
tion of that dream. After four or five months of
living in that border town, I met someone,
and—much to my dismay, though without any
regret—I found them to be not unpleasant com-
km.8 pany. On the contrary, I found them quite
pleasant indeed. When, shortly thereafter, in a
motel room, we were faced with the unavoidable
moment wherein we were supposed to be united
in one flesh, I turned down the opportunity. I

(1.16:44)
simply couldn't stand to be next to someone
else's body. Instead of making me feel alive, this

flesh repulsed me. I loved my Zolaida. When I knew this—when I realized that I no longer had anything to apologize for—I decided to return to her. It was the right time to do it. It was what km.7 I'd been waiting for: in other words, the final verdict. It was time for me to prove my unconditional love and devotion to Zolaida, above any other human being. I left Tijuana and returned home, content and anxious to see my love. But it was too late: Zolaida, my beloved baby, burdened by a guilt that wasn't hers to bear— because it was my own—had succumbed to her km.6 old habit of fasting. Her long, hungry penance (1.17:17) . . . her damned expiations! There was nothing my mother or Cecilio could do. She never allowed them to help her; she simply let herself die, just like her mother. That sense of guilt was hers again, that guilt she'd carried since she was four years old: it was Zoraida's weakness for that unfortunate hack of a writer, the pangs of km.5 (1.18:05) separation first between her parents and then between the two of us; the guilt of madness, of her degradation and flight from Zoraida; the crime of a father clouded over by the image of an early death; the shame handed down by the Opus Dei governess, that monstrous redhead, instilled continually in Zolaida from when she was six to when she was ten; the mortal sins that the Divino Verbo Encarnado nuns whispered km.4 into her ear as if they were the incontrovertible truth. Her anemia was already quite advanced, (1.18:56) and her starving had opened up a hole in the wall of her stomach; no medicine could cure her of that desire to cleanse herself of an invented fault, that blame that could not have been hers, that was actually mine, Solón's, and mine alone to bear. I'm the guilty party, the great poisoner, the god of my Zolaida, a dead god. That had km.3 been exactly why I fled to Tijuana: to be able to love her without shame, without fault, absolutely clean, once and for all, without a dark past, without a perverse dream coming to terrify me every night, to shatter our mirror of love, to lure me away from her, compel me to leave her, proving that I wasn't so much a man (1.19:27) as a slut with the outward appearance of a man, a man who acted and behaved like a woman. Do you understand me? My father had repeated it like a litany: I would never grow into a true km.2 man, no, I just wasn't cut out for the job. I was a shadow of a man, an incipient little boy, as he liked to say, beating my ass bloody with his belt. He shouted it out, right in front of my brother, until even I started to believe it, to believe him, the three of us shut up in the bedroom there while our mother waited outside the door, surely (1.19:58) dying of fright. And let me tell you this, Ricar-km.1 do: there's a chance that there was a grain of truth in what my father said, that it was more than just his wickedness talking. Only now, after all these months and years, have I discovered that, ultimately, I was not Zolaida's true love. I could never have been her one and only irreplaceable man. I knew it when I lost her, and when I finally reunited with my brother, (1.20:14) Cecilio.

XL

Just as he was putting the finishing touches on *The Abominable Tale of Solón and Zolaida's Love,* Elías saw the blue Ford turning onto Libertad, the only paved street in Las Rémoras. He double-checked the time on his watch (it was five in the afternoon) and realized that everything was coinciding just as he'd foreseen: the length of the drive (126.4 kilometers covered in one hour, twenty minutes, and fourteen seconds) matched perfectly with the time it took him to write—in one fell swoop—that story, and of course for Solón to tell it to Ricardo. It was a out-and-out miracle.

The car parked just in front of Tony's Lonchería. The sun was running lower in the sky now, but the heat continued to make it feel like a debilitating inferno even at dusk. Elías had set his notebook down next to him with his pen inside. Pili and Tony—together like some ill-conceived portrait of a father and daughter—neglected their duties, standing stock-still, paralyzed with curiosity and dying, like Elías, to see the three new visitors. Finally, as though in a vision from beyond, Solón emerged from the back seat, followed by Ricardo, getting out of the front. There was no doubt whatsoever; when the two novelists saw each other, everything was confirmed: this must be Elías, sitting there, unmoving, taciturn, under the sunshade . . . and this must be Ricardo, walking down the sidewalk, six or seven years younger—and still mildly astonished at the story Solón had told him—watching him expectantly, as if Elías were some sort of apparition, with a similar disbelief, but also happy, of course, to have found him. The similarities between them were shocking: despite their differences in age and the fact that Ricardo's hair was a shade lighter than Elías's, they looked like brothers. Or—at least—nobody would have doubted them if they'd claimed to be.

Cecilio started to approach them, but before anything else could happen, he was startled: he'd just stepped on a smallish lizard. He looked down at the smear on his shoe. Only in Las Rémoras could something like this happen. Only here do the animals prefer to die with their backs to the sun rather than moving from their chosen spots in the dust. Tony went up to him, undid his apron, and said:

"It's unfortunate; those weak little things sleep everywhere around here."

Cecilio nodded and quickly changed the subject, asking where he might be able to find the padre.

"Augusto Roldán?" Tony asked.

"Yeah, him."

"Up at the Altozano. If you'd like, I could take you. It's not far." He smiled. "Nothing is too far away in Las Rémoras. It's just that people here are so lazy that everything seems far away to them."

"Is something wrong?" interrupted Solón, not very interested in Tony's musings. "I mean, is my cousin still sick? We received a telegram . . ."

"Yes, I sent it," Elías spoke up. "I figured that he'd want to see you, which is why . . ."

He didn't finish. Nevertheless, Ricardo understood his other motive, the one that had really prompted Elías: since there was no public transportation to Las Rémoras, he'd needed to send a cable in hopes that Cecilio and his brother would find Ricardo and bring him along. And now here he was. Elías thanked them without saying a word.

"And how's he doing?" asked Cecilio.

"A bit better," said the writer. "I saw him around noon. You don't have to worry about a thing. I think the worst has passed. Santa and the doctor are with him now."

They all went quiet, out of suspense, not knowing what else could be said other than what was written. The August sky was like a dried-up spring, cloudless, and at times it seemed to want to reach down to the ground that ran so low and flat.

"*Bueno*, permit me to introduce myself," said Tony, who had intuited *certain* things in Solón and Cecilio that only *certain* men can intuit. "My name is Antonio Zubizarreta, at your service. I'm the owner of this establishment, and this is Pili, my assistant."

"Pleased to meet you," said the younger brother, his eyes radiating candor, while something indecipherable came into Ricardo's face that made him particularly difficult to look at.

"And this is Elías, our writer and local intellectual," continued Tony, his voice becoming a bit more singsong, pleased to be introducing his clients. "He's also the curator of our library."

"Actually, I live there," Elías said with a bit of a wince, and without taking his eyes off Ricardo, Cecilio, and Solón, still astonished at the incredible power fiction apparently held over life.

"So Ricardo," he said, "you're also a writer, no?"

"I try to be," Ricardo replied, looking at the ground, intimidated by the honor (or the ridicule) that his peer was conferring on him.

Pili, however, only stole fleeting glances out of the corner of her eye, not yet daring to gape openly. Then she finally came over to see what was up, just when a telltale blush came into everyone's face. They looked—their faces did—like dignified tutti-frutti.

"I'll take you if you'd like," Tony offered the brothers unabashedly. He seemed relaxed and at ease among these new visitors. "Pili, you're in charge until I get back."

"Shall we go then?" Cecilio asked Ricardo.

"If it's all the same to you, I'd like to stay here. I think I'll have something to eat," he lied.

"Suit yourself," said Tony. "Pili, please bring the young man whatever he wants. My treat . . ."

"Thanks, but . . ."

"Have a seat," Elías interjected, drawing up a chair. Ricardo sat down while the others—Tony, flanked by Solón and Cecilio—marched off under the blazing August sky. Soon they had disappeared from view.

Then, just as Elías was about to ask Ricardo something, Sigüenza's girlfriend interrupted them.

"What can I bring you, sir?"

"Please, call me Ricardo. And I'll call you Pili. So we're on a first-name basis now, all right?" he flirted. "But I'd like a glass of carrot juice or orange juice if you've got it, and a *torta*." He looked at her from head to toe.

Pili turned and left, happy, feminine, rolling her ample hips from side to side as she walked in a way that Sigüenza had never seen in all the years they'd been together. And had he been there to see it, he definitely would not have been happy.

One lone couple crossed Libertad then, hesitant and perhaps just a little bit sad. Something—the time of day, or the siesta—had cleared the street of passersby. Most people were probably at the beach sunning themselves, or at home seeking respite from the oppressive heat. Yet even so, all that solitude was rather odd. For whatever reason, most of the weekend visitors had already disappeared. All that was left was a tiny contingent determined to stay the full week: some folks from La Paz or Mazatlán, or others come from Santa Rosalía or Ciudad Insurgentes, and five or six Gringos at most—including, of course, Jenny, though nobody around town knew if she'd already gone or if she was staying at her establishment with the rest of the girls.

Pili appeared from inside the kitchen carrying a glass of carrot juice and a *torta* filled with chicken, avocado, and cream. They both thanked her—Ricardo more emphatically—while she strutted back inside, where she could watch them from the safety of the lonchería's battlements. Suddenly, Elías said:

"It looks like someone's got a girlfriend."

"Is it you?" Ricardo asked, laughing.

"Oh, I'm not talking about myself."

"I know: that Francisco Sigüenza guy. The poor asshole."

"An asshole yes, but at the end of the day . . ."

". . . He's still the town councilman!" Ricardo finished.

"They say he's going to marry her," spat Elías, sure this revelation would surprise this little seventeen-year-old Don Juan. But Ricardo wasn't perturbed in the least: in fact, he already knew. He remembered well that distant night on which he'd first imagined Sigüenza's lucky-dog face.

"And what about me!" Ricardo said. "If she throws herself at me, do you really think I'll be able to resist? Even if she were the governor's daughter! She's amazingly beautiful."

"Yes, she's beautiful, but so what?" replied Elías. "I'm telling you, she's in love with Sigüenza."

"Well, I'm telling you that she's not . . ."

"I'm just asking you to keep out of trouble," said Elías, as though he were addressing a younger brother.

Ricardo took a sip of his juice, just as Elías did with his coffee. They waited, looking off into the distance, towards the end of Libertad where the street comes to an end with the wharf and the little beach in the shape of a broken valve. And while it was truly incredible to have Ricardo there, Elías found it the most natural thing in the world to be with him, speaking in person to his own creation—who now was not so much a creation as a living being, something that moved without his consent: something free and real. And Ricardo could say the same thing, now that he had Elías there in front of him, plucked right from the pages of *Las Rémoras*. But neither of them dared to mention this. They preferred the comfort of silence, continuing to watch the two passersby passing, and the tiny sliver of sea that was visible from their seats, while Pili—ignorant of these complications—sat ready in a corner of the Lonchería and watched them, especially the younger one, bemused at the enormous similarity between them. Finally, Ricardo turned to Elías and said:

"I have a letter for you."

"Oh yeah? Who from?" the Rémorano asked, feigning a certain ignorance while he sipped at his coffee.

"I think you already know. Here it is," said Ricardo without caution or care, opening his satchel.

Elías—Ricardo could tell—took the letter with a heavy, tremulous hand; then he stowed it in his notebook without another word, without so much as a thanks. Ricardo took a bite of his *torta*, worked it over slowly in his mouth, and said at last:

"I was with her, you know."

"Well? Tell me," the writer said with a skeptical gesture, a little proud and fatuous. He didn't want to look weak in front of the younger man. What he should do was demonstrate a certain aplomb; he needed to hide the fact that he'd been so ravaged by love. Ricardo was aware of all of this, but it didn't matter to him; on the contrary, he quite understood. Which is why, amiably, without another word, he conceded: he was going to tell him as little or as much as he knew. He took a sip of juice, as if swallowing a vitamin or summoning up his strength, and began:

"I believe she loves you; at least, she confessed as much. Even though she didn't say it in so many words, she let it be known in other ways during our time in La Paz. Women, of course, never make things obvious, they never just come out with things. I don't know why. They hide everything, and you've almost got to guess. Being explicit is hard work for them, you know? The architect was right about that. But, Elías, who am I to tell you what she feels? You should know it better than anyone. So I don't think you ought to go around asking people. Just ask yourself and you'll see. *I* wanted to ask her, to convince her to return to Las Rémoras with me. But then I understood: everything ends, sooner or later, and that's why we have to learn to accept them no matter what the cost. We have to learn to take the bull by the horns before it runs us through and gores us. It's unfortunate that love has to be like that—like a bull. You fatten it up, you get into the ring with it, you feint, you execute a *pase de pecho*. You have to be wary, you have to protect yourself. It can fly into a rage. Nobody in their right mind enters the ring looking to die, but why do they go in at all? Why risk your life? Who knows! But people do it, no? The whole world does. The bullfight never ends, Elías. The difference lies in the fact that the greatest lovers—the most mature—only go through the motions. They don't really love anymore. Sooner or later you learn that you don't have to face down that colossal bull—sometimes it's better to play the clown. Roberta left because she came to realize that you were risking your life in the ring, and that frightened her. It all goes back to that moment when she decided once and for all that she was never going to enter the ring again. Not with you, not with anybody. She'd already done it once, and she has the fruit of that love with her: a son. And now, even with the best of intentions, you want to ask her to go once more into the breach, that she fall in love with you just like you want her to? No, no, that was never going to happen, she was never going to do that, Elías. There are people, like her, who learn their lessons the first time out. The lesson fills them, and it's enough for them." Ricardo paused to catch his breath, then continued: "Eventually Roberta decided that it wasn't right to prolong your suffering any further. And that's a symptom, believe me, a sure sign that deep down she did love you. At least, that's what I believe. Even when the moment of separation had arrived. Yes, she took it, took advantage of the circumstances. She knew that you were never going to leave her, so she took it upon herself to leave you. Think about it, Elías, you placed all the responsibility on Roberta's shoulders. You forced her to play a role that she had to reject." Here he took a sip of juice. "She also told me about Inés." Ricardo lowered his voice to a whisper, even though nobody else could possibly hear them, not even Pili, a few yards away. "You still think it was you who killed her, right?"

"What are you talking about?" the writer asked, raising an eyebrow.

"Well, we won't discuss it. But you should know that Inés was suffocated by Roberta's hand, and not your own. Yes, yes, I know, I was kind of dumbstruck myself at the news. But it's the clear and simple truth. She told me so herself. After you left that night, Roberta heard some scratching on the floorboards under the bed. At first she tried to ignore it, but then something reached out. And there she was, blue in the face. Maybe you did see her die, maybe you saw her last breath with your own eyes, but there have been cases where the dead simply refuse to die. I have no reason to lie to you."

"And then . . . ?" asked Elías. The umbrella above them wasn't offering much protection: the sun was almost perpendicular to it now, about to dip beneath the horizon.

"Then," the younger man concluded, "Roberta finished the job you'd started."

"So that was the real reason she left?" asked the librarian. "Because I'd implicated her? Made her my accomplice?"

"That was part of it, yes, but I think she was going to leave in any case. She had to. But I'm telling you, I really don't know. Maybe she explained things in that letter. You tell me, Elías."

"No, no," balked the elder writer. "You don't know. You don't know her like I do. She thinks she's omnipotent, you know? She took on the role of whore for everyone's sake; in other words, she didn't do it for anyone. Think about it: priests and whores aren't really all that different. Both provide the same service: they do what they do for others, not for themselves. That's why Saint Paul said it was better to save your heart for Christ than to give something of it to a woman. Whores don't share their hearts with anybody, really. Just love. And what a love it is! It's so complicated that, deep down, beneath all its convolutions, it must be rotting—rotting at its roots! You follow me? Love growing on one end and rotting on the other. Quite frankly, it's sickening. Nothing could stop her in her downward spiral of love. She was attracted to it, even. Now she's in a rush, a pointless rush. And when a woman decides she's not going to love anybody (at least in my understanding of the word love), then it's beyond impossible to be with her. In other words, there's no reason to hold out hope . . ." He took a swig of coffee. "One of those afternoons (maybe the last) when I sat like a statue on that rock over the beach, I wrote a final poem in my head, Ricardo, I wrote and rewrote and repeated it until I was exhausted. I wanted to put down, line by line, in cold detail, every ounce of skepticism that I'd been able to summon up since losing her, since loving her and losing her forever. (And others like her. Why not admit it?) Would you like to hear it?"

"I'm listening."

And this is what poured out of Elías's memory, without the least stammer of hesitation:

> After some years, you leave everything,
> You forget it all without much pain,
> Without the need for compensation,
> Even that which you desired most,
> And that which you have not yet needed.
> After all those years
> It is barely the rot of love
> —the improbable nostalgia of something—
> that takes root in the heart, in shadows,
> feeling its way,
> where it already inhabits you.

You learn about the pain nobody notices
And if someone looks it shames you:
You hide yourself, faint-hearted, in your collar.
Later . . . you want so little
Though you will inevitably be sad;
You fear nothing save love
And its capacity to destroy.

"It's good, Elías," was the only thing that Ricardo could manage to say, caught up in its cold cynicism, its architecture and prosody.

"Thank you, Ricardo, but it's trivial. When you really get down to it, you know, nothing and nobody has any real importance. Especially that fraud people call love. And this poem even less so . . ."

Ricardo looked on pensively, dubious. He cautioned:

"But in your heart you accept the fact that—at some point—Roberta did love you. You said so yourself, Elías."

"I never wanted to say that . . . I didn't think that's how it was."

"But you said it, you know? I think that, despite everything, you aren't quite so far off the mark as you think. She loved you. I don't know how much, but she did love you. She told me so. But I do, however, think that it's time for you to start to forget about her. You're right about that part."

"I know. I'm trying, at least. For me, it wasn't like it was with you and Laila. She didn't leave. You left. You fled from her." There was a note of recrimination in his voice. "You'll have to recognize that, Ricardo."

"So, because I left her, you conclude that I wasn't in love with her?"

"I never said you *weren't*." The writer was getting a bit agitated. "I'll even grant that you were. But in the end, you left her, which isn't as hard as being left. That's what I'm trying to say."

"It's not a question of how hard it was, Elías. It's just that, after the whole business with Inés the maid, leaving was the only option. You know that. It was the only thing to do. I didn't even do it consciously; everything was so cloudy and clumsy, without any sort of conviction or clarity. I was sick, I was feverish. There was something else: I was hopelessly in love with Laila. What other way out did I have? You know? I still haven't recovered. Sometimes I think that I'm living in a dream, in the pages of a novel, and for that reason I don't have to worry, I can be content in the knowledge that everything is going to come out all right in the end. Believe me, I really don't know why I did it."

"You know, that's almost exactly what happened to me, Ricardo." The writer said, then lapsed into a silent stare: warm and complicit.

"Yes, we're not so different after all, Elías. We both had to kill to get past our obstacles. And we did it because of love. How absurd is that! When someone's in love, they do things without thinking, or sometimes because they've thought too much. Love is a kind of madness, a sort of dementia." He had a distressed look in his eye. "Anyway, you didn't do anything. It was Roberta."

His accomplice was unperturbed. He'd been waiting patiently for the best possible moment to say it, to reveal it. And now was the time, just as it had been the proper time for Ricardo to reveal the true culprit behind Inés's death. Now it was Elías's turn.

"Of course, there's something you don't know, Ricardo."

"What?" The younger man felt some foreboding. Elías paused for effect, then, finally—as if giving his younger counterpart a gift or some bit of good news—he said:

"Inés, the maid, did not die."

First Ricardo thought he'd misheard. Then, almost immediately, he heard the older writer repeat:

"Yes, it's true. She's not dead."

"What are you talking about?" Ricardo stammered. "I killed her myself that afternoon."

"You didn't kill her. You only imagined it, Ricardo . . . You were living in a hallucination. You were being plagued by your love for Laila, which is what brought on the gastritis that Lascurain found so mysterious. Then came the fever . . . in your delirium, you convinced yourself that you'd have to kill Inés, right? But you didn't do it. You wouldn't have dared. I know." The writer smiled and finally said, "As you mentioned yourself, there are cases where the dead simply refuse to die."

"So I dreamed it . . ."

"No. What I'm saying is that you imagined everything, at every step along the way. Your maid's death was a false death, a death that I . . ." But Elías said no more. He didn't explain that the *presumed death* was a simple stylistic device that he'd employed, and which he'd intended to undercut later on. A device that, bit by bit, would have begun to take on enormous proportions in Ricardo's story, to the point of becoming a pretext . . .

"A reason for my coming to Las Rémoras. For us to meet. Right?"

They felt moored to their chairs, stripped of any desire to move. Despite all the obstacles and vicissitudes, the two of them—Elías and Ricardo—had come together, firmly connected under the tenuous twilight. The night—or the signs of its approach—was clear and splendid, and foretold even more calm and luminous things to come. A breeze like transparent threads of salt eased in from the depths of the sea, freshening the street, and even reaching as far as that house—the most distant of all—which had once been Inés's domain, but was now was run by Josefina. And still, despite all this—despite being the time of day when people usually took advantage of the cooler air to come out of their homes to gossip, flirt, and while away the few hours left before bed—not a single soul could be seen walking down Libertad or along the waterfront. In the meantime, Elías wanted to imagine again that wonderful encounter between Roberta, her son, and his character, Ricardo. The things that were said. He looked into the offing, through the gathering shadows, and he saw the houses of Las Rémoras, counted the scant few *tejocotes* that swayed in the wind, listened to the sweet chattering of the birds. He remembered everything, moment to moment, about Ricardo's story—the eventful journey, the train to Mazatlán, the ferry, Doctor Lascurain, Laila, Inés revived or Inés undying, Ricardo's mother, Federico Ross's novella, the meeting with Cecilio and Solón—but then, a second later, it all fell into a perfect oblivion, became sunk forever in the muck and mud of dreams and unreal fancies. Finally emerging from his heavy thoughts, Elías looked at Ricardo happily, feeling completely content within the space of their improbable good fortune. They each recognized themselves: they'd seen each other's faces somewhere before—in the mirror, probably. One was taller and more serious than the other, who was younger, less experienced. Elías drank the last of his coffee. Pili refilled his cup and Ricardo ordered another juice, *squeezed by your precious hands, Pilar,* he said, looking to make her blush. She walked off to fetch the juice, hips swaying again, feeling rather proud.

"You know, I like this very much," said Ricardo. "It's just as I imagined it!"

The librarian said nothing, simply smiled and that was all, taciturn and complacent like his alter ego. The greatest thing that had ever happened to him was going on right there and then: this meeting with Ricardo, right out of the book that he'd been writing. Roberta—if she would have had him—could also have been the greatest thing that ever happened to him. But she was now lost, completely lost. And there was no more time for useless lamentations. It was time to begin again.

A few minutes later, Pilar returned with the carrot juice. This time, she didn't say a word. She smiled at Ricardo and then returned to her post with the very same swagger Laila had shown entering and leaving his bedroom back in Mexico City. Then Ricardo turned to Elías and said:

"I have a question. Maybe it's a bit dumb, but . . ."

"Out with it."

"It's about . . ." He hesitated before finding the courage to ask. "What's the architect Jasso's name?"

"What do you mean, what's his name?" Elías laughed. "It's Jasso. Higinio Jasso . . ."

"Iginio with or without the H?"

"With the H, of course!" replied Elías.

"Are you sure?" the younger man pressed, still unsure.

"Don't tell me you've been writing Higinio without the H!"

"Yes, this whole time," Ricardo muttered. "That's why I was asking if you were quite sure."

"Look, if we see him, we'll ask him. Sound good?"

They both paused and took sips of their respective drinks, before Elías—tactlessly—asked:

"Tell me—honestly now—what did you think of Solón's story?"

"The truth is that I never would have thought that the two of them . . ."

"Well, I think you can see it coming as soon as he starts talking about that dream, that astral journey," Elías said.

"Anabasis. Like Sor Juana," Ricardo offered, gracious and academic. "It still all seems a bit incredible to me. And Solón was acting like it was nothing at all, right up until the very end, when we pulled into town!"

"Of course he did! That was the idea, Ricardo. That everything coincide perfectly!" He laughed. "If you knew how it ended, you wouldn't have gotten in the car with them, or anyway you probably would've made them pull over halfway here. Either way, we wouldn't have met . . ."

"You exaggerate," Ricardo replied. "You got the idea for adjusting the time from Federico's novella, right? That passage where he has that terrible dream, and he writes it all down in Paris after waking up. The time it takes to read the thing should coincide more or less with the time it took him—I mean *you*—to write it. 4:35 to 5:05 in the morning."

"Well, no, Ricardo. That's where you're wrong. I wasn't thinking of *Bodily Prayers* when I wrote *The Abominable Tale of Solón and Zolaida's Love*. If you must know, I got the idea from a story by Carpentier. He's one of my favorites . . ."

"And the name of the prostitute?"

"You mean Magda Gómez?"

"Yeah. Why Magda Gómez? I was a bit confused by that whole ending . . ."

"I'll say this: it bothered me too at first, but then I looked into it and eventually understood the complicated stunt that Federico was trying to pull. Remember the book he was writing in Paris? That's where he brings in all these novels that have in some way, shape, or form touched upon the theme of Hosea . . . which, ultimately, is the theme of Jesus Christ himself: the redemption of the whore via love."

"And the name?" pressed Ricardo.

"Magda, after Mary Magdalene, and Gómez, for Gomer, the prostitute Hosea was under orders from God to marry. In other words, it has to do with the two great Biblical whores, one from the Old and one from the New Testament, with the ultimate paradigm of Israel behind them, and with him—Federico—cast as a new Hosea, a new prophet come to redeem them. The name Yizreel is because their son—that of Hosea and Gomer—was named exactly that, and he represents a reconstituted, united

Israel. Federico, then, is both son and father . . . and in him, two great world religions are conflated."

"That's more than just a stunt . . . " said Ricardo, and they both fell into an erudite silence. They took comfort in their drinks and let the wind do the talking.

"Of course," Ricardo said suddenly, "That blue Ford is the same as in Ross's novella, right? I recognized it right away."

"Yes, it's the very same," granted Elías. "They were driving Federico around in that thing over twenty years ago. Who would have thought it . . . ?"

"He was very young, too, don't you think? He couldn't have been much older than fourteen then."

"Absolutely," answered Elías. "But, you know, it's different for everyone."

"So, what do you think about Federico's book?" Ricardo asked, mostly to change the subject. "It doesn't seem like Solón liked it much at all."

"Well, sure, what did you expect?" Elías replied, sounding quite informed. "Don't you see that they're characters in his story? Him and Cecilio?"

"But it's not like they came off all that badly. Actually . . ."

"They severed their ties with Ross a long time ago," said Elías. "And the reason for that wasn't what you think. It wasn't *Bodily Prayers*; it wasn't what was said in there or left out."

"So what—or who—happened?"

"What do you think?" countered Elías.

Ricardo took a few moments to reflect, mulled over a few new ideas, and then—surprised that he still hadn't fallen into the trap—he answered: "Zolaida!"

"Yes. Zolaida was the reason for the rift. Solón, that son of a bitch, blamed him, in part, for Zolaida's turning religious. He damned him to hell when he found out that Zolaida had starved herself to death."

"I hadn't thought about it like that," said Ricardo. "Solón said so himself in his story: Zolaida was the only daughter of Zoraida, the Chilean woman Federico met the same day that *Bodily Prayers* was published. But Zolaida had some affection for Federico—after all, if you think about it, the novelist really had been in love with her mother."

"Did you think I wouldn't hold a grudge?" Elías exclaimed, playing the part. "Solón pledged and promised that he loved her. But all that aside, he sent her up shit's creek without a paddle, knowing full well how weak and fragile she was, knowing about her propensity to fast when she was unhappy, and all that other ridiculous nonsense. She was anemic, always on the edge. And Solón loves her, despite all this, and then up and leaves, deciding that he has to settle his account with destiny first, thank you very much! Exactly what happened to poor little Miroslava Stern! Look, between you and me, Ricardo, do you really think that Solón never fucked that man in Tijuana?"

"I never even realized he was talking about a man. I thought it was . . . Anyway, that part is pretty vague. But yes, I believed him when he said that nothing had happened and that he'd found his only love in Zolaida. You should have seen the look in his eyes." Ricardo was a bit overwhelmed at hearing a different interpretation of *The Abominable Tale*, a deviation from the official version as told by Solón.

"Well, as far as I'm concerned, I don't believe him for a second. Why do you think I didn't get up from my chair to greet him? Going with those incestuous sons of bitches to see their cousin . . . !"

"Of course," Ricardo said, "Federico is their cousin as well."

"Yes, but on the paternal side."

"That means that Roldán and Federico Ross don't have any blood in common. They aren't real cousins."

"They don't even know each other. Though, the padre did

read Federico's book, for some reason. He's the one who lent it to me."

"You know what? Laila said that she loaned it to me, but to be honest I don't actually remember that," Ricardo mused. "According to you, I took it out of the library and never returned it."

"Well, like I said, you were feverish. She lent it to you; no doubt about it." He gauged the other's reaction, and then said: "So? What did you think? Did you like Federico's book?" He took a sip of coffee.

"At times I thought it was a bit too fragmented. The constant interruptions in time, the changing tenses, and—above all—I thought the philosophical disquisition fell a bit flat. The chapter he dedicates to Laila—I mean Laila's mother Laila—well, I wasn't expecting that. I never would have guessed that Octavio, her papá, was Federico's friend, the very same Octavio from the novella. Incredible, isn't it? The things you can find in books." He paused for a moment to let his excitement settle. "But the visits to *El Ranchito* and *El Ferry*, the trips to the beach, the scene with the aunt, and the one with the girl in the mirror . . . those are all quite good, aren't they? But you know, to my mind, Federico always seemed like something of an out-of-work romantic, an author démodé, in the gothic sense, I mean. The impossibility of fulfilling desire, the mother as eternal female, and above all the final chapter, the concurrent dreams, the autobiographical material, the anxiety that permeates everything, making everything into a kind of ghost story . . . But on the other hand, for me, the erotic scenes (much more than the truculent ones) are done with amazing skill. Unlike the tale of Solón and Zolaida, *Prayers* seems much less veiled, much more honest."

"More descriptive, you mean," Elías interrupted. "More descriptive sexually."

"Yes, much more descriptive indeed. But that's part of what I liked about it."

"Well, for me, a pornographic novel is precisely that: descriptive," Elías said. "Erotic novels, on the other hand, have to be more subtle, try to put less on display, if you will . . ."

"So you think Federico is an exhibitionist?" interrupted the younger man.

"I hadn't thought to put it that way, but now that you mention it, yes: I think so." Elías tipped his cup to get the last of his coffee, then remembered: "Juan García Ponce, author of *Inmaculada*, once said that decent people call their novels erotic, but since he wasn't a decent person, he always thought his books were plain old pornography, more or less. A question of taste, you see."

"Lawrence is of a different opinion, of course. He detested pornography."

"But Lawrence, as you know, was a rather eccentric example of what we might call straight-laced autoerotica."

"So did you like Ross's book?" Urrutia asked again.

"If only you knew, Ricardo, just how much I stole from that book in order to write my own! How could I not like it?"

"By the way . . . what are you calling your novel, Elías?"

"*The Longest Journey*," he replied, rather theatrically, since Ricardo clearly understood that it was a reference to his pilgrimage.

"But that's the same title as one of Forster's novels."

"Oh. I didn't know . . ." Elías was crestfallen. He'd never suspected that someone else could have usurped such a wonderful title. "What's it about?"

"Well, you're not going to believe it, but it's about exactly what you and I have gone through. It's the story of an encounter between two people."

"I see," was all that Elías could muster, a bit disillusioned and disappointed.

"So you say you were influenced by Ross's novella?"

"Indirectly, of course . . ." But then he decided he'd rather not explain it, and said instead: "Anyway, that critic's commentary . . . what does Fede say his name is?"

"Pereira, I think . . ." replied Ricardo, who evidently had a much fresher memory of the story than did Elías.

"His reading just seems stupid and superficial," he said, ill-tempered, before suddenly recalling a quotation Federico had used. "I'm not so sure that the 'philosophical' disquisitions you're referring to, Ricardo, are as empty as you think. As a matter of fact, I think they're the real meat of the book. Remember, above all, that *Prayers* deals with a naked memory constantly investigating itself, taking every turn in the road of time. Plus—and Federico says this himself somewhere—he exists outside of time, trying to avoid it as one might avoid a bad neighborhood. It has to be this way, understand? We can only transport ourselves through memory."

"But into the future!" Ricardo grumbled. "Doesn't it seem just a bit exaggerated?"

"But he never *was* in the future. *He will be!* He simply managed to transport himself there by virtue of memory. In other words, he remembered the future. *His* future. What happens, Ricardo, is that we're conditioned to only remember the past. And *Bodily Prayers* breaks with that habit temporality, shatters it, just like Fuentes does in *The Death of Artemio Cruz*. It's a story that takes place in space, not time, moving constantly, like the wind, and without regard for chronology or the natural succession of events. That's why it skips around from one scene to another, just as memory does when you're lamenting things that have passed you by. But I still believe that after reading the first few pages, anybody can figure out where Fede is going with it, and they can follow along without much difficulty. There are a fair number of keys and clues; for example, the age of the protagonist, the settings—in place and in time—and the famous "flashes of lightning." The four days—the four parts—are a strictly unconditional reference to those four successive and strictly chronological days in La Paz. That structure is the starting point for the alterations and iterations of linear time. I swear, I'd love to write something like *Prayers*, Ricardo. And Federico did it when he was twenty-one!"

"I hadn't thought of it like that, the way you've described it," Ricardo replied. "But what's really praiseworthy, I think, is the shadow of the mother hanging over everything, like an obstacle or impediment . . . and I like his use of the violet dress with the gold stitching, remember? You can feel it in every sequin: she possesses him completely. It's in the aunt, in the sister, in Epifania, in Laila, in the mirror-girl, even in the whore . . . !"

"I disagree. For me, the scene with the mirror is not Oedipal, Ricardo."

"In that case, what is it?" he asked, intrigued, maybe even a little concupiscent.

"Incestuous," Elías replied, thrilled to be revealing such a thing to the younger man. "The girl in the mirror can be none other than Selma. Well, that's how I read it. You'd have to ask the author, since who knows if Federico wrote it with that in mind."

"Do you know him?"

"No, but I'd love to meet him," Elías said, leaning back in his chair. Almost immediately, though, he realized something of supreme importance, turned to Ricardo, and asked: "I had a dream the other day; I don't remember anything about it, but I thought that you . . ."

". . . might be able to show you the description I wrote down myself, to see if it fits? I imagine so."

"Yes, maybe when I read it I'll remember."

"Don't get your hopes up. It's pretty experimental and absurd. It'd have to be, though, don't you think?" He opened up his satchel and produced his notebook.

Elías was about to start reading when a familiar voice—a muted cry, actually—caught their attention. He looked up from Ricardo's writing and saw a tall, spindly figure (which fit the voice quite nicely) coming into focus in the distance. Tony. First it was his mustachioed face and tall, shepherd's crook-like body that emerged from the twilight; then his bulging eyes and incredulous face. He was crying out to them as he ran down the Libertad sidewalk:

"Our padre is dying, muchachos! Roldán is dying!"

Pili was torn from her reverie, hearing Tony run up the street, now screaming as loud as he could. She hurried over to Elías and Ricardo, who were already on their feet.

"Augusto is dying. And he wants to see you both! Yes, yes, he wants you to come. He asked me to find you. Cecilio and Solón are with him. The doctor says that time is of the essence."

"But Tony, I just saw him at noon today and he seemed fine to me," Elías said.

"Roldán specifically asked for the two of you. He has to tell you something. Go. I'll catch up." Then Tony turned to Pili and said: "Muchacha, you'll have to close up. The whole world is there, outside the Altozano. All of Las Rémoras is waiting on news from Díaz Gros; you three are the only ones still missing. Sitting here, drinking coffee and chatting away . . . what the devil were you thinking?"

"That would explain why there's not a soul about," Elías remarked. He turned to his younger companion and said, "Let's go, Ricardo."

"But what the hell could the padre want with me?" Ricardo asked, worried. "He doesn't even know me. I'd just be in the way, Elías."

"If I knew why he wanted you there, I would have already told you," the librarian replied.

"Hurry!" Tony yelled again, getting angry.

And then they were both off like a shot and running through the Libertad blackness, slightly downhill, towards the waterfront and the bituminous sea. Then they bore left, passed the municipal building, and finally reached the small, almost insignificant Altozano. The clarity of the sky and the light of the stars was enough to illuminate both their faces: the look of compunction worn by Elías, and Ricardo's fear, his eyes ablaze with wonder.

There was such a crowd surrounding the Altozano, they couldn't find a way to get through; every step was blocked by the agglomeration of people gathered together for news of the padre, their spiritual father.

Finally, after some pushing and shoving and a few well-placed elbows, they managed to work their way through the first few rows of human fencing. Even at the door, though, and beyond that the corridor, the crowd prevented anyone from getting in or out. Elías shouted at the top of his lungs, but nobody paid him any mind. Then, at the other end of the line, they saw the drawn and anxious face of the doctor. He saw them too, and implored the people to make way, to move aside. Even that was to no avail. Finally—and with the dedication of kamikaze pilots—the two writers dove into the fray, finally surfacing (surrounded by some ten or twelve other people) in Roldán's bedroom. Santa wiped the sweat from the padre's face while Higinio and the other two hung back, rigid and contrite, against the wall. Joaquín, the fisherman, was watching his old ex-wife work. The heat hung close and heavy. Sigüenza and Rosinda (the city council secretary) were there as representatives of the State, mouse-quiet in the corner, awaiting the inevitable. Cecilio and Solón stood at one side of the bed, horrified, looking like two stuffed effigies, devoid of reason. They didn't even acknowledge the entrance of the two young men. Nobody really knew what had happened: suddenly, around three in the afternoon, with no warning, Roldán had lost consciousness and went livid in the face. A thick stream of blood more purple than red began to flow from his nostrils—and soon it began to look more black than purple. Díaz Gros had been doing the unspeakable: applying ice packs and draining fluids. Nothing worked. *It's happening again*, Elías thought in a flash, and then it faded quickly from his mind. *The real problem—the only one—was the affliction of having seen La Gringa, and the sadness eating away at his heart.* None of the old doctor's concoctions or compresses could do any good against that. First there was the fall up at the cemetery, just caused by the sight of her, and then her visit this morning, which he himself had been present for. As much of a priest as he was, Roldán was being hounded by the same dogs of regret that had chased down Rosales on the day that he died. The misfortune of ill-fated love. One had died for his love, Inés, while the other was dying from having met his ancient love again: Jenny the Gringa. And where, by the way, was she? Had no one gone to the brothel to inform her? Had nobody even thought of it? Would she already be on her way out of town? Neither Ruth nor Josefina nor any of the other girls were present in the bedroom either; maybe they were waiting with the masses outside.

Then, in the commotion and the heat that barely allowed the dying man to breathe, everyone watched as round old Santa bent down close to Roldán. He moved his lips, whispering something in her ear. Santa, who couldn't hear, looked up and made a shushing motion with her finger to her lips. Everyone fell silent, a silence that was magically transmitted outside, spreading from link to link, a chain of people succumbing to a reverential silence, as if words from the other side were about to pass through the padre's lips, and to be communicated to them by Santa. Finally, the old black woman spoke:

"The padre says that everyone must go, that he doesn't want anybody here. Only Elías and . . ." She had forgotten the other name.

"Ricardo?" Elías asked.

"Yes, the padre also asked for Ricardo."

"And who is this Ricardo?" Francisco Sigüenza asked from his post in the corner of the room.

"I am," he said, and as he looked at Sigüenza, he knew (this time from his own eyes) that that man truly was an imbecile: just as he'd imagined him that one night, walking along the waterfront after visiting Pili.

"And who are you, if I may be so bold?" asked the architect Higinio.

"He's a friend of ours," replied Solón, emerging from his trance.

"And who might *you* be?" asked Sigüenza.

"Augusto's cousins," Cecilio said.

And though that wasn't really a full explanation, nobody asked anything else. Santa bowed down again to listen to what the padre had to say, and then informed the group that he wanted her and the doctor to remain as well. This time, everyone there had some doubt as to whether she might be putting words in the padre's mouth, but nobody protested. Only Solón disregarded his cousin's wishes, and asserted that he would be staying put as well. Sigüenza replied that the man would either leave willingly with everyone else, or he would have the officers remove him by force. The cousin argued that they were family, but the councilman wouldn't have any of it. We don't know you around these parts, he said, before taking him firmly by the arm and leading him off down the hallway, past all the people waiting and praying. A path was formed, and the rest of the people gathered in Roldán's bedroom began to file out quietly, if reluctantly. Elías? Why the writer? they asked. Why should he enjoy such a privilege? Was Roldán going to leave him some inheritance? And the other one, Elías's counterpart, what was his reason for being there? Why had the padre sent for them? Díaz Gros finally shut the door and locked it. A general murmur surrounded the house. The night was still clear, and a few stars shimmered in the firmament, perhaps ready to fall from the sky if something extraordinary were to call them down. Although the breeze brought some relief to the Altozano, the municipal building, and perhaps even the trash heaps outside of town, the heat and humidity flushed the Rémoranos' grieved, suspenseful faces as they waited. Finally, standing at the foot of the priest's bed, Elías and Ricardo were able to hear Roldán's stammering. Díaz Gros hung back behind them, while Santa remained at his side to wipe the sweat from his brow.

"Ricardo. I knew you would come," Augusto began, his eyes glassy, his voice tired and thick. "Not for me . . . You don't even know me, do you? You came to Las Rémoras to find Elías, I imagine . . ."

Ricardo was hopelessly bewildered. So many things had been piling up in that one, torrid August. Santa made room for him and Elías to sit down on either side of the funerary bed. Above it, on the wall, hung the crucifix that seemed as ever on the verge of tumbling down. The padre, barely able to make out their faces through his cloudy eyes, struggled to continue:

"When I was very young, back before I had any idea what God was preparing me for, I met a young girl in La Paz . . . Yes, it was Jenny. You were right, you see, Elías: something suspicious was hidden there in *A Convert's Chronicle* . . ."

"Padre, you slept with her, didn't you?" prompted Elías, keeping his voice low.

"Yes, and she bore a son, the fruit of that relationship. You didn't know that . . . I didn't mention it . . ."

"Who?" Elías asked anxiously.

"She gave birth without ever telling anyone—not even me. At first she thought that Marcelo was the father. She would only realize her mistake later on. Which was for the best. If she'd told me that her baby was mine, I wouldn't have believed her anyway

. . . I would have thought that she was trying to sabotage my priesthood. Do you understand? How could I have believed her, after what had happened with him? With Marcelo? She only confessed it all to me eight years later, in a letter. She gave birth and left him . . . Her boy became the favorite son of Las Rémoras, that little town where she landed after fleeing La Paz. Here she met Santa and Joaquín, who were still married back then, and she, Santa, for better or for worse, was the one to raise him." The padre turned his head, trying to locate her, but he couldn't make out her face.

Tears began to spill down Elías's cheeks. Though he was holding Roldán's hand, he couldn't help but feel a certain amount of resentment towards the priest all of a sudden, a resentment tinged with grief, with not belonging. And for just that very reason, he tried to be strong by latching on to the only human characteristic that he had at his disposal at that moment: his confusion. Elías, Roldán's son? Him, the writer, the keeper of the keys to the library, the solitary, the orphan of the town, loved by all and yet related to none?

"Yes, that's the reason I came to Las Rémoras, Elías," said the padre. "That's why—when I got the letter your mother sent from San Diego—I asked to be transferred here . . . Las Rémoras had to be my parish. Because a boy—my boy—had been born on these shores. He was the son of this town, he lived here, and yet I was not in a position to be a father to him . . . a legitimate father . . . Forgive me," he pleaded with a sigh that sounded like it could have been his last. But then, in a voice barely above a whisper, he continued: "I believe that's why your mother chose Las Rémoras to be the site of her house of ill repute. In order to be near you in some way . . . Jenny, meanwhile, had an informant of sorts keeping tabs on everything you did, and that informant (as you must have guessed by now) was Inés, who nevertheless didn't think too highly of you, though I'm not sure why. She confessed everything to me just before she died, though she never knew that she was making her confession to your father, Elías. I had to bite my tongue. But I know that your mother's good intentions don't excuse her. Nor do mine . . . I didn't know that Jenny owned that brothel until just over a year ago. Actually, I've probably said too much already . . . Inés told me in confession. But then I understood, and I knew why Jenny had done it . . ."

Elías was lost in grief and shock, crying, not knowing who to turn to. But he hadn't let go of his father's hands. Finally, Augusto leaned in close to him and—with what strength remained in him—went on:

"As the two of you already know, the summer in La Paz that I met Jenny was when I had my first revelation from Our Lord, my first encounter with the Holy Spirit. I described it in my *Chronicle* . . . Like he did with Paul, Christ knocked me from my pride. It was then, during that summer vacation with my cousins, that I realized He had chosen me for the priesthood. When I returned to Mexico City, and against my parents' wishes, I entered the seminary. I straightened out my life, or at least I tried to . . ." His eyes clouded over, and he wiped away a tear before saying, "Five years later, I was sent to Querétaro, where I met a very beautiful and very devout young woman named Helena . . ."

"Helena . . . ?" Ricardo asked, his eyes bulging from their sockets like a racehorse's under the whip.

"Helena: your mother, Ricardo."

This didn't come as a shock at first, because Ricardo didn't believe it; he thought that he might be dreaming, or—why not?—that it was some sort of morbid joke that Roldán was playing. But then again, why the hell was a priest on his deathbed going to lie? How the hell could he be joking about something so serious, something so delicate? What was the sense in that? Nothing, that's what. So what the padre was saying now was the truth, and terribly so. This was his last testament—the testament of Augusto Roldán—and that was why he wanted them all there together. That was why Ricardo had come all the way from Mexico City: not only to get to know Las Rémoras and Elías, of course, but also so that he could come to know his true father. But then, who was the one he'd grown up with?

"She was married to your father, or—at least—she was married to the man you thought was your father. And that's how," he said, sounding like a psalmody, "you must love him, Ricardo. You must honor his memory . . . He was a student at UCLA when your mother was living in Querétaro, alone and bored with life in the city. With your grandmother, I should add. For some reason she'd moved in with her, and that's where we met and fell in love. It all happened so fast. Although I did everything I could to resist, the devil did his work too well . . . Can you imagine it? A seminarian and a married woman! By our own negligence, she became pregnant, and your father died thinking that you were his son. Your mother, and I thought that this would be for the best . . . or at least the most convenient solution. We never saw one another again, but I followed your progress through the letters she sent me: long letters in which she described your activities, your friends, your schooling, and your relentless drive to be a writer. I knew everything, Ricardo. I even knew that you would come here. I've been waiting for you. Your mother told me. In her last letter. Don't be afraid. Here, take my hand . . ."

"But how did she know? She never . . ." Ricardo was about to say that she'd never read *Las Rémoras* . . . but who knew? Maybe, without his knowing, she'd snuck into his room and read through that notebook with the torn-out pages. Maybe she'd known everything all along. Maybe it'd happened when he was sick, mired in delirium, those bottomless hours when he slipped into unconsciousness on account of his fever.

"You must understand," continued Augusto, father of them both, struggling heavily, "while Elías had neither a father nor a mother, you, Ricardo, had both . . . That's why I left. That's why I couldn't be near you. I did what I had to do. But I also want you to understand that you were always important to me, that I always kept you in my heart . . . I love you now and I loved you then—as my son. And although I never was able to see you outside the photos that Helena, your mother, sent me, I never stopped praying for you. I loved you and I asked God to help you the same way I asked God to help Elías . . . If He brought you both here to my side, it was for me to tell you what you now know . . . that you are brothers." He paused, weeping now in concert with Elías. "Yes, the two of you are brothers, and from this day forth that's how you must love and support each other. Especially you, Elías, because you're the oldest . . . I can bequeath you nothing, because I am nothing. I'm just a poor old padre filled with his sins, you see? I have no inheritance to leave you: besides God and his Holy Church I have nothing. And the two of you, you must know, also belong to Him . . ." He took a final breath, exhausted, and murmured, "But I can leave you my letters. Those from Jenny are for you, Elías, take care of them! And those from Helena are for you, Ricardo. They're over there . . . in that box on top of the writing desk. Keep them safe. You'll see that I'm telling you the truth. I love you both . . ."

He took them by the hands, and—with one last rattle, and despite Díaz Gros's best efforts, Augusto Roldán died. Bit by bit, his hold on the hands of his two sons began to loosen . . . yes, his two sons, his two young men, the only fruits of his only two sins, each of them, on opposite sides of the bed, shaken, cold with fear and shock, both now in tears. Ricardo somewhat less than Elías. The padre might have been his father, but he'd never known him up until today, and as such he couldn't find it in his heart to love the man, even in retrospect. He cared for him, sure, as one might care for a fictional character—a handsome, well-liked character from a book who dies in the final chapter—but not as a father.

Impossible. As Augusto himself had said just a moment before, his true father was another man entirely—the one he'd always had, despite the fact that he seemed rather far away indeed from the recent events of Ricardo's life—even if Roldán was in his blood . . .

Santa began to weep, and Díaz Gros succumbed to grief as well, which immediately infected the people standing out in the hallway and everybody else within earshot. Santa opened the door, and the look on her face confirmed the news without any need for words. The doctor placed a blanket over the padre's wan and haggard face, and then placed his hand on the shoulder of the writer. Finally Ricardo, taking the initiative, pulled his prostrate brother out of the bedroom. This time the people of Las Rémoras stepped back and let them through, almost as though afraid to touch them. When they reached the street outside the Altozano, Ricardo was able to make out Ruth and Josefina among the crowd. He separated from his brother to approach them and ask:

"And where's your madam? Where's Jenny?"

Contrite, cheeks ablaze from their tears and the heat, the two girls looked at each other as if they hadn't understood the question, or couldn't fathom what it had to do with the padre's dying. Finally, with her beautiful, tear-stained face and moist red lips (which Ricardo contemplated with fascination), Ruth said: "She left this afternoon. She was with us until five or six, giving us her last few instructions, and then she left. She was heading for the border, I think. She lives up there in San Diego. She'd been crying quite a bit, and she didn't want anybody to see her. She's usually so strong, I know, but something must really have bugged her. She was very sad."

Ricardo turned and went back to Elías. They embraced, and Ricardo was able to make out the warbling cries of the old mourners approaching. Yes, he said to himself, it was the same group of *plañideras* who'd attended Rosales's burial. Where would they bury the priest? In some special plot, near Inés but far from Rosales? Or maybe far from each? In that pantheon atop the only hill in Las Rémoras, overlooking the sea? The brothers were walking under cover of night, past the rundown city council building, which was being guarded by a single officer waiting for further orders, or—at the very least—a bit of news. They finally reached the waterfront, and the zephyr breathed out by the sea (like a sigh coming from a sleeping body) came to their aid, dispelling the heat and invigorating them. Ricardo made out the distant rocky crag where his brother had spent mornings, afternoons, and nights completely abstracted, meditating over his unfortunate love for Roberta. They passed Libertad and continued on to the other end of the waterfront, crossing Sardineros. Ricardo (who had, of course, written about it himself) saw Encaladores, where the town library was where Elías lived. They passed a few houses, and finally Elías stopped in front of one that the younger man didn't recognize, never having described it in detail in his novel. Elías —a bit more in control of his emotions by now, though still crying slightly—removed a key from his pocket and handed it to his brother, who opened the door to reveal a room replete with books: books on sagging shelves, books on the unswept floor, books on a beat-up writing desk, books in every corner and every niche. A proliferation of books, loose sheets of paper, pens, pencils, notebooks, and still more books. There might not have been a single other thing in the entire room—the aspect of the place was that of one original, primordial Book that had invaded everything. Only a single, tenuous light showed in one corner of the library-bedroom: one of those perpetual church candles.

"Don't you have any light?"

"Of course I've got lights," Elías replied, and hit the switch behind him.

"So why do you have that candle burning? For the saints?"

"It was for San Judas Tadeo, so that Roberta would return. But it doesn't matter anymore. Blow it out."

Elías dragged his feet, tired and disconsolate, while Ricardo eased into a wicker chair, the only bit of furniture in the room except the sagging bed and the desk crushed under all its books. Elías turned to his brother, scrutinizing him, and said:

"You know what? I want to go. I don't want to spend any more time in this town. Maybe I'll come back some day, but right now Las Rémoras has nothing to offer me. I'm alone . . ." He smiled. "Well, I guess I've always been alone."

"No more and no less alone than me, Elías. But we're together . . . Remember, we may both have just lost our father, but I lost another one just a few months back."

"Yes, I knew that he died. But you didn't love him, right?"

"I don't know . . . I think I may have. At least sometimes. The one I do love is my mother, but now . . . what good is it? I can't go back. Not now." Ricardo waited for a moment before daring, in a tremulous voice, to ask, "Do you want to go look for your mother? Do you want to go to San Diego?"

"No, no," Elías answered immediately, almost brusquely. "Not at all. You misunderstood me, Ricardo. I simply can't be *here*."

"You've got a lot of memories, right?"

Elías nodded. Ricardo got up from his seat.

"We'll go together, if you want," he said. He turned something over in his mind and then went on: "Maybe you want to stay for the funeral tomorrow? They'll have to send another priest to officiate."

"No, Ricardo, that's exactly what I *don't* want. Don't you see? Nobody knows you here in Las Rémoras. But I, on the other hand . . . I'm the son of this town, first and foremost, of Las Rémoras before Augusto Roldán. I was raised by Santa and Joaquín here, I grew up and worked in this little village. I fell in love with

Roberta here. I became friends with Tony, the architect, and even Rosales, who gave me the keys to this pigsty. I just can't stay here. I shouldn't."

"So what do you want to do?"

"I want us to leave this place as soon as possible, that's what."

"Tomorrow?" Ricardo offered with a hint of timidity.

"Yes, tomorrow. Or now even—but without telling anyone. Just like Roberta did when she left." Elías raked over his Roberta coals for a moment and then continued: "I don't even want to see Santa or Higinio first. Just you and me, Ricardo . . ."

"Where to?"

"North."

Just then they heard someone tapping at the door with self-conscious fastidiousness. They were taken aback, having no idea who it could possibly be at that hour, and they looked nervously at each other as if they might find the answer in each other's eyes. Elías approached the door with trepidation; finally, he gave it a tug, and there on the doorstep stood Pilar. Ricardo could see her there too: serious, beautiful, frozen in time. A midnight transfiguration; a true miracle sent from above.

"Where did you come from?" Elías asked.

"From my house," she answered, her face humble and ruddy.

"What do you want? Are you looking for me?" asked Elías. But then he understood: there was a suitcase at the young woman's feet.

Ricardo came over and picked up her bag, saying, "Come in, come in Pilar," and then he closed the door behind her.

"Thank you . . ." she murmured.

Ricardo offered her the room's only chair, and then leaned up against the writing desk. Several seconds passed, and with every one the silence became more and more uncomfortable. Finally, realizing that the young woman was too afraid to speak, Elías asked her amicably:

"So what's up, Pilar?"

She just sat there, her wide eyes focused on the younger of the two men, who—intrigued—awaited the parting of her marvelous lips.

"Tell us, what's going on?" Ricardo insisted, beads of sweat beginning to collect on his brow.

"I left home . . ."

What exactly did that mean?

"Why?" the two brothers asked.

"Because I don't want to marry Francisco," Pili said curtly, almost imploringly.

She couldn't have been more explicit. Ricardo's eyes lit up, and Elías's sadness and tears could suddenly wait for some other night, or maybe he'd even forgotten about Roldán entirely. All he felt was an ardent, burning curiosity.

"My mamá wants me to marry him, but I've already told her that I don't love him. She thought I was working to save up money for the wedding; at least, that's what I told her. But it wasn't true. I needed the money to get out of here," she said, confidently now and without fear. "I don't love Francisco. In fact, I detest him."

"And how is the town councilman taking this . . . ?" Ricardo asked craftily, drawing the story out of her like thread behind a needle.

"That's just it: my mother doesn't want to lose this opportunity for our family, even though she knows that I'm not in love with him."

"So why the hell were you ever engaged?" asked Elías, who definitely did not understand women.

"I never said that I wanted to be his fiancée, Elías. Some years ago, six or seven perhaps, he came to my mother to ask for my hand in advance, for when I grew up . . . I didn't know it at the time, but when I turned fourteen, he became my fiancé, *because yes*, my mother told me, it was the best thing for me. And I was foolish enough to believe her."

Neither Ricardo nor Elías had ever imagined this. The younger of the two brothers had believed from the beginning that on that night he'd described in *Las Rémoras*, when Sigüenza was walking along the waterfront, proud and happy after his visit to Pili's mother, it was because he'd just asked her permission to marry an eighteen-year old woman. But no. Pilar had been betrothed to Sigüenza since she was fourteen—like she said—and perhaps since the moment her mother was widowed and Sigüenza, taking advantage of the occasion, came to ask for her daughter's hand. It made him, Ricardo, suspect Sigüenza and Pilar's mother of plotting something behind her back.

"And the money?" Elías asked.

"The money's mine, and not for any wedding," Pilar replied, resolute. "Tony already paid me for my last few days. It's not much, but . . . He doesn't know I'm leaving."

"Where to?" asked Ricardo Roldán Urrutia.

"I don't know. I haven't decided yet," she said pensively, waiting, looking at the two brothers as a lapdog might, insinuating that she might have unintentionally overheard the contents of their discussion before knocking . . . in other words, that she was asking to go with them. The destination didn't matter; she would be happy. All she knew was that here, in Las Rémoras, her mother and Sigüenza were waiting . . .

Elías looked to Ricardo, who—though he didn't return the look—was quite obviously enchanted with the idea: Pili and him, Elías and him . . . what else could he possibly ask of fiction?

"For my part, I'd be honored . . ." Ricardo said.

"But how the hell are we going to get out of here, Ricardo? Have you even stopped to think about it?" argued his elder brother. "If they find us with her, we've had it. You most of all . . ."

And immediately he regretted his comment: Pilar blushed deep red. Ricardo did too. Then she said, with her downcast eyes:

"Elías, I have the keys to the Ford."

"What?" he asked.

"Yes, Cecilio left them in the ignition when the three of you arrived this afternoon. I was going to tell Tony, but in the rush to see the priest, I completely forgot." She paused for a moment, then qualified her answer: "Well . . . I didn't really forget. I decided to hold onto them so I could return them myself."

Before their very eyes, Pilar had orchestrated—better than either of them would have been able to—a plan for getting out of town. The three of them. She pulled the keys from the pocket of her dress and handed them to Elías, who—reflexively, almost automatically—took them from her. All he could think of to say was:

"And your things?"

"They're all right here."

"So what are we waiting for?" Elías exclaimed, happy all of a sudden to be bringing Pili along.

Ricardo beamed. "Just let me grab a few books," he said, "and we'll go."

"And if they do catch us all together?" asked Pilar. "What do we say then?"

Elías thought this over for a few moments and then turned to his brother:

"Nothing . . . Ricardo, you take Pilar's suitcase with you. Pili, you go on ahead and wait for us outside the lonchería. After that, it's you, Ricardo, and I'll bring up the rear. We'll all pile in the car and be off."

Meanwhile, Ricardo had already gathered together some half-dozen books, and Pilar had gone off on a circuitous route towards the lonchería—a measure that was not at all unwarranted, given the fact that her mother was likely on her way to Sigüenza's house to look for her at that very moment. After she left, Ricardo turned to his brother and said:

"Look! It's true. She really isn't in love with Sigüenza."

"What books have you got?"

Ricardo showed him the titles: *A Brief Life*, *The Green House*, *Hopscotch*, the *Quixote*, *Explosion in a Cathedral*, and *On Heroes and Tombs*. Then he tucked the books in his satchel, slung it over his shoulder, and grabbed Pili's suitcase in his other hand.

He cast one final look around the small house belonging to the brother he hadn't known before that day. Five minutes later, Elías did the same, packing his own satchel with a few clean shirts, a box of envelopes and poems in manuscript—memories, really—a couple of novels, and the notebook where he'd written the story of Ricardo, which up until recently had been known as *The Longest Journey*.

He put out the candle, his offering to San Judas Tadeo in exchange for Roberta's return, left the house keys in the front lock, and checked to make sure the other set—those to the blue Ford—were safely in his pants pocket. If anyone saw him, they would be suspicious; but if they asked him where he was going at that time of night, he would simply say: nowhere. But he crossed Encaladores, Sardineros, the waterfront, and finally Libertad without anyone seeing him, save for a couple of foreigners who couldn't be bothered to talk to him, and Rosinda, who didn't even notice. Although starlight fell clearly over the town and blanketed the waves out at sea, the night was still dark enough to protect him from impertinent or prying eyes. It had cooled somewhat, but the August climate respected no schedule: the heat was diurnal and nocturnal, it filtered down streets and entered into homes, soaking bedsheets with the sweat of Rémoranos who at that hour—it must have been past 11:00—where exhausted and interested in nothing else besides a good night's sleep.

In the distance he could make out the two tranquil figures of Ricardo and Pilar. There wasn't another soul down the entire slope of the street. Elías lengthened his stride, and finally he reached the lonchería—currently closed—and the blue Ford parked alongside it, right on the sidewalk. He opened the driver's side door and started the car. Perfect. There was plenty of gas in the tank, and the engine sounded good. He reached across and unlocked the other two doors so that his younger brother and Pilar could get in.

Everything told them to leave that night, right away, to leave Las Rémoras and head North. Elías had always wanted to go North. He felt less sad, less afflicted by Roldán's death. Despite everything that had happened—the innumerable appearances, disappearances, truths, the miracles, vicissitudes, the close encounters—he could count on his brother, Ricardo, as his traveling companion. And Pili was joining them. What more could he ask for?

Nobody in Las Rémoras saw them leave. Nobody even found out until the following morning. What will Tony think of us when he finds out? Elías wondered to himself as he gripped the steering wheel. And Jasso, the architect? Would he be disappointed to learn that his friend the writer was a car thief and murder suspect? Although—as Ricardo had pointed out—wasn't Roberta the one who'd smothered Inés in the end? Neither Higinio nor Sigüenza would ever find *that* out. Nevertheless, Elías mused as he watched the endless stripe dividing the highway, the incautious, arrogant, and obtuse councilman would be spitting fire when he (along with Pili's mother) realized that his fiancée had left him. Of course, his anger wouldn't last long; no doubt he'd quickly begin to devise another plan, about another woman. And Santa? She was a strong woman, if a bit emotional and sentimental. She'd demonstrated all her life that she didn't need to depend on anybody. First Joaquín had left her (or perhaps they left each other, who knows?), then the lawyer had died in the city council building, and lastly her beloved padre Roldán had abandoned her. (Maybe the good doctor Díaz Gros would take her on in his home?) After all that, what difference could it possibly make if I, a simple writer, were to leave without saying goodbye? Roberta didn't bother with farewells when she left with her son for La Paz, and Jenny didn't either. That Gringa didn't even bother to give me a kiss when she saw me that last night in the Altozano, the writer remembered sadly. What could anyone do then but wish him well? He asked to himself, pensive and disillusioned, stepping down hard on the accelerator whenever he could, whenever the sad and devastated Baja California Highway—Route 1 of the Republic, according to the maps—would permit it.

Ricardo startled him out of his pondering with a question:

"What are we going to do with our notebooks?"

"With our two novels, you mean?"

"Yes, Elías, *Las Rémoras* and your story about of my trip down here, *The Longest Journey*?"

"You know, I've been thinking about that," said Elías, and he lapsed back into contemplation. His passengers couldn't tell whether he was thinking about the people he was leaving behind, the novels, or just the road ahead.

"What novels?" asked Pili, intrigued.

"The novels we've been writing," was all the explanation that Elías offered. "I've been thinking about putting them together, you know? One of your chapters about me and Las Rémoras, followed by one of mine about your journey. Alternating and interlaced. I think we'll have to read both stories over again, calmly, to make sure of things. Obviously we'll have to cut my title, and use yours, *Las Rémoras*. What do you think?"

"It could work, Elías," said the other, looking honestly pleased with the idea. "Actually, I think it's fantastic. There's just one thing, though, about the title . . ."

"What's that?"

"Maybe we should give it a new one. What if some Gringo were to come across it one day? He wouldn't have any idea what Las Rémoras was."

"So what do you propose?"

"What about something descriptive? *The Obstacles*, perhaps. We've certainly overcome more than our fair share to get to this point."

"You know, I like the sound of that. Still, there's one enormous obstacle left to overcome," Elías cautioned, as if clipping his brother's wings.

"Which is . . . ?"

"Well, our encounter, Ricardo. I mean, everything that's happened today . . . Everything that happened from the moment you showed up with Cecilio and Solón and we finally met. Who the hell is going to write this final chapter in our story, Ricardo? Especially since there's been this distinction until now between your writing and mine. Ever since we've met each other, the situation has gotten infinitely more complex. Our two lives are confounded. They've became one."

"I don't think there's any problem," said Ricardo hesitantly, worried whether he'd be able to offer his brother (and himself, for that matter) a satisfactory alternative for ending their book. "We can reconstruct this final part without too much trouble. Write it together, I mean. We'll remember everything that we went through today; I mean, everything from the moment Cecilio, Solón, and I arrived in town until this very moment. It'll be a sort of apotheosis of what's come before."

Elías was astonished: his brother's solution was so simple, and yet it never would have occurred to him. That's what they would do: first alternate their chapters, and then reconstruct and rewrite the day of the padre's death, from 5:00 that afternoon to this very conversation in the old blue Ford, with the night wind dispelling the sultry August heat; but then, suddenly, his brother

Ricardo, still somewhat concerned, mentioned that they'd need to find a name with which to fuse the two stories, yes, a pseudonym for their book.

"I've already got one. Eloy Urroz," answered Elías, *outrageously* pleased with himself. "Eloy, of course. An 'E' name like my own, but one that sounds better than Eligio or Eliodoro or Eulogio, don't you think?"

"I like it already," exclaimed Ricardo, thrilled. "And Urroz for Urrutia, which is more phonetically pleasing than, say . . . Urruticoechea."

"Perfect," Elías concluded. "So when we've got it ready, we can send it out to a publisher under the title *The Obstacles*, as written by Eloy Urroz!" He said this all in a single breath, ecstatic really, and turned to look at Pili, who clearly didn't understand a word.

"Unfortunately, no publisher is going to believe everything that's happened to us, Elías," his younger brother said.

"Screw 'em. It's their problem if they don't believe it. What's important is that certain people can recognize the difference between things that really happened and things that didn't, and these people, I assure you, will believe us, without a doubt."

"You're right . . ." Ricardo said, lost in thought now. The verisimilitude of things—or the lack thereof—was really getting to him. Now, for example, he realized that two loose ends of their story remained untied, though neither of them had any desire to resolve them. He was thinking about the two letters from Roberta: one to him, and one to his brother. What did they say? What would they reveal? Perhaps they'd read them later, and then they would know. But later—not now. Those letters belonged to the past; they were, perhaps, the stuff of another book—first postponed, and then forgotten—the book in which Ricardo would finally give his description of the dream to his brother.

"Well I'll read your book, for one," Pilar said suddenly, replete with admiration for her two traveling companions.

"Really?" Ricardo asked.

"And if it's about the two of you, then it'll be even more interesting," she said, not without a certain feminine sweetness. "Is it some sort of biography, or something like that?"

"Not exactly, Pilar. It's really about two lives that intersect each other, two characters who meet," said Ricardo.

"Then it's the two of you?"

"Yes," replied Elías, who was obviously uncomfortable about describing the unfinished book.

"And who will you dedicate your story to?" Ricardo asked him.

"Well, who do you think?" Elías waited for Ricardo to say the words himself, and—finally—savoring his own anticipation, said: "To you, Ricardo, who else?"

"Because I already dedicated *Las Rémoras* to you, Elías. Didn't you know?"

"Honestly, I didn't," Elías answered, perturbed.

Not another word was said. They'd already settled everything with regard to their collaboration. They would wait and hope. In the meantime, the minutes snuck by with enormous stealth: they put miles and miles behind them without any sense of distance, completely oblivious to their sadness, far removed from the death of their father, Augusto Roldán, remembering it vaguely but without suffering. They felt light, ethereal, a bit more content. The wind rushed in through Ricardo's open window and flooded the car, refreshing their bodies, enveloping the three of them in a sort of smooth mist, in the pleasant and comforting air of things to come. Time passed, dauntless and intrepid, without revisions, without any oncoming headlights to destroy the peace of their tiny, rolling home, the sense of joy that sheltered the three of them inside their car.

No more than an hour later, just past Mulegé, Pilar—who'd been dozing up against the door in the front passenger seat—asked Elías:

"Where do you two want to go?"

Caught a bit off guard, the writer tried to gather up his half-thoughts and replied:

"I don't know, Pili. As far as this car can take us. As far as we have the strength and will to go."

"And if we spend all our money, Elías?" asked Ricardo, who'd heard everything quite clearly from the back.

"Well, we'll work for a bit and then be back on our way," he replied, sounding quite confident.

"Yes, but for how long, Elías?"

"I don't know just yet. The true traveler knows neither the shores he's bound for nor when he might return. It's a gamble. We're in no hurry, brother. Nothing stands in our way. We can cross the United States, if you want, even go to Canada . . . I don't know, and I don't think it matters much anyway. We're free and we're together."

"Yes, what else matters besides being together?" Pilar asked. "We could go as far as Alaska . . ."

An hour later—it was 1:30 in the morning, and the night sky was just as brilliant as it had been when they'd left Las Rémoras—Elías stopped the Ford on the shoulder. They were past Santa Rosalía, though not as far as San Ignacio. He and Ricardo got out, walked a few steps, melding into the desert shadows, just far enough that Pilar could no longer make out the outline of their bodies: two ghosts dissolving in the warm light cast by the stars. With their eyes ever on the horizon—that imprecise place where the blackness of the sky blended with that of the desert—the two of them dropped their pants down about their knees, and two gentle, simultaneous streams began to fall. Meanwhile, the vapor—with its warm smell of ammonia—floated up to their noses, reviving them, readying them to get back on the road.